HUGO
And The
MAIDEN

Minerva Spencer
writing as S.M. LAVIOLETTE

CROOKED SIXPENCE BOOKS are published by
CROOKED SIXPENCE PRESS

2 State Road 230
El Prado, NM 87529

Copyright © 2021 Shantal M. LaViolette

All rights reserved. No part of this publication may be reproduced, distributed, or transmitted in any form or by any means, including photocopying, recording, or other electronic or mechanical methods, without the prior written permission of the publisher, except in the case of brief quotations embodied in critical reviews and certain other noncommercial uses permitted by copyright law. For permission requests, write to the publisher, addressed "Attention: Permissions Coordinator," at the address above.

To the extent that the image or images on the cover of this book depict a person or persons, such person or persons are merely models, and are not intended to portray any character or characters featured in the book.

If you purchased this book without a cover you should be aware that this book is stolen property. It was reported as "unsold and destroyed" to the Publisher and neither the Author nor the Publisher has received any payment for this "stripped book."

First printing May 2021

10 9 8 7 6 5 4 3 2 1

ISBN: 978-1-951662-47-9

Any references to historical events, real people, or real places are used fictitiously. Names, characters, and places are products of the author's imagination.

Photo stock by Period Images
Printed in the United States of America

Chapter 1

London

Hugo tightened his grip on the Duchess of Beckingdon's narrow hips and plunged into her, filling the spacious bedchamber with the sound of skin slapping against skin, and making the huge four-poster bed shudder with his savage vigor.

He was servicing Her Grace exactly the way she liked it: rough, hard, and—yes—with lots of vulgar, earthy language.

"Admit you've been a wicked hussy and beg for what you need," he ordered, smacking her buttock hard enough to sting his hand.

Her spine arched and she gave a low, guttural groan. "*Please*, Hugo, I've been so naughty. Punish me with your cock. I—I *need* it."

A smile of genuine amusement twisted his lips as he grasped the thick silver and black rope of hair that had fallen over one of her shoulders, pulled her head back until her neck was arched at a cruel angle, and commenced to ride her even harder.

Hugo had to admit there was nothing quite like rogering a peeress of the realm as roughly as a stallion covered a mare. Not to mention making her beg for it.

Well, he reflected, that wasn't entirely accurate. Rogering a royal duke—something Hugo did three or four times a year—did outrank servicing a duchess.

He grinned at the obnoxious thought and leaned forward to bite her shoulder, not hard enough to draw blood the way he'd seen horses do, but hard enough to leave an angry red mark. And hard enough to send the duchess flying over the edge into bliss.

Hugo stilled, keeping himself buried deep inside her as she convulsed around him. He ignored his own incipient orgasm—like a good whore should—while she climaxed, her contractions exquisite agony around his aching shaft. When her shoulders began to sag with exhaustion, he reached beneath her and teased a second orgasm from her remarkably responsive body.

Hugo and the Maiden

He was ready to keep going, but again she begged. "Please, Hugo, no more. I can't bear it. Please—

So, that was it, then.

He gripped the base of his still erect yard to hold the sheath on his body while he pulled out. Even though he rarely spent in a punter—or a *client*, as Melissa liked to call them—he always wore a sheath. That was his only rule when it came to whoring and it was a rule he would never break; he had seen far too many old whores wandering the streets with faces like open sores, their minds eaten by the pox.

Lady Beckingdon gave a soft mewl of satisfaction and rolled onto her side, her tall, thin body tangling in the rose-colored silk sheeting that cost more than a housemaid earned in a decade.

Hugo stripped off the sheath and discarded it in the small brass rubbish bin tucked unobtrusively beneath a gilt-edged nightstand. Unlike the streets, or in some of the seedier brothels, you never needed to re-use such things at The White House—or Solange's, as it was now called.

Hugo pulled the bedding up over the duchess's slender form, once again impressed by her vigor. For a woman in her late fifties, she was far more active—and adventurous—than many of his younger clients. Sometimes she wanted him two or three times during an evening. Sometimes she wanted him *and* another man. That was fine by Hugo, she paid a packet for him, and he had no qualms about working tandem.

Hugo padded across the room and poured water into the wash basin. He took his time bathing the sweat from his face and neck before wiping down his chest and groin. He disliked leaving sweat to cool on his body and despised feeling sticky.

He cut a glance at himself in the oval mirror that hung over the tallboy dresser and then wished he hadn't. Every time Hugo saw his reflection it surprised and disappointed him. For some reason, he always looked different in his mind's eye: his nose smaller—aquiline and elegant—his lips fuller, his eyes a sky blue instead of the color of peat. In effect, Hugo imagined himself handsome. Or at least marginally attractive, and certainly not the dark-eyed, dark-haired, harsh-featured, and vaguely sinister looking man he saw in the mirror.

He would have liked to be taller and have the slim, graceful build of an aristocrat, but he was only of medium height and his hard, muscular body was sculped with brutal precision rather than sleek elegance.

Still, for all that he was such an ugly sod, it seemed that scads of women—and not a few men—couldn't keep their eyes or hands off him.

That was fine by Hugo. If somebody offered him enough money, he would fuck them—female or male, it made no difference to him.

They could beat him with birch switches and ride him as hard as a willful hack; they could have him beat *them*; they could dress up in a nappy and call him Papa, Hugo didn't give a damn. He only drew the line at anything involving children and animals.

Yes, even a soulless, damned-to-hell whore like Hugo had his limits.

He knew that most men, including several who worked in the brothel, believed that taking it up the arse was effeminate—not to mention dangerous and illegal. But Hugo didn't give a damn about any of that. He was in this business to make money, not to impress anyone—certainly not other whores or the punters who paid them.

Besides, male customers paid even more than women like the duchess did—both for what Hugo did with them as well as what he did afterward: which was keep his gob shut. Hugo kept mum as much for himself as anyone else. After all, if he were caught with another man, it wouldn't be just his client's neck in a noose. Being a sod was cause enough for death; being a poor sod was almost a guarantee that you'd get the rope.

Hugo poured fresh water over the soft cotton cloth and wrung it out before wiping down his arms and legs.

His popularity among their clients had never stopped mystifying him. There wasn't a night when customers weren't lining up for him. Of course, his appeal was limited to sexual attraction. Hugo's thin lips twisted with derision; people didn't flock to him for his sparkling conversation or lively wit. And none of his faithful clients ever made the mistake of imagining that they'd fallen in love with him.

He glanced over his shoulder at the duchess—not that he was supposed to know her name or rank, inside these rooms she was plain Mrs. Ellen Fletcher—to offer her a fresh cloth, but she was a silent lump on the bed, so he tossed the cloth aside.

The false names were another holdover of Melissa Griffin's—the prior owner of Solange's—many rules. But Hugo had been born to break rules and he made it his business to know exactly whom he was sticking his cock into. Why the hell would he put almost every penny he'd ever earned into Solange's unless he could control the variables of his whoring?

Hugo went back to the bed to snuff out the candle on the nightstand and check on Her Grace. He'd worn her out and knew from experience that she would sleep until it was time for her to go if he didn't wake her. Some nights he let her sleep, others he gave her more than she paid for—it was only good business. Besides, he didn't mind fucking her, not that he got any relief from it. It wasn't that he *couldn't* climax with a client, it was that he rarely let himself take that ultimate pleasure because all it did was fog his brain and make him feel like he was something other than a paid servant.

He was especially careful around such a rarified creature as a duchess—which were about as common as unicorns, in Hugo's experience—and always kept in mind that she was paying him for *her* pleasure, not his.

Hugo paused a moment to study her features. The duchess wasn't what you'd call beautiful, but she had a face that drew a man's gaze and held it. Even now, with mostly gray hair and deep lines around her eyes and mouth, she was a handsome woman.

She was also exactly twenty-five years older than him. Today was both their birthdays—although he'd not shared that information with Her Grace. While Hugo made it his business to know whom he was servicing, he also made sure his clients didn't know a damned thing about him. At least nothing but the bits of information he'd carefully created and provided.

The Duchess of Beckingdon reminded him of a horse with impeccable bloodlines. You could tell just by looking at her that she was the product of generations of careful breeding.

The same could not be said for Hugo, who resembled a street cur. Even his costly, tasteful clothing couldn't disguise his rough features or hide the fact that his eyes were permanently hungry, no matter how much he ate or how much money he had.

Hugo snatched up one of the heavy silk robes provided for both clients and their companions and slipped his arms into it.

Companion was yet another term of art that Melissa had coined. The word still made him laugh, even though he'd been whoring at

Solange's for well over a decade—the last three of those years as an owner. He frowned. Well, *co*-owner.

He tied the black silk sash around his waist and strode into the sitting room that adjoined each of the bedchambers on this side of the house—the *ladies'* side.

His own garments hung on the hooks where he'd left them, and he fished a ruby-encrusted silver case from his coat pocket. The case was a gift from the duchess and the vile cigars inside it were from one of his other clients—a member of the Spanish royal family if you believed what the man had told Hugo. The cigars stank, but there was something about them Hugo couldn't resist.

He poured himself a healthy measure of the fine brandy the duchess paid to have stocked and went to the huge fire that roared in the fireplace—yet another luxury the duchess paid for. He took a spill from a glass bowl on the mantle and lit the cigar, tossing the small twist of paper into the fire before lowering himself into the big leather wingback chair nearest the blaze. Even though it was late summer, he was cold. He was always cold.

"You are a terriblaay avertissmon for my cooking, Yougo. You 'ave no fat on you!" Oliver, the French chef who terrorized Solange's kitchen staff—as well as slaughtering the English language—had yelled at Hugo more than once.

Hugo ate almost constantly, but his body burnt food the way this huge fireplace consumed coal. No matter how much he ate, he remained lean, nothing but skin stretched taut over muscle, bone, and sinew.

He exhaled a plume of dirty brown smoke, his jaws tightening as he contemplated the woman who owned the other fifty percent of this venture and was occupying his thoughts far too often these days.

Laura Maitland was at least ten years older than Hugo and had been working at the exclusive brothel for over twenty years. She should have earned enough money to buy the brothel twice over. But Laura had a strong thirst for gin and cards, both of which had left her life in tatters.

It had been lucky for Laura that Melissa Griffin had discovered the other woman's addiction and taken charge of her before Laura could lose everything she had, including her life. Even with Melissa's help, it had taken Laura years to pay her debts and save any money.

Hugo and the Maiden

Three years ago, when Melissa sold the brothel, Laura had finally scraped up enough money to buy half.

Hugo had been furious. He'd saved for years to buy the place, but Mel refused to sell him the entirety of the business, insisting that she had an obligation to Laura. And so Hugo was stuck with Laura.

He'd had to put up with the woman's drunkenness for three long years. And he'd also had to advance her money repeatedly for her share of the business expenses. While she'd been drinking and gambling, Hugo had worked twice as much—taken twice as many clients—and saved every penny. He was ready to buy her out.

Hugo doubted that Laura would even consider an offer from him if she hadn't begun seeing a big, brutal bastard named Cowan Morgan about six months ago. It was the first time Hugo had known Laura to take a regular lover. But then she was getting a bit long in the tooth to attract the young, handsome men who'd once flocked to her in droves. It wasn't only her age, but all the drink that had taken its toll.

Cowan had been lurking around Solange's far too much for Hugo's comfort. But the man worked as an enforcer for the Welsh crime lord Bevan Davies, so Hugo couldn't exactly chase him off. Nobody in their right mind offended anyone connected to Davies.

And so Hugo had tolerated Morgan's presence. But the man was greedy and stupid and Hugo suspected that he might encourage Laura to accept an offer to buy her out. As dumb as Cowan looked, Hugo knew the man had to know that Laura lost more of the business every month she owned it.

Hugo didn't think it would be too hard for Cowan to convince her to sell and get away. Especially since Laura hated Hugo with such a virulent hatred.

Hugo grinned; there was nothing like a woman scorned when it came to hating.

The animus between them was mutual and dated back to his first week at the brothel, when Laura had shown up in Hugo's bedroom, naked beneath her dressing gown. He'd been bloody amazed at her cheek.

Hell! He had sex for a living—did the woman really believe that was how he wanted to spend his free time?

Not bloody likely.

That long-ago night—after he'd told Laura that if she wanted to have sex with him she could pay him just like any other customer—she'd shaken with fury. And had hated him ever since.

Laura wasn't the only person he'd angered with that sort of rejection. His steadfast refusal to take lovers had caused no small amount of heartburn over the years.

Well, that was too damned bad; the last thing he wanted was to throw his lot in with anyone else—especially another whore. Other people were a burden he didn't need. He'd spent the first twenty years of his life in poverty and want. He fully intended to spend the rest of it in comfort and luxury.

His plan for the future was a simple one: get control of Solange's—one way or another—and operate the brothel until he died. He had no desire to move to a cottage in the country and grow turnips and raise chickens—or whatever the hell it was an old whore did once they didn't whore anymore. He enjoyed what he did and had no interest in quitting.

He flicked the stub of his cigar into the flames and took another pull from his brandy. He didn't want a lover and he didn't want friends; all he wanted was money, lots and lots and lots of money. At the end of the day, money was the only thing that mattered. Without it, you were weak, vulnerable, and at the mercy of the rest of the world. And the world was a cold, cruel, ugly place and human beings were the worst part of it. The only person on the entire planet that Hugo trusted was Hugo.

And if that bothered other people? Well, they could go sod themselves. He didn't give a damn who hated him, how much, or why. In fact, he was used to people hating him. Hell, his own father had hated him so much that he'd sold Hugo to a stranger—and a twisted one, at that.

So, yes—thank you very much—he was quite comfortable with hatred.

"Mister Hugo?"

He looked up to find one of the maids, Mindy, standing in the doorway. She was pale, shaking, and wringing her hands.

"What's the matter, sweetheart?" he asked, putting down his glass and getting to his feet.

"It's Mrs. Maitland. Something has happened to her and—" She shook her head and looked away, biting her lower lip.

Hugo and the Maiden

Hope surged in his breast. "Is she ... ill?" *Or perhaps dead?*

God. He was *such* a bastard.

"Oh, please, Mr. Hugo, come and see, I—I can't bear to look at her."

Hugo couldn't bear to look at the woman, either. He decided poor Mindy was too overwrought to see the humor in such a comment.

He followed her from the room, not even bothering to put on his slippers. "Is Mr. Morgan with her?" he asked as they padded down the hushed corridor.

"No, sir. She's all alone."

Laura's quarters were in the same part of the house as his—the employees lived in one area—which meant he and Mindy had to go all the way to the other side of the building.

By the time they reached the stairs leading to Laura's apartment Hugo was breathing hard, mainly from suppressed excitement: if Laura died, Hugo had first right of refusal on her half of the business. He knew it made him a bad person to hope something had befallen her, but that's because he *was* a bad person. He'd made peace with that years ago.

Mindy stopped in front of Laura's door, which was ajar. There was a sliver of light coming from somewhere beyond the door and Hugo stuck his head inside.

"Laura?"

Blinding agony exploded in his skull, his vision went black, and Hugo dropped to the floor like a sack of potatoes.

"Tie 'is hands, 'e's a skinny bastard but 'e's strong," a voice he didn't recognize ordered.

Hugo shook his head to try and clear his vision, and promptly vomited from the pain.

"Bleedin' 'ell," somebody muttered.

Hugo tried to reach up and keep his skull from exploding, but his wrists had been tied behind his back. When had that happened?

"Pick 'im up."

Rough hands grabbed him around his middle and he went flying through the air and landed on something hard—a shoulder?—just before his head smacked into another hard object.

Blackness and pain pulled him under.

When he came to, he was lying face-down on rough, smelly leather.

"Wasss happening?" His words came out choked with drool.
"You 'ear that? The tough bastard is awake again."
Somebody chuckled.
"I fink he needs anovver sleeping draught."
Once again Hugo's head exploded.
This time, he gave up swimming against the darkness and slid into blessed oblivion.

Chapter 2

The Island of Stroma
North Coast of Scotland

Martha Pringle hurried toward the cluster of lights moving erratically at the north end of the island.

Everyone on Stroma knew when the church bell rang at this hour of the night that a ship had failed to clear the rocks. Now it was just a matter of how bad things were. Or how good they were—depending on a person's point of view.

She grimaced at the cynical thought. *You should be ashamed of yourself, Martha Jane Pringle.*

"Have a care, Martha, the trouble will wait for us to get there safely," her father said, his words more of a wheeze.

"I'm sorry, Father." She slowed her pace, if not for her own safety, then certainly for his. At seventy-six Jonathan Pringle was as agile as a man half his age. But Martha knew that old bones were brittle, and it would only take one break to put an end to his active existence; people did not mend quickly at his age.

"Did you bring the black bag, Martha?"

"Yes, Father."

"And the torches we made last month?"

"Yes, Father. I brought everything." Martha hoped most of it wouldn't be needed, and that the lights meant something other than what she feared.

They reached the tiny shingle beach in time to see several of the distinctive boats that the islanders called yoles push off the shore and head out toward the dark shadow near the rocks.

"My, that *is* a large ship," her father said as Robert Clark approached.

Mr. Clark was a strapping, handsome man who acted in the capacity of harbormaster, although Stroma had no actual harbor. Only small boats could be brought near Stroma as the beach was the sole point of access, with sheer, craggy cliffs bordering the rest of the island.

"Good evening to you, Miss Pringle," Mr. Clark said, nodding at Martha, his admiring look one that made her cheeks heat. Mr. Clark was attractive and unmarried, and Martha wasn't the only woman in their tiny village who found his person engaging.

"Good evening, Mr. Pringle," he said to her father. "She *is* a big vessel," he said in response to her father's comment, crossing thick arms over his muscular chest as he turned to stare out at the dark form. "Jem Packard got close enough to see she's called *The King's Folly*. I've never seen her in these waters before, so I reckon she must have wandered off course."

Martha could not tell from Mr. Clark's expression whether the ship had received any help *wandering* into the rocks that surrounded that part of the island. Although her father said nothing, she knew the question would be weighing heavily on his mind, as well.

The only area of dissention between the islanders and their vicar—an outsider to Stroma for all that he'd served the small community for two decades—was their wrecking activities.

To a man—or woman—they would have denied it, but the people of Stroma were known up and down the coast as wreckers: men and women who lured ships to their ruin and stripped them of their cargos.

Clark cleared his throat. "The ship looks like a transport, which makes me think her destination was New South Wales."

"You mean a ship for prisoners?" her father asked, his eyes widening in disbelief.

"Aye."

"And yet she is up *here*?" Martha asked.

"It is unusual, there is no denying that," Clark admitted. "My guess is the convicts were locked in the hold—maybe even chained. I think many won't make it out alive."

"Jesus wept," her father said, swaying like a reed in the wind.

Martha put her arm around him and sucked in a breath when she realized how fragile his shoulders felt beneath her hand. Jonathan Pringle had never been a big man, but he'd always been healthy. Now he felt as insubstantial as a bird.

"Martha brought our medical bag," her father told Mr. Clark. "Where would you like us to set up?"

"Actually, I think you should open up the meeting hall to treat survivors."

Hugo and the Maiden

"That's quite a walk. You wouldn't rather use the church?" Mr. Pringle asked.

The church was the largest building on Stroma and also close to the beach.

When Mr. Clark hesitated, the vicar smiled. "I know tomorrow is Sunday, but the Lord will understand why we can't have our usual service."

Clark looked uncomfortable. "We'll need the church for other purposes, sir. I'm afraid the dead will outnumber the living this night."

***

It was ironic that Hugo probably owed his life to being a piss-poor sailor.

From the moment he'd woken up half naked aboard the ship, he'd begun puking.

Shackled and chained to men on both sides of him and crammed in with convicts all around him, he'd quickly become the most unpopular man onboard: nobody wanted to get near him.

Sometime in the middle of the third or fourth night—he'd lost track—the prisoners around him had finally had enough of the inhumane conditions and began to riot. Hugo could have told them that his stomach was, by then, as empty as a killer's conscience and that if they'd but waited another few hours he would have coughed up his innards and that would have been the end of it.

But his fellow convicts had long since lost any interest in being reasonable. A riot with men chained to one another could only lead to one thing: some men living, some men dying.

Once the violence broke out, those in charge of the prisoners simply shut the two huge hatches to the ship's hold, periodically opening them just enough to toss down food and lower the occasional bucket of water.

Hugo discovered that the best way to avoid becoming a dead convict was to be so covered in puke that nobody wanted to touch you. So, he crammed his back up against the splintery hull and watched the fighting. Puking weakly from time to time.

It was soon evident which of the convicts had been arrested for crimes against property and which for crimes against their fellow man. The compulsion to steal a loaf of bread—usually driven by hunger— could not compete with the compulsion to kill or rape—two actions Hugo had witnessed more than once growing up in the rookeries.

Luckily for him, the two men chained closest to him were of the former variety. When the killing began, they both squashed themselves against Hugo like hens huddling for warmth, no longer put off by a little puke.

The three of them watched the horrifyingly lethal proceedings with growing terror as the days passed, their curiosity leavened with a healthy dose of self-interest.

It took no time for one prisoner to reach the top of the pile. The man was a mountain of a brute whose small, piggy eyes were those of a person who enjoyed exercising dominion over others. Once he'd made it clear that he was in charge, the situation in the hold settled into an uneasy peace.

But then no food or water came down the following day, and none the day after.

The big man—Graybow was the name tattooed in uneven blue letters across his massive chest—seemed to go mad on the third day, sawing off the foot of the man attached to him with a wicked, rusty blade he appeared to have snatched from thin air.

The prisoner on Hugo's right prayed loudly while the one on his left had taken up where Hugo left off and was puking—or at least heaving, since there was nothing left to bring up.

Graybow then sawed off the foot of the man on his left. When he'd finished, he forced the terrified prisoners nearest to him to form a human platform, which he climbed to reach the hatch doors, and began beating on them.

This went on for hours.

As the daylight that bled through the planks overhead faded, Hugo looked from the maniac's broad back to the rest of the convicts. Other than a few who were actively supporting Graybow—or themselves sawing off body parts of the men chained to them—most of the prisoners were as terrified as Hugo's two neighbors.

Hugo no longer had the energy to be afraid; he would rather die then and there—at least he'd escape the vile smell in the hold—than suffer through another day in Hell.

"Do you want to live?" The words came out of his mouth without direction from his brain.

His two companions' heads swiveled in his direction.

"You heard me," he said.

Hugo and the Maiden

When neither spoke, he turned to the one who'd been praying, a younger man who resembled a human matchstick with his flaming red hair. "What about you, Vicar? Do you want to live?"

The lad nodded.

Hugo turned to the other man. "How about you, Puker?"

Eyes wide, the second man nodded, too.

"Good, now shut up and listen; this is what we're going to do."

Chapter 3

Martha and several others worked quickly to turn the meeting room into a field hospital. There wasn't much they could do with the long wooden benches except cover them with sheets, blankets, and anything else that might cushion their patients and keep them warm.

Women from the small farms that dotted the island arrived carrying what little they could spare—which was still more than most could afford—and stayed to help once the patients began to arrive.

Stroma was a hard rock of a place that the rest of Britain had long forgotten. Although it was only separated from the mainland by the two miles of the Pentland Firth, the weather often ensured those two miles were as good as two hundred and Stroma could be cut off for weeks at a time from the outside world.

Of the three hundred and seventy-six people who lived on the island, only Martha and her father had moved here from the mainland. Jonathan Pringle had already been fifty-six when he'd accepted the long-vacant living on Stroma.

Not until Jonathan, his wife, and nine-month-old daughter arrived on Stroma did the vicar discover that the last clergyman to preach from the pulpit in the gray stone church building had been a follower of Mr. Penn, who—when he'd left to go to the Colonies—had taken half the islanders with him.

The remaining islanders had decided the village population could not survive another charismatic nonconformist and the church had been empty for decades.

As opposed as they were to a new spiritual leader, it hadn't taken long for the reserved but kind-hearted islanders to accept the soft-spoken vicar and his wife and baby.

"I've brought a can of hot lobster stew, Martha."

Martha looked up from the sparse contents of her medical bag to find Mrs. Morag Fergusson standing behind an enormous steaming cauldron.

"My goodness, Mrs. Fergusson. Please tell me you didn't carry that all the way here?"

Hugo and the Maiden

The older woman smiled, exposing a mouth missing half its complement of teeth. "No, Small Cailean brung it." Mrs. Fergusson's nephew, referred to by all as Small Cailean to distinguish him from his father, Big Cailean—who'd died many years ago—was easily the biggest man on the island, even though he was only sixteen. It was one of nature's jests that he was also one of its most gentle and timid. He smiled shyly down at Martha.

"Thank you, Cailean," Martha said.

His pale gray eyes slid away, his wind-reddened cheeks flushing darker, and he nodded. He rarely spoke and could not read or write. Martha had tried to teach him more than once, his huge form hunched over a tiny desk in the little schoolhouse where she often helped during the winter and spring, but the other children—from five to fifteen—would taunt him when she wasn't watching and he always ran away. Thankfully it never occurred to him to strike back at any of his tormentors, as much as they might deserve it.

"Get back down the hill, Small Cailean," his aunt ordered sharply. She tended to employ a rough tongue with her nephew, and Martha was grateful that Cailean didn't appear to notice. "They'll have need of yer back at the church."

Cailean scuttled out of the house and "down the hill," which was really a misnomer as the highest point on the island, Cairn Hill, wasn't even two hundred feet above sea level.

Just as Small Cailean left, Mr. Clark entered. "Are you ready, Miss Pringle?"

Martha nodded.

And then her patients began to arrive.

***

Some Hours Later ...

"Put me down, you great cabbage! Good God almighty—don't any of you people speak the King's bloody English?"

The voice cut through the din of the meeting house like a cleaver.

Martha tucked a stray lock of hair behind her ear and looked up to find the voice's owner a few feet away, swaddled and cradled like a baby in Small Cailean's arms. The giant was grinning as he stared down at the irate man, whom he held as easily as a child.

Martha stood up and stretched, biting back a groan before resting her hands on her hips. "I understand English, although I cannot say it is the King's."

The stranger's head whipped around and she startled. She didn't know what she'd been expecting—his voice and diction had been clipped and proper—but his face…well, it was all harsh angles and dramatic planes.

His cheekbones were like blades and his eyes were so dark you couldn't tell pupil from iris. They were also heavy-lidded and oddly tilted and it struck her that he looked like a satyr, or at least what she imagined one would look like.

"Who the devil are you?" he demanded, his black eyes sweeping over her quickly and dismissing her even quicker.

Martha's face burned under his cursory examination. "I am Miss Martha Pringle, and I would greatly appreciate it if you would not use such language."

He blinked, and his eyebrows, twin black-as-coal slashes, shot up until they disappeared beneath the sheaf of pitch-colored hair that hung over his forehead. "Is that so, Miss Martha Pringle? Well, perhaps you would tell this great bloody looby—"

Martha approached the man, as much as she didn't want to. "That is not the type of thing we call each other here, Mr.—"

His thin, mobile lips curved into an unpleasant smile as he crossed his arms, looking for all the world like he was lounging on a chaise instead of lying in another man's arms. If bloody, feces-smeared, vomit-encrusted, and soaking wet men did such a thing as lounge on chaises.

"What language are these people speaking?" the stranger demanded.

Martha gave him her most repressive stare, the one she used on recalcitrant students. "It is English as spoken by a native Scot, sir. That is where you are currently a *guest*—in Scotland, in the Orkneys. This is the island of Stroma." She hesitated and then added, "Small Cailean understands both English and Scots Gaelic—he knows two languages, which, I imagine, is one more than *you* know."

The man glanced around the meeting hall, his expression horrified, as if she'd just told him that he'd crossed the River Styx into Hades.

"How the bloody damned hell did—"

Martha spun on her heel.

"Oi!" he yelled after her. "Where are you going? I'm not finished with you. You can't just turn your bleeding—"

Hugo and the Maiden

"You needn't hold him, Small Cailean. Please put him on one of the pews and I will attend to him when he stops using such language." She tossed the words over her shoulder, ignoring the stranger's response, which was to squawk like an angry gull. If he was able to emote as loudly as that, he could not be too badly hurt.

Martha worked her way down the pews, on which the patients—all male—had been laid head-to-head and foot-to-foot. Every single man had horrible chafing on their ankles which she suspected was due to manacles. She splinted broken fingers, one broken wrist, stitched up a nasty gash, and smeared salve on raw wounds.

She was busy treating the seventh or eighth man, when her patient spoke. "He is the reason most of us are alive."

Martha looked up from his left hand, on which the two smallest fingers were broken. One of the things people learned on Stroma—which had no resident doctor—was to use splints, stitch small wounds, and do other general medical care. "I beg your pardon?"

"The, er, gentleman who was yelling—"

"*Get your big bloody paws* off *me!*" The words cut through the other chatter.

Martha's patient—surprisingly well-spoken for a convict—grimaced, "Well, the man who is *still* yelling is the same person responsible for most of us who are alive."

She glanced up at the yeller.

He was glaring repressively at Small Cailean, who appeared to have taken a liking to him and refused to put him down. Martha clucked her tongue before returning to her task. Small Cailean was sweet and gentle, but he did have a tendency to develop, well, *fixations*, and then cling like a burr. A *huge* burr.

"What is his name?" she asked her patient.

"I'm afraid we weren't in a situation where exchanging names was—well, let's just say the subject did not come up."

Martha didn't even want to think of the hellish conditions these men must have endured.

"He may be foul-mouthed and obnoxious," her patient continued, "but he stopped that maniac from killing a lot of us."

She looked up, arrested. "What maniac?"

Her patient turned an even paler shade than his already white skin, causing his many freckles to stand out even more. "A prisoner in the hold—Graybow was his name, or at least that was what was tattooed on his chest. Anyhow, he began inciting some of the others to, er, well to acts of extreme violence. Soon there were a dozen of them, slamming their chains against the hull and making a horrendous racket. The crew—there weren't nearly as many of them as there were of us—locked the hold shut, leaving us at that monster's mercy for days." He shivered. "When they stopped feeding us, Graybow sawed off the feet of the two prisoners next to him and it didn't seem like he would stop."

Martha sat rapt, his damaged hand forgotten in her lap. "And then what happened?"

"Well, that man"—he gestured to the obstreperous black-haired convict, who was currently asking everyone around him if they spoke proper English—"convinced everyone that we had to stop Graybow before he came after us. It took him a while to get enough people to agree, but finally we were able to rush him when his back was turned.

"It was the mouthy yeller who jumped on Graybow's back and wrapped the chain around his neck, squeezing, until the big bastard, er …" He paused, his pale cheeks coloring. "Begging your pardon. He, um, subdued Graybow until he was no longer a danger."

"Do you mean he—"

"I'll not say anything about that," the man said, his tone suddenly firm. "I *will* say that if that maniac Graybow had lived there would be a lot fewer of us breathing right now."

Martha held his gaze for a long moment. "Go on."

"That fellow took the blade that the monster had been using to kill and used it to pick open our manacles. He and one other man worked for hours freeing convicts. He kept on working even when the deck caught fire over our heads." He swallowed, his forehead suddenly sheened in sweat. "And if all that wasn't bad enough, the ship struck something hard and water came in faster than I would have believed possible. Men were screaming, fighting, and panicking, and yet he kept picking locks right up until the moment the water covered our heads. Those men who'd not managed to get free held onto men who were and pulled them down. Somebody grabbed one of my legs and I thought—I thought—" He began shaking.

"Shhh, it's alright Mr.—"

"Franks. My name is Albert Franks."

"You mustn't agitate yourself, Mr. Franks. You are safe now."

Hugo and the Maiden

As Martha finished splinting his fingers and smearing his scratches and abrasions with rapidly diminishing salve, she couldn't help casting another glance at the savior in Mr. Franks's story.

A less likely looking hero Martha had never seen.

***

Hugo could not understand a damned word anyone said—except for the stern-faced school mistress who'd scolded him and then left him with one of the hugest men he'd seen in his entire life.

Hugo stood five foot ten inches in his stocking feet and weighed a good thirteen stone, but this man was a bloody giant and he held Hugo as if he were a babe. And the woman had called him *Small* Cailean? Hugo shivered at the thought of a *Big* Cailean.

At his shivering the big man propped Hugo on his hip like an infant and solicitously pulled the blanket up to his chin.

Hugo smiled up at him. "Er, thank you, Small Cailean."

The man's response to his weak thanks was a blinding smile, confirming Hugo's suspicion that he must be a bit touched in the upper works. Well, touched or not, Hugo owed him his life because he'd certainly saved his worthless hide.

For all his great size Small Cailean had moved swiftly and nimbly over the jagged rocks that ran from the shoreline out to sea, to where even more were hidden, one of which must have taken down the ship.

Hugo had managed to swim to one of the jutting, half-submerged rocks after he'd escaped the hold, but he'd not had the strength to do much more than hold on with one hand, his body floating like a piece of kelp in the frigid water.

He'd become so cold that he actually felt hot as a lassitude curled around him, until his fingers began to slip from the rock.

And he'd not even cared.

The giant had picked up Hugo as easily as he would a crab clinging to a rock at low tide. He'd then proceeded to carry him for what seemed like miles without even breathing hard.

So, of course Hugo was grateful, but the man—Small Cailean— refused to relinquish him, and it was bloody embarrassing to be carted about like a wounded lamb.

"Thank you," Hugo said for the dozenth time. "You can put me *down* now. Just put me there, on that bench, and then you can go and do ... well, whatever it is that you do." He gave the grinning giant a hopeful smile. "Really, I shall be fine until, erm ..." He looked across the room at the prickly female, who seemed determined to treat every other man before him. And all because he had not told her his name.

Hugo studied her humorless face as she spoke to one of the men she was treating. The man said something to her and she *smiled* at him.

Well, the little shrew. He'd just have to show—

The sound of guttural syllables slamming together made Hugo look away from the schoolmistress. An old woman had come to stand beside the giant, apparently for the sole purpose of gaping at Hugo.

He smiled at her. "Hello—do you speak English?" He enunciated each word clearly.

The old lady chuckled, as if he'd just said something amusing.

Hugo gritted his teeth and looked away, pulling the rough homespun blanket more tightly around his naked torso as he gazed around at the rude stone walls, some manner of pitiful assembly room. His attention settled on the ginger-hackled man who'd been manacled beside him, the man that Hugo had called *Vicar* because of all his praying.

Hugo hadn't wanted to know any of his fellow prisoners' real names, no matter that he believed several of them probably innocent of the crimes they'd been accused of.

Take Hugo for example; he was guilty of plenty, but petty thievery was not among his many crimes.

He'd been naked when they took him from Solange's and naked when they'd kept him crammed in some vile cell. His captors had finally given him clothing that appeared to have been specifically calculated to make him look like a clown—trousers that fell only to his knees and a shirt so voluminous it might have served as a circus tent—for his brief moment before the judge. A very suspicious-looking judge.

When Hugo had opened his mouth to ask what court he was in, the guard had struck him so hard that his head was still ringing days later. So, he'd stood there before the bench, too dazed to speak while they'd accused him of petty thievery and sentenced him to seven years transportation in less time than it took to drink a pint.

Afterward the guard stripped Hugo of his embarrassing clothing and shoved him into a different cell, this one with people he came to know all too well during the week or more that they'd waited. New prisoners had been added daily, each one claiming innocence.

Hugo was familiar with criminals—he'd grown up in the rookeries, after all—and he knew that every convict insisted they were innocent. But there'd been startling similarities in all the stories that he'd heard while in that cell: every man had been arrested at night, they'd all been denied any access to the normal rights afforded even the lowliest of criminals, and all of them had sounded and behaved like the tradesmen or clerks they claimed to be.

A shadow fell over Hugo and he looked up.

"Well, Miss Martha Pringle has returned." He bowed as effectively as a reclining man could bow. "To what do I owe the honor?"

"I will take a look at your leg, if you can manage to be civil." She had the sort of blue eyes he loved—the type that he would've liked to have himself. Except his eyes would never have contained such a severe, humorless expression.

It took every bit of restraint he could muster to gaze into those judging orbs and say, in a treacly voice, "I would be most appreciative, Miss Martha Pringle."

Her surprisingly sensual lips curved into an ironic smile. So, she wasn't entirely without humor.

"You can put him down, Small Cailean."

The young giant complied without hesitation—after refusing Hugo's fifty entreaties. So, the man *did* understand English.

She lowered herself to the bench and Hugo turned onto his side to accommodate her, the action causing the blanket to slip. He wouldn't have thought she noticed his bare chest and abdomen if he'd not seen the red stain spread up from her hideous, high-necked gown.

Hugo grinned as she lifted the blanket from his legs and gingerly felt around the shallow gash on his shin. Too bad it wasn't his thigh that she had to examine. He moved slightly and the blanket opened to his navel, exposing the taut pale skin just above his pubic hair.

Her fingers squeezed the swollen, oozing wound and he jolted. "Great fucking hell!" he yelled, his eyes leaking tears.

Her mouth compressed into a thin white line.

"I'm sorry, I'm sorry," he said, holding up his hands in a placating gesture. "I shouldn't have said that. You just surprised it out of me."

Her eyes narrowed, but she merely turned to her bag.

Hugo hastily pulled the blanket tight around his body, no longer interested in teasing her.

"What is wrong? Is it broken? It feels bloo—"

She glanced up sharply.

"It feels broken," he meekly amended.

"It is not broken. The skin is torn, and you are bruised." She closed her bag of medicines and stood.

"Is there nothing you can do?" he asked, frantic that she seemed to be leaving. "Doesn't it need to be stitched to stop me from bleeding to death? Are you *finished* with me?"

"The best thing for both the cut and the swelling is soaking your leg." She turned to Hugo's savior. "Take him down to the cove, to the flat rocks. The tide should be high enough that he can sit with his leg in the water but not get the rest of him wet."

"*What?*" Hugo shrieked. "Don't you have anything for the pain? I'm in a great deal of pain and—"

Small Cailean leaned down and scooped him up.

"Good God! You want me to *dangle* myself in the water? Are you mad? It's blo—it's *freezing*."

She gave him a smile—her first—and it was every bit as superior and smug as her resting expression. "The water is cold, but the night is quite pleasant. I'm sure if you keep your blanket wrapped securely around your person that you will be fine."

So, she'd noticed that slipping blanket ploy, after all.

Hugo bit his lip, preparing to beg her. But Small Cailean was already heading toward the door.

Chapter 4

Martha had sent her father to bed hours earlier. He tired so quickly these days and the number of dead men that they'd seen tonight had been enough to crush anyone's spirit.

Between Martha, Mr. Clark, Mr. Joe Cameron—the man who owned and operated their tiny inn, taproom, general store, and post office—and Brian Boyle, who worked a number of jobs in their tiny community, including that of sexton—they were able to distribute the ambulatory prisoners to the villagers who had room to house them. Only one of the injured men—a boy, really—was too injured to walk.

There were seventeen men in need of shelter and Martha kept five. While the meeting hall could have held many more men, five would be plenty to feed and care for. The tiny cottage where she and her father lived was right near the meeting house, so she could conveniently bring food to them.

"You believe most of the crew made it to the mainland?" she asked Mr. Clark once they'd sent the last prisoner off with a crofter and his wife.

"Four lifeboats were seen heading toward Gill's Bay."

"Will they make it?"

"I should think so—the water's calm enough and they've plenty of moonlight."

"Then how is it that the ship's captain didn't see the rocks?"

Mr. Clark shrugged, his usually full and smiling lips compressed into a line. The treacherous rocks that flanked Stroma to the east were not a matter for discussion. Martha knew, even though he'd not said it, that the crew had decided to take their chances rowing to the mainland rather than making the far shorter trip to the island. The Stroma islanders had a bad reputation as people who wouldn't just watch a ship founder, they would help it along and dispatch any survivors who might make it to shore.

Martha tried not to think about that.

Besides, matters had changed greatly in the years since her father had come. While it was true that cargos often went missing, there were far fewer human casualties.

"One of the men I spoke to said the crew were fighting among themselves," Joe Cameron said.

"Yes, I heard that from several of them myself." Martha looked at Mr. Clark. "Do you know what might have happened?"

"There was obviously something wrong as the ship was indeed bound for New South Wales." Mr. Clark shrugged. "It's anyone's guess as to what happened since we only have the prisoners' side of the story."

"It's a disgrace that the crew left the prisoners trapped below," Joe said, echoing Martha's thoughts exactly.

Mr. Clark looked considerably less outraged, and Martha experienced an unhappy pang at his unchristian response.

Brian Boyle eyed the door to the meeting hall. "I can't feel good about leaving you up here with those five men, Martha—no matter how pitiful they're looking right now,"

"Aye," Mr. Clark agreed. "Especially that *one*. He's a bad 'un."

The other men nodded, knowing exactly which one he meant, although nobody had yet managed to get his name.

"He is more bark than bite," Martha assured them. "And all five of them could hardly lift their arms to feed themselves they were so exhausted. They won't be causing trouble tonight."

The men hemmed and hawed but finally moved off toward their various dwellings.

Mr. Clark was last to leave. "Are you sure about this, Miss Martha? I could bunk up along with them in the meeting hall?"

Mr. Clark had an aged mother and a widowed sister with two children to care for. He left before light most days to fish, so keeping him here would only make his life that much harder.

"That is a kind offer, but I shall manage. Good night, Mr. Clark."

"And good night to you, Miss Mar—"

"Great bleeding bollocking hell! What the devil is *that*?"

Martha grimaced. "Oh dear. It sounds as if Small Cailean might have left Lily behind. I'd best be off."

Mr. Clark frowned, but nodded and headed down the path toward his cottage.

Hugo and the Maiden

Martha knocked sharply on the meeting hall door. "I wish to come in, are you—" She hesitated, trying to think of the least embarrassing way to ask if he had covered himself. Seeing so much of his body earlier had been an unprecedented experience, one she would not be forgetting soon.

She'd seen men without shirts, of course, but never had she seen a body like his. Even the men on the island, who were well-muscled from days of grueling work, could not compare. He was as hard as stone, defined and distinct as if someone had created him with a sculptor's chisel. His pale skin was almost completely smooth but for a fine trail of dark hair that grew down the center of his body, between the stunningly delineated muscles of his abdomen, disappearing into the—

The door flew open and Martha squeaked in surprise.

It was the troublemaker, of course.

Small Cailean must have made him a crutch because he was standing beside the door, shrouded in blankets, his face tight with pain, and his dark eyes wide with something that looked like fear.

"It's over there." He pointed to the far corner of the dimly lit room. "Some manner of beast that slithered onto the bench and tried to come at me beneath my blankets. It tried to bite my co—"

Martha cleared her throat.

He stopped abruptly.

"You needn't work yourself into a lather—that is only Lily."

He eyed her apprehensively. "What is a Lily?"

"Lily is an otter. Small Cailean's otter, to be precise. He must have left her to comfort you. He likes you a great deal, it appears."

"Why the bl—" His jaw snapped shut at whatever he saw on her face. "Never mind." He turned and stumped back to the bench he'd claimed for himself. He'd taken two blankets and wrapped them in creative ways to cover up most of his body. The other four men, she saw, were in various stages of sleep. Two were snoring and two others were looking as if they'd like to.

Unlike her obstreperous, otter-fearing guest, the other men had clothing, albeit tattered and grimy.

Martha could not understand why nobody had thought to bring the man at least a nightshirt, but it was too late to ask for such a thing now and her father's clothing would be far too small for such a muscular, broad-shouldered man.

She went to where Lily must have hidden after being yelled at. "Come here, little girl," she cooed, making the kissing sound Small Cailean used to call the young otter.

Lily came out grudgingly, her dark eyes full of reproach as she scampered into Martha's outstretched hands.

"There's a good girl," Martha praised, holding her just like you would hold a baby. Which is what Lily was, a spoiled little baby.

Martha walked back to the foul-mouthed convict. "See," she said, stopping in front of him. "Lily is just a sweet little girl." She scratched the otter under her chin and Lily's eyes closed and she made a soft rattling sound in her throat.

The man shuddered. "It's a rat. The most enormous, filthy rat I've ever seen."

"Shame on you," Martha said, only partly jesting. "Lily is a sea otter. And she's very clean and well-mannered, aren't you, Lily?"

"Ha! She tried to sneak beneath my blankets—you call that manners?"

"Otter manners."

To Martha's surprise, he laughed. As it did for most people, laughter transformed him. He still looked like a wicked satyr, but he looked like a younger, less intimidating wicked satyr.

"What is your name?" Martha asked before she could stop herself.

He regarded her from beneath heavy eyelids that were fringed with long and lush feminine eyelashes. Martha swallowed, suddenly uncomfortable as she recalled her glimpse of his *distinctly* unfeminine body.

"What would you like my name to be, darling?" His voice was like velvet and even Lily perked up at the sound.

Martha's face heated, which only angered her more. "I am *not* your darling."

He gave her another of his crooked smiles. "Hugo."

"I hardly wish to call you by your Christian name."

"My surname is Higgenbotham."

Martha frowned at the unusual name. "Your name is Hugo Higgenbotham," she repeated, feeling rather silly as her mouth struggled with the tongue-twisting syllables.

He gave a chuckle that made her belly clench. "No. I just wanted to see what those gorgeous lips of yours looked like when you said the word Higgenbotham."

Hugo and the Maiden

Martha's jaw sagged. Lily, sensing her sudden change in mood, sat up and chittered nervously.

Hugo Whatever His Name Really Was merely chuckled. "Careful, your rat is getting excited."

Martha was seized by such powerful emotions—anger, shock, and something else, something less familiar—that she was shaking. "I find it hard to believe that you are mocking me after I have done everything I can to help you."

"Not everything, sweetheart." He scooted until he was against the back of the bench and patted the smidgeon of space in front of his hips. "You could toss that rat outside and crawl under these blankets and keep me warm."

To say she'd never been so shocked in her life would have been an understatement. She was so shocked she needed a whole new word for it.

But that wasn't what bothered her.

No, what bothered Martha was how tempted she was to do exactly what he suggested.

***

Hugo knew he was acting like an arse but he couldn't stop himself. He wouldn't even know how; he couldn't recall a time when he'd *not* behaved like an arse.

Now might be a good time to embrace a change, a cool voice in his head recommended as Hugo watched the woman—Miss Martha Pringle—turn on the heel of her sturdy brown boot and march back the way she'd come, snuffing out the only source of light, a candle that gave off more smoke than illumination, on her way out the door, leaving only the moon to light up darkness.

Hugo considered calling after her—not apologizing, exactly, but perhaps *charming* her out of her mood. It had always worked well for him with women in the past, but then he'd not been lying wrapped in a scratchy blanket, beaten like a piece of flotsam, and without so much as a pot to piss in or a window to throw it out of before.

He was too bloody tired and achy to beg or charm. He'd beg and charm tomorrow.

He grunted and lay back on his hard bed.

Hugo told himself that he should be grateful he wasn't still covered in puke, chained to other men, and trapped with a maniac in the hold of a prison ship.

He chewed his lower lip, which had become painfully chapped from being deprived of water for days. Well, other than salt water.

Thanks to the burning planks over their heads, the scene in the hold when the boat hit the rocks had been a Boschian vision of Hell. Water rushed into the damaged hull, dousing flames, while men screamed and fought against both fire and the freezing darkness of the ocean, crawling on top of each other to beat against the hatches, drowning those beneath them.

Right about the time they broke the hatch doors open the ship began to move—an unimpeded drift—and Hugo had realized the vessel was sinking.

Those men who were not able to make their way out scrambled to keep to the part of the hold that held a pocket of air, clinging to the ship's ribs like wet rats.

Hugo followed the flicker of feet, the bare soles ahead of him like the pale bellies of fish, disappearing through the jagged hole

"It's sinking," he'd yelled as he stroked through the water toward the crack.

"I can't swim," one of the men screamed.

You'd better give it a shot, Hugo thought as he'd sucked in all the air he could hold and plunged into the blackness.

His lungs were on the point of exploding when he finally broke the surface. The sea wasn't rough, but the rocks caused strange and powerful currents that pulled at his legs like freezing claws. Cries had filled the darkness as others who were less fortunate either gave up looking for land or struck the jagged rocks lurking below the water.

The moon was almost full, which made him wonder—even in his battered, water-logged state—how the devil the captain had managed to hit the rocks?

Or perhaps he'd died in the fire? Or abandoned his ship?

Even bobbing in the water, Hugo had been able to see a goodly distance ahead, so he struck out for what looked to be shoreline. But he'd only taken a few strokes when his leg slammed into a submerged rock. As he'd clung to the same rock that cut him, waiting to die in the freezing water, he'd stared at the ship. Through his haze of pain, it had looked like there were men fighting on the flaming, wildly tilted deck of the ship.

Hugo and the Maiden

Hugo thought about that now as he wrapped his blankets tighter around his cold body. He must have imagined it because that would have been madness, wouldn't it?

He pushed the unpleasant thought aside and yawned, his lips twitching into a tired smile as he thought about Miss Martha Pringle with her sensual mouth, rebuking gaze, and curvy sinner's body. He couldn't recall meeting another woman quite like her.

Hugo suffered an uncharacteristic pang of remorse as he recalled the way he'd treated her. She'd been kind to him and he'd been a rude, vulgar arse. Tomorrow he would do better.

He yawned again, unable to keep his eyes open a minute longer.

That night, instead of having nightmares about burning ships and bloody killers, he dreamed of liquid blue eyes and full, smiling lips.

Chapter 5

The following morning Small Cailean was waiting for Martha on the stone steps to their little house, with Lily draped across his massive shoulders like a luxurious living scarf, gazing worshipfully at him.

He leapt to his feet and Martha smiled up at him. "Good morning, Cailean. You are just in time to help me carry breakfast over to the meeting house."

Cailean shifted from foot to foot, clearly eager to visit his newest pet.

"Come inside," she said, leading him into the tiny kitchen. "I can see you are excited to see the man you rescued, aren't you?"

Cailean spoke less than a few sentences a year but something about the obnoxious man appeared to have captivated him and he mumbled a word that sounded like, "Braw."

Martha snorted. She could think of a lot of words to describe Mr. Hugo *Higgenbotham* but the Scots word for *wonderful* was not one of them.

His body certainly fits that description, a sly voice in her head pointed out.

Heat crawled up her neck even though—thank goodness—only Martha could hear the scandalous thought.

Cailean carried the large pot of porridge while Martha brought bowls and spoons and a jug of milk. She preceded him and opened one of the double doors for the giant man. The slate building had tiny windows which somebody long ago had filled with stained glass that caused the plain pews and gray stone floor to look magical in the early morning light.

Cailean and Martha paused as they took in the scene: all the men were sound asleep. She glanced around at the various lumps under blankets and decided a hot breakfast was more important than sleep.

"You can put it over there, please." She made no effort to keep her voice down and pointed toward a bench which had been covered with oil cloth and still held a mostly empty pitcher of ale left over from last night.

Hugo and the Maiden

"What bloody time is it?" a muffled, surly voice demanded from beneath the lump of blankets on the front pew.

Martha closed her eyes briefly; clearly she would have to pick and choose her battles with Mr. Hugo Whatever His Name Was or they'd be brangling all the time. She took a deep breath and began to portion the food into bowls.

The other sleepers were roused either by her actions or Hugo's complaining, so Martha had Cailean distribute the food to four of the men, leaving the complainer to her.

"Mr. Hugo." Martha stood in front of his motionless form, which was entirely shrouded with a blanket. When he still didn't move, she said, "I've got your breakfast. If you do not take it, I'll share it out for the others and you'll have nothing until the noonday meal."

The blanket moved with grudging slowness.

His hair, which was salt-encrusted and stuck in all different directions, was a thick black thatch that almost touched his shoulders; it was longer hair than she'd ever seen on a man. The planes of his face were even harsher in the morning light.

He was not a handsome man, but somehow he had the most compelling face she had ever seen; it was difficult to pull one's eyes away from him.

At least it was difficult for Martha.

His squinty gaze slid from the steaming bowl in her hands to her face and narrowed with suspicion. "What is it?"

"Does it really matter?"

He cocked his head to the side and pressed his expressive lips into a prim line—an imitation of *her* expression, Martha surmised. "Oooh, look who isn't in a good mood this morning."

Martha ignored his taunt and set the bowl down on the bench not far from his head with a loud *thunk*. She went back to her serving area and picked up the jug of milk. The other men were digging into their bowls like they'd never seen food before and had eaten at least half before she could offer them some milk.

"It's sweetened with honey," she said to Albert Franks.

"Yes, please, Miss Pringle—thank you so much, this is manna from heaven."

Mr. Franks's shocking red hair and pale freckled skin made Martha smile. "You are welcome."

She moved along to the next man, whose name she could not recall. Like two of the others, the man was young, skinny, and didn't want to meet her eyes. Interestingly, only Mr. Franks and Hugo behaved like they were not guilty. She suspected Mr. Franks might actually *be* innocent, but Hugo, on the other hand?

Martha snorted.

"What are they getting?" The peevish voice interrupted her musing, but Martha ignored him, making her way to the last two men before going to where Hugo sat away from everyone else, as if he were special.

Small Cailean certainly thought he was. The big lad was gazing down at him with the same expression Lily was giving *him*: one of rapt adoration. Who knew what the sweet giant saw in the unpleasant man?

Hugo had not yet touched his food. Instead, he was giving her small serving station an enquiring look, his beak of a nose twitching. "No coffee?"

"I'm afraid not."

He gave a pained groan. "Why did I have to wash up on the only rock in Britain too savage to have coffee?"

"You didn't wash up, Small Cailean rescued you. And we *do* have coffee, but we save it for special occasions."

"Special occasions? I'd say today is a bloody special occasion since I'm still alive."

Martha turned on her heel at the foul word and handed the pitcher to Small Cailean. "I shall leave him in your hands."

"Wait, where are you going?"

Hugo sounded pleading and pitiful, but Martha was not drawn in. She slammed the door behind her and headed back to the cottage, where she put on her bonnet and changed into the nicer of the two cloaks she owned. Although it was only early fall on Stroma the mornings were cool.

Martha found her father in the box room they'd converted into a tiny study. "I'm going down to see what news there is, Papa."

He glanced up, his mind slow to follow his vision. "Ah, Martha. What's that you say?"

"I'm going to the inn." Martha avoiding using the pub's name—the Greedy Vicar—which she knew pained her father, even after all these years.

Hugo and the Maiden

He gave her an absentminded smile. "Very good. And, er, the gentlemen in the hall?"

"I've given them breakfast and Small Cailean is in with them."

"Ah, yes, he's such a good lad. So gentle. Um …" He paused and she knew he'd lost the thread of his thought. Fear slithered down her spine. He'd become so *vague* lately.

He pushed up his spectacles and that is when she noticed his hands.

"Father." He jolted at her sharp tone and she softened her voice. "Let me see your hands."

He offered them to her, as trusting as a child. Ink stained his thumb and two fingers of his right hand, but all ten digits were a disturbing shade of blue.

"You are freezing, Father."

"No, no. It's quite pleasant in here."

The sun shone through the east-facing window, turning the air shimmery with heat; it *was* warm. Martha held his frozen fingers for a moment between both of her hands, trying to chafe some warmth into them.

His crystalline blue eyes sharpened, and his face creased into a smile, changing in an instant from a confused, vague stranger to the father she knew and loved. "Don't you worry, Martha. It's just a bit of sluggish circulation that will be fine when I get moving." He squeezed her hands.

Martha wasn't so sure, but what could she say? He was quite an old man for anywhere in Britain, but especially for Stroma, where the harsh climate aged people and took most before their time.

"I will be back in plenty of time to make the noonday meal." Whose ingredients she would need to beg Joe Campbell to give her on account as their monthly budget was not sufficient to feed seven people, or eight if Small Cailean chose to stay.

"Very well. I shall see you when …" But his gaze wandered back to his book before he finished.

The Greedy Vicar was the social center of Stroma. Of the almost four hundred people who lived on the island perhaps one hundred lived in or near Uppertown. Another fifty or so lived in Nethertown, at the other end of the island, and the rest lived on the area known as The Mains—the agricultural center of the island.

As Martha walked toward Uppertown, she looked out over the Pentland Firth; the water between Stroma and the mainland was as smooth as proverbial glass, although she knew that could change without warning if the wind picked up.

The tiny inn/taproom/store was crowded when she entered.

"Miss Pringle!" a half-dozen voices called out.

Martha was busy greeting several of her father's parishioners when Mr. Clark approached her. For once, he was not smiling.

"Do you have a moment, Miss Pringle? Joe said we can use the small parlor."

Martha followed him into the Greedy Vicar's *only* parlor, small or otherwise. She pulled off her ancient leather gloves and then untied her bonnet.

"I'm afraid I have some bad news, Miss Pringle."

"Oh?"

"A handful of the prisoners you tended last night disappeared just before dawn. Have you checked yet to see if yours are all there?"

"My goodness! Yes, all five of mine are still in the meeting hall."

"The escapees took Lem Kennedy's boat."

Martha grimaced. "Ah."

Mr. Clarke nodded wearily. Lem Kennedy was one of the island's more fractious residents. He vocally advocated leaving the shipwreck victims to their fate rather than offering any help. He was also known to have a number of objects of questionable provenance tucked away in the caves not far from his cottage.

"There *is* some good news," Mr. Clark said. "When I went over this morning to look for Lem's boat I learned that all four lifeboats made it to shore and there were ninety-eight men aboard them: forty-two crew, the rest, er, passengers."

"Did anyone know how many were in the hold?"

"It would appear that between ours and theirs—both living and deceased—another thirty convicts and seven crew are unaccounted for."

"Dear Lord," Martha whispered. "Thirty-seven missing. Did you find out what the ship was *doing* up here?"

"The captain was not among the survivors and the crew had several different versions of a similar story, but none of them make sense. The constable thinks it was mutiny. As far as he could establish, some of the crew were determined to get the ship to Sutter's Cove."

Hugo and the Maiden

"Ah." Sutter's Cove was a well-known haunt for criminals.

"It appears the crew haven't been paid in a while. No doubt the ship would have been stripped of its valuables and sold to a buyer not overly concerned with legality. The constable is quite overwhelmed and the convicts that came on the lifeboats have been disappearing into the countryside like weasels into a cornfield. We'll have to keep the ones we've rescued for at least a week before somebody from Thurso can collect them."

Martha nodded absently. "The islanders should be warned to keep an eye on their boats."

"We've already spread the word." He hesitated. "And how about you, Miss Pringle? Has he—well, have any of the men given you any trouble?"

"No, they are behaving like gentlemen." That wasn't entirely a lie. "And the one you are thinking of is called Hugo." She hesitated and then added with a smirk, "Hugo Higgenbotham."

Chapter 6

Hugo reclined on his bench and flexed his injured leg while his brain worked on a plan for getting off this bloody island.

It had only been three days and already the gash had dried up and the swelling had gone down. He hated to admit it, but Miss Prissy Pringle had been right about the cold salt water and its healing properties. He wondered if he shouldn't ask—

The door to the meeting hall opened and the woman herself entered, followed by Cailean, who was carrying a long board that was a piece of ship's planking with the words *he Royal Cond* in faded, scrolling black script.

"Good afternoon, gentlemen." Miss Martha smiled at the other four men but ignored Hugo.

Well, he supposed he'd earned her treatment over the last few days. Despite his resolution to behave like a gentleman, he couldn't seem to stop himself from saying shocking things to tease her and elicit that delicious blush. After he'd complimented her trim ankles yesterday—which had all but begged for his attention by peeking out from beneath her too-short hem—she had stopped speaking to him.

Cailean, on the other hand, only had eyes for Hugo.

Hugo grinned at the big man and winked. "How are you this fine afternoon, little brother?" he asked, chuckling when the big lad colored up at the pet name. Hugo was relieved to see that the giant had come without his rat this time.

"I have a special treat today. Mrs. Couch sent over a wheel of her cheese and we've got fresh bread and salted fish to go with it."

Salted fish. Hugo bit back a groan; who would have ever guessed that he'd be trapped in a place where salted fish was considered a treat?

Miss Pringle turned to Cailean, who hadn't stopped staring at Hugo. "Can you bring in the keg, Small Cailean?" She cut Hugo a narrow-eyed look while the lad went outside and returned with a keg, his huge arms making it look tiny.

"Joe Cameron has also kindly offered up this cask of home brew."

There was a murmur of genuine appreciation from the other four and Hugo realized he'd better join in or risk looking like an ingrate.

Hugo and the Maiden

"What generosity and kindness the people of Stroma are showing us—and you more than anyone, Mistress Pringle." He employed an exaggerated, expansive tone of voice, as if he were declaiming from a stage.

Her plump, sensual lips—which did not match her small, serious nose or chilling blue gaze—tightened and she turned back to her makeshift tray.

"Any more news today?" Hugo asked.

"I have no new information about survivors." She paused and then added, "However, Mr. Clark just shared the news that a constable will be here sooner than he expected."

"How much sooner?" Hugo asked.

"You'll only have to spend two more nights on the island."

The earlier excitement about cheese and ale dissipated in a heartbeat and Hugo glanced around at the others. All the convicts except Franks looked as guilty as foxes caught with hens between their jaws.

Well, this wouldn't do. The only way to manage this sort of news was to give the impression of cheerful acceptance. And then run like hell the moment the islanders' backs were turned. Although how the bloody hell you were supposed to run from an island would require a bit of thinking.

Hugo decided now was as good a time as any to begin his campaign of cheerful acceptance.

"I wanted to thank you for your generosity, Mistress Pringle." He turned to the giant, who'd slowly inched closer until he was practically in Hugo's lap. "And you, too, Cailean." Hugo held out his hand and the other man stared at it. Hugo wiggled his fingers until Cailean extended a paw almost twice the size of his.

"*Bloody hell,*" he murmured as Cailean's hand gently engulfed his.

He released the giant's hand and turned to Miss Pringle, whose ironic, skeptical expression said she was not fooled for even an instant. Well, no matter, she'd not even seen the tip of the iceberg when it came to Hugo's charms. No woman could hold out against him for long.

***

Martha was surprised to see Mr. Higgenbotham up and about; she would have guessed that he was an idler. But he had risen early every morning and seemed to be moving around without his crutch today.

She studied him out of the corner of her eye as he sat on the bench beside his neatly folded bedding, doing something with his hands that held Small Cailean enraptured.

By rights Mr. Higgenbotham should have looked ridiculous in the mismatched clothing she'd gathered from various islanders. Martha had not been able to find a coat or vest to fit his broad shoulders, so he wore only a wooly jumper with his trousers. The trousers were a good three inches too short and had to be held above his narrow hips with a length of rope.

Instead of looking foolish, the soft, gray fabric molded to his body when he moved, emphasizing, rather than concealing, both his muscular thighs and bottom as well as the considerable bulge of his manhood.

Never in her entire life had Martha looked at a man *there*—not even Mr. Clark, whom she'd walked out with more than once.

She told herself that the fabric was so thin and worn that it was difficult *not* to catch a glimpse. But that was a lie; she never just *glimpsed*. It was as if a team of oxen dragged her eyes to the front of his hips and then parked them there.

Martha had seen male dogs and horses aplenty, and Mr. Higgenbotham appeared far closer in size to the latter.

The loosely knitted sweater that stretched across his shoulders was the sort that island men wore while fishing: a boat-necked garment with raglan sleeves that was easy to pull on and off. Whoever had owned the sweater before had been smaller than Mr. Higgenbotham, and the striped pattern was distorted by his muscular chest but then loose around his narrow waist.

It was also too short to cover a full two inches of his tightly woven and extremely mesmerizing stomach.

To Martha's horror, every time she saw him, saliva pooled in her mouth and her fingers actually twitched to stroke and explore the tantalizing ridges and veins that disappeared beneath the low-slung trousers.

Only his footwear did not create uncomfortable sensations between her tightly clenched thighs. On one foot he wore a sturdy brown boot that looked at least a size too large and on the other—amazingly—he wore a gentleman's dancing slipper, which could only have come from a wrecked ship because she had never seen a man on Stroma sport such footwear.

Hugo and the Maiden

Martha raised a hand to her mouth to cover her smile as she stared at his feet.

"I shall see you later this afternoon, little brother," Mr. Higgenbotham said to Cailean, who stood and gathered up Lily to leave.

Martha waved to Small Cailean as he left and then, against her better judgment, crossed the room to see what Mr. Higgenbotham was working on.

"Good afternoon, Mistress Pringle." His lids lowered and the smile that curved his thin lips made something low in her belly—something *beneath* her belly, truth be told—tighten, sending sparks of pleasure shooting through her body.

His nostrils flared as he watched her, almost as if he were scenting something.

Martha suddenly knew—she just *knew*—that he was aware of what his suggestive, naughty looks did to a woman. Did to *her*.

As he appeared disinclined to do anything but smirk, it was up to her to end the uncomfortable silence. "What were you showing Small Cailean?"

He wordlessly handed her a tightly braided cord.

Martha ran a finger over the intricate braiding. "Why, this is lovely," she said, looking up and catching him staring, his expression brooding. "The work is so perfect and uniform—even with this rough old rope. Where did you learn such a thing?"

"I worked for a whip-maker when I was younger." He smiled up at her, his teeth white but crooked, the canines wolfishly sharp. "He didn't hesitate to use those implements on me when my work was anything less than perfect."

Martha hated how her face heated constantly in his presence; why was he able to make even the most repulsive subject sound wicked?

"That's dreadful," she said firmly, refusing to be baited by his mischievous look. "I do not condone whipping children—or anyone, for that matter." She handed him back the length of braid.

Amusement glinted in his dark eyes. "I do not condone whipping, either. At least not for children or animals."

Martha frowned. She was just about to ask him exactly for *whom* he did condone it when a voice spoke beside her.

"Miss Pringle?"

She startled and turned to face Mr. Franks.

"I'm sorry, miss, I didn't mean to scare you."

Martha gave him a genuine smile, grateful to him for breaking the spell Hugo seemed to weave around her without even trying. "How are you feeling today, Mr. Franks?"

"Fit as a fiddle, miss, and ready to do something to earn my keep."

"Why do I think that you might be exaggerating slightly, Mr. Franks?"

"No, miss. I feel better than I've felt in weeks."

Hugo snorted but Martha ignored him.

"Well, since you're offering, Cailean just left to do his weekly peat deliveries. I'm sure he would appreciate it if you brought ours up here for him."

"Thank you, miss. It would be my pleasure."

"Anything I might do?" the convict named Devlin asked.

"Perhaps you might carry all the bedding outside to the cauldron that's heating over the fire."

"Allow me to do the wash for you, Miss Pringle," the prisoner named Parker offered. "I worked in a hotel in London and often did such work."

A man doing washing? Martha looked at his eager face; well, why not? "Thank you, Mr. Parker, that would give me more time to prepare our next meal."

Lorn Smith, the youngest of the prisoners—who had a broken leg that prevented him from walking—gave her a pained look. "I'm sorry, miss, but I'm good for nothing."

He couldn't have been more than fifteen and Martha wondered what a mere boy could have done to deserve banishment to the other side of the world.

"Don't fret yourself, Lorn, I've got potatoes for you to peel."

He grinned as if she'd just promised him a shiny guinea.

"And what about me, Mistress Pringle?" a low, velvety voice asked beside her. "How may I serve you?"

Martha forced her face into stern lines, hoping that would disguise the pounding in her chest, and turned. It was all she could do to keep her eyes from dropping to his hips, checking to see if he was really as big as she'd seen yesterday.

Instead, she met his mocking gaze. "Can you walk without aid of your stick, Mr. Higgenbotham?"

Hugo and the Maiden

His lips twitched at the sound of the faux name. "Yes, but not very quickly, I'm afraid."

"You won't have to walk fast to do what I need."

"And what is it that I can do for you ... mistress?"

"I have a rather important job in mind for you."

"Anything you desire," he said in a voice heavy with ... something.

Martha smiled sweetly and Hugo's dark eyes widened. "The three chamber pots are in desperate need of emptying and cleaning."

A snorting chuckle came from young Lorn and Martha almost laughed, too, as Mr. Hugo cut the injured boy a filthy look.

"I'm not sure I can walk that far," he said, no longer sounding teasing or sensual.

"You've only to take them as far as the pit out back of the building. I'm sure you can manage such a short distance if you take your time. It will be good exercise for your leg."

His sour expression was more than enough reward for the disturbing effects that his wicked body, looks, and words had on her.

***

Hugo dumped the last pot into the pit, grimacing and squeezing his eyes shut at the pungent odor that emanated from the narrow, deep hole.

He walked just far enough away to gulp in fresh air and then paused to stretch his leg, working the knee carefully while flexing his foot. It hurt like a bastard, but the deep gash was dry and pinky-red rather than puss-yellow. The wound had started to shrink and pull on the healthy skin, which hurt more than the wound itself had. He wondered if the woman would give him some type of salve if he asked.

Do you think that you can ask for something without saying the words bloody *or* fuck?

Hugo ignored his irksome inner voice, instead turning to gaze out over the small valley that was south of the meeting house. He shook his head at what he saw. Not in a million years could he have imagined that a place like this godforsaken island even existed in Britain.

Growing up in the desperate, grinding poverty of St. Giles, he'd not believed there could be anyplace worse than London's rookeries, but he'd been wrong.

The Stroma islanders were as poor as the denizens of St. Giles but they seemed content—*proud*, even—to live and labor on this frigid rock at the arse end of the world.

Take Miss Prissy, for example. She was no longer young—although her smooth skin and bright blue eyes said she couldn't be much more than twenty—but she was still young enough that she should want something better from her life, something far away from *here*. She still had a bit of bloom left, but when that was gone, she'd be forced to pick from the pitiful stock of islander men he'd seen these past few days.

Since most of the younger people, male and female, seemed to have left the island, Martha's only real choice for husband was the ruggedly handsome and pompously stuffy Robert Clark.

Hugo had seen the looks that Clark gave the vicar's daughter when he thought nobody was watching. If Miss Prissy wasn't careful, she'd find herself leg-shackled to a man with the personality of a halibut and stuck on this rock for good.

Hugo snorted as he considered Clark's furtive, hungry glances. Perhaps the only good part about being a whore—aside from the money—was that it freed a man from being a slave to the demands of his cock. If Hugo wanted a fuck, he'd pay for one—not bloody court and marry some female. Not that any decent woman of good sense would have him for a husband, of course.

The hungry looks that the upstanding Mr. Clark gave the upstanding Miss Pringle when he thought nobody was watching were positively wolfish. Hugo would wager everything he had—which, admittedly, wasn't much at the moment—that the wholesome Mr. Clark went home every night and fisted himself raw to randy thoughts of prim Martha Pringle.

No doubt the two would marry, she'd squeeze out a couple of brats, and they'd eke out their meager living eating salt fish and wearing woolen clothing harsh enough to scrape off what little bit of skin the vile winds didn't already scour from their bodies.

Hugo shifted and winced as the abrasive wool of his trousers rasped over his bare cock.

You're spoiled, lad, his mental companion sneered. *Too many years wrapping yer arse in silk has made you weak—soft.*

Hugo snorted at that last accusation as he rubbed a hand over his midriff, which was as hard as the wooden pew he was currently using

Hugo and the Maiden

for a bed. Soft was one thing Hugo Buckingham was not. Especially his cock, which was taking an inconvenient interest in Miss Pringle's delicious little body as well as her pouty lips and amusingly rough tongue.

Hugo suspected the erection he'd woken with this morning was not so much the product of the erotic dream he'd enjoyed about Miss Pringle as it was the result of his near-death experience on the ship. He knew from his younger, wilder, days that brushes with danger could leave a man with a ferocious desire for sex.

And there was also the fact that he'd not *used* any of his erections for weeks. He'd been a whore since he was fourteen, and—with the exception of the few times in his life when he'd been too ill to work—he'd rarely gone a day without engaging in some form of sexual activity.

Back when Melissa Griffin had owned Solange's she'd ordered him to take brief holidays every year. What Mel never knew was that Hugo had spent those holidays at an expensive London hotel where he'd continued to work, taking those clients who were eager enough for his body and skills that they would risk coming to him outside the safe confines of the brothel.

Hugo gingerly lowered himself to his knees to grab a fistful of sawgrass to scour out the shitty pot. He held his breath as he scrubbed, thinking about Melissa, the closest thing he'd ever had to a friend—although he wasn't sure Mel would say the same about him.

The gorgeous red-headed madam was also the only woman Hugo could recall ever lusting after—before now—although not for love or marriage.

Hugo had wanted Mel for the same reasons England's most rich and powerful men had paid a king's ransom for one night with her: not for her beauty—he knew a dozen women more beautiful—but because she was utterly unattainable, at least emotionally.

A man could buy Mel Griffin's body—although she'd refused to sell it to Hugo, no matter how much he'd offered—but he could never have the rest of her: at least not until Mel met Lord Magnus Stanwyke.

Hugo snorted. The most sought-after madam in Britain caught by a bloody vicar. How was such a marriage even legal?

He shrugged away his annoyance: it was done now, Mel was married and disgustingly happy, with one brat and another on the way. Who would have ever believed that a whore could be so content as the wife of a clergyman—especially such a moralizing prick as Stanwyke?

Hugo tossed the shit-sodden grass into the pit and straightened his aching leg with a groan before limping over to the bucket of used wash water.

He still corresponded with Mel—even though she'd refused to give him any guidance when it came to running Solange's because her husband forbade her to have any involvement with a brothel.

It would never cease to amaze him that there was a man alive that Mel Griffin would take orders from. But everyone, apparently, knelt to somebody.

Everyone except for Hugo.

Hugo enjoyed exchanging letters with Mel, and not only because he knew it drove her blond god of a husband half-mad to know his wife kept in touch with him.

He grinned at the thought, dumped some of the old wash water into the pot, and swirled it around before tossing it into the stunted foliage.

It was the last of the shit pots, so he limped back to the meeting house with the clean vessel, placed it inside, and then sat on the steps and watched the washing process that was taking place in the sheltered area between the tiny cottage and meeting house.

Devlin and Parker were stirring the steaming cauldron and talking in low voices like a pair of scheming witches. Hugo would have bet his left ballock they were discussing how to get the hell off this bloody rock.

It was a sign of Miss Martha's innocence that she had told them when the authorities would come from the mainland with a prisoner manifest.

Young Lorn wasn't in any shape to make a run for it, but the rest of them were healthy and hale enough. Although Hugo doubted the ginger-hackled man—Albert Franks—would try to escape.

It should have been obvious even to an idiot that Franks had never committed a crime in his entire life. He must have crossed somebody with enough money to have him scooped up and sent to the other side of the world. It fascinated Hugo to wonder what a mild-as-milk man like Franks could have done to so anger a person that they would have him kidnapped and transported.

Hugo extended his gammy leg and flexed it. He had no money, barely enough clothing, and no boat. There was only one way to acquire all three of those things: steal it from these impoverished rustics.

Hugo chewed his lower lip as he considered the little stone house the vicar shared with his daughter. None of the vicar's clothing would fit him, Hugo knew they had no boat, and he doubted they possessed a single coin between them.

But the vicar must take a collection from his parishioners, mustn't he? Even on an island as poor as this one there was a church near the little cluster of shacks they called a town.

Although he'd never stepped foot in a church in his life, Hugo knew about the concept of tithing—a way for the church to suck money out of their flock the way a poor man sucked the marrow from a bone. Ten percent of what they earned was the figure he'd heard. With Hugo's luck the islanders would pay with fish or produce or livestock.

Hugo snorted. He could just picture himself heading south with a sack of mackerel over his shoulder and a laying hen tucked under his arm.

Miss Pringle came out of the tiny stone house. She ignored Hugo and went, instead, to the two men laboring over the caldron of laundry. The sleeves of her unfashionable day dress were rolled up to her elbows and her thick corn-silk-colored hair—her best feature next to those sinner's lips of hers—had come loose in places and strands adhered to her damp temples. He'd seen no maid or scullery lass so Hugo knew she must keep house for herself and her father. And now there were the five of them—strangers she was feeding and tending.

At least one of whom was contemplating stealing from her.

It took him a long, disoriented moment to identify the sensation that crept over him: shame.

Since when had he been afflicted with such a loathsome emotion?

Hugo scowled and dragged his attention back to the business at hand: escaping. Besides, if he stole anything from the Pringles, he'd send back ten-fold when he got to London.

He couldn't leave tonight for several reasons: his leg needed another day's rest and he had to assemble money, clothing, and find a boat. Which only left tomorrow night. His stomach churned at the thought of waiting, but he had no choice.

Miss Pringle and the two convicts chatted like normal people, a skill Hugo had yet to learn. At his age he'd probably never learn to get on with people other than whores. Actually, he didn't get along with most whores, either. Take his business partner, for example—because that is obviously the person who'd engineered this stunt. Laura hated him enough to banish him to a living hell on the other side of the world.

Yes, Hugo had quite a way with people.

He shrugged. So what if he couldn't conduct meaningless chatter and people didn't like him?

He pushed himself off the steps and headed toward town, his mind back on business. He might not be well-liked or be able to behave like a normal person, but he was the bloody best at deciding what he wanted and then taking it from whomever he had to, without even a grain of remorse.

Chapter 7

Martha tried to stay away from Hugo—she refused to call him Mr. Higgenbotham in the privacy of her own mind—but he was like the proverbial flame to her moth.

Her father was eating at Mr. Stogden's, an older man who lived alone on the southwest side of the island, so she took her meal with their guests.

She'd made a fish stew for dinner and they ate with the meeting house doors propped open since the summer had been unusually warm and pleasant for Stroma.

"Thank you, Miss Pringle," Mr. Franks said as he took both his bowl and Lorn's. He seated himself across from the younger man on a pew somebody must have helped him turn around. Between the men was a stool with a board and chess pieces on it. Martha had brought the game when Mr. Franks had mentioned he might teach Lorn how to play to while away the time.

Parker and Devlin sat together on another bench, talking quietly while Devlin employed a needle and thread, doing a remarkably neat job of stitching up a rent in his coat.

That left Hugo, who was sitting at the makeshift table with Small Cailean, chuckling about something. No doubt he was corrupting the younger man. It was Martha's duty to see that didn't happen.

She strode purposely toward the two men. "May I join you?"

Hugo stood immediately and gestured to his stool. "Please, sit here, Mistress Pringle."

"Oh, I didn't know there were only two seats. I wouldn't want to—"

"It's no bother. Please, sit."

"Thank you."

Hugo fetched the spent keg that was waiting to be returned to Joe Cameron and put it down between Martha and Cailean. When he sat, his chin barely reached the table.

Small Cailean made a soft, huffing sound and then quickly covered his mouth with his hand, as if laughter were something bad.

Martha couldn't help smiling; Hugo did look rather silly.

"Look at you two," Hugo said, shaking his head, "Making fun of a chivalrous man like myself."

"Why do I find it difficult to think of you and chivalry in the same breath, Mr. Higgenbotham?"

He placed his right hand over his heart. "You wound me." Before she could respond he asked, "Tell me, how long have you lived here, Miss Pringle?"

The polite question surprised her. Gone was the surly, imperious man who'd arrived in Small Cailean's arms only a few nights ago.

"We moved here from Leeds when I was nine months old."

Hugo ate another mouthful of soup before turning to Cailean. "And what about you, Master Cailean—an islander born and bred?"

Cailean nodded, his shy expression joined by a flush of pleasure, making Martha realize that most of the islanders never asked him questions—or talked to him, at all. They just gave him orders.

"And what about *you*, Mr. Higgenbotham?"

"*Moi?*" He splayed his right hand over his chest, his eyes wide. "Why I've only come to Stroma quite recently."

Cailean chortled and Hugo's lips curled up at the corners, the expression making him look more like a satyr than ever.

"I meant where are you from, Mr. Higgenbotham?"

Martha could see that it amused him that she continued to call him by a name she knew to be false rather than use his Christian name.

"I'm from London." While his smile didn't disappear, his dark eyes shuttered.

"London is a large place; from what part do you hail?"

"A place called St. Giles." He cut her a sly look. "You've heard of it?"

Who in Britain hadn't heard of the infamous enclave? "It was once a leper colony."

He blinked. "Really?"

Martha experienced a flare of pleasure. *Take that, Mr. Higgenbotham, you don't know everything, do you?*

"A very long time ago, perhaps one hundred years after The Conquest. St. Giles was the patron saint of lepers, you know."

"I *didn't* know that, but it certainly sounds right. It's the worst cesspool of humanity in the entire country, but I've never seen a leper. Well, perhaps social lepers, if there is such a thing." He smiled wryly. "Tell me, how is it that you know the history of lepers in St. Giles?"

"I like to read. And I help at the school when it is in session."

"Oh? A teacher?"

"Nothing so grand—'a helper' would be more accurate." She hesitated and then asked, "Did they not teach the history of London in your school?"

Hugo laughed. "They barely taught English."

"But you read—I saw you with the books I brought yesterday—so you must have learned something."

He finished his soup and sighed with obvious pleasure, patting his stomach, which was as flat and ridged as a washboard. "Thank you for the delicious meal, Miss Martha."

Martha was not entirely sure she approved of his form of address. Also, she was not going to let him evade her question.

"Was your school really so terrible?" she persisted.

"No, they did their best with too few teachers and too many pupils."

"If you don't mind my saying so, your accent does not strike me as one from the, er, rookeries." Martha could see by his knowing grin that he was amused, rather than insulted, by her clumsy probing.

An expression that looked very much like fondness flitted across his hard features. "A friend of mine told me that my accent was execrable, so I made her help me with my *el oh cue shun*."

He had female friends? Why did that sound so ... unusual, for a man and woman to be friends? Did Martha have any male friends? Small Cailean was a friend, of course—although they didn't discuss things.

Mr. Clark was a suitor, but Martha wasn't sure she would call him a friend. Why was that? They discussed matters concerning the island, of course, but rarely anything personal. Could that still be considered friendship?

"Where's your fur scarf today, little brother?" Hugo asked Cailean, interrupting her musing.

The boy gave another of his silent laughs, whether at Lily being a scarf or at having a nickname, she didn't know. Martha liked how Hugo included the quiet giant in conversations. She was guiltily aware that she'd not done as much of that as she should have.

"Well," Hugo said, standing. "I believe it is my turn at the dishes today." He took his bowl and Cailean's before glancing at Martha's.

"May I take that, Miss Martha?" he asked, his lips curved into that slight smile that did such unnerving things to her body.

What was wrong with her? It was just a smile!

Martha handed him the bowl, jerking back her hand when his finger brushed hers.

She watched him walk—although it was actually more of a strut—the short distance to the bucket of water the men used to wash their dishes, unable to keep her gaze from lingering on his muscular bottom and the band of pale flesh between the low-slung trousers and the hem of his too-small sweater.

Martha might be inexperienced, but she was not stupid. She knew the sensations flooding her body and causing parts of her anatomy to tingle and swell were of a sexual nature. She'd had similar experiences in the past. For example, when Mr. Clark came to walk out with her, she'd often felt a pleasant fluttering in her stomach.

But this feeling was no mild flutter; it was raw, primal, and frightening.

What was happening to her?

***

Stealing a boat, Hugo decided, would be far easier than he'd thought. Even though convicts had already stolen two crafts, the fishermen still left their boats lying about on the shore.

Hugo could just go down to the small beach and pick one that didn't look leaky.

After thinking about it long and hard he'd decided against stealing a coat or better pair of shoes—even though the undersized dance slipper on his right foot felt more like a rat trap than footwear.

It wasn't his conscience that kept him from pinching a pair of shoes, but lack of availability. Spare clothing was rare on the island, and spare footwear even rarer. Most people only owned a single pair of boots or shoes, which meant that he would have to steal the items off somebody's body while they were wearing it. Even Hugo drew the line at that.

But money was another matter; money he could not do without.

He needed to find the church strongbox—if there was one. If there wasn't, then Hugo didn't know what he'd do.

He refused to steal from the Pringles, who'd fed and sheltered him. Besides, the more time he spent around Miss Pringle, the more he suspected that she would sense his presence in her house even in her sleep.

Hugo was an expert when it came to recognizing desire and lust and could spot a virgin from fifty paces away. Poor Martha Pringle was currently being violated by thoughts she'd never imagined herself having without bursting into flames.

Yes, Miss Prissy Pringle wanted him badly—or at least her body did. Hugo knew that the physical sensations she was experiencing were wreaking havoc in her erstwhile safe and predictable world.

Unfortunately, he didn't have the excuse of being a virgin to explain his own reaction to the woman. He was—quite astoundingly and unwillingly—fiercely attracted to the vicar's prim daughter.

He'd never had such a strong physical reaction to anyone before. Why Martha Pringle—a censorious, repressed, prudish vicar's daughter—exerted such a pull on him, he simply couldn't comprehend.

His body didn't care that his mind was annoyed or offended. In fact, it would be fair to say his body *rejoiced* in her innocent prudishness.

Every single time her harlot lips pursed in a virtuous scowl as her gaze lingered on his crotch—which happened whenever she saw him—he became hard.

Every single time he made her blush or gasp or frown, he became hard.

In short, every single thing she did or said made him hard.

Hugo had no idea why. Perhaps it was witnessing the way her disapproval of him warred with her obvious desire? As virtuous as she was, she couldn't stop herself from wanting him—even though she wasn't sure exactly what it *was* that she wanted. Somehow that restored his faith in human nature.

He took a great deal of pleasure imagining her lying in her bed at night rubbing that itch between her legs while trying *not* to think of him.

Hugo was a bad person for thinking such a thought and he was doubly bad for enjoying it so much. But as bad as he was, even he refused to obey his body's commands and debauch the vicar's daughter.

He pushed the virginal temptress from his mind and turned his attention toward finding a way to get into the church.

So he could rob it.

"Oh God," he muttered, shaking his head. He was going to Hell. But then, had there ever really been any doubt of that?

Chapter 8

As luck would have it, it was the vicar himself who told Hugo the location of the church collection money.

Hugo was braiding rope on the meeting house steps when the vicar came ambling over to see what he was doing. "Why, that is lovely work, Mr. Higgenbotham."

"Thank you, sir." Hugo imagined what the old fellow would say if he knew Hugo's facility was the result of making whips, crops, and floggers for erotic punishment.

He was accustomed to using the finest, most supple leather, but the only materials available on the island were scraps of fishing rope. It wasn't bad rope, but it didn't offer much comfort or cushion to a person's hand if you needed to carry a bucket a long distance. So, he'd decided to braid several pieces together to make thicker handles for the buckets that Cailean carried all over the island like a beast of burden. Other people had seen the handles and the requests were pouring in. One old man had even offered to trade him a pair of gloves for two handles.

"Could you make one of these just as thick, but longer?" the vicar asked, the question pulling Hugo from the hypnotic task of braiding.

"I can make them as long as you want, although I'd need longer pieces than the pitiful scraps I'm using for this one."

"I can get you longer rope," the vicar said, his pale cheeks flushed with excitement. "Would you mind taking a walk down to the church so I could show you what I need?"

It was all Hugo could do not to leap to his feet and cheer.

So off they headed.

Their pace was, by necessity, snaillike as the old man was as thin and fragile as a twig.

"You are an exceptionally well-spoken man, Mr. Higgenbotham. What did you do before you were, er, put onboard that ship?"

"I own properties in London, which I lease for income." That wasn't entirely a lie.

"Ah."

Hugo and the Maiden

A pregnant pause followed as they strolled down the hard-packed road that linked both ends of the island. Hugo suspected that knew what the old man would say even before *he* did.

"I do hope you will pardon my temerity," the vicar said, his pale, papery cheeks coloring, this time with embarrassment rather than excitement. "But I can't help thinking that you and Mr. Franks seem, er, out of place among the others. I only say this based upon my impressions after calling on all the rescued men to offer the opportunity to unburden their consciences."

Hugo smirked at the man's careful substitution of the word *rescued* for *convicts*.

The vicar had offered the same chance to the five men at the meeting house. Hugo had politely declined, not wishing to contemplate either his tarnished conscience or how many years of the vicar's life it would take to listen while Hugo unburdened it.

"Out of place?" Hugo said when it appeared the older man was waiting for an answer.

"You both seem like good men to me. How did you come to be in the hold of that ship?"

He experienced an odd sensation at hearing this kind and intelligent man's description of him. Nobody, to his knowledge, had ever called him *good*.

Even Melissa had often told Hugo that he was a soulless bastard only out for his own gain.

He *was* a soulless bastard out for his own gain and the vicar was wrong, of course—that went without saying—but Hugo decided he liked that this saintly man had a good impression of him.

I wonder if he'll feel that way after you steal church money and abscond with it?

Hugo scowled. *I'll send him back a hundred bloody pounds to cover whatever I take.*

He glanced down at the vicar, whom, he saw, was patiently waiting for his story.

"It is widely accepted that every man in Newgate has been wrongly accused," Hugo said.

The vicar chuckled. "Oh, I daresay that is true." He cut Hugo a surprisingly shrewd look. "I'd also say some of those men *are* innocent—or at least no guiltier than many others who are walking free. Being confined is not, in itself, proof of criminal behavior, Mr. Higgenbotham."

"You are a philosopher, sir."

"So my daughter tells me. But we were speaking of you," he reminded Hugo gently.

Hugo sighed. He'd tell as much of his story as he could without shocking the old man into heart failure.

"I believe my business partner paid to have me abducted and wrongly accused of theft. I was given no opportunity to provide a defense before I was convicted. Afterward, I was put into a cell with other men who had similar experiences.

"I've done more than my share of questionable things in my time," Hugo confessed, not wanting to look the other man in the eyes when he said that. "But I'm innocent of what I've been charged with. I would wager my left bal—er, a good deal of money," he amended, "that the same is true of Albert Franks." Hugo chuckled. "In fact, Mr. Franks has the look of a man whose mind has never been violated by an illegal or immoral notion in his entire life."

The vicar nodded as he followed Hugo up the steps to the stone church. "I concur that Mr. Franks radiates innocence."

Hugo pulled open the heavy door and entered a church for the first time in his life. He was more than a little surprised that the clouds didn't part and a bolt of lightning didn't strike him dead.

The vicar led him to a stone bench whose wooden top lifted to reveal rolls of canvas, a toolbox, and other bits and bats.

"What I'd like is one of your braided pulls for our church bell," the vicar confessed as they studied the contents of the bench.

As they discussed the best way to replace the worn ties with something sturdier and yet still attractive—a task that Hugo would never actually complete—Hugo thought about the vicar's earlier statement: that Hugo was a good man.

There'd been a time in his life—for most of it, really—when he would have felt proud to have deceived another person so thoroughly.

Now, all he felt was a profound sense of loss.

***

Hugo waited until two hours after dark to make his escape.

The vicar had left him alone in the church to work on the new braided ropes, trusting him in a way that made Hugo want to scream.

Hugo and the Maiden

Didn't these people know the island was infested with criminals? Hadn't they learned their lesson already?

He'd easily found the church collection—a handful of shillings and pennies—in a small wooden box with *no* lock.

As he'd sat looking at the pitiful little pile of coins he'd decided that it felt *worse* to take such a paltry sum than it would have felt to take a thousand pounds. He didn't want to take it, but he desperately needed it—and it wouldn't be nearly enough.

But it was all he had, so he'd scooped it up and wrapped it in a square of torn canvas and tucked it into his trouser pocket, briefly wishing he had a way to leave a note in the box assuring the vicar that he would reimburse him. But he didn't have ink, quill, or paper, so wishing was pointless.

After stealing God's money from the vicar Hugo lost all interest in any further thieving.

He had wanted to bring food with him but decided he'd forage once he'd made it across the firth. Besides, he seemed to have lost his appetite along with his will to steal—an affliction he could not recall experiencing before.

Carrying only his shoes and the stolen coins, Hugo tiptoed out the door in his bare feet. He went round to the back of the meeting hall and sat on the ground to put on his shoes. His left foot was calloused and bleeding from the ridiculous dance slipper, which already had a hole the size of a guinea in the sole.

Well, it couldn't be helped.

Once he was shod, there was no putting it off. He decided to stride down the main road rather than skulk. After all, the bloody island had no trees, so skulking would be difficult to pull off in any case.

As he headed for the narrow path, he cut the little stone house one last glance. "Goodbye, Miss Martha Pringle. I hope you enjoy a long and happy life," he whispered, stunned by the hollow feeling in his gut.

Hugo shook himself. No doubt he was feeling odd because he'd not been able to eat much at supper, which had been—

"Good evening, Hugo."

Hugo leapt a good foot in the air and his throat constricted to the diameter of a pin, yet he still managed to utter a mortifying squeak. He spun around and found Mr. Pringle sitting on a low stool on the side of the cottage.

They stared at each other, the only sounds Hugo's labored breathing and the surf, which was audible from anywhere on the small island.

Mr. Pringle lifted up his hand and Hugo squinted: he was holding a pipe—a meerschaum.

"It is my most persistent vice," the vicar admitted, his voice low but not a whisper. "I don't smoke it any longer—it upsets Martha too much—but it still makes me feel meditative to simply hold it."

A compulsion to confess struck him. "I took—"

"I know you took the money."

"What? How? You never returned to the church, did you?"

"No. But I could see it in your eyes. Not *what* you were going to do, only that you were going to do something that made you uneasy. It was simple to guess what."

"I'm going to send you back your money and a good deal more."

"I don't doubt it."

Hugo gaped at the unexpected response.

"Did it ever occur to you that you could simply *ask* me for the money?"

Hugo scoffed. "And you would have given it to me?"

"Yes. The money you took is for those who need it. I believed your story about being innocent of what you were charged with, Mr. Higgenbotham."

He heaved a sigh. "Buckingham."

"I beg your pardon?"

"My name—it's Buckingham." That was another lie, but a much older one. "I only told your daughter it was Higgenbotham to tease her."

The vicar chuckled. "It makes her smile whenever she says it—and Martha is such a serious girl that I love seeing her smile."

Hugo had no idea what to say to that.

"I won't tell them about the money, but you must know that they will come looking for you. Taking a boat—even for temporary use—is a grave infraction to people who rely on such things for their livelihoods. If you do this tonight, Mr. Buckingham, you will have no defense when the authorities apprehend you. And I think you must know they *will* catch you. Have you ever lived in the country before?"

"No."

"I thought not. You will be an easy target. But if you stay—"

Hugo and the Maiden

"If I stay I shall be an even *easier* target," Hugo said with barely suppressed anger.

"Not if I help you."

"I beg your pardon, Mr. Pringle, but how can you help me?"

"The word of a clergyman carries weight in this area. Not only that, but it is my understanding there was something odd about the ship you were on. The fact that a convict transport was up near Stroma, for a start."

"But how can you help me?"

"I won't tell you *how,* I just give you my word that I *will* see to it that you are not taken back when the constables or runners or what-have-you come to fetch the prisoners."

Hugo wondered if he were dreaming. "Why? Why would you do such a thing?"

"I want a favor."

"I beg your pardon—did you say you wanted a favor?"

"Yes."

"May I ask what kind of favor?"

"I believe you just did." The vicar grinned impishly. "I'm sorry, that was childish. As to the favor—I will tell you what I want after I have guaranteed your freedom. That is the bargain, Mr. Buckingham."

"How do you know I'll keep my part of the bargain?"

"That is entirely up to you." The kindly old vicar suddenly looked terrifyingly stern.

Hugo glanced away, unable to bear the other man's piercing gaze, which seemed to burn its way into his soul. Or what he supposed was his soul, not that he'd ever given the matter much thought.

Mr. Pringle stood, the action accompanied by creaks and pops as his old body straightened. "I will leave you to your decision, Mr. Buckingham." He smiled, once again a kindly old man. "I'll have my answer one way or another come morning." He disappeared around the corner of the house.

"Fucking hell," Hugo cursed under his breath. A favor? Just what did the old gimmer want from him? What *could* he want? Money? Hugo had already offered him that.

Hugo stared across the firth, the distant mainland visible under the partial moon. His mind played out his escape: he would row across—it was not far, two miles he'd heard a local say. It was a beautiful, calm night, so he'd have no problems. If the headland was as rugged as

Stroma—and there was no reason to believe it wasn't—the cliff faces would outnumber the beaches and it might take him a while to find a place to land the craft. And then he would begin his six-hundred-plus-mile walk to London.

Hugo groaned. It sounded like a bloody nightmare.

He stared at the silent, dark stone house. But what if the vicar was wrong? What if he couldn't save Hugo when the men came to take them?

He thought about Mr. Pringle's eyes—they were faded and old and did not see clearly, but they'd held a degree of certainty Hugo did not think was feigned. If the vicar said he would set him free, the man would.

"Bloody hell," Hugo grumbled. He glanced around and noticed that—while he'd been dithering—his sore, bleeding feet had already led him back to the meeting house.

It must be a dream. He, Hugo Buckingham, a man who never trusted a soul, would trust this ancient vicar he'd met not even five days ago?

"You're a mad bastard, Hugo," he whispered as he dropped onto the meeting house steps and removed his shoes before opening the heavy door on the right, wincing as it gave a low but audible groan.

Hugo barely took two steps into the darkness of the meeting house when his head exploded.

Chapter 9

As usual, Small Cailean was waiting outside the cottage door at dawn to carry the porridge out to the meeting house.

"Good morning, Cailean. Thank you for helping me today."

Cailean gave him an abstracted smile, his thoughts obviously on the man who was currently occupying far too much time in both their thoughts.

Martha had woken up early that morning, determined that today she would *not* follow Hugo Higgenbotham around like a lost puppy.

He was a convicted criminal; he only flirted and teased her because she was female, not because he had any real interest in her; and he would be gone in less than two days.

So, those were three good reasons to avoid him.

Armed with her new resolve, she marched to the meeting house and then stopped abruptly. The cracked oar that she used to stir the laundry was jammed through both handles of the double doors.

"What in the world?" she muttered.

She turned to Small Cailean. "Why don't you put that on the step," she spoke in a gentle and calm tone even though the hairs on her neck prickled.

After they'd both put down their burdens, Small Cailean had to yank hard on the oar to free it.

"Will you wait for me over there?" Martha pointed to the corner of the building. "If anything happens, I want you to run as fast as you can to the village, all right?"

His face crumpled and his chin wobbled; Martha hated herself for frightening him. She laid a hand on his massive shoulder, which was trembling. "It will be all right, Cailean. Really. Go ahead," she prodded, waiting until he was cowering beside the building before opening the door.

Martha didn't know what she'd been expecting, but it certainly wasn't the sight that greeted her.

***

Hugo had been saying the same word for hours, "Fuck, fuck, fuck, fuck, fuck …"

Except his mouth was stuffed with a rancid rag and he was gagged so it sounded more like: "Fuff, fuff, fuff, fuff …"

Here he was yet again, tied up and naked. Would the humiliation never end?

And the worst of it? It was all his fault. He should have ignored the vicar's bloody conscience-twisting offer—since when did he have a conscience?—and just kept walking. The old man wouldn't have stopped him, why hadn't Hugo just stuck to his plan?

And he should have known Parker and Devlin were up to something. He *would* have known it if he'd not spent his time agonizing about robbing the islanders and sniffing around the vicar's far-too-interesting daughter.

Hugo had to give Parker and Devlin credit; he'd not heard a sound before they fell on him in the darkness.

"Sorry to steal the togs right off your back, mate," Devlin whispered in Hugo's ear while Parker bound both his knees and his ankles together with his *own* bloody braided rope. "But I'm sure you know 'ow it is because I saw you eyeballin' my boots these past few days."

The man was correct; Hugo had considered stealing his boots but gave up the plan when he saw that Devlin slept with them on his feet.

Once they'd stripped and bound him, they laid him on the cool flagstone floor in front of his sleeping bench. "Don't want you to fall off an 'urt yourself," Devlin whispered.

After that, he heard them tie up Franks and the boy, Lorn, neither of whom put up a struggle. Hugo could only assume the other two would be similarly stripped and bound.

So, there they lay, just like three game cocks, stripped, plucked, and trussed.

He enjoyed the briefest of moments contemplating the expression on Miss Pringle's face when she opened the door in the morning. But his amusement was short-lived. What if the men went into the vicar's house and stole something?

Or worse, what if they *did* something?

Hugo squeezed his eyes shut against the images that crowded his head, his temples throbbing with impotent rage and no small amount of worry.

Hugo and the Maiden

He didn't know a damned thing about Devlin or Parker—they could be forgers, or they could be murderers or rapists.

Don't borrow trouble, the voice in his head advised, good advice for a change.

Besides, surely the men would be more interested in escaping than committing more crimes?

Hugo could only hope.

As the minutes turned to hours, his bound hands and feet swelled and became numb, so he gave up on trying to free himself from his bindings. He drifted in and out of a miserable doze for a few hours. But it was a nightmare-riddled sleep that left him even more exhausted.

It was his bladder that woke him. He tried to be thankful that he'd taken a piss before bedtime, so he didn't really start to suffer until just before dawn.

There was only a hint of pale gray light coming through the windows when Hugo decided he could wait no longer.

He'd just rolled onto his side—rather than urinate on his stomach—when he heard movement outside the meeting house and the door swung open.

If he'd not been in excruciating pain both inside and out, he would have laughed. He doubted the modest young woman could have looked more shocked if she'd opened the door to a full-blown Roman orgy.

Her hands flew to her mouth and her eyes grew comically huge as they rested on his Man Thomas, which—predictably—did some significant growing of its own now that it had an audience.

Hugo closed his eyes, rolled onto his back, and let his head drop to the hard, gritty floor with a dull *thunk*. Naked, bound, *and* sporting a cock stand—and to think he'd spent the night believing things could not get any worse.

***

Martha would never be able to look Hugo in the face again without bursting into flame.

His sexual organ, she could now verify, was prodigious. Or at least it seemed so to her. For all she knew an organ that length and girth lurked in every man's trousers.

Not only had it been huge, but it hadn't looked at all like she'd expected—not that she thought about such a thing. Or at least not much.

It had been ridged and curved and darker than the rest of his skin. The top had been domed and fatter than the shaft.

And most shockingly, it had moved independently of the rest of his body when she'd looked at it—almost like it was sentient.

Martha shivered—how was it possible for a woman to take such a monstrous instrument into her body?

The wanton, wicked, and unholy though made her shiver with another emotion entirely and she fled to the back of the meeting house, leaving Cailean to untie Hugo.

Fortunately, the other two men, while missing their shirts and trousers, at least retained their smallclothes. As Martha liberated Lorn and Mr. Franks, she tried not to think about why it was so easy to keep her eyes away from their hips.

Once the men were free, Martha left Cailean in charge and ran all the way to the Greedy Vicar. The first thing she noticed after flinging open the door were four strangers standing at the bar talking to Joe Cameron, the innkeeper.

Joe smiled. "Ah, here is the lady who has been taking such good care of five of your survivors. You know Mr. McCoy, do you not, Martha?"

Martha knew of the arrogant sheriff from Wick, but she was too breathless from running to speak.

Mr. Clark, who was sitting at a table enjoying one of the Greedy Vicar's hearty breakfasts, shoved back his chair and strode toward her. "Miss Martha, is something amiss?"

"The prisoners ..." She paused, panting.

Shock and fear tightened Mr. Clark's handsome features. "Did he do something—"

"They've run," she wheezed out.

"All of them?"

"No, just two."

"Two of them escaped?" McCoy repeated, his expression grim.

Martha nodded and McCoy turned to the men beside him and they spoke among themselves before he glanced at Mr. Clark. "My men could use help from somebody who knows the island."

Mr. Clark hesitated; the other islanders would not approve of assisting any arm of the law—for any reason.

"I'll help," Clark said.

Hugo and the Maiden

Martha somehow suspected that the gleam of anticipation in his eyes was because he believed Hugo was among the escapees. He must dislike Hugo a great deal because his cooperation with the authorities would not endear him to his neighbors, many of whom kept stills or ill-gotten goods hidden on their property.

Martha lingered to watch the men split into two groups and leave while other islanders began to trickle in, no doubt having seen McCoy's boat and wondering what was afoot.

She'd just declined—with regret—Joe Cameron's offer of breakfast and was about to go back to the meeting house when she discovered that Mr. Devlin and Mr. Parker were not the only ones who'd disappeared.

***

The final count was twelve missing.

As Martha headed back to the meeting house, she couldn't help wondering how twelve men had sneaked away in the dead of night unnoticed. Something told her that they'd had help.

Cailean was standing with her father when Martha arrived.

"It seems Mr. Devlin and Mr. Parker weren't the only ones to run last night," Martha told her father.

Hugo's blanket-shrouded figure appeared in the open doorway of the meeting house. "How many?"

"Twelve."

"Bloody hell! How the devil did so many get off the island?"

For once, she ignored his foul language. "Nobody knows. There are no boats missing."

"That means they had help."

Albert Franks appeared beside Hugo, wrapped in another blanket, reminding her that she'd forgotten to beg for more clothing when she'd been at the pub.

She also recalled the other, not-so-good news she had to share.

"What is it?" Hugo demanded, as if he counted mind-reading among his many annoying abilities.

"Mr. McCoy is here from Wick with the ship's manifest."

"Bloody fucking wonderful." The furious man whirled on his heel and stomped back into the meeting hall, his blanket fluttering behind him like a cape. "I don't suppose there's another pair of trousers lying about?" he shouted from inside the building, the glass in the windows vibrating with the strength of his anger.

Albert slumped as if the weight of the world had descended on his shoulders.

Martha knew exactly how he felt and there was no lying to herself about the reason: Hugo was leaving today.

Chapter 10

After Martha had delivered the unhappy news to the men who remained in the meeting house, both she and vicar went off, heading in separate directions.

That left Hugo, Albert Franks, and the boy—Lorn—to ponder their immediate future.

Hugo was too infuriated to even think straight; what a fool he was to have listened to the vicar. He could be gone right now.

Marth returned an hour later carrying an armful of clothing.

"Here, let me help you with that, Miss Pringle," Franks said, forgetting that he was wearing a blanket and treading on it, yanking it off. "Oh, I beg your pardon," he murmured, scrambling to cover his drawers.

Martha appeared too distracted to notice and wordlessly left them to divide up the castoffs.

Hugo had just finished tying on yet another pair of too-short trousers with rope when an old farmer name Sutherland showed up leading a mule.

"Will you two gentlemen excuse us?" she asked Hugo and Franks, gesturing Mr. Sutherland into the meetinghouse.

"What do you reckon is going on in there?" Franks asked Hugo.

"Nothing too sordid," Hugo said, amused when the younger man's fair, freckled skin flamed.

There was still no sign of the vicar twenty minutes later—a fact which did not make Hugo happy—when Miss Pringle opened the door.

"We'll need your help getting Lorn onto the mule."

Hugo gave the woman a searching look, but she ignored him.

Lorn was a twig of a youngster and Hugo easily carried him out without any help from Franks.

Without saying a word to anyone, Mr. Sutherland led the young boy off on the mule.

Martha turned to Hugo and Franks after they'd gone. "Mr. Sutherland will keep Lorn at his farm until the boy is well." Her kissable lips compressed into a thin line. "He is only fifteen. He stole a silver snuffbox and was sentenced to seven years." The disgust in her voice was enough to let them know what she thought about *that*.

"Mr. Sutherland's youngest son just went off to take a job on the mainland, so he needs help on his farm. Once his leg is healed, Lorn will get another chance here if he wishes to take it."

"I don't suppose Mr. Sutherland needs an older son?" Hugo asked, only half in jest.

"Perhaps two?" Franks piped up.

"I'm sorry," she murmured, visibly unhappy.

The poor girl's misery was almost palpable, and Hugo felt bad for her, even though he would be the one suffering if Mr. Pringle didn't live up to his promise.

"Where is your father?" he asked.

"He's gone to speak to Mr. Stogden." She hesitated and then asked, "Did you wish for spiritual guidance?"

Before Hugo could answer, Clark strode up from the direction of town. "Miss Martha," Clark said, giving her a brief nod before turning to Hugo, his gaze hardening. "McCoy and his men are back from searching the island and they're ready for you."

"Did you catch the conspirators?"

Clark came closer, as if to menace him; Hugo wished he would bloody well try it.

"And how do you know they got help, Higgenbotham?"

Hugo saw Martha's lips curling up at the corners at Clark's use of his false name.

"Were you in on the escape?" the sanctimonious bastard prodded. "Is that how you knew?"

Hugo smacked himself in the forehead with his palm. "Blast. That's what I forgot to do after I helped them all escape last night—go *with* them! You're a bloody genius, Clark."

Franks laughed and Martha pressed her lips together and looked down at her shoes.

"Think you're clever, don't you?" Clark demanded.

"Not too clever if I'm still here after helping the others on their way."

"I'm here to escort you and the others to the village."

"We're ready to accompany you," Martha said coolly, giving the pillar of the community a frosty look.

Clark's forehead furrowed under her speculative gaze.

Hugo and the Maiden

Well. This was an interesting development. What had the male manifestation of masculine moral perfection done to cause Miss Martha to be displeased with him?

Clark pulled his attention from Martha and frowned at Hugo and Franks. "Where is the third one?"

"Oh, did I say there were three?" Martha asked. "I must have been addled—three escaped, only these two remain."

"But—"

She narrowed her blue eyes, her cute little jaw jutting out. "Yes, Mr. Clark?"

Hugo wondered if the man was stupid enough to ignore the danger signs and persist in his questioning. Especially with a woman he was clearly hoping to marry.

Clark stared at her for a long moment and must have decided likewise because he nodded abruptly. "Fine. On you go, you two." He gestured to the path.

Hugo and Franks walked—shoeless—in front of Clark and Martha.

It didn't take long to get to the little town and the entire way Hugo wondered what the old vicar was doing. And, more importantly, where he was. What if Pringle returned after Hugo was gone—packed away like a salted herring in the hold of some bloody ship?

Hugo's jaw was so tightly clenched that it ached. Good God, he'd been an idiot to place his trust in a forgetful old man who was likely taking a kip somewhere after his busy morning.

A veritable crowd had gathered outside the Greedy Vicar and Hugo reckoned most of the population were assembled to watch the festivities. As he looked from face to face, he wondered which of the people present had helped the convicts off the island.

Lined up against the side of the church—which was conveniently located a stone's throw from Stroma's only taproom—were seven men: seven men who'd been too stupid to leave with the others last night.

Men like Hugo, in other words.

Clark frog-marched Hugo and Franks toward the seven and then stood facing them, his arms crossed over his chest, his gaze pinned on them—well, on Hugo—as if they might try to run.

Hugo ignored him and surveyed the crowd for Mr. Pringle's distinctive white head.

A man who must be the constable or sheriff or whatever, shoved his way through the throng, two human oxen in tow.

"These are the last of them," Clark said to the newcomer, his words earning him some nasty mutters from the accreting crowd.

Hugo blinked at the hostility. Why were they behaving in a distinctly unfriendly manner toward Clark?

"My name is McCoy," the humorless-looking lawman loudly proclaimed as he unfolded several water-damaged sheets of paper and then looked up at Hugo and Albert. "I don't suppose you two lads will behave and tell me your real names?"

"Albert Franks," Franks said without hesitation.

McCoy didn't acknowledge his answer. Instead, he continued flicking through the papers, as if unaware or uncaring of the tension his continued silence was generating. Or, more likely, he was the kind of man who fed on the misery of his captives.

"And what about you?" McCoy asked a long moment later, without lifting his eyes from the list.

"Hugo Buckingham."

Clark made a soft *hmmph* and for a moment Hugo wondered if the other man would bring up the fact that he'd given the islanders a different surname. But one look at Clark's smug smirk told him that the other man was so certain that Hugo was a criminal that no other evidence would be needed.

McCoy continued studying the names for a good ten or fifteen centuries before he finally looked up. "Not surprisingly, neither of those names is on the ship's manifest."

Franks heaved a sigh and looked ready to faint. "Thank—"

"But that hardly means anything, does it?" McCoy asked. With an authority figure's unerring nose for a troublemaker, he directed this question at Hugo.

Hugo smiled. "I daresay a clever person might invent a name to evade transportation."

His words drew a few chuckles from the crowd.

But not from Martha Pringle.

She stood alone at the forefront of the crowd, her hands clenched into fists, and her mouth compressed as if she were in pain. Bloody hell! The woman's heart was in her eyes and she was all but bleeding for them—for *him*. When had another person ever been so anguished on his behalf?

Hugo and the Maiden

That was easy to answer: never.

Hugo wished that he could tell her not to waste all that emotion on him or his eternal soul; he wasn't worth worrying about and certainly couldn't be saved.

McCoy raised the list and gave the sheets a shake, the gesture pulling all eyes back in his direction. "In addition to a host of criminal charges—including smuggling and engaging in fraudulent impressment in the name of His Majesty's Navy, to name but a few—the captain of *Fortune's Lady*"—he paused to enjoy the snickers at the unfortunate name of the now splintered vessel—"was also a casualty of his mutinying crew."

McCoy paced in front of his enrapt listeners like a hawker working a crowd. "It seems the good captain was concerned about confusing his legal and illegal human cargo and gaining the wrong kind of attention when he reached New South Wales, so he had the King's prisoners strip and made additional notations to the original manifest." His piggy little eyes flickered over the convicts, again coming to rest on Hugo. "Or maybe he just wanted to see all you lads get your kit off."

There were gasps mixed in with the laughter this time.

"*Mister* McCoy," Clark chided, his face taut with anger. "There are women and children present."

Hugo glanced at the woman Clark was concerned about, but Martha was staring at him so fixedly that he knew she'd not heard the chivalry the other man had exhibited on her behalf. Hugo gave her a quick smile and a wink, which woke her from her daze. Even now—when they both knew he'd be on a boat bound for the other side of the world by the time the sun set—Hugo had the power to make her blush with just a look.

Poor girl. She'd probably end up with only Clark to teach her about her sweet body and all the wonderful sensations it could both give and receive; it was a bloody shame.

Hugo pulled his gaze away from hers and looked at the man in question.

Clark had placed his meaty fists on his hips and was staring down the vulgar lawman. Hugo felt a grudging respect for him in that moment, no matter that he was a moralizing, tedious pillock. At least he stood up for Miss Pringle and behaved as a gentleman *should* behave when it came to the woman he loved. Not that Hugo knew much about such things.

Hugo's fecund imagination was suddenly assaulted by an unwanted vision of Martha and Clark in a darkened room, Clark lifting Martha's flannel nightgown only as far as her waist before covering her small body with his larger one and rutting into her with all the finesse of a boar.

Any respect Hugo had for the other man dissipated like a fart in high wind, blown away by the sudden fury that surged through him at the imaginary vision.

Or perhaps that is jealousy you're feeling, Hugo.

Jealousy? *Jealousy!*

Ha! He'd never been jealous in his life—and certainly never when it came to sex, which represented nothing other than money in his mind.

"All right, all right, step back," McCoy said to Clark with a dismissive wave.

Once Clark had backed away, McCoy jabbed a thick finger at Albert Franks, "The only ginger-haired convict on this official manifest is in his forties—a wee bit older than you, I'd say. If you're not on my list, then I won't get paid for you. That means I don't want you." He held up a hand when Franks opened his mouth. "And before you ask, no—I won't bring you to the mainland. I'm not a ferryman."

He turned away from Franks, his muddy brown gaze settling on Hugo.

Hugo recognized the glint in McCoy's eyes: it was the look of a man who enjoyed inflicting pain for the sake of it. Their interaction, Hugo knew, would end either with him in chains or publicly humiliated, or likely both.

"Now you, Mr. *Buckingham,* well, you're a bit more difficult to discard—dark hair, dark eyes, on the tallish side"—he shrugged—"all around you're nothin' of any note."

Hugo hated himself for feeling insulted at the oaf's casual dismissal of his appearance—all the more so because he believed it was accurate: he really wasn't anything special.

At least not until he took off his clothing.

"You don't match any of the descriptions...*exactly*, but you come close enough to one—perhaps two—of the men to deserve a closer look." He glanced at the list, although Hugo was certain he'd already memorized both names and descriptions and was merely flexing his power for his audience. "Let's see—the first you resemble is James

Hugo and the Maiden

Assent. You fit the physical description and look about the same age." He looked up. "And how old would you be, Mr. Hugo Buckingham?"

"Thirty-two."

McCoy narrowed his eyes at Hugo's flat tone, and he reminded himself to act humble. Or not very smart. Or humble *and* not very smart.

Hugo fixed a fatuous expression on his face and added, "Sir."

McCoy nodded, visibly appeased.

So, a gullible, stupid bully, it would seem.

"It says short brown hair." He examined Hugo with exaggerated care. "I suppose yours might be termed on the longish side ..."

"Yes, sir," Hugo said, prepared to lick the man's boots—or anything else he might want licked—if that was what it took to keep him off the next convict ship.

McCoy's lips curled into a smug smile at Hugo's obsequious tone. "It says here that Mr. Assent has a scar from a knife wound on the right buttock." He grinned. "Kinda' amusin' that—Mr. *Ass*ent," he repeated, just in case there might be somebody in the crowd who needed it spelled out for them.

But his wit hardly earned him a chuckle from the increasingly grim islanders, so McCoy continued, "This should be simple enough to confirm drop your trousers and let's have a look."

The crowd erupted and a familiar voice cut through the noise. "Surely you don't mean for him to do so right *here*?"

All eyes turned to the vicar, who was making his way through the crush of bodies. He looked entirely awake, his blue eyes sparking with anger.

Hugo's knees almost buckled with relief.

"Who the devil are you?" McCoy demanded.

"I am Jonathan Pringle, vicar of St. Andrews," the vicar said in a voice Hugo supposed must be the old man's pulpit voice.

"Er," McCoy said, his arrogance dimming beneath the vicar's Old Testament glare.

But then somebody in the crowd snickered and McCoy frowned, his lips compressing into a stubborn line. He said, in a loud, belligerent voice, "If nobody wants to see this man's arse, they should shut their eyes. Now, *Buckingham,* turn and drop 'em."

Hugo was vaguely aware of Clark trying to hustle Martha away, but he was too concerned with obeying McCoy's command smartly to be able to spare any worry. Besides, Martha had seen a good deal more than his arse that morning.

Clark had bound Hugo's hands tightly enough that he fumbled with the rope holding up his trousers; abject terror shot through him when he couldn't loosen the bloody knot. He imagined himself back in chains simply because he couldn't pull down his damned trousers quickly enough. Fueled by that fear, he tore open the knot and the threadbare garment dropped to the ground before he could grab it.

Several high-pitched gasps from the crowd told Hugo that more than one woman had stayed to watch.

"As smooth as a baby's bottom—no knife wound to speak of." McCoy's voice brimmed with ugly amusement. "All right, Buckingham, pull 'em up."

Hugo bent to pick up his pants, the action earning him a few more gasps, before turning to face McCoy, awkwardly tying the rope at his waist.

"Are you convinced, sir?" Mr. Pringle demanded.

McCoy shrugged. "I'm not quite certain yet."

The crowd rumbled, no longer amused by the show. "I'll agree you aren't Mr. Assent," McCoy said with a smirk. "But there is another name on this list that fits your description."

"I would like to have a word with you, Mr. McCoy." The vicar's voice was stern, but not loud.

McCoy blinked. "Er—"

"It will take no more than a moment."

McCoy took a deep breath, his eyes on the restless crowd. "Very well, but I can spare only a minute or two."

"Step into the church, if you would."

Every eye followed the two men as they disappeared into the church. And then every eye came back to Hugo.

He let his gaze wander over the faces. Some were flushed, a few were judging, and some were amused.

And then there was Clark, who radiated fury and disgust.

Hugo winked at him and then looked at Martha, whom he'd purposely kept until last.

Even from where he stood, Hugo could see that her eyes had darkened. She was flushed and her chest rose and fell quicker than it should have for a person at rest. Hugo smiled at her.

Clark stepped in front of him, blocking Hugo's pleasant view.

Hugo and the Maiden

"I don't know what you've got planned, *Buckingham*, but you don't fool me. I can smell the rot on you."

"Are you sure that's not your own upper lip you're smelling?"

Several of the islanders laughed.

Hugo saw Clark's fist coming and was able to duck, dodging what would surely have been a painful blow.

"Mr. Clark!"

Martha's horrified voice must have pushed through Clark's rage because his second swing never came to fruition. Instead, he seemed to shake himself, and dropped his fist to his side, his face fiery as he realized what he'd done.

Silent disapproval rolled off the gathered islanders: What kind of man struck somebody whose hands were tied?

The door to the church opened and everyone turned as one, momentarily forgetting about Clark. McCoy's expression as he came toward Hugo was difficult to read, but Hugo would have sworn the man looked ... frightened.

McCoy stopped in front of Hugo and said, "Pull up your left sleeve."

When Hugo complied, McCoy nodded. "No tattoo, you are not the man on my list." He spun on his heel, as if he couldn't stand looking at Hugo a second longer. "Cut Mr. Buckingham and Mr. Franks loose."

Hugo's heart pounded in his ears. He was free! He was free!

Now all he had to do was get his un-scarred, un-tattooed arse back to London and kill the bitch who'd done this to him.

Chapter 11

At the urging of what seemed like half the island population, Hugo, Albert, Mr. Pringle and Martha lingered at the Greedy Vicar after McCoy and his prisoners headed back to the mainland.

Mr. Clark, Hugo couldn't help noticing, was not among those celebrating Hugo and Albert's liberation.

The three men enjoyed a pint of ale and slice of mutton pie, courtesy of Joe Cameron, while Martha drank a tiny cup of chocolate and nibbled a slab of bread slathered in butter and strawberry preserves. Hugo had never seen a person enjoy a thimble of chocolate so much. Orgasmic, that was the only word for her expression.

By the end of his meal—and not two hours after he'd exposed his bare arse to the citizens of Stroma—Hugo had received five offers of work. Either the islanders were impressed with what they saw, or—far more likely—they would support any person who got one over on the local constabulary.

The best offer, Hugo reckoned, was from Mr. Abel Stogden.

Stogden was a gruff old man who earned his crust cutting flagstone and selling it to a buyer on the mainland. Hugo thought his job sounded the most promising, but that might have been because he didn't really *understand* most of the others.

He suspected Martha had listened to his conversations, although she'd remained unusually quiet, and he was hoping she might have some guidance when it came to translating the other offers.

Unfortunately, Martha was no longer giving him the yearning looks she'd shot his way when she'd believed that he headed off to the far side of the world. She was now regarding Hugo as if he were a problem that she wasn't sure she was interested in solving.

In any event, Hugo was full of good food and ale and optimistic about the future for the first time in weeks as he followed the Pringles and Albert back to the meeting house

"You may stay at the meeting house as long as you need to," Mr. Pringle said when they reached the stone cottage. He glanced at his daughter. "But you'll need to arrange with Martha when it comes to

Hugo and the Maiden

food or laundry and whether she has time to provide such services." Mr. Pringle patted his daughter's shoulder before climbing the stone steps. "It's been a taxing day, my dear. I'll leave you young people to your own devices."

Hugo almost asked if he could have a minute of his time, but the old man looked so exhausted that he decided to wait until tomorrow to ask about the mysterious favor he now owed him.

Once the door shut behind him, Albert turned to Miss Pringle. "Please, you must tell me what I can do to help—not for future bed and board as the Wilsons offered me a job with both—but for all that you've already done for me."

Her smile was sweet and gentle and—Hugo couldn't help noticing—not an expression that she ever turned in his direction. "It's been a long day, Mr. Franks. Perhaps we can speak about the matter after church?"

"Of course, miss." He smiled shyly. "And ... thank you for everything." He turned and disappeared into the meeting house.

Her eyes swiveled to Hugo. "And you, Mr. Buckingham."

Hugo grinned. "In the flesh—but not as much as this morning."

Her jaw sagged.

"I need to ask you something," Hugo said hastily, before she slapped his face, stormed into the house, and slammed the door. "It's not anything salacious," he assured her, when she took a step back.

"Hmm."

"Is that a yes?"

She crossed her arms. "Get on with it."

"Did you hear my conversations with, er ..." He racked his brain to recall the names he'd memorized when he couldn't understand anything they said. "Mr. Craig, Mr. Donald, Mr. Smith, and, er, I think another Mr. Smith—Brian, maybe? And Mr. Stogden."

"Oh, do you mean those conversations in which the islanders were all falling over themselves to give you work?"

Hugo chuckled. "They do seem inordinately fond of me, don't they?"

"It's more that they despise McCoy and all men like him."

"How kind of you to keep me from getting a big head, Miss Pringle."

"I'm far too late for that. Do you know what a wrecker is?"

76

Hugo blinked at the change in subject. "Er, somebody who wrecks things?"

She gave him a look that could strip the barnacles off a ship's hull. "Wreckers are coastal folk who lure ships to their doom and then collect the cargo."

"Ah. But surely not the people here?"

"I will cast no aspersions, Mr. Buckingham. Aside from wrecking there is also the issue of illegal spirits. A goodly number of the islanders brew to supplement their income. They are, quite understandably, wary of anyone who might be in league with the excisemen."

"I see," Hugo said, feeling rather stupid for not discerning that fact earlier. So that was why they were angry with Clark.

"*Hmmph*. But I believe you had a question."

"Of those offers of work, which one do you advise me to accept?"

"Why are you asking me?" she asked with no little suspicion.

He scratched his head and grimaced; he was determined to wash his hair tonight even if he had to do it in freezing saltwater. "Er, mainly because the only one I could understand even a little was Mr. Stogden." He thought that might have been a smile tugging at her lips.

"Mr. Craig offered you work on his yole—it is his boat," she said when she saw his perplexed expression. "Mr. Smith, Mr. Smith, and Mr. Donald are fishermen *and* crofters, and need help around their farms."

"Thank you." Hugo hesitated, "You know I am city born and bred. Could you tell me a little about what these jobs entail?"

"Mr. Craig's work will probably be the least physically strenuous, although your days will be long. Crofter work is non-stop and you would labor from dawn to dusk, it will require a certain facility with animals—sheep, pigs, fowl, perhaps a mule. Lots of cleaning out of animal enclosures and such. As for cutting flagstone, well…" She let her gaze flicker over him and then swallowed, the flush he loved so well creeping up her neck. "I'm sure you can guess it is excessively hard work, but Mr. Stogden pays almost twice as much as the others."

Hugo considered her information. Mr. Craig would doubtless kill and throw Hugo over the side of his fishing boat before an hour was out—unless the man enjoyed cleaning vomit from his yole. And farm work sounded very…smelly.

Hugo nodded. "Mr. Stogden it is, then. Thank you."

Her expressive eyebrows arched.

Hugo and the Maiden

"Why do you look surprised?"

"You don't strike me as the kind of man to have done much strenuous work"

Hugo felt oddly insulted. "Are you saying you think I lack the physical strength, Miss Pringle?"

A layer of red washed over the pink already staining her cheeks and she grabbed one of his hands and turned it palm up, her rough finger pads tracing his smooth palm.

She looked up, her eyes very blue against the red of her face. "Your skin is so soft it's obvious you've never done an honest day's work in your life."

Hugo took a step toward her, closing the distance between them. "Why, Miss Pringle, how observant of you to notice my...skin."

She pressed her lips together.

"And you might be pleasantly surprised to learn just how *hard* I can work, when properly motivated."

She dropped his hand as if burned, took a step back, struck her heel on the step, and would have fallen on her arse if Hugo hadn't caught her. He should have let her go once he'd steadied her, but his body wanted what it wanted, and right now it wanted to feel Miss Pringle.

Although her body was firm and muscular from all her physical labor, her breasts were small and deliciously soft as they pressed against his threadbare shirt, warming his chest. She had nice, womanly hips—at least as far as he could tell without a more thorough examination.

Hugo imagined how fetching her bottom would look bent over in front of him, his fingers digging into her hips, his cock sliding into her body.

That was all it took to make him harden against her flat belly.

Awareness—slowed by her own animal arousal—gradually dawned in her eyes. Her jaw dropped and those kissable lips quivered—anger, desire, confusion, and a dozen other emotions flitting across her face quicker than a flight of swallows.

And then her body stiffened like a plank and she shoved him back.

Hugo immediately released her.

She clamped her jaws shut, brushed off the front of her dress, inhaled enough to strain her plain frock to its limits and said, "Church begins at eight o'clock. Sharp."

She was gone in a flurry of skirts before Hugo could tell her that he'd not be attending church tomorrow. Or any other day, for that matter.

He adjusted his throbbing erection before wandering over to the meeting house, where he found Franks looking at something on the bench beside him.

"What are you doing?" he asked.

The younger man jolted. "Oh, Mr. Buckingham."

"Call me Hugo."

Franks's gaze dropped to the front of Hugo's thin, obscenely tented trousers and he blushed almost as prettily as Miss Martha. Hugo saw the truth in the lad's wide green eyes, which was riveted to his cock. Bloody wonderful—*just* what he needed right now—an infatuated pup.

"Well?" Hugo prodded.

Franks blinked and wrenched his eyes up to meet Hugo's. "Uh, what was that, again?"

"What's on the bench beside you?"

"Oh. I'm calculating how much I will need to get back to London," Franks said, scribbling on the small scrap of paper with a graphite stick.

Hugo dropped down beside him. "What do you do in London, Franks?"

"Call me Albert." His attempt to sound like Hugo was adorable.

"Very well, what do you do in London, *Albert*?"

"I'm a clerk at a solicitor's office. At least I was."

"Huh. What the devil did you do to end up on that ship?"

Albert's smile dropped away. "I think my employer is responsible for my abduction."

"That bad of a clerk, were you?"

"What?" His eyebrows knitted. "No, of course not."

Hugo chuckled.

"Oh. You were speaking in jest."

"Yes."

"Er, I invented something and asked him to assist me with the patent process." He cut Hugo a shy look. "I am a man of science—not a solicitor. I only took the position to make money while I pursued my invention."

"What did you invent—if you don't mind telling me, that is."

Hugo and the Maiden

"Of course I don't mind telling you."

"Perhaps you should. Look what happened the last time you shared the information."

Albert stared blankly, making Hugo feel bad for teasing the boy, but—really—you'd think Franks would have learned his lesson already. And that lesson was: you should guard any information that involved money with your life.

"I am usually an excellent judge of character." He must have seen Hugo's skeptical look because he added, "Except for that one time—but he was my *employer*." He sounded amazed, as if thieving employers were such a rarity in this world. "But my heart tells me that I can trust you."

Hugo suspected he was being guided by some other organ—one closer to his waist—but kept that observation to himself because young Albert had the look of a man who'd not yet identified his own sexual proclivities.

Instead, he said, "I thought men of science only trusted their intellect."

"I aspire to be a Renaissance man."

"Ah." Hugo said. "That has something to do with using both science and art to inform one's thinking, does it not?"

"Just so," Albert said, looking inordinately pleased.

"Admirable. So, go on, then, what is it—this invention of yours?"

Several long minutes later, Hugo held up his hand. "That's plenty, thank you."

"But I'm just getting to the interesting part." Albert's eyes shone with enthusiasm.

"I didn't understand a bloody word you just said, Albert, so I'll be unable to understand *the interesting* bit, either."

Albert's face fell.

"Come now," Hugo said, feeling like an ogre for taking the wind from his sails. "You must be used to people not comprehending this…this, well whatever it is."

"Yes, since I left school, it has been difficult to find like-minded men of science."

Hugo wanted to tell the boy that he should bugger the science and go get his corn ground by a like-minded man. But he didn't.

"Cheer up," he said, clapping Albert on his slender shoulder. "You're a free man now. Tell me about these Wilsons you'll be moving in with?"

Albert brightened. "Mrs. Wilson needs help while Mr. Wilson is fishing." He paused, his expression pensive. "I have never actually *been* on a farm, although of course I understand the underlying concept. Have you?"

"No. City born and bred." Hugo pushed up off the bench.

"What do you suppose Mrs. Wilson shall have me doing?" Albert asked, a pucker of concern between his eyes.

"Probably birthing cows, slaughtering hogs—thing of that nature," Hugo said.

Albert's eyes threatened to roll out of his head. "No, do you really think so?"

Hugo turned away to hide his smile. "Oh, I daresay you'll become accustomed to it in no time."

He left the boy to his worries and went to investigate the benches where Devlin and Parker had slept. The two men had left their bedding, so he now had two more blankets and could fashion a pillow out of one.

When he walked back to his bench, he saw Albert was rolling up his blankets. "Makin' a break for freedom already?" Hugo teased. "I was jesting about the cow and hog thing. Miss Martha told me it's mainly feeding sheep and fowl, lots of shoveling manure, and bringing in the harvest."

The boy sagged with relief but continued rolling the blanket. "I'm to go to the Wilson farm tonight. Mrs. Wilson said there will be work that need doing early in the morning before church." He tucked the blankets under his arm and stood. "But I'll see you tomorrow then, at church."

Rather than tell Albert that he'd be nowhere near the church, Hugo just smiled. "Good luck to you, Albert." He watched the younger man leave, glad to be alone for the first time in weeks.

It was stuffy inside the meeting house, which had been shut for a good part of the day, so Hugo propped the door open. The sun was only just dipping low.

A huge yawn distorted his face; he would go to bed early tonight. But not before he washed himself, which he'd not been allowed to do this morning before being shoved into smelly clothing and dragged off.

Hugo and the Maiden

The first order of business was to haul water.

He could wash his body in cold water, but the clothing required warm if he was to rid the shirt and neckerchief of the stench of another man's stale sweat. As for the vest Martha had found for him? Well, it was best not to wash that at all as it looked held together by threads. He still did not have a coat, but that was fine as the weather was quite warm, although he'd been told it would cool down quickly in the coming weeks. Hugo planned to be long gone before then.

He unearthed the buried pocket of coals in the fire pit where Martha heated the big wash caldron and fed in some dry grass and a little peat until he had a flame large enough to heat the water.

While that was heating, he took a bucket of cold water into the meeting house and stripped down, using his bunched-up shirt as a washcloth. It was not the best bath he'd ever had, but he felt wonderful after it. Hugo could not abide dirt, especially on his person.

Once he'd washed his hair—twice—he wrapped one of the blankets around his waist and shook out the others.

It was a shame he didn't have some of the lye flakes that Martha had used for her laundry, but he did a creditable job using some scrubby plant that had lavender flowers and smelled quite nice.

Once the old garments were as clean as they were likely to get, he squeezed them dry and hung them outside.

The five men had tracked dirt into the meeting house, so Hugo found a broom and dustpan. He had only intended to sweep the area near his bedroll, but once he'd started it seemed wise to keep going.

When he'd finished with the floor, he made his bed on the flagstone rather than the bench, which he found difficult to turn on without falling off.

All that scrubbing and sweeping had worked up a sweat, so he left the door open. It was almost dark and he doubted anyone would be coming around so he pulled the blanket off his hips and folded it into a pillow before lying down on his bed, not bothering to cover himself, letting the cool breeze dry him.

Lying there naked on the floor reminded him of that morning and he smiled, his cock twitching at the memory of Martha's stunned but hungry gaze as she'd stared at him: naked and erect.

Hugo could spot the lust in Martha as easily as he could in Albert. It wasn't much of a skill after thirty years of living, but it was—other than whoring, braiding whips, and wielding them—pretty much all he had to show for himself.

Anyhow, it didn't matter if Martha wanted him. Mr. Pringle had saved Hugo's life so the last thing he was going to do was thank him by deflowering his daughter.

Still, that didn't mean he couldn't have her any way he wanted inside the privacy of his own head. He smiled at the thought and reached down, his cock lengthening as he relived the feel of her breasts pressed against his chest.

He gave himself a long, leisurely pull, luxuriating in the slow thickening of his shaft and drawing out this phase of arousal—willing to wait for his first orgasm in weeks—and making it last. His slit wept heavily, as if making up for lost opportunities, quickly producing moisture enough to slick his shaft.

His fingers tightened as he pondered his unexpected attraction to the proper young woman who'd given him this impressive erection. Martha Pringle was pretty enough, and she was one of the few young women he'd seen in the past few weeks, so he supposed it was only natural that she would figure in his fantasy.

Hugo sighed; that was a lie. Or at least an oversimplification.

His attraction to her was more than just convenience. He also enjoyed their verbal jousting and he adored making her stern little face flex into a smile.

And then there were the innocently lustful, needy, and *wanting* looks he'd caught her casting in his direction.

Those yearning looks—to be wanted with such ferocity—were like an aphrodisiac. His heavy eyelids drifted shut and he fisted himself with slow, firm strokes as he recalled that morning, and the greedy way her gaze had slipped down to his hips and then jerked back up. And then slid down again and again in those few precious seconds.

The memory of her raw desire made his balls tighten and he spread his legs and reached between his thighs, pulling at his sac with his free hand, holding tight to the memory of her wide eyes, her flushed cheeks, her plump lips that he imagined wrapped around his cock, sucking him *so* bloody hard—

Hugo flung himself into bliss, his spine arching until he hurt, until only his shoulders and heels were on the floor, his buttocks clenching and thrusting as he pumped himself with savage strokes, fucking his fist as if it were *her.*

Hugo and the Maiden

He spent so hard that ribbons of hot seed crisscrossed his chest and shoulders. Even after nothing more came out, he continued milking himself, until his touch hurt, the mingling of pain and pleasure making him feel alive. Alive and free.

Sated and boneless, he lowered his exhausted body to his blanket and heaved a huge, contented sigh.

He was drifting in a pleasurable post-orgasmic daze when a sound startled him. He opened his eyes and glanced around. But there was nothing, only the breeze gently rattling the open doors on their hinges.

Hugo enjoyed a long, languorous stretch before picking up the corner of the bottom blanket and wiping the cooling spunk from his skin; he would wash the blanket tomorrow.

He'd begun to get goosepimples so he padded over to the doors and closed both before wrapping the lightest blanket around his hips so he'd be decent in the morning.

After all, he thought with a huge yawn, it wouldn't do to shock the vicar's daughter two days running.

Chapter 12

Martha had not seen Hugo for a week—not since he left the meeting house last Monday morning, heading out for his first day of work.

She'd watched him from the safety of the house, lurking in the kitchen window and spying like a sneak thief, consuming him with her eyes as he left, his few possessions in a neat bundle under one arm, his step jaunty.

Every day she'd expected him to call, or at least stop by on his way to the Greedy Vicar, where Albert told her he'd seen Hugo give a letter to Joe Cameron, who collected the mail for the mainland.

Tuesday through Friday she'd told herself he was probably too exhausted from his first week of strenuous work to do much other than eat and sleep.

But when she went to the Greedy Vicar late Saturday on the pretext of buying something or other, she learned that Hugo had been in earlier, not to the taproom, but to purchase some items from the small store.

And *still* he'd not stopped by.

Martha told herself she was grateful for his absence, good riddance to the man. Besides, Mr. Clark had been coming by and asking her out walking more often. Martha wished she were more excited about his attention, but she was still displeased by his willingness to expose his neighbors to possible prosecution merely to spite a man who turned out to be innocent. Well, at least innocent of whatever had landed him on that ship. She had a strong suspicion that Hugo Buckingham was guilty of plenty of other things.

When it came to Robert, Martha had reminded herself that it wasn't her place to judge her fellow human beings, and so she'd gone walking with him and they discussed the matters they'd always talked about: his work, her day, his sister and mother, her father—all the while carefully avoiding any mention of the man who now stood between them.

Although Martha didn't see Hugo during the day, she saw him—to her lasting mortification—every night in her dreams.

Hugo and the Maiden

What she'd witnessed last Saturday night in the meeting house had been shocking. But surely such a vision should have become mundane after the fiftieth time she'd relived it—or certainly by the hundredth. Yet the images burnt into her mind's eye had not lost their potency. Indeed, they'd become more powerful, escaping the confines of her dreams to spread into her waking hours.

Like right now.

She was supposed to be cleaning the meeting house; instead, she was standing motionless, her mind's eye filled with images of Hugo stretched out on his back, naked, the last sullen rays of the sun painting his rippling muscles and pale skin a dull, devilish red. The thick muscles in his biceps and forearm bulged while he stroked himself, the thrusting of his hips primal and savage.

To her shame, she had begun to tingle and swell between her thighs. She'd squeezed her legs together to stop the tingling, but that had only intensified it.

One squeeze had led to another. And another. Until soon she'd found herself clenching along with his thrusts.

Each stroke had tightened him like a clock key turning a spring, his impossibly hard body arching until his back no longer touched the floor, his movements becoming less controlled, guttural sounds escaping his open mouth, his head thrown back, eyes closed in ecstasy—

And then Martha's own pleasure had seized her, the intense physical sensations doubling her over until her forehead rested on the cold flagstone step. Part of her mind—the tiny part that was not given over to sensual gratification—shrieked at her to leave, to run, to get away before Hugo saw her.

Please, Lord, she'd prayed, even while she'd continued to flex her inner muscles to draw out the pleasure, *I know I'm a wanton sinner, but if you let me get away from here without him seeing me, I'll never do anything like this again.*

Martha knew—even as she made the promise—that it was a lie, perhaps the first lie she'd ever consciously told God.

She'd backed away on her hands and knees, and, when she was sure she would not be seen, pushed to her feet, still backing toward the house. And that was when she brushed against an empty peat crate and knocked it over, the soft *clunk* sending her fleeing the short distance back to the stone house as if the hounds of Hell were on her heels.

Once inside the house she'd collapsed against the door. A quick glance at her watch had shown that barely ten minutes had passed since she'd gone outside to see where the smoke was coming from.

Her entire world had changed in ten minutes.

She'd barely slept that night. Every time she had closed her eyes, she saw him again. The delicious explosion had occurred twice more, no matter how much she tried to prevent it.

The same thing had happened every night since. Martha was beyond hope—utterly lost to the pleasures of the flesh: a child of Onan, as it were, not that she'd ever suspected that applied to women.

"Martha?"

She squeaked and jumped at the sound of her father's voice, clutching her broom to her chest. Would he know what she was thinking just by looking at her?

"In here, Father," she called out in a quavering voice.

The door opened and the vicar stood in the doorway. "Hello, my dear. I just wanted to let you know I was back from visiting young Lorn."

"How is he?"

"It will be a while before his leg mends, but Mrs. Sutherland has already installed him in Denny's old room and Lorn will probably be too plump to move by the time he's healed."

"I am so happy to hear it." She glanced at her watch and saw it was after two. "Do you want me to come in and fix you something?"

"No thank you," he said, patting his non-existent paunch, "Mrs. Sutherland puts on quite a midday spread. I shall be working on my sermon in my office if you should need me."

Martha looked into his faded blue eyes and saw no condemnation of her—no disgust that she was an immoral wanton. Was it really that easy to hide thoughts that burned like fire inside her body? Is that what other people were doing while they were walking about the island?

Martha sighed and closed her eyes, resting her forehead against the cool stone wall. But Hugo was there, waiting for her.

Chapter 13

Hugo soon discovered that getting back to London was not going to happen as quickly as he'd hoped.

Once the euphoria of being free dissipated, he was in the same situation as before: he either needed to earn or steal his way back south.

Given his recent brush with transportation, he had no interest in breaking the law.

So that left working—at least until he could send a letter to Melissa and ask her to advance enough money for his journey. But before he could send a letter, he needed money to buy paper, ink, and a quill. He knew the vicar would have given him as much, but he was tired of relying on the poor old man and his daughter for everything from the food he ate, to the clothing on his back.

Fortunately, this was the busy time of year on Stroma and strong backs were in demand. While the men fished as many hours as they could, the women tended the crofts, caring for livestock and bringing in the harvest without the aid of their menfolk in many cases.

The Stroma crofters grew potatoes, hay, oats, and a variety of vegetables. But in the main, they grew corn. Most of the crofters kept laying hens and other fowl, a pig, a sheep or two, and some even a mule, although the plough was not employed on the island.

The island, fascinatingly enough, did not have one single tree. The main source of heat—peat—they had to import. Bringing the soft fuel to the island was the chief expense of most islanders, so a great deal of the local economy was barter, a skill which Hugo quickly mastered. He had two—well, he actually had *three*—valuable skills, but one would likely get him lynched. And so he sold his strong back and his braided cords.

Once he'd put his mind to earning money rather than stealing it, he labored every waking hour. He spent his days working for Mr. Stogden, who allowed Hugo the use of a structure on his land that resembled a lean-to, but more substantial and built from stone. It would never serve as a dwelling in winter, but Hugo hoped to be gone before it became too cold.

Hugo liked Mr. Stogden: the old man kept to himself and had no interest in socializing—unlike just about everyone else on the bloody island.

It wasn't that Hugo wasn't fond of a chin wag every now and then with whores, thieves, flashmen, and others of that ilk. But just what the hell would he have to talk about with a fisherman or farmer?

Would they swap stories?

If any of the islanders ever learned that he'd earned money by servicing other men's wives or taking it up the arse, they would likely drive him from the island with pitchforks and torches.

That knowledge hung in the back of his mind like a specter and made avoiding socializing with *decent* people an easy decision.

Besides, he didn't have time. After his long day at the quarry Hugo worked braiding cords. He first finished the vicar's bell pull—free of charge—and then took a steady stream of orders from other islanders. In order to spend his evenings braiding, he needed to purchase peat to have firelight to work by.

Luckily Mr. Stogden kindly advanced him his first week's wages after he'd worked only two days. "I can see you'll be worth the money," the old man had said when Hugo had shown his surprise. Naturally, Stogden's kindness had made him work even harder. So maybe the old man was just a savvy businessman.

Hugo used the advance to purchase fuel and a few necessities—like a quill, ink, and parchment—from the tiny store. He'd quickly learned that he had to add the Greedy Vicar to the short list of places to avoid on the island.

Another was the vicar's house, which Hugo avoided diligently in case his curious cock led him into trouble: namely into Mr. Pringle's daughter.

But his cock couldn't be blamed for needing to steer clear of the little pub. No, it was the islanders themselves who kept him at bay. Not out of cruelty, but because they liked him too much. Each time he showed his face in the tiny taproom somebody would insist on spelling him a pint.

Which meant that Hugo had to reciprocate.

It wasn't that he was clutch-fisted—oh, very well, so he was a bit tight with his money—but this wasn't a bloody holiday. Hugo needed money to get the hell off this rock. Buying pints for strangers—no matter how nice—was hardly going to get him to his goal any faster.

Hugo and the Maiden

And so, he'd only gone to town a handful of times, even though he was itching to see if the mail boat had brought a letter for him.

He'd just finished his twelfth day of work at the quarry when Mr. Stogden came strolling up to his lean-to.

"I've got something for you, Mr. Buckingham."

Hugo looked up from his washing—which he did every day—and wiped his hands on the cloth he'd thrown over his shoulder. The older man was holding an expensive-looking cream envelope.

Hugo smiled: Melissa.

"I can see from your expression this is good news," Mr. Stogden said.

"I hope it is good news, sir." The envelope had been franked by Melissa's father-in-law, the Marquess of Darlington. Well, *that* was interesting.

"That's the first of those I've seen."

Hugo assumed he meant an aristocrat's frank.

"Lord Darlington—he's a marquess when he's out and about, isn't he?" Stogden asked.

"Yes. But this letter is from his daughter-in-law who is an acquaintance of mine."

The old man's craggy face was hard to read. "Hmmph. Well, if you're going to be off will you give me notice? I've not got another man to take your place—at least not one as hardworking as yourself."

Hugo's face warmed at the rare compliment from the reserved man.

"Of course, sir. Would a week serve?"

"Sounds fair enough. Well, I'll leave you to enjoy your letter."

"Thank you for bringing it," Hugo called after him, only now recalling his manners.

The old man just waved a hand and kept walking.

Hugo felt an odd combination of relief, hope, and regret as he looked at the letter. He was relieved to know he wasn't utterly cut off from the outside world, he hoped Mel had some money for him, and he actually felt the tiniest speck of regret that he would soon be leaving.

That last thought gave him pause; since when did he like to engage in grueling physical labor from dawn to dusk, sleep in an animal enclosure, dress in castoffs, and cook his own meager meals?

Cutting flagstone might be physically exhausting, but at least there weren't lazy employees, complaining clients; and he could leave his work behind at the end of a day.

Running one's own business, Hugo had quickly learned, was not all beer and skittles.

That didn't mean he had any intention of remaining on Stroma. Even the people born and bred on the island wanted to get the hell off it. Still, the simplicity of island life had its appeal.

Martha Pringle's pretty face flitted through his mind, but he quickly banished her. He hated admitting—even to himself—just how hard it had been to avoid her. The sooner he got off Stroma the better it would be for *that* innocent young woman.

If he were leaving soon then he'd need to go by the Pringle cottage and speak to the vicar about the favor he still owed him. But right now, he needed to set aside his letter and finish his washing—he wasn't gone yet and he'd rather not work in dirty clothing tomorrow.

After he'd hung out the last garment to dry, he picked up his letter and sat in the shadow of the old stone trough. Hugo slid his finger beneath the thick blob of sealing wax, unfolded the letter, and smirked; there were four sheets with overlarge writing. Melissa must have enjoyed making the marquess pay for such an expensive letter.

Hugo's letter, by contrast, had been written and then cross-written, the words so small Melissa would have needed a magnifying glass to read it. He'd purchased only one sheet of paper, a tiny jar of ink, and a ragged quill from Joe Cameron's store.

Tucked between the third and fourth pages were two bank drafts: one for and one for £200.

Hugo smiled; Mel had come through for him, as he'd known she would.

The £20 was small enough that Joe Cameron should be able to give him half in goods and half in cash. The £200 was an outrageous sum and he'd need to take it to a bank on his way to London..

He'd not wanted to borrow so much, but he had no idea what mess awaited him in London, or how long it would take to regain control of Solange's.

He spread out the letter.

Dearest Hugo:

I received your letter the very morning we were setting out to spend a month with Magnus's family at their seat. Yes, they now invite me to their home. I never

Hugo and the Maiden

believed it would happen, but after giving birth to one perfectly delightful grandson—and another child on the way—my in-laws have become almost amenable to the whore their son married.

Hugo snorted; nothing felt quite as good a bringing a peer to their knees, something he knew from personal experience.

What a dramatic life you have: kidnapped, transported, and then shipwrecked! You might even surpass Joss when it comes to high drama, although perhaps not scandal.

Hugo sniffed at the mention of his old nemesis from Solange's, a whore named Joss Gormley. Hugo had long suspected that Melissa had allowed Gormley into her bed—albeit long before Hugo knew her—and he'd never quite gotten over the spark of envy he felt for the man.

You should sell your story to the papers, Hugo, although nobody would ever credit it as being true.

"Very droll, Melissa."

I received a letter from Daisy only a week before yours and it was absolutely full of gossip about Solange's.

Daisy was a mutual acquaintance who'd worked at Solange's when it was still called The White House. Daisy now ran an inn in France with her husband, but kept in touch with several women who still worked at Solange's.

Daisy mentioned how everyone at Solange's was stunned when Laura told them that you'd decided to take an extended holiday and see the great sights of Europe.

"That fucking bitch," he hissed at the paper, squeezing it as tightly as he'd like to squeeze Laura Maitland's neck.

Hugo heard a scuffing sound and looked up; Cailean hovered uncertainly a few steps away. Hugo had been so caught up in his letter he hadn't hear the boy's approach. As always, he had Lily draped around his neck.

Hugo still hadn't gotten accustomed to the oversized rat, but he no longer shrieked like a little girl when he saw her.

He grinned at the sweet giant. "Well, look who's come to see me." He waved him over. "Come here, little brother."

Cailean smiled and shuffled over to him, stopping close enough to Hugo that they could bump shoulders, the boy's preferred manner of showing affection. The gesture brought Hugo's face perilously close to the otter's ass, but he supposed that was better than its sharp-toothed face.

Hugo knew Cailean could speak, but other than that first night, he'd not heard him utter a word. The boy kept him company around the firepit most nights and also showed him some of the island's secret coves and how to access the tiny, secluded beaches.

Hugo had wanted to see the system of caves the islanders called the Gloup, but Cailean broke into the shivers when he suggested it, so it was something he'd still not explored.

"Are you done working?" Hugo asked.

Cailean did odd jobs like delivering peat, loading boats to go to the mainland, or anything that required a strong back.

The boy nodded.

"Well, that's something to celebrate, isn't it? Go look in the lean-to. There's a paper sack you might find of interest." Hugo had begun keeping a few sweets for the boy after he realized Cailean didn't receive pay for his work. Instead, the money went to his aunt, who kept him.

That hardly seemed fair, especially since it would have taken only a few pennies to make Cailean happy. Hugo didn't agree with the general consensus that Cailean was touched in the head. The more time they spent together, the more Hugo believed that the reverse was true.

At first, he'd thought the younger man was twenty-five—based on his size and build—but had been stunned to discover he was just sixteen.

Cailean was quick to pick up new skills—Hugo had set him up with some rope to braid and he was doing a fine job, even with his massive fingers. Cailean also had a nearly perfect memory and could count cards better than anyone Hugo had ever met. Who knew what else the boy would be capable of with a bit of schooling?

Cailean returned from the lean-to with the bag in his hand, too polite to open it, and offered it to Hugo.

"It's for you, little brother," Hugo said. "I'm sorry there isn't much, but when I'm done reading my letter we can go to the Vicar and raid Mr. Cameron's sweetie cabinet. Sound good?"

Cailean smiled.

"Good, go relax in my luxurious palace and I'll not be two ticks," Hugo said, waiting until Cailean disappeared back into lean-to. Hugo was likely to swear a bit more before the letter was over and displays of temper terrified the gentle boy.

He turned back to the crumpled sheets of paper.

Hugo and the Maiden

Daisy also said Laura has made some rather unpleasant changes. One of which was taking on Bevan Davies as a partner.

"You duplicitous fucking whore!" Hugo shook with fury. "Bloody Bevan Davies." Of all the slimy bastards in London, why did it have to be Bev?

The man had been a force to be reckoned with in St. Giles when Hugo had been a lad and had only become more powerful over the past fifteen years. He was greedy, brutal, and vicious. And now, it appeared, he co-owned Hugo's business—or all of it, if he knew Bev.

He wanted to bloody weep.

I don't know what you plan to do, Hugo, but you know where I stand on the matter of Solange's. If you have any say in the matter, I recommend that you close it and invest your money elsewhere.

"That's bloody well enough for you, isn't it Mel?" he irrationally demanded of the paper.

Frustration and fury threatened to blow the top off his head. Just because Melissa had married an extremely wealthy man and could afford her fancy morals didn't mean *Hugo* could.

He'd worked like a dog since becoming co-owner of the brothel. Unlike Laura, he'd not quit taking clients. In fact, he taken more than ever before.

While he'd managed to put some money in the bank these past three years, he'd poured most of his earnings back into Solange's. He simply did not have enough money saved to quit working. He had enough to live modestly for a few years—if he were frugal—but he didn't want to live modestly; he'd spent most of his life on his knees so he could live *well*.

Even though I know you will deny it, engaging in the flesh trade is a soul-destroying business.

"Ha! You say that now, but that was your life for *years*, Mel." How like people to judge others once their own situation was all nice and secure.

Just because Mel was suddenly suffering pangs of conscience didn't mean Hugo was. He had no conscience—he never had.

"Blasted moralizers," he muttered.

I know you, Hugo—you have the façade of a cold, heartless, selfish man and often you can be that man. But I've also seen you give money to street urchins and feed a starving kitten.

"Christ," he muttered. "Will I never live down that damned kitten incident? Who the hell *wouldn't* feed a kitten if it showed up on their doorstep, Mel?"

The letter didn't answer him.

Hugo had only meant to give the mangy little beast a bit of milk before shooing it away, but of course some whore—every single one of whom had big mouths—had caught him feeding the thing and engaged a bloody town crier to spread the news.

Then the blasted women had taken the cat as some sort of mascot. The cat—*Hugo*, they'd had the nerve to call it—still lived in the kitchen, so fat and lazy he was more likely to be caught by a mouse than the other way round.

Hugo called him Tiger—but only when nobody else was around. He could tell by the way Tiger perked up around him that the cat remembered it was Hugo who'd first fed him.

Or maybe he perked up because Hugo was the only one who knew how much Tiger liked having his fat chin scratched.

Hugo rolled his eyes at his stupid thoughts and turned back to the letter.

I know you must find the prospect of a new way of life intimidating. But you are not without friends, Hugo. Joss and his wife are talking about sponsoring another orphanage and Magnus and I are also in dire need of kind, trustworthy people to help out with our new school for older children.

Hugo snorted rudely. "I'll do that right after I fart guineas, Mel." Jesus. Hugo running an orphanage. What would the woman come up with, next?

You are welcome at Stanwyke Park—by me, at least—if you should wish to visit on your way south.

I ask that you send me a letter to let me know you have received the bank drafts, and also to let me know your plans.

Take care, my friend,
Mel

Hugo chuckled at the thought of stopping by a marquess's grand estate. He wouldn't, of course, but he was relieved to see that Melissa hadn't become so proper that she didn't enjoy spreading a little bit of mischief.

Hugo stared at the bank drafts. So, he could leave after he'd given Mr. Stogden his notice. All he needed to do was visit the vicar and settle up with him.

Hugo and the Maiden

He ignored the thumping in his chest—and lower—at the thought of seeing Martha.

No, you are going to see the vicar—not his daughter.

"Fine," he groused. "I'm not going there to see her."

He smirked as he folded up the letter. Just because he wasn't going there to see *her*, didn't mean he couldn't enjoy himself if she happened to be there.

Did it?

Chapter 14

"Martha is at the lady's sewing group this evening," Mr. Pringle informed him. "I'm afraid she won't be home until quite late."

Hugo was stunned by the wave of disappointment that swamped him. Just when had he started missing the sharp-tongued, bossy woman so much?

This was not good. Not good at all. How could he be such a fool?

He shoved away his concerns; he could ponder his unwanted attraction to the virginal miss later. On his six-hundred-mile journey south.

"Er, I was just popping by to let you know that I'll be leaving next week." Without the hope of a good verbal jousting with Martha on the horizon or the possibility of making her blush, Hugo just wanted to finish his business with Mr. Pringle quickly.

But the vicar had other plans. "I was just about to put the kettle on." He stepped back and gestured for Hugo to enter.

Hugo had never been in the house before and hadn't expected it to be so small and ... *sparse*. It was almost monastic, not that Hugo had any personal knowledge of monks.

"Leaving us so soon, are you?"

"Yes, sir. But I wanted to repay my debt to you before I go."

"Ah, well, it's nice of you to call."

His vague answer made Hugo wonder if the man had forgotten all about the favor he'd exacted.

Hugo was debating with his conscience whether or not he would remind the vicar when the old man said, "You must mean the favor you promised me."

So much for the vicar's rotten memory.

"Yes, sir."

"I was, in fact, thinking of calling on *you.*" Mr. Pringle paused, his blue eyes going hazy and his forehead creasing. "Although I must admit I don't know where I would find you these days, as you're not staying in the meeting house." He blinked owlishly up at Hugo, turned, and then tottered toward a tiny kitchen.

"I'm staying out at Mr. Stogden's."

"Ah, yes. That's right, that's right. Now I recall. Abel told me that when I stopped in to check on how you were managing."

Hugo frowned. Check on him? Just what the hell did that mean?

He shrugged the thought off, more concerned about the old man's faulty memory. How had he forgotten where Hugo was living and working?

Oh well, it was none of his concern.

"Now where did Martha put the kettle?" the vicar mused.

The kitchen held the smallest cookstove he'd ever seen. There was a kettle on top and steam was blasting from the spout. "Er, I think—"

"Oh, there it is." Mr. Pringle stared at the stove as if he'd never seen it before. "Why, it looks like I already boiled the water. Excellent, excellent," he murmured to himself. He grabbed a medium-sized Brown Betty from the counter and spooned black gold into the pot—enough for two, Hugo could see.

Hugo held his breath as Mr. Pringle picked up the boiling kettle and poured. Some of the boiling water went into the teapot and more onto the counter and floor, barely missing his slippered feet.

"Er, can I help you with anything, sir?"

"Ah, yes—Martha made some biscuits the other day." The vicar set the kettle back down on the stove with a loud clang and turned, an impish look on his face. "She thinks I am too doddering to know that she spends money on sugar for my sweets rather than a new ribbon or trinket for herself. But I notice." He tapped his forehead in demonstration of his mental acuity. "The tin is in that cupboard, bring it to the table." He carried the Brown Betty to the small table, the little teapot looking as if weighed a stone in his fragile old hands. "Grab two plates and mugs while you're about it."

While his back was turned, Hugo quickly moved the kettle off the stove, where it was once again belching steam.

When he returned to the table with the requested items the vicar was humming softly as he lifted the lid to examine the tea he had only just spooned into the pot. As absent-minded as he seemed, Hugo wondered why Martha left him alone in the house.

Not your affair, Hugo.

True. He would be gone from this island—this life—in a week. Hugo set out the chipped, mismatched plates and mugs before prying open the dented old tin. The aroma that hit him made his mouth water.

Hugo looked up and met the vicar's expectant stare. "Shortbread."

The vicar grinned when Hugo's stomach grumbled. "Go ahead, have a piece now, before your tea."

Hugo hesitated for a heartbeat. "Well, if you *insist*."

They both chuckled as if they were indulging in something guilty, and then sat and munched the sweet, buttery slabs in silence.

Hugo was almost finished with his piece and gazed longingly at the container; he could eat the whole damned tin himself. He had a fondness for sweets. But no, he couldn't ask for another—they were for an old man who had few enough pleasures in life.

He popped the last bit in his mouth, determined to savor it.

"Do you find my daughter attractive?"

Hugo tried to catch the soggy piece of cookie that flew out of his mouth, but it was too late. He was grateful that it hit the wall behind the vicar rather than his host's face.

"Damn!" Hugo said, and then, "Oh, sorry." His face and neck burned, and it took him a moment to identify the foreign feeling: it was embarrassment. When was the last time that anything had embarrassed him?

The vicar chuckled. "I shouldn't have blurted that out—it was my fault."

Hugo happened to agree.

The vicar poured their tea while Hugo braced himself for whatever was coming next. His appetite—even for delicious shortbread—was now gone.

"I am dying, Hugo."

Hugo's head whipped up and, again, the old man chuckled. "Oh, not right *now*."

He huffed out a breath. "I'm pleased to hear it, sir."

"I'm doing a wretched job of making my point."

Again, Hugo silently agreed.

"I don't wish my daughter to know, but I saw a physician when I was last on the mainland. He told me my heart was weak and could give out at any time. Indeed, he seemed surprised it has lasted this long. He said that anything that elevated my pulse might be the end of me." His

Hugo and the Maiden

lips twisted into a scowl and he glared at Hugo. "I ask you, why would a person want to live if they had to avoid everything that makes their heart race?"

Hugo didn't see much point in that kind of life either. "Er—"

"I've had chest pains," the vicar confessed, sparing Hugo from having to speak. "Each one is more difficult to recover from than the last and it is becoming impossible to hide them from Martha. I doubt I will survive this winter."

Hugo's nose and eyes prickled, and he had to swallow. Several times. Dammit! What the hell was wrong with him? The salt air must be rotting his brain.

He set down his mug with a thump, sending tea sloshing over the sides. "It's a brutal environment in the winter, I'm told," he said, hoping the vicar didn't notice his hoarse voice.

"Yes, it is. It took my wife our first winter here. Martha was not yet two. It is not an easy life."

Hugo thought that was the understatement of the decade. Even this early in the fall the conditions were inhospitable.

"Can't you go south, sir?"

"I have nowhere to go."

"What about the watering holes that are supposed to be good for one's health—Bath? Harrogate?"

"I do not have the means to go to those places."

"Surely the Church should take care of such things after a lifetime of service?"

The vicar waved a dismissive hand, visibly bored with the topic of his health. "I know you received a letter franked by the Marquess of Darlington."

Hugo blinked.

The vicar laughed. "You cannot keep exciting news like that secret on a small island. You mentioned you will be leaving soon.

"Er, yes, that is correct, sir."

"You must have worked hard to save enough money already."

"My friend, Lady Magnus, sent me a bank draft. She is Darlington's daughter-in-law."

"Mm-hmm, mm-hmm." He nodded. "And how much is that for?"

The question startled a laugh out of him.

The vicar smiled and raised a hand. "Bear with me, Hugo, I do have a point I wish to make aside from prying into your business."

"Two hundred pounds." He didn't mention the smaller draft.

"Two hundred pounds," Mr. Pringle repeated, his tone one of awe.

Hugo squirmed. He knew that amount sounded like a fortune to a man like Jonathan Pringle—indeed to anyone on this island—but he dealt in such sums often. As a whore, he had commanded the highest of prices. And since he'd purchased half the brothel, he'd earned even more.

"Do you know what that tells me, Hugo—receiving a draft that size?"

"No, sir."

"That you are a man who powerful people will send a large sum to upon nothing more than a request."

Hugo wondered what he'd say if he knew that the signature on the draft was that of an ex-madam. "It is a loan, and I shall have to pay it back, Mr. Pringle."

"Yes, yes, of course. But you *can* pay it back, can't you?"

"Er, yes, sir." Christ, he bloody hoped he could.

"And not only because you are a man of means, but because you feel morally obliged to repay your debts?"

"Of course." How the hell had the conversation strayed in such a bizarre direction?

"I know you have amassed your wealth in questionable ways, Hugo."

Hugo's jaw dropped and Mr. Pringle chuckled. "Actually, I didn't *know* that—not until I saw your reaction; I was just speculating. Your expression tells me I guessed correctly."

It was Hugo's turn to laugh. "You're as wily as a fox."

"I am not completely without guile," the vicar admitted, his smile slowly fading. "I won't ask what you did to earn your money. It is not your past that concerns me, but your future."

Hugo thought about testing the vicar's belief in his own words and disclosing that he made his money from buggery, sucking cock, and bedding other men's wives. He could just imagine the effect such words would have on the old man's fragile heart.

No, it would not be Hugo Buckingham who would be responsible for *that*.

Hugo and the Maiden

Instead, he said, "I beg your pardon, sir, but why should anything about my life concern you?"

"I think you can guess the answer to that, Hugo."

The only reason Hugo could think of was so outlandish that he refused to speak the words out loud and give them life. "I cannot."

Amusement glinted in the vicar's pale blue eyes. "We shall come back to that in a moment. What I want to know is if you will resume earning your living by illegal means? Or will you continue as you have these past weeks on Stroma—a hardworking, trustworthy man?"

"It's not that simple, Mr. Pringle."

"Oh, and why is that?"

"I have a lot to protect and that means I may have to do things I do not like to protect it."

"I see."

Hugo looked away from his suddenly piercing gaze. "If I told you otherwise, I would be lying, sir. You cannot imagine the things I've done to earn my money."

"You are doubtless correct in that—I am not a worldly man. However, I sensed something happened in your heart the day McCoy did not take you back with the others—some fundamental change—or was I wrong?

It was true that Hugo felt different now, but that was likely because he was working night and day and too exhausted to think of anything else but his next meal. Life on this remote rock was as different from life in London as it would be on the moon.

"I don't know if I've changed, Mr. Pringle. But what I *do* know is that even if I walk the righteous path for the rest of my days I am not, at my core, a good man. I am ruled by selfish impulses—greedy and acquisitive impulses and I can't change my stripes. I like—no, scratch that—I love creature comforts and material possessions. I crave luxurious surroundings, fine clothing, excellent food, and all the other hedonistic pleasures money can buy. I've been poor once and I never want to be poor again."

"But that is not all you are, Hugo—a collection of wants and desires. You are a good man—I have evidence of it."

Good God! Would the man not have done already and simply tell him what he wanted

"What do you mean?" he asked wearily when he'd taken hold of his temper.

"You have been gentle and kind to Cailean Fergusson, a boy who can give you none of the things you listed above."

"He saved my *life*, sir."

"Then why don't you simply send money back to him when you reach London—just as you offered to do for me that night—rather than befriend him?"

Hugo sputtered. "I said I was selfish, not a monster. I like him and I've only been kind to him—it costs me nothing. You are making something out of nothing. You know me as I am here Mr. Pringle, in a place where my options have been limited to working or stealing. Have you forgotten that my first choice was to steal?" Hugo's face burned and he threw up his hands, slumping in his chair. He hated articulating his shortcomings. "Can we please move to the heart of the matter, Mr. Pringle? Why did you ask me whether I found your daughter attractive?" Although Hugo had more than a sneaking suspicion.

"I am a father who wants the best for his child—his only child."

Well, that was easy enough. "The best for your daughter is—as much as it pains me to say—Robert Clark. The man is an insufferable prig, but he is steady, dependable, and has already made it his business to protect Martha." The words were like acid on his tongue, but they needed to be said. "Your daughter would know what she was getting with such a man. He would take care of her and never give her cause for worry."

"Oh, I agree; Robert Clark is the more decent, morally upstanding man."

His words were unexpectedly painful.

"But I'm not sure what Martha needs is the more decent, morally upstanding man. My daughter is spirited and delights in being challenged. I think she will gradually lose her light with Mr. Clark. Not because of any cruelty on his part, but simply because he is a prosaic, unimaginative man who will not appreciate Martha's intelligence and passion for life."

Hugo wanted to argue that Martha was rather prosaic herself, but then he remembered the way her eyes had burned when she'd believed he and Albert were about to be hauled off in leg-irons. And how she'd lied to Clark to rescue young Lorn. And how she'd had to bite back a smile every time her gorgeous lips mouthed the foolish word *Higgenbotham*.

Hugo and the Maiden

Hugo stifled an irritated groan. What did any of that matter? So what if she was spirited and passionate? What was that to him?

He met the old man's pale gaze. "If you think Clark will dim her, er, light, she doesn't need to marry him. I'm sure there must be other hardworking, fine young men here. Or perhaps on the mainland."

"It's not only that, Hugo, it's also that life on this island is so very, very hard." He leaned across the table and grasped Hugo's hand and Hugo gasped at his ice-cold fingers.

"Life on Stroma killed my wife, Hugo. I do not want the same for Martha. I want to know my Martha's future is secure—that she is with a man who will take care of her, but also challenge her. I have seen the way you look at her."

Astonishingly, Hugo's face heated.

The old man smiled. "Not only *those* looks, Hugo, but the ones you give her when you think nobody is looking."

"Oh, and what looks are those?" Hugo wanted to sneer but the question came out like a plea—*did* he look at her in some way he didn't realize? Was it possible there was more to his attraction to her than simply wanting to fuck her?

"She fascinates you."

Hugo opened his mouth to deny the vicar's words, but he realized they were true. He *was* fascinated by her goodness and her spirit. He'd never met anyone so giving, whose passion seemed to be making others feel safe and loved and cared for.

"And I have seen the looks she gives you."

Hugo bit his tongue to keep from making a pitiful arse of himself and begging the old man to tell him more. The last thing old Pringle needed was encouragement in whatever mad scheme he was hatching.

But the vicar was relentless. "These past two weeks you have stayed away from her on purpose, haven't you? You have done so because you did not want to toy with her affections."

Hugo shrugged, even though he knew it was childish and rude.

"I know you have. But staying away is hurting my daughter. Each day Martha's bright eyes have become a bit duller. My heart aches for her; you will know how it is when you have a child of your own. You want to see them happy and will move heaven and earth to make that happen. And it seems to me that you, Hugo, are what she wants to be happy."

Hugo's head spun as if he'd just guzzled a pint of gin. This man could not be saying what Hugo was hearing. He wanted to tell him to stop—to shut up, to quit dangling some fantasy in front of him. Hugo opened his mouth to tell him that he'd send money to express his gratitude, and that was his final offer.

But the cold, boney fingers tightened around his hand with surprising strength and Mr. Pringle leaned closer. "I saw the way Martha looked when she thought McCoy might take you away; it would have broken her heart. The same thing will happen when you leave a week from now: it will break her heart. I don't want to think of how painful it will be to look at my beautiful, kind daughter once her heart is broken." His jaw tightened. "I will do everything in my power to see that doesn't happen."

When Hugo merely stared, he cocked his head, his expression softening. "You both care for each other already and I believe it could grow into something more if given a chance."

Christ! Did the man really think that being with him was favorable to being a fisherman's wife? He should have had more than his heart examined by that physician.

Hugo bit his tongue; he could not say any of that.

Instead. he said, "Do you not have any family she could go to?"

"No. There is no family on either side. Her mother was an orphan and I—well, my siblings were older and have all passed on. I am all she has."

Hugo ground his teeth, his thoughts flitting around in his head like moths trapped in a lantern. "What makes you think she'd accept me if I offered for her?"

Where the hell had those words come from? What in the name of all that was holy would I do with a wife? I've never even had a lover for more than a week!

Hugo wanted to howl. Why had he asked the man such a thing?

He could see by the vicar's slight smile that he knew he'd set the hook deep. The sneaky old bastard.

"You won't know the answer to that until you ask her, Hugo."

Hugo gaped, his brain spinning like a toothless gear. But then the gear caught on something.

"Sir, you know she'd never leave Stroma without you, and I have to leave. If I don't go back to London soon there may be nothing to go back to."

Hugo and the Maiden

They held each other's gaze and Hugo had to admit the man would have made a fine card-player.

The vicar nodded. "You leave that to me, Hugo."

Hugo groaned, not caring that he sounded like a spoiled child. "Please let me set you up in a cottage someplace with a generous allowance—anywhere you like. That way Martha doesn't need to marry Clark, or me, or anyone else. It's the least I can do to thank you for saving me. If not for you, sir, I'd be spending the next seven years in chains."

"But I don't want money." Mr. Pringle's snowy white eyebrows slammed down into a straight line. "You promised me a favor—or have you forgotten that, Mr. Buckingham?"

Hugo recoiled; the old man looked downright frightening. In fact, he looked like God. Or at least how Hugo imagined God would look.

"Yes, yes of course I did. That's what I'm trying to—"

"Do you have feelings for Martha? Or have I misinterpreted what I've seen?"

Hugo stared into the other man's clear eyes. If he said *no* he was certain the vicar would release him from his obligation.

He opened his mouth to say exactly that, but his lips refused to form the word. Instead, he said, "I *do* like her, Mr. Pringle—but—" It was as if somebody else had taken possession of his mouth. What in the name of God was wrong with him? Why did he say that? Why would—

"Go on, son," the vicar urged.

Hugo stared at Mr. Pringle, searching for the right words—or any words, really. He more than liked Martha, but he didn't think lust was what the vicar had in mind. And lust was pretty much all Hugo had to offer a wife.

Wife?

He choked back a hysterical laugh. He must be out of his bloody mind to even be discussing this.

"I will make you a bargain," Mr. Pringle said.

"*Another* bargain?" Hugo squawked.

The vicar ignored him. "You were planning to leave next week?"

"Next Tuesday, or Wednesday at the latest."

"Stay two weeks—just fourteen days. Stay and pay court to her—every day—as you would any young woman. If, by the end of two weeks, you still do not wish to marry her—or her you—I'll consider your debt to me paid in full."

Hugo knew Martha found him attractive—or at least she wanted him in ways she didn't understand, physical ways. But she was pragmatic; just look at how long her courtship with Clark had been going on. She would never agree to anything in fourteen days. Especially not with Hugo.

He could stay the two weeks and discharge his debt and leave Stroma a free man. In every sense of the word.

"That's all you want from me?" he asked.

"All you have to do is demonstrate a good faith effort when it comes to courting my daughter." His blue eyes turned hard. "I would say *two weeks* of spending time with a pretty girl is a fair exchange for *seven years* in New South Wales."

The old man certainly knew how to turn the screws. Hugo had made a promise, and he would live up to it.

"Very well, Mr. Pringle, I will stay for two weeks and do my best to, er, court Martha."

Mr. Pringle's smug smile told Hugo that he'd never had any doubt on the matter. Then the old man's smile dimmed slightly. "Er, I would ask you not to tell her about this."

"I'm not stupid, Mr. Pringle. It would be worth both our lives if she learned you were bribing a man to court her."

The vicar winced.

"Don't fret, I can keep my mouth shut. I'll pay court to your daughter, although I'm not really certain what that means." Hugo's idea of courting Martha would be stripping her naked and licking every part of her body.

Somehow, he didn't think that was what the vicar had in mind.

"I am sure you will come up with several activities you both would enjoy," Mr. Pringle said.

Hugo choked back a laugh. Oh yes, he had no shortage of ideas when it came to entertaining himself with Martha.

He sighed at the thought of postponing his return to London. Oh, well. What did an additional week matter? He suspected the same mess would await him whether he returned in two weeks or two months.

The vicar held out a hand, as if to seal their agreement. "You'll see, Hugo—the two of you won't even need two weeks to learn to love one another."

Hugo and the Maiden

Hugo just nodded and shook his hand.

He should have told the old man that he'd already lost; Hugo had never loved anyone except himself and he never would.

***

When Hugo entered the tiny pub a few minutes later he easily spotted a familiar flame-red head. "Ah, there you are, Albert, I was hoping to see you this evening."

Albert looked up from the small booklet that he always seemed to have his nose buried in, his face breaking into a big smile when he saw Hugo. "I thought that I'd missed you; I heard you were here earlier."

Hugo dropped onto the stool beside him. "I just popped in with Cailean before going to have a chat with the vicar about something. But I wanted to talk to you and figured you might be here."

"I've not seen you in days; you've turned into quite the hermit lately."

"Yes, well, those days are over." Hugo nodded at Joe, who lifted a glass and pointed to the beer tap. "Please, Joe—and another for Albert while you're at it, please."

"Oh, thank you," Albert murmured. "Your letter is all the locals are talking about," he said, giving Hugo a curious look.

"Good Lord—I only read it myself a few hours ago."

"Well, you know how things are here. So, it's from a duchess, I hear?"

Hugo laughed. "Close. My friend is married to the youngest son of a marquess."

"Ah."

Joe set down their pints. "Thank you, Joe—pour one for yourself when you get a chance. And please add them to my account."

The innkeeper smiled, clearly well pleased that Hugo would be spending a goodly chunk of the smaller draft in either his pub and store. "Ta, Hugo."

Hugo slid Albert's beer across the bar to him and raised his glass. "Here's to getting off his island," he said in an under voice.

Albert raised his pint and they clinked glasses. "I'll drink to that—although it will still be a while for me."

"Not anymore. I've got enough to send both of us home, Albert."

"Oh, but I can't take money from you."

"It's just a loan—and I know you're good for it." Virtue oozed from Albert; giving him a loan was as safe as putting his money into a bank.

Albert's green eyes widened. "Really? I mean, are you sure? I shan't be able to repay you—not right away, so—"

"We're going to get our hands on that patent of yours, Albert. You're going to become a screamingly wealthy man and then can repay me."

Albert grinned and raised his glass again. "Now there's something I can drink to. When do you want to leave?"

"When can you go?"

"Hmm." Albert scratched his head. "The Wilsons asked that I give them a week's notice."

"Good, tell them tonight. I have to wait two weeks, but we can at least get you on the road."

"I could wait for you?"

There was no reason for Albert to wait an extra week just because Hugo had to.

Not to mention you're hoping you might be here a bit longer. Maybe even long enough to do what Mr. Pringle wants you to do ...

That thought had never entered his mind.

Liar.

Hugo brutally crushed any thoughts of a future with Martha—at least any future beyond the next two weeks. What the vicar wanted and believed was nothing but an old man's fantasy. The reality was that Hugo would be leaving Stroma as an unmarried man once he'd repaid his debt to Mr. Pringle.

He grimly took a long pull from his pint. "You needn't wait for me, Albert. And I won't be more than a week behind you."

Chapter 15

Martha was sitting in the meeting house darning one of her father's socks when Hugo appeared in the open doorway.

At first, she thought she'd imagined him, but then she remembered the only way he appeared in her mind's eye these days was without any clothing.

And in a state of animal arousal.

Today he was clad in a shirt, neckerchief, trousers that actually reached his ankles, boots that matched, and a waistcoat she had never seen. It looked as if his hair had grown longer since she'd last seen him, although she knew that was hardly possible in two weeks. His skin was no longer a pale from being locked in the hold of a ship, but a golden brown. He was thinner and he resembled a satyr more than ever. Cutting flagstone was brutal work and she knew men needed to eat almost constantly to do such work. She doubted he was getting enough to eat.

She berated herself for caring.

"Good afternoon, Miss Pringle. What a delight to find you here."

As always with Hugo she took refuge in sarcasm. "Well, if it isn't *Mr. Buckingham* himself."

He sauntered into the meeting house as if he owned it. "At your service, ma'am." He dropped a ridiculously graceful court bow. "I would ask how you've been doing but I can see you are blooming."

"Did you need something?" she asked coolly.

He put his hands in his trouser pockets and leaned up against the doorframe, more at ease than he had any right to be. "Are you angry with me?"

"Of course not," she said, seething. "I just never expected to see you again." She grimaced; could she sound more like an infatuated, lovelorn idiot if she tried?

"I think you missed me."

If Martha trusted her aim, she would have thrown her darning needle at his head.

He strolled over and lowered his long, powerful body onto the bench beside her, sitting so close their legs almost touched.

"What are you doing?"

"Sitting." His expression was as innocent as Cailean's. "I was wondering, Martha, if—"

"I did *not* give you leave to use my name."

One moment he was sitting beside her, the next he was down on his knees in front of her, taking her hand—the one with the sock rather than the needle. "I beg of you, Miss Pringle," he said, his eyes dark and soulful, "please allow me the inestimable privilege of using your Christian name."

She snatched her hand away. "You are incorrigible, but I suspect you already know that."

"I do," he admitted, gracefully rising from his knees, brushing off his trousers, and sitting back down on the bench. "But perhaps with your influence I could become ... corrigible."

"I'm not sure that's a word."

"It has to be."

"Why does it *have* to be?"

"Well, there is indifferent and different, insolent and solent."

Martha snorted. "I know there is no such word as solent."

"If that is true, you should be honored."

"And why is that, pray tell?"

"Any man can bring you flowers or baubles, but not just any man can create a new word for you."

Martha ignored his foolishness and narrowed her eyes at him. "I see you have new trousers, shoes, and a vest."

He looked down at said vest, fingering the lapel with his long, tapered fingers, which were no longer white and soft. Martha couldn't help noticing the blood blisters on his thumb.

"My other waistcoat came apart while I was washing it, so I purchased this one from Willy MacLeod's wife. She said he'd eaten too many dumplings to fit into it."

"I don't recall a time when Willy could have fit in that."

"Well, Willy's loss is my gain—or perhaps I should say Willy's gain is my gain." He grinned and she had to bite her lip to keep from smiling. His eyelids lowered and his nostrils did that ever-so-slight flaring thing that made her stomach flutter. Although, quite honestly, most of the things the irritating man did made her stomach flutter. "Tell me, Martha, do I look well in it?"

Hugo and the Maiden

Martha pursed her lips and yanked on the darning yarn with an unnecessarily vicious tug. "You know you do."

"Then perhaps you would like to come out walking with me and my waistcoat—be seen out and about with us?"

"I would have thought you were too busy planning your journey south to bother with walks." Once again, she wanted to chew out her own tongue.

He smirked. "Will you miss me when I'm gone, Martha?"

"No."

He laughed.

"When are you leaving?"

"Not for another two weeks."

Joy leapt in her chest, but she immediately suppressed it. It didn't matter how long he was here; he was still leaving.

"But let's not talk about my departure. Come for a walk; it is too lovely an evening to darn socks."

"You wouldn't say that if it was your sock I was darning."

Hugo lifted the right leg of his trousers to expose an ankle boot with no stocking showing. He also exposed a fine expanse of muscular calf in the process—although it was nothing she'd not seen before. "I eschew socks." He leaned toward her when she ignored him. "I'm serious, Martha—why not come walking with me?"

"Because she's already agreed to come out with me."

Martha jolted. She'd been so fixated on Hugo that she'd noticed nothing else. Hugo, she suspected by the sly smile curling his lips, had known Mr. Clark was nearby and had wanted him to hear the invitation.

"You should be on your way, Buckingham," Mr. Clark said, marching up to Martha and taking her hand.

Martha frowned at his proprietary gesture. He was more interested in thwarting Hugo than walking with her, she was sure of that.

Based on the knowing, amused glint in Hugo's eyes, he'd guessed that, too.

Martha cut Mr. Clark a stern look and then turned to give Hugo a tight smile. "Come back tomorrow evening, Mr. Buckingham. I shall walk with you then."

***

Hugo was waiting on the cottage steps when Martha opened her door at seven o'clock the next evening.

Instead of the newer outfit he'd worn yesterday, he was dressed in the clothing that she'd scrounged for him. It was a disgrace to call them clothes, but the ragged garments were spotlessly clean.

"Oh, you're here," she said foolishly.

"I was a few minutes early, but didn't want to appear over-eager, so I waited outside."

"But you thought you'd tell me that you were over-eager, just in case I didn't happen to notice."

He grinned. "You know me so well."

"Ha."

"I thought we might take a walk down to the Greedy Vicar if you'd let me treat you to a hot chocolate."

"You are a spendthrift, Mr. Buckingham. You needn't put yourself into debt because of me."

"Oh, trust me—the thought would never enter my mind. Everything I do, I do for my own satisfaction."

"Hmmm." She cut him a speculative glance. Like everyone else on the island she knew that an aristocrat had sent him a letter containing a bank draft so large—twenty pounds—that Joe hadn't been able to cash it.

"I'm surprised you aren't already gone. I thought you were eager to get off the island and go back to—well, back to whatever it is you do."

Martha began walking before he offered her his arm—which is what Mr. Clark always did. But she suspected that she wouldn't be able to think *or* walk if she touched any part of Hugo.

"I've decided to give Mr. Stogden two weeks to secure another employee."

"That is thoughtful."

"Thoughtfulness has nothing to do with it. My behavior is entirely self-serving."

"How so?"

He gave her a warm look. "It means I get to spend more time with you. Life is too precious and brief to deny ourselves every sensual pleasure, wouldn't you agree?"

Martha's face heated at his blatant innuendo. "That sounds like the philosophy of a hedonist."

"Absolutely! My goal is unfettered pleasure."

"You're a care-for-nobody, in other words," she suggested.

Hugo and the Maiden

He gave her a look of mock surprise. "Why, Miss Martha, I feel as if you know me better than I know myself."

"Hmmph. I spoke to Albert earlier today and he said you are paying for his transportation to London and gave him the name of a friend who will put him up when he reaches the city."

Hugo frowned. "Did he." It wasn't a question.

"*He* says you have been generous to him. One might say ... selfless, almost."

Hugo's mouth twisted into a pruney shape. "Mr. Franks needs to keep his opinions to himself."

"Why do you wish to pretend as if you care only about yourself?"

"It's not a pretense, trust me."

Martha could see by the stubborn set of his jaw that she would get nowhere on this subject. "Tell me, Mr. Buckingham—"

"I insist you call me Hugo."

"Tell me, *Mr. Buckingham*, what is it you do in London?"

"I manage various business concerns."

"That sounds considerably less strenuous than cutting flagstone." It also sounded very vague.

"Are you wondering how I maintain such a magnificent physique while engaging in such sedentary work?"

Martha's face burned. "I'm wondering no such thing."

He chuckled. "A man can always hope."

Really! He was a menace to a woman's peace of mind. Why did she enjoy his company so much when he always made her feel so skittish?

And why didn't she believe him when he claimed to be self-centered—what sort of person would say that if it weren't true? How come she persisted in believing that there was more to him than frivolity and selfishness? And why was he so much more intriguing than Mr. Clark—whom she knew to be a good man, at least in most matters?

Just what was wrong with her? Was she like a magpie and Hugo the new, shiny object that caught her attention? Could she really be so shallow?

Martha had—grudgingly—accepted that a great deal of her feelings for him were physical in nature. But that wasn't all of it. There was just something about him that seemed to call to her.

Every instinct screamed that she should send him off with a flea in his ear, but she could not make herself do it. The two long weeks that he'd avoided her had been dreary—frighteningly so—and she was in no hurry to return to those tedious days.

Besides, he would only be here for a short time and then he would be gone. Forever. Surely there was no harm in enjoying him before he left?

The thought of Hugo leaving forever made her stomach churn as if she'd just eaten bad fish.

She bit her lip to keep from groaning at her own stupidity. What was wrong with her? How in the world could she have become so attached to the man in such a short time? Was she really in danger of falling in love with him?

Or even worse, had she already fallen?

Chapter 16

Hugo was late.

He was also filthy, which he hated. He had planned to wash up and change his clothing before going out with Martha—the seventh evening they'd spent together out of the last ten—but the day had been chaotic and long.

The driller he worked with, Gerry Boyle, had suffered an accident that crushed his arm. Hugo and one of the other men had carried the injured man on a stretcher to Nethertown. When they'd arrived, Mr. Stogden had a boat waiting to take Gerry over to the doctor on the mainland.

The entire process had left Hugo dirty, exhausted, and scared—for Gerry. He liked what he knew of the hardworking man, who had a wife and three young children. The Boyles had a tiny bit of land, but it wouldn't be enough to sustain them without Gerry's money from cutting stone. Hugo imagined that, in addition to physical pain, Gerry was probably worrying about his family right now. That was what happened when somebody allowed themselves to care for other people: they became a burden.

As Hugo made his way toward the Pringle cottage, he thought about what the vicar had said about life on Stroma aging people.

There was plenty of aging going on in the rookeries, but Stroma had brutal weather to contend with as well as geographical isolation.

Gerry had been able to go to the mainland today because the weather had cooperated. What would have happened if it had been storming and a boat couldn't get across? A person could die so easily while help was only a few miles distant.

The lights were on in the windows of the Pringle cottage and Hugo grimaced as he realized how late he was. He wouldn't be surprised if that bloody Clark had taken advantage of the situation and stolen a march on him.

He raised his hand to knock but the door opened.

"Oh, Hugo," Martha said, her expression anxious.

"I'm sorry I'm late it—"

"Hush, you needn't apologize." She took his hand and gave it a gentle squeeze. "I heard you helped bring poor Gerry to Nethertown." She drew him inside and led him toward the small table where he'd had tea with Mr. Pringle. "Mr. Stogden went with him to the mainland?"

"Yes," Hugo said, more than a little distracted by the feel of her small, work-roughened hand on his. She was so *small* physically and yet so … potent.

She released him to reach for the kettle, and Hugo immediately missed her.

"Would you like some tea?"

It took a moment for his befogged brain to translate her words. "Er, please. I would love some."

Hugo took his hand from the table and rested it in his lap, covering his half-hard cock, more than a little alarmed by what a simple touch from her did to his body.

Martha bustled around the small space far more efficiently than her father had.

Hugo glanced around—where *was* Mr. Pringle? "Is your father here?"

"No, he's gone to sit with Gerry's wife, Adele."

Even a whore like Hugo knew he shouldn't be in the house alone with a young unmarried woman—not unless he wanted to destroy her reputation.

"I should wait outside," he said when she turned to place cups and plates on the table.

Martha smiled. "Nobody will think the worse of me for giving you a cup of tea and a few biscuits after the day you've had."

"But—"

"If it makes you feel better, I can open the front door."

As she left the room Hugo marveled at how quickly their roles had changed. Since when was he such a knight protector? But he knew the answer to that: he didn't want to repay Mr. Pringle's kindness with scandal.

Nor do you want to be forced into marriage.

The thought drove him to his feet just as Martha entered the kitchen.

"What is it?" she asked.

"I'd rather have a pint," he lied. "If you don't mind being seen with me in all my dirt I'd like to go down to the Vicar as we'd planned."

"I don't mind."

"Good, I'll wait outside for you." Hugo darted out the door before she could stop him.

He was pacing and delivering a lecture to himself on the subject of proper behavior when Martha opened the cottage door.

He stopped in mid-stride and looked up at her. She had tucked her lovely hair under an old straw hat and had tossed a crocheted blue shawl around her shoulders.

She was the most beautiful thing Hugo had ever seen.

"Hugo?"

He jolted. "Hmm?"

"I'm ready."

They set off.

"What did you do today?" Hugo asked, not wanting to think about his own day.

"I transcribed my father's last sermon for him."

"You transcribed it?"

"Yes, he keeps a record of them all, a leather-bound book just for that purpose, but his handwriting is dreadful, so I copy it into the book for him. It is also an opportunity to read his words over. Sometimes, on a Sunday there are things to distract me."

Hugo felt a twinge of guilt at her words; he'd never heard her father speak.

There it was again—another bizarre feeling assaulting him: guilt. Hugo had always been the most guilt-free person in Britain and now he was—

"Martha?"

Hugo and Martha turned to find Mrs. Fergusson, Cailean's aunt, rushing toward them.

"What is it, Mrs. Fergusson?" Martha asked.

The old woman's expression was tense and pinched. "It's Small Cailean."

"What about Small Cailean?" Hugo asked before Martha could speak.

"He didn't come back last night and he's not back again tonight."

"Who saw him last?"

"Er, my lad, Hamish."

Hamish Fergusson was one of Cailean's principal tormentors; Hugo had already given the lad a stern talking-to about teasing his giant but gentle cousin.

"Did your boy do something to him?" Hugo demanded, not bothering to hide his displeasure.

"Oh, boys will be boys, you know. It's nothing that—"

"Where was he last seen?" Martha cut Hugo a worried glance.

"He was off looking for Lily."

"What happened to Lily?" Hugo asked, dread pooling in his chest.

"Well, the boys were just playin' and—"

"What did they do to her?"

The old woman flinched at the cold menace in his tone.

Martha laid a hand on his shoulder. "Hugo, perhaps you should—"

"No, Martha—I want the truth." He frowned at Mrs. Fergusson. "And I want it *now*."

"Hamish said they chased Lily into the Gloup," Mrs. Fergusson blurted.

"Bloody hell!"

"But they didn't mean—"

Hugo turned away from her before he said something he'd regret. "I've not been into the caves because Cailean is terrified of them," he admitted to Martha. "Do you think he would have braved his fear if Lily went in there?"

"Cailean knows the entire island like the back of his hand, Hugo—the Gloup included." She turned to the older woman. "What is the tide tonight?"

"It's almost low slack."

"That's a bit of luck, Hugo. Low slack is the only time you can access the cave," Martha explained.

"So we can go now, then?" Hugo said, trying not to think of the boy and his damned rat scared or hurt someplace. Dammit! He should have known something was amiss when Cailean hadn't shown up to visit him yesterday evening.

"Have you looked elsewhere for him, Mrs. Fergusson?" Martha asked.

"I've got Hamish and the boys lookin' for him around Swilkie Point and—"

Hugo and the Maiden

"He's hardly likely to answer the same people who drove him into hiding, is he?"

Mrs. Fergusson recoiled from Hugo's anger.

"Who do you know who's not out tonight?" Martha asked softly, giving Hugo a chiding look.

Hugo knew she meant the fishing boats. Almost every fisherman on the island was out on the water taking advantage of some sort of fish run.

"Jem Packard isn't out—I saw the *Louise* on the beach." Mrs. Fergusson stared worriedly at Hugo.

Bloody right she should.

"Hugo and I will fetch oil lamps and get over to the Gloup. You go ask Jem if he will take the *Louise* out and check some of Cailean's favorite places."

"Aye," Mrs. Fergusson nodded. "I'll get Hamish to take me where they've already looked and we'll look again. He'll not be afraid if I call for him."

"Good," Martha said. "You go on now. We'll get back to you as soon as we've had a look."

Martha turned to him as Mrs. Fergusson hustled away. "The last time Cailean slept in the caves he got a proper scolding after the entire island was out looking for him. That is likely why he was too terrified to show them to you. Still, searching for Lily would have made him swallow his fear. And perhaps he was trapped down there by the tide."

"But *two* nights?"

"Come, let's get the lanterns." She smiled up at him. "Don't fret, Hugo. I know you love him and—"

"I don't love him," Hugo quickly denied. "I mean, I *like* him, of course. I just think that, er, well." He grimaced. "The man saved my life—did you know that? If he'd not found me that night I would have died. And I know he doesn't like being in the dark when he's alone—" He cut Martha an embarrassed glance. "He likes me to walk him home from Mr. Stogden's when there's no moon," he explained. He shoved a hand through his hair. "He loves that bloody rat. I can see him risking his life for her."

"It is all right to worry, Hugo. That's what we do with people we care about—worry about them." Martha's tone was one of gentle amusement.

***

Hugo filled two lamps while Martha left a brief note for her father. She didn't think he'd be coming home until late since poor Adele had been almost hysterical about Gerry, but she didn't want him to worry if he returned to find her gone.

"Tell me about these caves," Hugo asked as they started toward the Gloup.

"The Gloup has been used for smuggling over the years," she said. "For all I know it could be in use right now."

"Smuggling what? I wouldn't have thought anyone here could afford the goods that are usually smuggled."

"And you'd be right. It's mainly used to store spirits that are made here before they're taken to the mainland. There are also items collected from, er, well—"

"Wreckers store their booty in the caves," he guessed.

"Sometimes."

"Good Lord, why would anyone carry things all the way down into a cave that you can only reach for an hour a day?"

"You can reach it anytime by boat."

"Might it be dangerous for Cailean—for *you*—to go down there?"

"None of the locals would hurt Cailean."

"Except his own cousin."

"They're just boys, Hugo."

His expression was skeptical, but he didn't argue.

They came to the sloping rock pathway that led down into caves and had to go single file, each holding a lamp as they picked their way down.

"The caves branch off in several places," she said. "We'll keep on the one heading north."

"Why that one?"

"The others become quite small." Her voice bounced off the hard rock that was now on three sides of them.

"How long do we have before we need to leave?" Hugo held her lantern when she needed both hands to climb over a pile of rocks. Once she was down, he handed her both lights so he could do the same.

"We can stay in the main cave forever without drowning. It only gets blocked off because part of the passageway fills with water.

Hugo and the Maiden

He took back his lamp and they continued. "I'm surprised enterprising young boys like Hamish aren't down here making mischief."

"They know better than to trifle with the men who use these caves," she said as they approached the tunnel opening.

Hugo lifted his lamp and stared into the gloom ahead. "I'll go first."

"Once you reach the section that is submerged daily the rocks will be slippery with seaweed, so you must be careful."

Hugo's dark eyes glittered in the yellow light of the lantern. "Are you worried about me, Miss Martha Pringle?" he teased. "You know what worrying about somebody means, don't you?" he asked, turning her own words back at her.

"I'm not worried about you, Mr. *Buckingham*. But that's my father's favorite lamp you're holding. I should hate for you to trip and break it."

He chuckled, the sound echoing eerily in the darkness ahead.

The ground ahead was sharp and rocky, punctuated by areas that were smooth with pebbly sand.

"Did you mark the time when we came down?" Hugo asked.

"We have a bit less than an hour and it takes about ten or fifteen minutes to get to the main cave."

"We'll be cutting it close."

"Yes, but we wouldn't have any more time at the next low."

The air was so humid it was like breathing water.

"I can't believe anyone would come all the way down here just to distill some of that wretched corn liquor."

"Oh, you've had some of that, have you?"

"Unfortunately."

Martha chuckled at his obvious distaste. "You'll need to toughen up if you're to ever make an islander, Hugo Buckingham."

An uncomfortable pause followed her words, reminding her that he would be gone soon; he would never become an islander.

"Tell me about where you live—your house in London," she asked, hoping to get his mind off the task at hand.

He hesitated so long she thought he might not answer—she had noticed that he was close-mouthed when it came to his personal matters, although he certainly didn't mind asking other people questions.

"I shared a house with some others."

"Do you have an office near the—where did you say you worked? The Exchange?"

"Yes."

"I thought a person required a great deal of—" Martha's face became hot as she realized what she'd been about to ask. "Er, I didn't mean to—"

He chuckled. "Are you trying to discern whether I am a wealthy man, Miss Pringle?"

"Of course not."

He stopped so suddenly that Martha bumped into him.

"What is it?" she asked.

He crouched down and then turned, his expression grim as he moved so she could see what he was looking at: it was dried blood, and a great deal of it, splattered over the rocky floor of the tunnel.

Martha raised a hand to her mouth. "Oh no! Do you—"

But Hugo was already walking.

Chapter 17

There was a distracting buzzing in Hugo's head. Or maybe it was outside of his head.

Either way, it was maddening. A vision of quiet, gentle Cailean with his head split open flickered through his mind's eye and the buzzing intensified.

"Hugo. Hugo? *Hugo!*" Martha's breathless voice came from behind him.

"What?" he barked.

"We don't know it is Cailean's blood."

"We don't know it isn't."

"We won't be of help to anyone if we hurt ourselves before we can get there." Her hand landed on his shoulder. "Please." She was panting so Hugo stopped. "Thank you."

They stood for a moment while Martha caught her breath. "That blood could be any number of things, Hugo. I know for a fact that Bridget Simpson's dog has been stealing hens. And then there's—"

"It's all right, Martha. I've calmed down." She gave him a doubtful smile, which Hugo returned. "Shall we carry on?" They walked in silence for a while.

"You mentioned some other tunnels," Hugo said a short time later. "Should we check those first or go straight to the main?"

"If he came after Lily he might have gone into any of the passageways and not all the way to the still cave."

"And you say this still is no longer in use?" he asked, more to hear her voice rather than any real interest in island brewing.

"Not after some long-ago customs agent or exciseman found it. They destroyed it, but the name stuck."

"The islanders didn't replace it?"

"No. The caves are used for smuggling, but nothing so permanent as brewing anymore."

Hugo couldn't imagine spending any time down here no matter how good the money might be. The stench of seaweed, fish, and rot that clung to everything on the island was especially strong.

"Right ahead is the first tunnel that branches off," Martha said.

The tunnel in question looked like more of a hole. They'd only gone about ten feet in when the passage narrowed dramatically.

"This would be a devil of a place for a man as tall as Cailean," Hugo muttered, already bent nearly double.

"Why don't you let me go first?"

Hugo didn't like that idea. At all. "I can go a bit farther." Unfortunately, that was *all* he could go. He dropped to his haunches and turned to Martha, who was still upright. Hugo grinned up at her. "Why, you're just a little thing."

"I am five foot one- and three-quarter inches."

"Ah."

She pursed her sinful lips and looked down her small, straight nose at him. "So, have you changed your mind about letting me go first?"

"All right; but be careful. And go slowly—if you slip and sprain an ankle it would be difficult to—"

"Why, Hugo—are you *worried* about me?" She was smiling—no *grinning*—down at him.

"No, I'm worried about how sore my back would be having to carry you."

She laughed.

"Go on with you," he said gruffly.

"Yes, Mr. Buckingham."

"How very obedient you are, Miss Pringle. I *do* like the sound of that."

She edged around him and proceeded into the darkness. "I wouldn't become accustomed to it, Mr. Buckingham," she tossed over her shoulder.

The light from her lamp disappeared far too quickly. "Keep talking to me, Martha."

"Do you miss me already?" Her voice sounded hollow and bounced off the walls—an odd, soggy echo.

"Do you like living on Stroma—or would you like to one day leave?"

"I could make a case for either." Her voice was far too faint for his liking.

"Martha? How far—"

"Oh, Hugo. Oh, no!"

Hugo and the Maiden

"What is it? Martha? *Martha!*" Hugo snatched up the lamp and started after her, his knees bent as he all but crawled forward. "I'm coming. Just—"

"I am not hurt. But I've found a dead otter."

Hugo sank to his haunches in relief, blood pounding in his ears. Thank. Bloody. Hell.

"Hugo?"

"What is it, darling?" The word slipped out, and the silence that followed was a good eight-months pregnant.

"This isn't Lily."

"Can you tell the difference between one otter and another?"

"Can *you* tell between one dog and another? Or between two cats?"

That was true; he'd know Tiger anywhere.

"Oh, heavens," she said, which was as close as Martha ever got to cursing. "It's just dreadful—so many cuts and gashes. I can't believe the poor creature made it this far."

"From a knife or another animal?"

"Um, I don't know. It could be either."

"Are there any animals that might have done this?"

"Well, male otters can be quite vicious." She paused. "I believe this is a boy otter."

Hugo heard her mortification at having to articulate such a thing and couldn't help laughing.

"You are not a nice man."

"I know," he agreed. "Now get back here."

***

By the time they crept out of the dead otter cave more than twenty minutes had passed.

"We have to hurry, Hugo," Martha said, frowning at the watch pinned to her bodice.

"Is the next cave like that?"

"Even narrower."

"I think we should get to the main cavern first and look at smaller ones on the way back if we have time. What do you think?"

"We could split—"

"Don't. Just don't even say it."

"Are you afraid to be alone?"

"I'm not bloody keen on caves or dead animals or a tide about to rush in and drown us."

She laughed.

"I'm delighted to amuse you, Miss Pringle. How much farther?"

"No more than a few minutes."

Hugo stopped. Martha wasn't expecting it and staggered. He caught her, one of his hands on her waist to steady her.

Martha had never been this close to him; he was like a furnace. And so very, very ... hard.

"Listen," he said softly, leaning close. "I think you were right about splitting up. It's possible whoever killed that otter is still down here."

"Who would—"

"I don't know, maybe one of the smugglers you've mentioned."

"I can't believe that. It was probably just another otter."

"Maybe, but I don't want to take any chances. I want you to hang back. If there is somebody, er, well, unsavory, ahead I want you to run and bring help."

Martha hesitated, but then nodded; it was a solid plan. "All right." But the thought of leaving him was . . . painful.

His stern expression shifted into a sweet, gentle smile that Martha wouldn't have believed his wicked lips capable of forming. "A kiss for luck."

And then he lowered his mouth over hers and physical sensation swamped her. His lips were warm and firm; his scent was an earthy mix of male sweat and fresh air; and his body felt huge and hard against hers.

The tip of his tongue, soft and slick, flicked over her tightly pursed lips and she relaxed under the gentle caress. He made a low rumbling sound in his chest and then pulled away. Martha swayed toward him, her body following his.

"Sorry our first kiss was so quick and clumsy, sweetheart," he murmured in a husky voice. "But I had to taste you. Now stay here." He turned and was gone in a heartbeat.

Martha stared after him, her jaw sagging. He'd called it their first kiss. That implied there would be more, didn't it?

***

Hugo and the Maiden

Hugo's heart was pounding—partly out of worry for Martha's safety and Cailean's whereabouts, but mostly because of inconvenient-as-hell lust.

He was disgusted with himself; how could he be hard at a time like this? There must be something deeply deviant about his character: he was marching into a potentially dangerous situation and sporting a full-blown stand.

His mouth pulled into a grin. Well, why the hell not? After all, he did all his best work with an erection, didn't he?

The cave widened abruptly, becoming almost twice as broad and several times higher than the passageway. Hugo caught his breath. Good God; it was like a bloody cathedral. The light from his lamp cast eerie shadows in all the nooks, crannies, some of which looked deep enough to be tunnels or other caves.

A scuffing sound echoed in the room and Hugo pivoted, his right hand clenched into a fist and at the ready.

Martha jumped and yelped. "It's me! I'm sorry—"

"It's all right," he whispered, although he doubted anyone lurking in the caves could have failed to hear her screech. "Come along and stay close. Let's make sure we're alone."

It took a good ten minutes to check each of the caves.

It wasn't until they entered the third system of tunnels that they found evidence of human habitation; somebody had spread out knitted blankets where deep sand covered the hard rock floor.

"Those must be the blankets Mrs. Mason said went missing."

Hugo gestured to a pile of what looked to be chicken bones. "Maybe it wasn't the dog taking the Mrs. Simpson's hens, after all."

In the next cave they found the remains of a fire. "How could anyone have a fire in here?" Hugo asked, his voice echoing eerily.

Martha lifted the lantern and they both looked up. The ceiling went and up and up, narrowing like a chimney before disappearing into darkness.

"I know where this comes out," Martha said. "There is a crack in the earth."

Hugo scattered the fire pit ashes with his boot. "I wonder if this is where the convicts hid before getting off the island?"

"If so, that would certainly mean the islanders helped them."

Which is what Hugo had suspected all along.

"Well, none of that matters now," he said, and then paused.

"What's that?"

"What's what?"

He laid a finger across his lips and they both froze to listen.

Martha recognized the sound, first. "Oh no, Hugo—that's water!"

Hugo grabbed her hand, and they ran.

Chapter 18

There was about eight inches of water in the tunnel that led out of the main cave.

"Can we make it?" Hugo asked.

She chewed her lip and frowned as a swell rolled in, doubling the water level in the blink of an eye. "I don't think it's worth the risk."

"How long will we be here?"

"Um, twelve hours."

Hugo said something astoundingly vulgar. "Sorry," he muttered abstractedly.

"Somebody might come get us by boat when Mrs. Fergusson tells people where we've gone." Martha didn't add that was extremely unlikely with the herring run going on. None of the Stroma fishermen would want to interrupt laying out their drift nets to rescue two people who were perfectly safe.

Well, except for Robert.

If he learned she was in the Gloup with Hugo he'd come get them—or at least Martha. She grimaced at that thought.

Hugo paced a small circuit of the cavern, frowning. "I'm relieved Cailean's not down here but I wish we'd had the time to look in that other tunnel."

"I know you are, Hugo, but we didn't."

To her surprise, he chuckled. "Very well then, I'll stop fretting like a hen with a chick. We are here for the nonce and that is that. I suppose we should extinguish one of the lamps so we'll have enough oil to make our way out. How long do these things usually last?"

"They were full, so perhaps another four or five hours." She shivered; it would be utterly dark if they turned both off.

"What is it, Miss Martha—afraid of the dark?" he asked, his taunt an echo of her earlier teasing.

"You are so droll, Mr. Hugo Buckingham." Martha extinguished her lamp and placed it against the cave wall. "You should shorten your wick," she told him.

For some reason that made him laugh, but he turned the key-shaped knob until the light was a mere glow.

He pointed toward where the water lapped gently at the sandy shore of the cave. "How high will that get?"

"Perhaps a foot?"

"Let's stay here, then."

"Shall we bring over the blankets to sit on and fetch some water from that smaller cave?"

"Good idea." He lifted the lamp and led the way.

Martha found part of a clay jug and held it beneath the rivulet of water dripping from the darkness above them. "It's fresh," she said, offering some to Hugo.

He glanced at the cave wall, which was slimy, and pulled a face. "I'll have some when I get desperate."

"Is that how all city dwellers are—pernickety?"

"That's how *this* city dweller is but help yourself."

Martha did. Once she'd had enough to drink, they returned to the main cave.

"How about here?" Hugo asked, pointing to the deepest sand.

"We'd better double them," she said. "This sand is damp."

Once they'd laid them out one on top of the other Hugo gestured with a sweeping bow. "After you, my lady."

Martha fingered her shawl, wondering if she should lay it out somewhere not so close to Hugo.

"Come now, I won't bite." His smile exposed the pointy canine teeth that Martha had noticed before; they looked perfect for biting.

But it would be churlish to argue—where else was he supposed to go—so she lowered herself onto the far edge of the blanket, wishing she'd worn her cloak. The air in the caves was cooled by the ocean water; it would be a chilly twelve hours.

Hugo sat with a soft *thump* beside her and extracted a waxed cloth from the pocket of his worn coat. "How fortunate is this?" He unwrapped one of the fried hand pies the fishermen took out on the water with them. "It's a bit crushed for living in my pocket all day, but beggars can't be choosers."

Martha looked up at his face, and then wished she hadn't. Being this close reminded her of their brief kiss and made her wonder if he would kiss her again.

He cocked his head. "Martha?"

"Hmm?"

"Some pie?"

Hugo and the Maiden

"Oh, thank you," she murmured, taking the piece of pastry he offered.

They munched in silence, until Martha could not bear the tension a moment longer. "Are you looking forward to leaving Stroma?".

He snorted. "God, yes."

Martha flinched at his fervid tone.

He grimaced. "I'm sorry. I didn't mean I was happy to get away from the people—from, er, you, Cailean, your father," he added somewhat lamely. "I just meant I have business that is desperately in need of my attention."

"Albert told me that he believes his employer paid to have him taken. You've never explained what happened to you."

"I'm not certain who paid to have me kidnapped, thrown into jail, and then falsely charged and transported."

"You're not sure?" she repeated tartly. "Just how many people would want to do that to you?"

He smiled, but it didn't reach his eyes. "I suspect it was my, er, business partner."

"Why would your business partner have done such a thing?"

"I think she wants to—"

"Your partner is a *she*?"

He took a big bite of pie and chewed; his gaze speculative as it rested on her. "Mmm-hmm."

"That's, er, unusual, isn't it? A woman who engages in business?"

He kept chewing, but his lips curled up at the corners.

"What?" Her face was hot. "I'm just making polite conversation."

He swallowed, his smile turning to a grin.

"You are a very annoying man."

"So I've been told. Often."

"By whom?"

"Anyone who knows me, people who've just met me—the list is a long one."

"I believe it." Martha opened her mouth, but then closed it.

"What?" he asked, tucking the empty cloth back into his pocket.

"What what?" she repeated.

"I can see you are dying to ask me something. What is it?"

"I'm not *dying* to ask you anything."

"Suit yourself." He shrugged out of his coat.

"What are you doing?"

He winced at her shrill tone. "Don't worry, I'm only taking off my coat."

"Why? It's cold in here."

"Because I'm going to use it as a pillow."

"Oh. You're going to sleep?"

He sighed. "It's been a long day, Martha."

Martha looked at the dark smudges beneath his striking eyes and felt a pang of guilt for begrudging him some sleep. She edged as unobtrusively as possible toward the outside of the blanket.

He smirked. "You needn't fret; I won't do anything, er, untoward."

"I'm not worried," she lied.

He snorted and flopped onto his back, tucking the coat under his head. And then he yawned and closed his eyes.

How could he possibly sleep in this situation? Clearly her proximity meant nothing to him. At least not what it meant to her. Her skin was behaving strangely—flushing hot and then turning clammy and cold. And she couldn't seem to breathe normally.

And yet he was completely relaxed.

She studied him in the low light of the lamp. He wasn't classically handsome like Robert, but he was the most attractive man she had ever seen.

Like his body, his face was chiseled and composed of hard, stark planes. His nose was big—a veritable beak—and his thin-lipped mouth was permanently curved into an almost-smile. This close to him she could see the half-moon-shaped curves that bracketed his lips.

His eyelashes were thick and black, like his hair, and fanned out on his sun-bronzed skin. He must have bought a razor, because the hairs on his face were only just sprouting, as if he'd shaved that morning. The neckerchief he wore did a minimal job of covering his throat. Martha saw that he had to shave all the way down his neck, just like her father did.

His face and throat looked damp and dewy—the constant humidity on Stroma had some benefits—and she knew that his skin would taste salty, both from sweat and the sea air.

Her mouth watered to lick him. Right *there* in that hollow…

Martha had to swallow several more times to keep from drooling like some sort of maniac.

Hugo and the Maiden

Her gaze wandered lower. His shirt was threadbare and gritty; he'd obviously not had time to go home and clean himself or change from his work clothing today.

The thin cotton did nothing to hide the dark circles of his nipples. The shirt was too small for his broad shoulders and powerful chest and had come untucked, baring an inch-wide strip of muscular midriff.

Martha's pulse sped as she studied the fascinating ridges of his lower belly; there wasn't so much as an ounce of fat on the man. The muscles flexed slightly with each breath he took. She pushed a finger into her own belly; it was soft, with only a hint of muscle.

Her fingers twitched to feel him. To trace the prominent vein that pulsed beneath the thin skin; to explore the fascinating line that began just above the blade of his hip and cut diagonally, delineating the smooth muscles of his flank from his striated abdomen; to caress the intriguing trail of downy black hair which disappeared beneath the low-slung waistband of—

Don't look. It's wicked, Martha.

A team of oxen couldn't have stopped her gaze from venturing lower.

Her jaw sagged at the unmistakable ridge thrusting against the thin fabric and her eyes jerked up to his face.

He was looking at her, his eyes hooded, his expression almost ... stern. "What are you doing, Martha?" His voice was low and gravelly.

"N-nothing."

One of his eyebrows cocked.

"Just looking," she amended. As if to demonstrate, her willful eyes slid back down to his hips.

Yes, he was still erect.

Martha was trying to yank her gaze away when he palmed the hard ridge and squeezed.

A small whimper escaped her parted lips

The muscles in his forearm rippled as his fingers flexed. The outline of his organ was ... well, she knew what it looked like in the flesh, of course, but she thought that maybe she had exaggerated its dimensions in the weeks since seeing it.

She hadn't.

"Martha."

She swallowed and looked up.

"You shouldn't be staring at me like that while I'm trying so hard to behave."

"B-behave?"

He nodded slowly, his features shifting into something almost feral as his arm flexed and pumped, just once, before his hand dropped back to his side. "Yes, I'm behaving like a gentleman and you're—"

She snorted. "You call what you just did behaving like a gentleman?"

"I'm *trying* to behave like a gentleman," he amended, "but you aren't making it easy by staring at me like that."

"Like what?"

"Like you want to lick every inch of my body."

An outraged yelp broke out of her and her face—which was probably glowing brighter than the lantern—scalded at his amused, knowing expression. "How dare you—"

He rolled his eyes in an odious, dismissive way. "Don't bother to deny it. I recognize desire when I see it."

For a moment, Martha could only gape, her mouth opening and closing like a fish gasping for air. She struggled for a cutting set-down—or even an un-cutting one—but came up with nothing. And then she looked—really looked—into his dark eyes. The truth struck her like a whack to the head.

"You desire me, too," she blurted.

He only stared.

"You k-kissed me earlier."

His jaw flexed, and some unidentifiable emotion flickered across his face. "I shouldn't have."

"Why? Do you have a sweetheart in London? Or a w-wife?"

"No. And I don't want one, either."

Martha recoiled from his cold look and sharp tone. "Don't worry; I wasn't suggesting I wanted the position."

"Good."

Hurt and anger roiled in her belly. "Why have you been walking out with me? Just to toy with me?"

"I'm doing it because…"

"Why?" she prodded.

He hesitated so long she'd stopped expecting an answer when he finally said, "Because I like spending time with you." The words were warm and comforting, but his gaze was … grim.

Hugo and the Maiden

"If you like spending time with me then why do you look so unhappy?"

"Because what I want can't lead to anything good."

"What do you w-want?"

He gave an agonized, frustrated groan. "I want to fuck you, Martha—that's what I want from you. That's *all* I want."

"How *dare* you!"

He caught her wrist before she could get to her feet. "I'm sorry, I should never have—" He stopped, muttered something she couldn't hear, and shook his head. "No, I'm not going to apologize for what I am."

"You mean vulgar and odious?" She pulled on her arm, but he wouldn't release her.

He had the temerity to smile, although it was short-lived. "Among other things." The look he gave her was penetrating and direct. "Listen to what I have to say—don't run off."

She ground her teeth, desperate to blister his ears.

But then she recalled that she'd started all this by staring at his body like some sort of depraved person. She heaved an exaggerated sigh and nodded. "Fine."

He released her arm. "I'm not who you think I am." His lips flexed into a grimace. "Or maybe I am." He shook his head, as if to dismiss the comment. "What I'm trying to say, is that I might not have been guilty of the crime that landed me on that ship, but I have done many things far worse than thieving."

"You mean like what you did to Graybow?"

His dark eyebrows slammed together. "How did you know—oh, Albert told you. Just wait until I see him ag—"

"Please don't blame him; he told me about it that first night. He said that what you did saved him—and lots of other men, too. So, if that's the kind of *bad thing* you meant, then it saved the lives of other people."

"That's true, but I didn't have to kill him to do that. I could have just choked him until he was unconscious." His jaw flexed. "But I chose to kill him."

"Albert said that he'd already killed other men—several others."

"If it had been your father on that ship, do you think he would have killed Graybow, or merely left him stunned?"

Martha opened her mouth, but then closed it.

"I thought so," he said. "Anyway, that is the least of the bad things that I've done. And I will do more after I leave this island. It is in my nature to be selfish, Martha. It was selfishness that made me kiss you earlier." He lowered his voice. "There is no future for us, Martha. Somebody like you needs—"

"Somebody like *me*? Just what does that mean?"

He groaned. "Christ."

"Do not take the Lord's name in vain in my presence, Hugo."

"See?" he said, "That's just one of the many reasons why I can never be the man you want or need."

Martha scowled, hoping it hid her pain. "You presume too much, *Mr. Buckingham*. I never for a minute thought of you … that way."

His lips quirked into a disbelieving smile. "Oh really?"

"Despite what you seem to think, I am not *angling* after you. I'd all but forgotten about you until you began coming around again."

"Is that so?"

"It *is* so," she insisted, beyond infuriated by his snide, mocking tone.

He snorted.

"I was only being kind when I agreed to walk out with you," she said. "After all, I'm betrothed to Robert Clark."

Hugo's eyes bulged.

Martha bit her lip. Hard. Why had she said such a thing? Robert had never asked her to marry him, and she wasn't sure that she would say yes if he did.

She wanted to yell—or hit something. Or somebody. What in the world would Robert say if he learned what she had just said?

Martha opened her mouth to take back her spurious claim.

"Congratulations to you both." Hugo sneered. "I'm sure you will make each other very happy."

She flinched, stung by his nasty, condescending tone. "Why Mr. Buckingham, could it be that you are jealous?"

"Ha! That's not jealousy, sweetheart, that was sarcasm. And more than a little relief. I think you're perfect for each other."

Martha refused to let him see how much his words cut her. "Think whatever you like in the privacy of your own mind," she retorted. "But I'd appreciate it if you didn't mention this to anyone. It's a private matter."

Hugo and the Maiden

He gave a rude hoot of laughter. "As difficult as it might be for you to believe, the subject of you and *Robert* rarely comes up in any of my conversations."

"Good. Now, if you don't mind, I would like to get some sleep."

He pushed up off the blanket and shook out his coat before slipping it on. Instead of going elsewhere to lie down he relighted the other lamp.

"What are you doing?"

"I'm suddenly not sleepy," he snapped. He began to stalk across the sand but then stopped and turned. "Will you be all right here by yourself?"

So, he wanted to get away from her? Fine.

"I'll be better by myself." She turned her back on him. "Please don't disturb me when you come back."

Martha's ears strained for some sound, but there was nothing other than the gentle lapping of the water.

The tears she'd held back suddenly broke free. *Say something, Hugo,* she willed him. *Don't leave like this. Tell me ... something.*

But the light in the cave flickered and grew dimmer.

And then Martha was alone.

Chapter 19

"Well done, arsehole," Hugo muttered under his breath once he'd left the main cave.

He stopped and glared at the rock walls around him.

What the hell was he doing? The last thing he wanted to do was creep around these bloody caves. Still, it was better than sitting beside Martha after hearing that she was betrothed to Clark.

Hugo clenched his jaws hard enough to make his teeth hurt; he wanted to hit something—to break something.

Why the hell had she only told him that *now*—after he'd spent ten days making a fool of himself over her? If she'd admitted to being betrothed when he'd asked her to spend some time with him, he could have passed the message along to the vicar and he'd be in London right now.

Maybe it took a few days with you to convince her that Clark was the more appealing option.

Hugo snorted contemptuously. That would be fine by him. As if he had ever wanted to saddle himself with a wife! And a vicar's daughter, at that.

Liar.

Hugo ignored the mocking laughter in his head and stomped down the tunnel that led away from the water—and away from Martha—and deeper into the island. He didn't get far before the cave shrank to the diameter of a badger hole.

Well, good. Because he had no desire to wander off, he'd only needed to get away from Martha before he said something he'd regret.

His crude words—about wanting to fuck her—came back to him in a rush.

Hugo scowled. Fine, before he said something *else* that he'd regret.

"Bugger." He lowered himself to the rocky but dry floor of the cave and leaned against the wall, grimacing at the cold that penetrated even through his coat and shirt.

He yanked his thoughts away from Martha, only to have them slide in another—even more unwelcome—direction: Cailean.

Hugo and the Maiden

Where the hell was the boy? He knew this island like the back of his hand. If he was missing, then something was wrong. Hugo should have guessed that Cailean wasn't down here. Regardless of what Martha said, Cailean had looked genuinely terrified when Hugo had suggested exploring the caves.

It sickened him to think of his cousin Hamish and cadre of bullies finding the boy while Hugo was stuck down here. He couldn't do a damned thing except pointlessly fret about the lad for the next twelve bloody hours.

Speaking of pointless, what about that argument you just fled from like a vaporous miss?

Hugo gritted his teeth, but he didn't try to argue. For once, the voice in his head was right: their disagreement had been foolish and pointless.

But then so had entertaining the futile hope that there could ever be something between them. All she felt for him was animal attraction. He knew better than anyone that physical attraction could happen between strangers and even between people who hated each other. It had nothing to do with the finer feelings that led to love or marriage.

Hugo could only be grateful that he'd kept his pitiful feelings for her to himself.

"Feelings," he scoffed, absently grabbing a handful of sand and letting it drain through his fingers. Since when did he give a damn about—or even notice—any *feelings* other than the desire for money, security, and physical pleasure?

It was being on this bloody island and out of his element that was causing him to behave like such a gudgeon. Once he was back in London—back in the only milieu where he really belonged: a whorehouse—he could forget this whole nightmare had ever happened.

But first he had to get through the next five days, thanks to his asinine promise to the vicar to extend his stay. He couldn't believe that he'd allowed Mr. Pringle to talk him into courting Martha. He'd enjoyed spending time with her these past few days, of course, but it had been pointless.

Well, not entirely pointless. His lips curled into a smug smile; he'd hugely enjoyed annoying Clark with his presence.

But his amusement at that thought was short-lived. He tossed the handful of sand onto the ground and brushed off his palm before leaning back and closing his eyes. He was bloody exhausted; today had been one of the worst days in memory. Not as bad as the day his father had sold him, or as terrifying as being abducted and tossed naked into the hold of a convict ship, but still the sort of day he never wanted to re-live.

Being stuck in this cave while Cailean might be hurt somewhere was bad enough but learning that Martha and Clark were betrothed had made things even worse.

And imagining Martha married to Clark—making love to him?

Hugo scowled; no, he couldn't bear to think about it.

Sleep. Or at least get some rest, he ordered himself.

Several minutes passed. His body refused to unclench and his mind still raced.

Go back in there, apologize, and quit sulking.

Hugo opened his eyes. He refused to crawl back there with his tail between his legs and—

You're wasting precious lamp oil sitting here.

Hugo perked up. Yes, that was why he needed to go back; not because he wanted to be near her, but to preserve the lamp oil.

Martha was curled up on her side on the blanket, as close to the edge as humanly possible. He decided not to offend her sensibilities by lying beside her. He found a spot that had more sand than rock and settled down.

"Hugo?"

He was just about to snuff the light but paused. "Yes?"

"I'm sorry if I was snappish with you."

Hugo hesitated, and then said, "I'm sorry, too."

"You don't need to lie over there on the sand. We can share the blanket."

He opened his mouth to say he was fine, but then noticed she was shaking. "Martha, are you cold?"

"J-Just a little."

Hugo got up, shrugged off his coat, and draped the ratty garment over her shoulders.

"What are you doing?"

"I'm not cold," he lied.

Her body remained tense for a moment, but then relaxed. "Thank you."

Hugo reached for the lamp and snuffed the light.

Hugo and the Maiden

The darkness was so complete it was almost tangible. And it was also damned chilly. Hugo wrapped his arms around his torso, closed his eyes, and tried to listen to the sound of the water rather than the chaos of his thoughts.

Where was Cailean?
Had somebody hurt him or Lily?
Would Martha be happy with Clark?
Would Solange's still be his when he returned to London?
Would—

Hugo must have drifted off to sleep at some point, because he was wakened by something warm and soft and fragrant pushing against his side. "Martha? What's wrong?"

"I'm so cold, Hugo." Martha's words were broken by the sound of chattering teeth.

Hugo was awake in an instant. In fact, he was astounded that he'd ever slept he was so bloody cold.

"Have we slept long?" he asked.

"I haven't slept at all, but it's maybe an hour since you turned off the lamp." She sounded miserable.

"I can keep you warm, but I need to hold you." He gave a snort of laughter. "I know that sounds like I'm—"

"I understand."

Hugo turned onto his side and she immediately pressed her back against his chest, her bottom against his crotch.

Hugo gritted his teeth, grateful he wasn't hard, but not sure he could maintain his slumberous state for long. Still, he pulled her closer, tucking her into his chest. "Lift your head," he said. When she did, he slid his biceps under her. "Go ahead, you can use me as a pillow."

"It won't be too uncomfortable?"

"If it is, I will tell you."

After a moment's hesitation she lowered her head onto his arm. "Better?"

"Much." After a few moments her body stopped its violent trembling. "Thank you, Hugo."

"You're keeping me warm too." Lord. Was she ever.

"You must be freezing without your coat. Do you—"

"I'm fine." Hugo snuggled a bit closer. "I wouldn't have thought it would be so cold."

"Did you find anything interesting in the other rooms?"

"No, the tunnels are just as you said and too small for people."

There was a long silence, and then, "I can't sleep, Hugo."

"Maybe once you warm up."

"No, it's more than that."

"What is it?" he urged.

"I don't know. I just feel ... unsettled."

"Well, being trapped in a cave might do that to a person."

"I was feeling this way before we got trapped. I've just been feeling ..." He felt her shrug. "It will sound foolish."

"Tell me anyway."

"I suppose the best word for it is *fey*."

"I don't know that word," he admitted.

"It just means you have a feeling of impending dread—that something is wrong."

"That doesn't sound like a good feeling." Hugo wondered if what she was sensing was her father's ill health. He thought Mr. Pringle owed it to Martha to warn her, but it was no business of his.

"Do you mind talking for a while?"

"I thought that's what we were doing?"

She chuckled. "I meant about personal matters?"

What could be more personal than admitting to a feeling of impending doom?

"You don't have to if you don't want to," she said quickly.

Talking about personal matters only meant lying, but what did it matter at this point if he told her more lies? He'd be gone in a short time and never see her again.

"What did you want to ask?" he said.

"I was just curious about growing up in London."

Ah. That was easier than he thought. "It's nothing like here."

"I could have guessed that much. Tell me about it."

"Tell you what?"

"You mentioned you worked for a whip-maker. How old were you?"

"Fourteen."

"Did you have to leave school?"

He could hear the disapproval in her voice. "Yes, but that's not unusual where I'm from. Most people leave school much younger—ten or eleven—to start working."

Hugo and the Maiden

She clucked her tongue. "I suppose it isn't so different than here—many children work on their family boats or farms. But most can get schooling in the winter. Did you father apprentice you to him?"

Hugo smiled faintly. "Yes, that is exactly what happened."

"You said he beat you. Was it—"

She sounded so anguished—so sad—for him that he regretted ever mentioning Caton's predilection for whippings.

"It didn't happen often," he lied. "He wasn't a bad man, just ... impatient." And exceptionally horny for a man his age.

Hugo decided to leave out that tidbit.

She paused, and he suspected she was wishing that she'd never brought up the whip-making. "Er, do you have brothers and sisters?"

There was a subject Hugo didn't often think about. "Yes, eight."

"Oh, goodness. *Eight?*"

"Mmm-hmm."

"You must be very close if you had such a large family."

Hugo tried to recall an image of any of his brothers and sisters, but he couldn't summon any faces—which was odd, considering he'd not been that young when he'd left home. But his siblings had all been so much older and all he could remember was that they'd considered him an annoyance.

"Er, we're not as close as we used to be."

"Oh."

She sounded so disappointed that he amended, "Mainly because we all live so far apart. But we visit each other."

"That sounds lovely." She sounded much happier at that, but also wistful. "Do you have a favorite?"

"Favorite what?"

"Sibling."

"Oh." Faces and names drifted around in his head, nothing but pieces in a bland flavorless stew of memories. "Er, Susan." At least he thought there'd been a Susan.

"Is she older or younger?"

"Older. They were all older."

"Were? Did something happen?"

"No, no, nothing happened. It's just a figure of speech."

"The youngest child of nine. I'll wager they spoiled you rotten."

"Yes, they spoiled me," he agreed.

"What did your father do? Was he a man of business, too?"

Hugo's father was the one he remembered best. Maybe that's because he was the last one Hugo had seen. He could still see him in his mind's eye. He'd had thin, sandy hair and a worn face; his rounded shoulders had been slumped as he took the money Mr. Caton gave him. And then he'd turned and walked away without a word or backward glance.

"Hugo?"

"Hmm?"

"Your father, what did he do?"

"He sold things."

"Things? You mean he was a shopkeeper?"

"Something like that."

"Do your parents live in London?"

"Yes."

"They must be worried sick about you." Her voice pulsed with sympathy for Hugo's mythical loving, worried family.

"They're accustomed to me working hard and not hearing from me for long periods of time." Sixteen years, in fact. "I doubt they are worrying." That was certainly true.

"You must have worked hard to become so successful. Your family must be so proud of you."

Hugo made a non-committal noise. "Are you warmer, yet?"

"Yes, I'm quite cozy." Her bottom wiggled adorably—and dangerously—against Hugo's groin. "What about you?"

"Much better. Tell me about your family," he said, trying to take his mind off his cock, which was nestled between her cheeks and showing signs of liking it there.

"There isn't much to tell. My mother didn't have siblings and my father's were all older. It is just me and Papa." She hesitated and then said, "I have always yearned for a big family."

"You'll be happy with Clark, then—he has a large family, does he not?" There, that took care of any incipient erection he might have worried about.

Her body stiffened. "Erm, yes."

She was silent so long he thought she'd fallen asleep.

But then she said, "You said earlier that you don't have a sweetheart in London. Why is that?" Her voice was so soft he barely heard it, even in the quiet of the cave.

"I work too much," he said. *And nobody other than another whore would understand and accept the nature of my work.*

"But since you come from a big family you must want children of your own some day?"

He snorted. "Good Lord, no."

"You don't like children?" She sounded horrified.

"I don't dislike children, I've just never imagined myself as a father." *Nor can I imagine the patter of little feet up and down the corridors of Solange's.* "What about you?" he asked, already guessing her answer.

"Yes, I want lots of children."

Hugo could picture her imaginary offspring: strapping sandy-haired boys with bovine expressions like Clark's and blonde, blue-eyed little girls with their mother's sparkling eyes and zest for life.

Why did the image leave him feeling so utterly exhausted?

He waited for more questions, but they never came. Instead, her body gradually softened against his and her breathing turned deep and regular, until he knew she was asleep.

Hugo stared into the darkness: he'd never felt so awake in his entire life.

***

"Hugo!"

Hugo's eyes flew open and he squinted against the blinding light. "Wha—?"

Something huge fell on him—something warm and squirmy with sharp elbows. Hugo struggled to breathe.

"Hugo!" Cailean bellowed in his ear.

"Cailean, you're crushing him." Martha's voice seemed to come from a long way off.

"Let Mester Hyougo up, lad," a male voice ordered.

Cailean rolled off him, grabbed him under the arms, and yanked him to his feet.

"Thank you," Hugo gasped, looking from Cailean to the man holding the lamp. "Mr. Packard?" he said stupidly.

"Aye."

Something suddenly occurred to him and his head whipped around. "You're safe, little brother! I was bloody worried about you!"

Cailean flung his arms around Hugo and squeezed.

"*Urgh*, Cailean—" Hugo patted his massive shoulder and squirmed until Cailean released him.

The lad caught Martha up in a similar embrace and twirled her around in a circle, kicking up sand.

"Cailean! Put me dooooooown!"

"He was right worried about the two of you," Packard said. Or at least that's what Hugo thought he said. He still had a difficult time understanding most of the islanders.

"Do you know where he was?" Hugo asked, rubbing the sleep from his eyes.

"Hidin' with Lily in one of the caves on the east side."

"Why?"

"Din't say."

Hugo yawned. "What time is it?"

"Barely dawn." His gaze strayed to Martha, his blue eyes sharp and speculative.

"Nothing happened here," Hugo hastened to assure him. "I know you saw us sleeping on the blanket, but—"

"Aye, aye. Come along now."

Hugo couldn't help thinking the man looked a bit grim. Well, likely he was losing good fishing hours to rescue them.

They folded up the blankets, handed Martha into the boat, and then Hugo and Cailean pushed it off, Cailean jumping aboard last. Hugo had imagined the cave was farther inland, but it turned out that the tunnel was twisty, rather than long. Outside it was a beautiful morning, the water around Stroma like glass, the sun just barely over the horizon.

Martha fussed absentmindedly with her hair and dress, no doubt wondering what she'd say to her father about being in the Gloup overnight with Hugo.

He turned to find Cailean regarding him with a worshipful stare. "Is Lily safe?"

Cailean nodded, but his gaze turned to one of worry, and he glanced toward Jem and then at Martha, clearly wanting to say something.

"What is it?" Hugo asked.

But Jem just shook his head and Cailean looked away. What was going on? Would the islanders really be so offended that he and Martha had gotten stuck while looking for Cailean?

Hugo and the Maiden

Hugo bristled at the thought; he dared anyone to so much as look sideways at Martha. Especially Clark; the man had better mind his step.

Hugo would speak to the vicar, himself, and assure him that nothing inappropriate had happened. Thankfully, he could do so with a clear conscience. Aside from a chaste kiss, he had behaved like a complete gentleman for the first time in his life. It was about as enjoyable as he'd always suspected it would be.

He could also tell the vicar about Martha's betrothal, which would put an end to any other foolishness. Hugo wouldn't say anything to the vicar, now, but he would send back some money after he got home, just to thank him for all that he and Martha had done for Hugo.

It took less than ten minutes to get from the caves to the beach at Nethertown, where a great number of yoles were up on the sand.

Hugo frowned; was it Sunday today?

"Why are none of the boats out?" Martha asked.

Jem's jaw moved back and forth, his gaze shifty.

Martha looked at Hugo and he shrugged.

Only then did Hugo notice all the people standing higher up on the beach. "Jesus," Hugo muttered under his breath. It looked like the entire population of the island, even Gerry Boyle, had gathered to greet them. He swallowed. Were he and Martha really in so much trouble?

"Jem?" Martha's voice was unnaturally high.

Robert Clark stood at the front of the crowd and he and two other men came forward to catch the yole.

Before they even reached the shore Cailean scooped up Martha and hopped into the frigid water, which came to his knees.

Hugo scrambled toward the bow as the two men beached the boat. "What in the—"

"Put her down right now, Cailean," Robert Clark ordered, his expression stern. The huge lad jolted.

"It's all right, Cailean," Martha soothed. "You can set me down."

He did so, and then scuttled away from Clark, visibly frightened.

"You've scared him." Martha frowned at her betrothed. "There's no reason to—"

"There's been an accident, Martha."

Martha looked over the crowd of people. "Is somebody hurt? My father—where's—" Her eyes darted wildly before settling on Clark again. "Where's my father?"

Clark cleared his throat. "There was a fire at your cottage and—well, I'm sorry, but your father was there. He must have been sleeping when—"

"No." She shook her head violently, backing away from Clark as if he were attacking her. "No. You're lying—" She stumbled, and Hugo lurched forward to catch her.

Martha twisted in his grasp, tears streaming down her face as she stared up at him. "Hugo—tell him he's lying!"

Hugo slid his arms around her slender, shaking shoulders, his gaze riveted to Clark. For once, the other man's face contained only sorrow, no dislike or fear.

"What happened?" Hugo asked as he stroked Martha's back.

"Maybe a candle fell over or the vicar put something on to cook and forgot about it." Clark shrugged. "It's hard to say."

Hugo thought about how absentminded Mr. Pringle had been the day he'd invited him in for tea. And then he thought about the vicar's expression when Hugo had told him that Martha would never leave the island without him.

I'll take care of that, he'd said.

Hugo's stomach churned, as if he'd eaten something rotten. Had this been Mr. Pringle's way of *taking care* of things?

"It can't be right, can it, Hugo?" Martha's fingers dug into his waist.

"I don't think Mr. Clark would lie to you, love," he said quietly.

But Martha didn't seem to hear him. "He can't be gone. He was here just hours ago—he can't be gone so fast, not without some sort of … *warning* or chance to say goodbye. That's not how it's supposed to happen. Is it?"

Hugo frantically searched his mind for something that might comfort her. But, in his experience, that is exactly what happened to the people you cared about: they left you when you least expected it and without warning.

Clark laid a hand on Martha's shoulder. "Come, Martha. My mother and sister are waiting for you at the house. We will take care of you."

Hugo felt her body stiffen slightly and he held her gaze, looking for some clue as to what she wanted—needed.

Hugo and the Maiden

Her eyes pled with him—begged him to do or say something that would take away her pain and return her life to the way it had been yesterday, when her father had still been alive.

But he couldn't give her that. Nobody could.

She dropped her gaze and stood unresisting as Clark slid his arm around her shoulders.

Hugo swayed toward her as Clark led her away, his hands twitching to grab her back. But she wasn't his to comfort, was she? She had told him only hours before of her betrothal.

Martha had an arm around Clark's big body and clung to him, her feet stumbling as the crowd parted for them. She sobbed like her heart was breaking.

Hugo suspected it was. And there wasn't a damned thing he could do to help her.

Chapter 20

Hugo dried his face on what used to be his second-best waistcoat but was now his hand towel, and then washed the rag in the rapidly cooling wash water and hung it out to dry.

There. Now he was ready for work tomorrow. His last day of work, in fact.

The day after—Saturday—Packard would ferry Hugo over to the mainland where he'd engage a room at the inn, purchase some clothing and shoes, and then hire a post chaise to take him south. A seat on the mail would be far cheaper, but Hugo refused to be crowded into a small space with far too many other bodies.

He emptied out the wash water and turned the pot upside down, staring at nothing while he tried to ignore the heavy feeling that settled over him whenever he thought about leaving this wretched little island. But there was no reason to delay any longer. He'd already extended his stay by another week because it hadn't felt right to bugger off right after Mr. Pringle's funeral.

He'd stayed so long that he was now leaving on the same day as Martha's damned wedding. He was sorely tempted to go to Mr. Stogden tonight and tell him that he wasn't coming to work tomorrow, that he was leaving Stroma a day early.

Hugo was trudging toward Stogden's house to do exactly that when he recalled that he'd promised to eat his last dinner on the island with Cailean tomorrow at the Greedy Vicar.

Hugo muttered a vulgar word and turned back to his damned lean-to.

He was looking forward to seeing Cailean and some of the other islanders, of course, but he wasn't looking forward to encountering Martha and Clark together. He'd been avoiding the Greedy Vicar because Martha had been staying in the tiny inn's guestroom until she was married.

It wasn't that he couldn't stand seeing Martha happy—although that might have been difficult—but rather that she didn't even look like her normal self.

Hugo and the Maiden

He knew she was grieving for her father, of course, but beneath that grief Hugo saw a sort of resignation, as if life had now divulged everything to her and her future held no surprises or secrets.

Hugo suspected that was exactly what marriage to Robert Clark would be like: they would have children, he would fish, she would work their small piece of land and take care of their family, and they would scrape by.

It was a grim future, in Hugo's opinion.

Not that being married to a whore would be any rosier.

You promised the vicar that you'd try.

Hugo gritted his teeth against the familiar, annoying refrain; it was like a Greek chorus had taken up residence in his bloody skull.

The woman had been *secretly* betrothed to Clark. What was he supposed to do, club her on the head and drag her to London? If the vicar had known that his daughter's affections were already attached—or if he'd known the truth about Hugo—he wouldn't have wanted Martha anywhere near—

Something big and warm landed on his shoulder and Hugo yelped and spun around.

Cailean was cringing, his eyes as round as coach wheels.

"Oh, sorry for screeching, little brother—you scared me." Hugo forced a soothing smile but then frowned when he saw Cailean's cheeks were wet, his eyes red-rimmed. "What is it?" His eyes narrowed. "Has Hamish been bothering you again?"

Cailean shook his head violently.

Hugo grunted. "Good." He'd given Hamish Fergusson's arse a proper kicking for teasing Cailean. "What is it, then?"

Cailean reached out, as tentative as a child, and took Hugo's arm.

"You want me to go with you?"

Cailean nodded.

Hugo followed, but the big lad didn't release his wrist. The boy had stuck closer than ever to him since Lily's desertion. It turned out the female otter had a love interest—a boy otter who had a rather nasty disposition as far as Hugo could tell. Hugo had named the new otter Joss, since the big, brutish-looking bastard reminded Hugo of his nemesis from the old days: Joss Gormley.

Hugo had passed that little tidbit along to Mel in his last letter, certain she would be amused and share it with Joss in her next missive to the other man.

He knew he should feel bad about naming a snaggle-toothed water rat after Joss when the real Joss had offered Hugo the use of Lady Selwood's—his wife—London house while Hugo sorted out his business.

The gesture was a kind one and Hugo was grateful. Doubtless he should show his gratitude by treating Joss with more respect.

But Hugo wasn't ready to change the tenor of their relationship at this point. Besides, he doubted that Joss would even know how to deal with a polite Hugo.

Cailean yanked on Hugo's arm, almost pulling him off his feet. "Slow down, little brother. There's no rush."

Hugo glanced around; Cailean was leading him in a familiar direction: toward the Gloup. He wanted to run in the opposite direction. *Please, God, not another night in the Gloup.*

But God wasn't listening.

Cailean started down the ravine-like path that led toward the caves and Hugo dug in his heels. "Cailean, I don't think—"

Cailean jerked Hugo's arm so hard it was either go along with him or lose a limb.

"All right, all right. But you'll need to let go of my hand so I can—"

Hugo let out an undignified squawk as an otter loomed out of a crack in the wall at them.

Well, perhaps *loomed* was a bit of an exaggeration, but still ...

"What's going on?" he asked Cailean.

The lad pointed to the grasses and dried kelp behind Lily. A small rill trickled down the cave wall, close enough for the otter to drink or wet its fur, which they seemed to like.

Hugo squinted and leaned closer. "Is that—" He jerked back when a tuft of dried grass moved. "Good God—Lily has babies." They were two tiny brown lumps and Lily was trying to shove them farther back into the crevice/nest.

Hugo clapped Cailean on the shoulder. "Congratulations, Cailean, you're an uncle. So, what are they called pups, kits, hatchlings?"

Cailean's pale blond eyebrows knitted.

"What's wrong? Aren't you happy for Lily and, er, Joss? At least I guess he's the father." Hugo glanced around for the male otter but, thankfully, didn't see him.

Hugo and the Maiden

Cailean leaned down, as if to touch the babies, and Lily made an angry chirping sound, her expression decidedly unfriendly. Cailean cut Hugo a look of profound sadness.

Ah.

"It will be all right, Cailean," Hugo said. "She's just a new mum. Give her a bit of time and—"

Strident chittering came from the left and Hugo whipped around: it was Joss.

He was standing on his hind legs, his mouth open, holding a clam in his sharp-clawed hands. Or paws.

"Christ, that thing has some teeth," Hugo muttered, grabbing Cailean's arm. "Come on. We're upsetting them, little brother. We'd better—"

Cailean spun around and bolted up the path.

"Cailean, wait!" Hugo called as the lad scrambled up the trail, sobbing.

Joss bared his teeth and loped toward Hugo, looking more like a weasel than a sea otter.

"Bloody hell." Hugo backed away—he didn't like turning his back on the creature—his feet sliding on the scree.

The otter snarled.

"Oi!" Hugo yelled.

The creature jolted at the loud sound and stopped.

"That's right," he snapped, pointing a finger at the animal. "You mind your manners. And you." He turned to Lily, but the female had disappeared deeper into the nest. Hugo frowned over at Joss, who was slowly advancing on him, once again baring his teeth. "You watch yourself, lad," he warned.

And then he turned and ran like a coward.

Cailean was nowhere in sight when Hugo finally scrambled to the top. It was almost dark and Hugo would break his neck if he went looking for him at night. He'd check on him in the morning, before he went to work.

As Hugo trudged back to his lean-to, he thought about Cailean and what his life would be like without his otter. Lily had been with the boy for almost three years. Before Hugo came along, the otter was his only friend. And now Hugo was leaving.

"Shut up, Hugo," he ordered himself as he approached his encampment.

He stopped and frowned; the flaps on the lean-to were down. He thought he'd left them up, which he usually did until he went to bed.

He strode to the lean-to and pulled back flap. "Martha," he said, sounding breathless to his own ears. "What are you doing here?"

"Hello, Hugo."

She was sitting on his worn but clean bedroll. Mr. Stogden had given him a heather-stuffed pad to go under his blankets and Hugo's little bower was both comfortable and fragrant.

He stepped back. "Does Clark know you're here?"

"It's not his business."

Hugo gave an unamused bark of laughter. "I beg to differ. I'm sure he would, too. Martha—"

"I told him I couldn't marry him."

Joy and dread leapt in his chest. "Oh?"

"I thought about what you said—that night in the Gloup."

"What did I say?"

"That you weren't a good man. That you'd done bad things and would likely do them again."

"Er—"

"I don't care."

"You don't care about what?"

"About what you used to do."

"But you don't know what I've done."

"No."

Hugo felt like they were having two different conversations. "Uh—"

"My father kept his journals—there were five of them, in all—in the church beneath the strongbox. There was a hollowed out area in the stone floor where he kept the other church valuables."

Hugo knew all that since he'd stolen the church money. He kept that piece of information to himself. "And?" he prodded.

"I—I didn't want to read them at first. I knew it would be too painful. But today I just felt—" She shook her head. "It doesn't matter what I felt. I read them. Well, not all of them, obviously, but I started at the most recent and went back several weeks—to the night of the shipwreck. There were entries that mentioned you."

"Yes, I stole the money, but—"

"I know," she said quietly. "I also know that my father offered to help you if you stayed. And that he did help you with Mr. McCoy."

Hugo and the Maiden

"That's true."

"He wanted a favor in return."

His little peat fire sent shadows dancing over her face.

"Yes," he said, carefully.

But when she spoke, it wasn't what he'd feared. "He said that you were a good man, even if your past was, er, checkered." She swallowed and it looked like hard work. "He also said—" Her voice broke and she cleared her throat. "He also said that he thought you might, erm, care for me."

Hugo opened his mouth, but he couldn't seem to force any words out.

She pinned him with her gaze. "Do you?"

It was Hugo's turn to swallow—several time. "Er—" He experienced the oddest sensation just then; like he was watching himself from somewhere outside his body. He wasn't impressed by what he saw: His mouth hung open, his eyes bulged, and he looked like an idiot. A terrified idiot.

"Never mind." She pushed to her feet and shoved past him.

Hugo grabbed her upper arm lightly and held her. "Just ... *wait* a moment, Martha." This close to her he could see her face was scarlet.

"Wait for what? For you to come up with some pablum? You should have seen the expression on your face."

"What do you mean?" he asked, even though he knew.

"You looked horrified and terrified."

That was an accurate assessment. Fortunately Hugo didn't say that out loud.

She yanked her arm. "Just let me go."

Hugo held her in place. "I do care for you, Martha. But you don't understand…"

"I don't understand what?"

Why had he returned to his lean-to? If he'd gone looking for Cailean he could have avoided this confrontation. Why hadn't—"

"You say that you care for me?"

He nodded dumbly.

"So why would you stand by while I married Robert?"

"Because he is the better man. Er, for you," he added, just because he couldn't bear that she thought he meant Clark was better in general.

"How do you know that?"

"Um—"

She made a noise that was amazingly similar to the one Lily had made earlier. "Just because I don't have much experience with—well, with life, I suppose—doesn't mean I don't understand my own feelings. Shouldn't I be the one who decides who is best for me?"

"I just think that right now—so soon after your father's death—isn't the best time to make important decisions."

"Is that why you pushed me into marrying Robert?" she scoffed.

It was Hugo's turn to sound like an angry otter. "Now wait just a minute, Martha. I didn't do any such thing. You *told* me that you were secretly betrothed. Or have you forgotten that?"

She bit her lower lip—the same lip he'd dreamed about biting times beyond counting. "I made that up."

"*What?*"

"I thought that maybe you'd say or do something if I told you that."

"What exactly did you expect me to say or do after you'd told me you were promised to another man?" he sputtered. "Challenge him to a duel?"

"Oh, don't act so innocent!" She jerked her arm away. "You knew Robert wanted to marry me and yet you kept asking me to spend time with you. Or was that only to goad him?".

"No, of course not."

Although he *did* enjoy goading Clark and behaving flirtatiously with Martha was the quickest and easiest way to do that. Still, he could hardly say that, at least not without destroying her. "That was different," he added lamely.

"Different how?"

Hugo's normally crafty brain seemed to have abandoned him. "Um, I asked you to spend time with me because I didn't think you were betrothed."

"Well, I'm not betrothed, now."

"Martha, the entire island is coming to your wedding in less than two days."

"Not anymore."

He felt like he was in one of those dreams, the ones where he tried to run, but couldn't seem to get anywhere.

If you really want to get rid of her all you need to do is tell her who you really are. And then watch her go sprinting back to her good man.

Hugo and the Maiden

Nausea rose in his throat at the thought of confessing who he was. *What* he was.

Hugo ground his teeth; his own shame infuriated him. He had *never* lied about who he was to anyone, nor had he been embarrassed by what he did for a living.

And yet he couldn't seem to stop lying to Martha.

"I'm sorry."

Hugo looked into her stricken eyes. "For what?"

"I can see from your expression that you are searching for a kind way to reject me. That you just don't want to hurt me."

She was offering him a way out, and Hugo opened his mouth to take it.

But nothing came out.

She made a gulping sound and her eyes got glassy. "I shouldn't have put you in this position. It's my fault that—"

"Oh, Hell," Hugo muttered as a soft sob broke out of her. "Come here." He pulled her into his arms. "Shh, shh." He patted her back, trying to ignore the way her breasts pushed against his chest. What kind of pig thought about soft, lovely breasts when a woman was in mental anguish?

Hugo held her and let her cry, rubbing her back the way he'd seen people soothe crying children.

He closed his eyes; she felt good in his arms—she fit, as if she belonged. As if her body had been made for his.

Hugo shoved aside the insidious thought, but it kept pushing its way back in.

There was no way he could take her with him. Being with her on Stroma was one thing—it was a place out of time, where he didn't have to *be* Hugo Buckingham—but in London? He couldn't hide who he was, what he did, where he came from. There simply—

"I'm sorry for being a watering pot. But I miss my father so much, Hugo." She whispered the words into the worn material of his vest, her hot breath causing goosepimples to break out all over his body.

"I know," he said, even though he didn't know. When had he ever loved anyone like Martha had loved her father? Never. Not even close.

"I can't seem to stop feeling alone."

"I'm sure that is normal, sweet—er, Martha. After all, you lived with him all your life."

"I'm lonely when I'm with Robert and feel even lonelier when I imagine being married to him." She mumbled something into his clothing.

"Er, I'm sorry, I didn't hear—"

"I said, *then I thought about you, Hugo.*"

"Um—"

"I realized the last time I felt safe and happy was down in the Gloup."

"Oh. Well, that's natural since you didn't know about your father back then and—"

"No, it's more than that." She nuzzled closer, her body soft, curvy, and delicious. "I can't stop thinking about you."

And Hugo couldn't stop thinking about her breasts and the way they were rubbing against him. *Thrusting* against him.

Only a genuinely selfish, thoughtless bastard would become hard right now, Hugo.

Hugo gritted his teeth and didn't even bother to defend himself; he was a bastard.

The sudden stiffening in her back told him that she'd noticed *his* sudden stiffening.

"Ah, Christ, Martha—"

She flinched at his blaspheming.

"I'm sorry," he hastily said. "I'm, er, well—"

Hugo tried put her at arm's length, but she clung to him like a barnacle, too innocent to realize what she was doing to him. "Um, you should let me take you back to your room at the Vicar, darling. This isn't a—"

She nuzzled closer, her hips pressing hard against his.

Hugo groaned and his eyes rolled back in his head. "Martha—"

"It's all right, Hugo, I know what you want."

He opened his mouth.

"I—I want you, too, Hugo. You don't need to do that other thing this time—I want to stay."

Chapter 21

The words hadn't even left her mouth before Martha wanted to snatch them back.

Hugo took her by the waist and firmly set her at arm's length. "What *other thing?*"

You want to tell him, admit it. Shame flooded her, but she couldn't deny it.

Hugo caused sensations in her body that she'd never even dreamed of experiencing—and he'd barely touched her.

She'd only told him the partial truth about why she'd broken off with Robert. She suspected he wouldn't like the full story, which is that Robert had walked her to her tiny room at the Greedy Vicar and Martha had invited him in.

He'd hesitated, trying to be a gentleman, but Martha had insisted. She'd *needed* to know what it felt like to kiss and touch him.

It had felt like nothing.

Well, that wasn't entirely true, it had felt embarrassing—like she was kissing her brother.

"Martha." Hugo's warm, calloused hand slid beneath her chin and he forced her to meet his gaze. A notch had appeared between the elegant arches of his eyebrows. "What other thing?"

Every second she hesitated, his eyebrows drew down more. Now that she'd piqued his curiosity, he would not leave it alone.

Martha stared into his dark eyes and knew—with every particle of her being—that if she didn't say something to him before he left Stroma, she'd regret it for the rest of her days. It would be better to speak and face rejection than to remain silent and never know.

"I saw you the night in the meetinghouse, after you washed your clothes, and you had a blanket wrapped around you and—"

Realization dawned as slowly as a sunrise and his silent, speculative regard made her face hotter and hotter.

"Hmm. This sounds like a conversation best enjoyed while sitting." He gestured to the bedroll where she'd waited for him.

She sat, leaning against the stone wall, and he lowered himself beside her.

"So, you were spying on me."

"I was *not* spying."

"Then what were you doing?"

"I was—I wondered—"

His smile grew with each sputter.

Martha shut her mouth.

"Why are you telling me this now?" He sounded genuinely perplexed.

She could hardly tell him the truth, could she? That she couldn't stop thinking about him. That it was his face she wanted to see when Robert kissed her? That Robert's hands on her body made her feel worse than unmoved, it made her feel as if she were being ... unfaithful.

"Martha?" he prodded.

She could tell him none of those things because she was a coward. Instead, she said, "I feel guilty." That wasn't entirely a lie ...

"Why?"

"Why?"

"Yes, why do you feel guilty?" he asked patiently. "After all, it's not your fault if you caught a glimpse of me doing *that*. In fact, most people would say I should not be doing *that* anywhere at all, and certainly not in the middle of the meeting house with the doors wide open." He stopped abruptly and frowned. "Tell me, how long did you stay to watch?"

"Um."

"You stayed *um*? How long is *um*, Martha—more than a minute? Less than an hour?" His voice was low and compelling—almost menacing.

Just tell him. You know you want to.

"Erm, until the end."

His expression was inscrutable.

"Won't you say something?"

"Did you think about me—after? When you were alone in your bed?"

"*What?*" she shrieked, recoiling.

"You heard me."

"But—"

"No buts." The harsh lines of his face were stern and intense. "You wanted me to know that you watched—don't deny it. If you'd said nothing I would never know. Now you've told me. So now answer my question: did you think about me when you were in bed."

She sucked in a breath, squeezed her eyes shut, and nodded.

He gave a low, satisfied chuckle and cupped her jaw. "Look at me, Martha."

She opened her eyes to find that he was no longer leaning against the wall but was facing her.

"You came here to seduce me tonight, didn't you?"

She opened her mouth to deny it, but nothing came out.

"It's all right; you don't need to answer that." He caressed her cheek, his expression thoughtful. "It arouses me to think of you watching me when I was naked and hard."

She sucked in a noisy breath at his provocative words.

"I especially like to imagine you thinking of me later when you were alone. Did you touch yourself?"

Martha's jaw sagged.

His soft words cut the invisible threads that were holding her together and she began to unravel. It was an effort to breathe and there was no way she could form a word.

But he didn't seem to care about an answer.

"I remember what I was thinking about that night—as I pleasured myself. Do you want to know?"

Martha had to breathe through her mouth to get enough air.

"Do you?"

She gave a jerky nod.

"No, I want you to say it: *Hugo, what were you thinking about as you stroked yourself to orgasm?*"

A strangled squeak came out of her gaping mouth.

Hugo swept his thumb lightly over her lower lip, his skin salty on the tender flesh. "I adore your mouth, Martha." His gaze remained on her lips while his thumb moved back and forth. "Shall I tell you what I was thinking that night without making you beg? Would you like that?"

Their eyes locked and the expression in his was hard—almost cruel.

She nodded.

"I was thinking about you and that mouth of yours." His jaw tightened and his nostrils flared. "I've pleasured myself almost every night, thinking about you, your mouth, your body."

She could hear her ragged breathing even over the drumming of her pulse.

"Just looking at you leaves me aroused and wanting." He stroked the corner of her mouth. "You saw just how hard I was that night, didn't you? That was your doing." He caught his lower lip with his sharp teeth and shook his head. "Lately, once isn't enough. Sometimes I get hard during the day."

He kept saying that word: *hard*. It was doing things to her body. Her lungs labored and the place between her thighs throbbed so loudly she could actually hear it: *thud thud thud*.

When he lowered his mouth over hers, Martha felt as if she'd been waiting for him all her life.

His words were crude, but his mouth was so soft, so gentle. He sipped at her lips, stroking her jaw, chin, and throat with his rough fingers. "Mmm," he murmured, nibbling her lower lip and then sucking it into his mouth.

Martha's head spun drunkenly.

He released her lip and pressed butterfly kisses on the swollen flesh. "You taste as good as you look. I'd like to eat you."

Martha gaped, doubtless resembling a rockfish that had been brought up from a great depth.

Hugo slid his hand behind her head. "Lean back, sweetheart, I need to kiss you properly."

Good Lord! There was more? That was *nothing* like Robert's kiss. "Pr-properly?"

"Well, maybe *im*properly would be a better word for it." He chuckled and it was the sort of low, growly sound that Martha imagined a dangerous jungle panther would make right before it pounced. "And please breathe, I don't want you dropping into unconsciousness."

It was a relief to let her head fall back, to let him support and cradle her in his arms while his mouth reclaimed hers.

"Just relax and let me please you," he murmured. He kissed and licked at the seam of her mouth. "Open," he whispered. His tongue invaded her parted lips and he explored her, light teasing touches on her lips, her tongue, and even her teeth.

Martha struggled to keep pace with his wit-scattering kisses, but sensation swamped her, overwhelming her body and mind.

When he finally pulled away, his breathing was as labored as hers and his eyes burned. "I've wanted to touch you for so long." His wicked lips quirked in a way that always presaged something outrageous or teasing. "Well, maybe not that first night, when you were so cruel to me, but—"

"*Cruel* to you? I wasn't—"

"—I thought of you even more over the days that followed." He made a clucking sound with his tongue. "Good thoughts, for the most part—even though you made me clean chamber pots."

She opened her mouth and he laid one elegant finger across her lips. "Shhhh," he whispered, stroking lightly from her jaw to her throat, where he paused, his long-fingered hand easily spanning her and lightly and squeezing. His eyes had gone vague—as if he were somewhere else—while his fingers stroked the fabric of her high-necked gown, the rough pads snagging on the worn cotton, *scritch scritch scritch*.

The sound appeared to shake him from his reverie, and he lifted his hand and looked at his palm, a wry smile on his mouth as he raised his eyes to hers. "My hands are not so soft and white now, are they?"

Martha took his hand in hers and traced the soft blisters and hardening calluses. "No, but they are still beautiful."

His lips flexed slightly at her compliment. "May I untie your cloak—before it throttles you?"

"I can do it." She reached for the worn tie with a shaking hand.

"No, let me. It will be a novelty for me to remove your cloak while you get to do it every day."

A choked laugh broke out of her at his foolish words, his whimsical answer somehow soothing her raw nerves.

"That's better," he said, deftly opening the knot that was indeed pressing against her throat. "Kissing and touching and exploring each other's bodies is not serious business, Martha, it should be savored and celebrated." He tucked a lock of loose hair behind her ear, his fingers never ceasing their soothing yet inciting caressing. "You have lovely hair, so glossy and thick, not unlike Lily's silky texture."

Again, she laughed. "Did you just compare me to an otter? The same creatures you call rats?"

He grinned. "I'm terrible, aren't I?" This close to him she could see his pupils were swollen. "You'll have to think of some way to punish me."

His words were innocent, but she sensed there was some other meaning behind them. And she burned to discover it, to explore this complex and confusing man. But she was so wretchedly ignorant that she couldn't even think how to go about beginning such an exploration.

"I was so well-behaved that night in the Gloup, wasn't I?" he asked, the question breaking into her thoughts. "I wanted to touch you so badly."

"Er, you did?"

"I can't recall a time when I've denied myself what I wanted—especially when I wanted you so very much."

His words were like something out of a dream. He'd *wanted* her? Martha opened her mouth.

"I restrained myself, but every man has his limit, Martha." He eyes dropped to her mouth and his pupils flared. And then he jerked his gaze back up. "And I think you came here tonight to push me past mine"

Once again, she began to speak, but he pulled away, until they weren't touching.

"I'm giving you the opportunity to leave … now. You don't have to go back to Clark. You don't have to marry him or anyone else. I will make sure you are taken care of—that is a favor to your father, not to you, so you needn't feel beholden to me. I owe him that much, at least." He paused, and then added, "You don't need to give yourself to me, Martha."

Her addled brain clumsily sorted through what he'd just said. He was offering to take care of her, not to marry her or spend the rest of his life with her. He felt obligated to help her—because of her father.

What he'd left unsaid, but what Martha had heard, nonetheless, was that wanting her physically—both now and that night in the Gloup—had nothing to do with love or marriage. If she wanted either of those things from him, she should leave. Now.

If she gave herself to him, it should be for reasons of her own.

Because if she stayed—if she succumbed to her desire for him—she would be a soiled dove in the eyes of decent men. Men like Robert.

But whether she gave herself to Hugo or not, Martha knew—without a doubt—that she would never want to marry anyone else: she loved him. She wouldn't—couldn't—stop loving him just because he didn't feel the same.

So, she could either take this much of him and be ruined, or she could take nothing at all.

The decision was surprisingly easy.

Hugo and the Maiden

Martha grabbed his head and yanked him down.

For a moment—a moment that lasted years—Hugo's body didn't yield to her; he remained rigid and unresponsive. And then he muttered something vulgar and claimed her mouth, thrusting his warm, silky tongue between her lips.

***

Hugo knew that only a few words from him—the truth about who and what he was—would drive her away forever. If he really cared for her then he should speak up and save her.

But he was covetous and lustful and selfish—why should that surprise him?

Hugo didn't just want her; he wanted to make sure that nobody else could have her. He wanted to ruin her chances with Clark or any other decent man. He wanted to leave her with only one choice: Hugo.

And so he lowered his mouth over hers.

She opened beneath him, soft and willing and sweet, and he plunged into her deep and rough, wanting her to know just what kind of beast she was giving herself to: not a kind, gentle man, but a crude, lustful brute.

He willed her to pull away and save them both—to slap him across the face and leave without looking back.

Instead, she clutched his hair even harder and moaned softly, inviting him deeper, innocently trusting herself to the worst man for miles.

Hugo had doomed them both.

He rewarded her trust by ravaging her, until she was breathless and whimpering. He took and took and took, and still she offered more. When her tongue tentatively stroked his own, Hugo stilled his pillaging and slanted his mouth, opening wider to give her access, inviting her to join in her downfall.

Had he ever enjoyed a kiss this much? Her joy in discovery made him realize that he'd never just kissed a woman for kissing's sake. After all, whores weren't hired for their kissing skills, were they?

Whores.

He imagined her expression when she learned he was a whore, and he jerked back.

"Hugo?" Martha blinked up at him. "Is something wrong?"

Her wide-eyed blue gaze was like the dangerous beauty of a whirlpool and Hugo allowed himself to be pulled down and down. Her eyes were easily the most expressive he'd ever seen, and right now, her pupils were huge with desire. For him.

You can still salvage this, a sly voice taunted. *It's only a kiss. So far.*

He didn't want *only* a kiss. He wanted all of her. Would taking her for himself—not just for tonight, but for all the days and nights ahead—really be so bad?

After all, Mr. Pringle had wanted Hugo to get his daughter off this godforsaken rock. It was Hugo's duty to do what the vicar had wanted and marry her. He'd given the man his word.

Ha! The word of a whore.

Mr. Pringle had seen goodness in Hugo.

But he didn't know you, did he, Hugo?

No, the vicar had no idea what sort of man he'd entrusted with his daughter.

Hugo shifted until he was no longer touching her—he couldn't think straight with her in his arms. "Why did you agree to marry Clark, Martha?"

She knitted her brow. "Why are you asking me such a question?"

"Because a short time ago you wanted him enough to marry him. Yet now you are with me. You are in pain—confused—what if—"

"I was *wrong* to accept him."

"What if you are *wrong* again? If there is even a chance for you and Clark then you should go." The words tasted foul in his mouth.

"Are you saying—"

"I'm saying that staying with me tonight doesn't just mean tonight, Martha. I won't do that to your father." He knew his face had twisted into an ugly sneer. "I might be rotten to the core, but at least I can keep my word. And if you stay, it means you will marry me, Martha."

"Are—are you saying you l-love me?"

It wasn't the question that Hugo had expected. More fool him; what young woman didn't dream about falling in love?

He looked into her eyes, which bled emotion, and knew that he could lie about everything else in his life—and he would bloody well do so if she accepted him—but not this.

Hugo wanted her *intensely*, more than he had ever wanted anyone else in his life. His desires had always been money and what it could buy for him: security and safety. Wanting money was easy—you just found a way to make it.

Wanting another person? Well . . .

Hugo and the Maiden

"I don't have much experience with love, Martha—hell, I don't have *any* experience with it. I doubt that I'd recognize it if it crawled up my trouser leg and bit me on the—well, I'm sure you take my meaning. I like you a great deal and enjoy your company more than anyone else's. And I find you desirable—*very* desirable." She turned a fetching shade of pink, just as he'd known she would. "But love?" He shook his head. "If I don't know what that is by the age of thirty-two, I doubt I ever will. I don't—"

"I love you, Hugo."

Hugo's jaw sagged.

"That's what I discovered after I read my father's journal—when I allowed myself to feel, instead of just doing what I thought my father would have wanted and marry Robert. I love you."

A groan broke out of him at her declaration, and she flinched.

Hugo took her by the shoulders when she would have turned away. "I wasn't groaning because you said, well, you know"—Hugo couldn't even say the blood words. "Christ," he muttered, and then grimaced when she jolted. "I'm sorry."

If she found his habitual taking of the Lord's name in vain, just wait until she learned about the rest of him. But Hugo had no intention of confessing the crimes of a lifetime to her.

Even so, she should know what kind of man he was.

"I've made a great deal of my money in ways which are both illegal and immoral. I am not a good man, Martha. It's my nature to get what I want by any means. That's the way I've always been, and I don't see myself changing."

"These—these *things* you've done, are you saying they would make me not want to marry you if I knew?"

Hugo gave an unamused bark of laughter. "I think what I've done would make you not want to even look at me."

"Why won't you just tell me?"

Yes, Hugo—tell her why you can't share the truth. Tell her it's because nobody in your life has ever loved you—or looked at you the way she does—and you want to see just how badly she wants you and if she'll take you without knowing the truth.

Hugo couldn't deny all that, but he was hardly going to admit it.

"I'm not ashamed of what I've done, Martha, but I also refuse to lay my past out for inspection—yours, or anyone else's."

"That's not fair, is it?"

"That's another thing I am not: fair."

"Have you murdered somebody, er, *not* in self-defense?"

"No," he said.

"Are you married?"

Hugo laughed, genuinely amused. "Murder and marriage are closely linked in your mind, are they?"

She didn't laugh with him.

"No, I am not, nor have I ever been, married." *Nor did I ever bloody believe I would be.*

"Do you have children?"

"No."

"Are you cruel to children or animals?"

Hugo blinked. "I can't even recall the last time I was around a child. But, no, I have never been willfully cruel to a child—well, at least not since I was a child, myself. And *no* as to the other."

She stared at him with the same burning intensity she had the day McCoy came to take the prisoners back to the ship: with her heart in her eyes.

"You mentioned the way you made your money. Are—are you planning to do the things you did … again?"

How should he answer that? Would he whore again?

Just thinking about going back to that life—to whoring seven days a week—made him feel tired. But if Laura had destroyed everything he'd worked for, then he'd do whatever he needed to do to earn money. He always had.

"Short of murder or abusing children and animals, I'll not make you any promises. I will do whatever I need to do to provide for myself and anyone under my protection. That is what I can offer you, Martha."

She regarded him solemnly for a long moment and then laid her hand on his forearm and they both stared at it, as if it were some exotic butterfly perched between them. Her hand trembled as she slid it up his bicep, over his shoulder, and up his neck, not stopping until she cupped his jaw, her fingers as work-hardened and calloused as his own.

The raw emotion—the love—in her gaze humbled him. Hugo vowed that he would do all he could humanly do to make sure that she was happy and well-cared for.

The only thing he wouldn't do is give her the truth, a truth that would only hurt her, anyway. Wasn't that enough?

Hugo and the Maiden

It would have to be.
Hugo kissed her palm. "Will you marry me, Martha Pringle?"

Chapter 22

His body tighten beneath Martha's hand; it thrilled her that she could make such a strong, powerful man feel so deeply.

But it also pained her that he didn't love her or trust her enough to tell her the truth about himself. But the thought of living without him—no matter what he had done or might do in the future—pained her more.

"Yes, I'll marry you, Hugo Buckingham."

One minute they were sitting side by side, the next Martha was lying on her back, Hugo looming over her, his hands planted on either side of her shoulders.

"Martha," he whispered, giving a slight, wondering shake of his head. "You need to understand what you will be getting. What you saw me doing that night? Fisting myself? That's me, Martha. I'm crass and earthy and I like being that way. I'm not a gentleman—I'm not … couth. I don't like furtive trysting in the dark—I like fucking in all its forms."

She gasped.

Hugo nodded, as though she'd said something. "And I like saying the word *fuck*—and cruder words besides. I won't be the kind of husband to visit you weekly and mount you in darkness. I want to know every part of your body, intimately, and I want you to learn all about mine."

His eyes roamed her face. "I've never had a lover before." He chuckled when her eyes bulged. "No, I don't mean that I'm a virgin. What I mean is that I've never been with anyone that mattered, anyone I cared about."

Martha's heart leapt; caring wasn't love, but it was better than nothing. Was that pathetic? Perhaps, but she would take what she could get.

"I know what you are like, Hugo. Do you think I don't? You are irreverent, clever, and, yes, vulgar—but I like you just as you are. You don't have to—"

He crushed her mouth with his, the kiss savage and hungry. Martha opened to him and slid her hands into his thick, wiry hair. He kissed her until they were both breathless and then nuzzled her chin to tilt her head back, lowering his mouth over the base of her throat and sucking.

She pushed herself against him, unable to get close enough, one hand gripping his neck and pulling him tight while the other stroked the impossibly hard lines of his shoulders and back. Only when his hair tickled the top of her breast did she realize that he'd opened the wooden buttons on her dress.

"Up a bit," he said as he tugged both the bodice and worn chemise down her shoulders. She shivered, and not just from the cool night air. "I'll warm you," he murmured, and then something unspeakably soft caressed her nipple. "Martha." The word was a damp, hot whisper against the tight pucker of flesh.

A soft grunt of pleasure slipped from her mouth as he sucked her nipple, not stopping until it was a hard, needy bud. Her body arched in wanton invitation, pure pleasure driving away any self-consciousness.

"Touch me." He took her wrist and guided her hand beneath his untucked shirt.

Martha's fingers brushed hot, silky skin stretched taut over muscles that were as hard and sculpted as the wooden ships the islanders made.

He hissed in a breath and flexed beneath her questing fingers. "So good," he praised, licking and nibbling and sucking. "Unbutton my vest," he ordered softly, his teeth grazing the thin skin over her ribs.

Her hands worked awkwardly between their bodies, and when she reached the last button, he sat up, reached over his shoulder, and pulled both his vest and shirt over his head.

Martha had seen his upper body before, but never so close, and never with the invitation to touch. She stroked from his tantalizingly hard belly to his smooth chest.

He growled and dropped onto his elbows, capturing her mouth. Their kisses became frenzied and so did Martha's hands as she explored the broad flare of powerful shoulders that tapered to the tight twist of muscles at his waist. And below that…

He flexed his hips as he thrust against her, the action causing the impossibly tight globes of flesh to harden even more.

"I want to touch you, Martha."

Fear and anticipation swirled in her belly. She swallowed. "You mean you want to—"

His mouth pulled up on one side, his eyes hooded. "We will save that for our wedding night. But tonight … tonight I want to explore you and bring you pleasure."

What did he even mean?

His hungry expression turned almost gentle as he kissed the tip of her nose. "It's fine if you'd rather wait until we are—"

"No, I want you to t-touch me, Hugo."

He pushed onto his knees and his gaze dropped to her chest, which she'd somehow forgotten was uncovered, and he cupped her breasts with his big, warm hands.

Martha bit her lip just in time to catch a whimper.

"You're so beautiful." His dark eyes moved lower.

The mortification at what he was seeing crumbled beneath the raw desire in his gaze and heat pooled in her belly.

"Hugo? Should we—maybe close the flap on—"

"No. It would be too dark without the firelight. I need to see you."

Martha knew she should insist—what if somebody saw them?

But she wanted to see him, too.

He stared down at her as he casually thumbed her already hard nipples, each touch sending painfully pleasurable bolts to her tightly clenched thighs.

A guttural sound slipped from her mouth and she thrust her chest up at him as he lowered his mouth. He didn't suck, as he'd done before, but dropped frustratingly soft kisses, stroking her with one hand while his other pulled the bunched fabric around her middle lower and lower.

"Lift your bottom, darling."

She obeyed and he shoved the dress and chemise down, his gaze dropping to the triangle of dark curls. Instead of touching her there, he rubbed her stomach in a circle. His mouth curved as he caressed, the circles becoming larger and larger, and lower and lower until . . .

Martha stiffened when he brushed her mound and he paused, his dark eyes locking with hers. "Do you want me to stop?"

"No."

His eyelids lowered and his lips curved into a faint but well-pleased smile. "Spread your thighs for me, Martha."

The muscles in her legs jerked and jumped to do his bidding, shame mingling with want as she opened herself to him. He caressed down her belly and over her mound, stroking the seam of her lower lips, the pressure he exerted never quite enough to touch that exquisitely sensitive part of her.

Martha pushed her pelvis up on his next stroke.

He chuckled, his hand not ceasing its heavenly work. On the next stroke the tip of his finger slid between her lips and she whimpered. "So wet and swollen, and it's all for me, isn't it, Martha?"

Martha wasn't in any condition to speak.

His stroking became rhythmic. "Your little bud is engorged—needy." Hugo groaned. "Chri—*fuck* I want to put my mouth on you."

Her entire body shook at both his crude language—she was not so lost to pleasure that she didn't notice his hastily-caught blasphemy—and shocking words: *his mouth*?

"I have been dreaming about this every night." He stroked from the part he called a *bud* to her entrance, and then he pushed a finger inside her.

Martha gasped and her body clenched.

"You're so tight, sweetheart." He began to work her with gentle strokes, his chest rumbling with a sound that was remarkably like a purr.

Finally—*finally*—he touched her sensitive core.

Martha couldn't help it; she moaned, her body going liquid as his thumb circled the source of her pleasure while he eased another finger in beside the first, the stretch both uncomfortable and wildly erotic.

"Have you ever felt yourself inside?" He pumped her harder and deeper, as if to demonstrate which *inside* he meant.

A choking sound escaped her parted lips and he chuckled. "I'll take that as a *no*. You feel like hot, slick velvet inside, Martha. I can't wait to watch you explore your body." He did something with his fingers that made her whine and buck. "You are so close," he said, working her toward her climax with shocking ease. Martha tried to hold back, to draw out the pleasure, but she was no match for his magical hand.

"Come apart for me, Martha."

She exploded at his command and lost herself in pure bliss, only vaguely aware of her hoarse, desperate keening and his soothing voice as she drifted.

It was the tickle of hair on her belly that brought her back to herself.

She shoved up onto her elbows, her arms shaky and weak. "Hugo—what—"

"I'm going to use my mouth on you." He opened her with his thumbs

"Hugo! That's—

"Oh, Martha." His tone was reverential. "You have the most beautiful cunt I have ever seen."

Martha's mortified yelp turned into a moan when he lowered his mouth over the already stimulated bundle of nerves, shattering her with the soft wet heat of his mouth.

"Hugo," she whispered, more than a little reverence in her own tone.

The urge to give herself up to pleasure, to collapse and close her eyes, was almost overwhelming, but she needed to see—to bear witness to his exquisite wickedness. His dark head bobbed between her spread thighs as he laved her with the flat of his tongue, again and again and again.

Martha began to shudder as the now-familiar pleasure built, incited not only by physical sensation, but also by the sheer depravity of the act—the knowledge that Hugo was touching such an intimate, private place with his mouth.

Her climax hit her like a bolt of lightning and her back arched, her heels digging into the bedding as she ground herself against his mouth, grunting and mewling and all but sobbing.

"That's right, darling, let it all go."

Her body clenched and released, clenched and released, until she was as limp and wrung out as a rag.

When Hugo pulled away, she opened her woozy eyes. He'd pushed up onto his knees, a hand on the front of his trousers. Instead of untying his makeshift belt, he stroked the obscene bulge over the thin fabric, the muscles in his forearms ropey and taut. "I will be a long time getting to sleep, Martha."

She reached for his belt, but he shook his head and leaned away.

"Not tonight, darling. We should get you dressed, and I'll walk you back to the Greedy Vicar."

***

Hugo couldn't believe those words had just come out of his own mouth.

Hugo and the Maiden

He'd never been this aroused in his entire life. What difference would it make if he took her? Especially after what they'd just done. They were going to be married; did it really matter if he had her maidenhood now or two days from now?

And yet...

"Hugo?"

"Hmm?"

"I have a question."

His body stiffened, and not in a pleasurable way. Questions, in his experience, were never good.

"Yes," he said cautiously.

"Why did you avoid me for two weeks after taking the job for Mr. Stogden and then suddenly come back?"

"I tried to stay away so I wouldn't be tempted to do something like we just did." He gave a harsh, unamused laugh. "Clearly I wasn't too successful."

"Oh." She dropped her gaze to her body, saw she was naked, and jerked the edge of the blanket to cover herself.

Hugo wasn't a religious man, but even he knew the Biblical story of Eve, and how she'd covered her body after making love with Adam. Something Hugo had just said had shamed Martha.

"What did I say to hurt you?" he asked.

"Nothing."

"Martha, look at me, love." Her eyes, which had been hazed with pleasure only a short time before, were now clouded with pain. "Remember what I said earlier—about me having no experience with this sort of thing?"

She gave a grudging nod.

"That means you have to tell me when I say something rude or hurtful. That wasn't my intention, but it seems to have happened."

Martha filled her lungs and exhaled slowly before answering. "It's only—well, it just sounds like you didn't *want* to like me."

And that, as the saying went, hit the nail on the head.

Even Hugo—as oblivious as he was—knew he couldn't say that.

Instead, he said, "I just believed that you would be better off with Clark."

The furrows on her forehead deepened.

Hugo tried again. "It was not easy to stay away from you, Martha." That, at least, was not a lie. "Can't you just accept that I was trying to do the right thing by you?"

Emotions galloped across her pretty face like a herd of horses. He couldn't identify the one that finally settled, but at least she nodded. And then she brought his hand to her mouth and kissed his palm.

The tender action left him breathless.

"Your poor hands," she murmured, kissing his fingers. She lingered over the large blister on his thumb, kissing it and then—God save him—licking it with her kitten tongue.

"Fucking hell, Martha."

She dropped his hand like it was a hot coal. "I'm so sorry—did I hurt you?"

Hugo took her hand and clamped it over his pulsing cock in answer.

"Oh." Her plump lips parted in surprise, which of course made him even harder. "How long can you stay—"

"A long time," he assured her. His ability to stay hard for hours—in addition to his remarkable recovery time—was but one of the things that made him so successful in his business.

Her fingers tightened around his shaft and he gritted his teeth and lifted her hand. "We need to get you back to your room at the Vicar." *For my own sanity.*

"Can't I stay just a bit longer?" She leaned into him, sighing in a way that squeezed his chest.

"Just a bit," he said in a raspy voice.

Hugo laid down beside her and she tucked the blanket under her arms. "I feel guilty."

"About what we did?"

"Oh, no—of course not."

It was unnerving how much her words relieved him.

She kissed his hand again. "I adored what we did. I can't wait to do it again. Er, and other things, too."

His jaw sagged. *This* was prim Miss Martha Pringle? While his brain boggled at the words coming out of her mouth, his prick pulsed joyously; never in his entire life had he wanted to have sex with anyone so badly.

Hugo wasn't sure if he was entirely happy about that …

Hugo and the Maiden

"Er, what makes you feel guilty then?" he asked when he saw she was staring at him.

"Is it bad of me to want to leave Stroma?"

He snorted. "I'd say it's a sign of intelligence." He lightly caressed her cheekbone with his thumb. "Why did your father come here to begin with, do you think?"

"He said that he wanted to be somewhere his services would be needed."

"Did your mother like it here?" Hugo suspected that the wife of a vicar had to go wherever her husband could get work.

"I don't recall my mother. My father said she was never quite robust after I was born but that she was the one who wanted to come to the island. She caught a chill that became worse. The storms were terrible that winter and he could not get her to a physician in time."

"You've never met any of your mother's people?"

"My father said she was an orphan." She hesitated. "I've been thinking about your family, Hugo."

Her words sent a spike of anxiety to his chest. "Oh?"

"Won't they want to see you get married? I mean, I know not all of them, but maybe one or two?"

He'd completely forgotten that he'd spoken of his family that night in the caves. What the hell had he told her?

"Do you want to wait to get married until they can come?"

Hugo had to bite his tongue to keep from laughing; they'd be waiting a very long time.

"They're not exactly the traveling sort of people." Only after he said that did he recall that he'd told her all of them had moved out of London. He really needed to get his lies straight.

"Er, we don't need to have the banns read?" he asked, hoping to move the subject away from his family.

"No, in Scotland a willing couple can marry without such formalities.

"Well, then. The curate is coming out to Stroma for a wedding; I think we should give him one."

Her expression was, understandably, tense.

"Or we can wait, Martha. I can always go down to London and then come back when—"

"No, Saturday is the best idea. You'll want to leave immediately after?"

"I'd prefer to spend our wedding night somewhere other than this lean-to or the spare bedroom at the Greedy Vicar."

She chewed her lip.

"What is it?"

"Have you thought about Small Cailean? He will miss you—he's become so attached. And his aunt, well…"

"What are you saying, Martha?"

"His aunt takes care of him, but she doesn't—"

"She doesn't treat him like he is a person," Hugo finished for her. More like a dog. Or a draft animal.

"She does her best, but I don't think he is happy here."

Hugo groaned. "God, Martha. Are you suggesting what I think you're suggesting?"

"Is your house in London too small?"

He laughed before he could stop himself. Solange's was enormous, with plenty of rooms.

Martha frowned. "Why is that funny?"

"Having enough room isn't the issue," he said. "Why are you saying this? Did Cailean tell you about Lily?"

"Cailean doesn't really communicate with me—or anyone—like he does with you."

Hugo pushed down a surge of pride.

"Why, what did he say about Lily?" she asked.

"She's got a family and wasn't too friendly about including Cailean."

"Ah, well, that was bound to happen eventually. I thought she would have gone off long ago."

"I can't imagine Cailean would be happy in London, Martha."

"Why not?"

"It's noisy, crowded, and there aren't the sort of places he seems to like—beaches, the sea, plenty of countryside to explore."

"I think he spends so much time wandering because he doesn't like to go to his aunt's house."

Hugo suspected she was right.

Still, when he tried to imagine the shy, gentle young man in London, he just couldn't envision it.

Yet when he tried to imagine Cailean on Stroma without Lily or Martha or Hugo, he didn't *want* to think about it.

"Good Lord, Martha. What are we going to do about Cailean?"

Chapter 23

Hugo hadn't expected that he'd have to face any questions about Martha until after work—when he'd agreed to meet her at the Greedy Vicar.

But the people of Stroma once again surprised him.

"You're a good lad," Mr. Stogden said once his last day was finally over. "If you ever need a job, you're welcome back here."

Hugo was humbled by the compliment "Er, thank you, sir."

"I understand you're to marry Martha Pringle."

Hugo gawked.

Mr. Stogden chuckled. "Even a hermit like me gets news like this quickly." His face became stern. "I know the vicar regarded you highly, Hugo. He would be pleased with this," Stogden said, adding to Hugo's surprise. "Clark is a solid man, but Mr. Pringle wanted the best for Martha. And life on Stroma—well, let's just say that I encouraged my children to find work elsewhere." He paused, his eyes suddenly as flinty and hard as the stone in his quarry. "You make sure you do well by her, Hugo Buckingham."

"I'll do my best, sir."

Stogden handed him a small stack of coins. "Here is your pay." He smiled and winked. "I hope to see you down at the Vicar later so I can buy you a congratulatory pint."

"I'd like that, sir."

It didn't take Hugo long to clean up and change into his better set of clothing, and he was soon on his way down to the tiny pub. While he wasn't looking forward to the grilling he'd likely face, he could hardly leave Martha to answer all the questions alone.

"Evenin', 'Yougo."

He turned to find Jem Packard ambling toward him.

"Hello, Mr. Packard."

"I gather I'll not be takin' you over quite so early tomorrow?"

Hugo snorted and resumed his trek. "Does everyone on the island know?"

"Aye, and probably on the mainland, too." Jem fell into step beside him. "Martha says that you'll get married when the curate comes tomorrow."

Hugo didn't hear any judgment in his tone.

"Yes, that's right. I'll still need you to take us over after the wedding breakfast—weather permitting, of course."

Jem didn't answer immediately

They trudged in silence.

"Aye, reckon I can do that. You talked to Clark?"

Hugo glanced at the older man; Jem had never been this chatty with him before. "No. Why should I have?"

Jem shrugged. "No reason."

Hugo suspected there was one but that he was too dense to have guessed it.

"I need to stop by Mrs. Fergusson's," Hugo said as they neared the small stone cottage where Cailean lived with his aunt and cousin. "Are you going to the Vicar?" That was a stupid question, where else would he be going?

"Aye."

"Tell Martha I'll be along shortly."

Jem looked like he wanted to say something, but just nodded and continued down the path.

Hugo took a deep breath and then knocked on Mrs. Fergusson's door. He heard the woman yell inside the house and a moment later the door opened.

He grinned up at Cailean. "Ah, just the man I was looking for." Cailean stepped back into the house without looking at him.

"What's wrong?" Hugo asked. "Cailean?" But the boy shuffled into the little kitchen with his eyes downcast, leaving Hugo to follow.

"Who was it?" Mrs. Fergusson snapped rudely, not turning from the cookstove where she was cutting potatoes into a pot.

Hugo bristled at her tone; why did she have to speak to her nephew so harshly? "Good evening, Mrs. Fergusson."

She yelped and spun around, flustered. "Oh, Mester Yougo, er, I didn't—"

"I want to take Cailean with me," Hugo blurted, spurred by anger into speaking bluntly. Hugo turned to the lad. "I'm sorry, I should have asked you before—"

Cailean flung his arms around him.

Hugo and the Maiden

"Cailean," Hugo wheezed, pounding on the other man's back when he couldn't force any words out.

"Let 'im go, Cailean," the old woman scolded.

Cailean's vise-like grasp fell away and Hugo sucked in a lungful of air. Yes, one of his ribs definitely felt bruised.

"You awright, Mester Yougo?"

He met Cailean's worried stare first. "I'm fine." He smiled to show he meant it. "I take it that's a *yes*?"

Cailean nodded vigorously.

Hugo looked at his aunt. "Mrs. Fergusson?"

She swallowed under his harsh stare and glanced at her nephew. Hugo saw regret flicker across her face and knew that she would miss the lad, even though she viewed him as a burden. "You'll take care of 'im, aye?"

"I will."

Mrs. Fergusson said something in Scots to Cailean, but Hugo recognized the word *Martha*, so obviously she already knew about their impending marriage.

Cailean nodded at whatever she said, and the old woman turned back to Hugo. "I told him to be a good lad and mind you and Martha."

Hugo suspected Cailean didn't need to be told that, but he understood it was probably the old woman's way of showing that she cared.

"If he doesn't like it in London, I'll make sure he gets back to you safely," he promised her.

Beside him, Cailean bounced on the balls of his feet, staring at Hugo as if he were a god.

Bloody hell.

"You want to come over to the Vicar to see Martha?" Hugo asked, more than a little embarrassed by Cailean's worshipful stare.

Cailean bolted out of the kitchen and Hugo smiled at the old woman. "I guess that's a *yes*, too." He hesitated, and then added, "I hope you'll come and enjoy a celebratory glass of sherry with us, Mrs. Fergusson."

Her wrinkled face creased into a smile. "Aye, thank you. I'll be over in a bit."

Hugo left, pleased with himself for offering the olive branch.

The Vicar was already crowded when Hugo and Cailean arrived. For a moment, everything went silent, and Hugo felt the weight of several dozen eyes.

But then somebody yelled, "Hugo!" and the room erupted into warm, noisy chaos as the people he'd come to know over the past weeks shouted out congratulations, clapped him on the shoulder, and generally roasted him on his impending nuptials.

Martha sat at the table closest to the tiny bar and Hugo made his way over to her, having to stop frequently for good wishes and congratulations.

"Good evening, Mistress Pringle," he teased.

She gave him a shy smile, her cheeks rosy. "Mr. Higgenbotham." Hugo laughed.

"Hello Cailean. I hope—" Martha bit her lip and looked at Hugo. "Cailean has agreed to join us."

Her smile was glorious. "Oh! I'm so happy to hear that."

Hugo grinned at Cailean, who looked fit to burst. "Why don't you go tell Joe what you want to drink, Cailean. And bring me a pint of bitter, if you don't mind."

The lad nodded and darted toward the bar.

Hugo dropped into the chair next to Martha with a sigh.

"I'm so happy he's coming with us, Hugo."

Her adoring look made him want to preen like an idiot. "Well, me too," he said gruffly. So," he said, changing the subject, "Was it a rough day?"

"Not as bad as I feared."

"Everyone I talked to already knew," he told her. "You must have been busy."

"I only had to tell Joe and Mary and they did the rest." She hesitated and then added, "But the day felt endless; I'm glad you're here."

Warmth spread inside him at her words. "Me too," he said quietly, and then noticed the slight tightness around her eyes and frowned. "Was anyone unkind about our decision to marry so quickly?" *Like Clark.*

"No, not at all," she assured him. "It's just, well, I—I spoke to Mr. Clark first thing—I felt he deserved to know before anyone else. He was a perfect gentleman and wished me all the best."

"Of course, he was." Hugo scowled at the surge of jealousy in his belly.

"Everyone understands why we are doing it this way." She gave him a reassuring smile. "People like and respect you, even though they've not known you long, and they care about me and are happy for us both."

Hugo wasn't so sure of her assessment, but, as the evening wore on and more people came to congratulate them, and he realized that she was right. The people of Stroma saw Hugo as a man who'd been wronged by the law and worked hard over the past weeks. Also, many of them still hadn't forgiven Robert Clark for the help he'd given McCoy. The cynical part of Hugo—the larger part—suspected that was the true reason that so many people seemed happy about Martha's decision to marry Hugo.

Whatever the reason, Hugo's face hurt from smiling by the time the little taproom began to empty out.

"Do you need a lantern?" Martha asked as Hugo walked her upstairs to the inn's one guestroom.

"No, there's moon enough." Hugo opened the door to her tiny bedchamber.

She cut him a furtive glance. "Well, good night, then."

Hugo caught her arm before she could slip away. "Surely I can give you a kiss?"

She blushed adorably. "Well—"

Hugo gave her a chaste peck on her flushed cheek.

She frowned. "Is that all?"

Hugo laughed and claimed her petal-soft lips with a real kiss. "Sleep tight, Martha. I'll see you tomorrow." He winked. "At our wedding."

He'd only gone a short way up the road when he noticed somebody with a lantern approaching from a cluster of cottages.

Hugo stopped. "Good evening, Clark."

Clark didn't stop walking until he practically stood on Hugo's toes. "I've been waiting for you, Buckingham."

If Clark thought his behavior was intimidating, he was deeply mistaken.

Rather than step back, Hugo stepped forward. "Why, Robert," he purred suggestively. "I didn't know you cared."

Clark jerked back so fast that he stumbled and Hugo caught his arm before he could go arse over tip.

Clark yanked his arm away. "There's something rotten about you, Buckingham." He snorted. "Even your name sounds false."

He was right about that much, at least.

"I think what you are trying to say is '*congratulations, Hugo.*'"

Clark's jaw moved from side to side, his hands fisted at his sides.

Hugo's body remained taut as he waited for the other man's attack.

But then Clark's shoulders slumped and all the rage seemed to drain out of him. He shook his head, his expression one of resignation and disgust. "I can't blame Martha for choosing you—she's just a simple country lass who lost her father and is confused and scared. Life on the island is hard and I'm sure that London must sound exotic and appealing to her. But she belongs here with people who will care for her. I think you know that Buckingham. If you care for her then you should think of her best interests. Don't do this to her; don't take her away from the only home she's ever known."

Clark's threats had only amused him, but Clark's plea?

Well, that was another matter, entirely. Maybe his words wouldn't have been so affecting if Hugo didn't completely agree with the other man.

"Martha is a grown woman," he said. "She can make her own decisions."

"Do you even love her?"

"What I feel for her is none of your concern."

"Well I *do* love her," Clark said.

Fury—and something very much like envy—flared inside him at Clark's claim, and the ease with which he made it. Hugo sneered. "How nice for you, Clark. But Martha doesn't love you; she loves *me*. And that's what matters, isn't it?"

Clark gave him a sad look. "You don't love her, do you? You're the sort of man who can't love anyone but himself. Because if you did, you'd do what was best for her and leave her alone." Clark turned on his heel and headed toward the little stone cottage that Hugo knew he shared with his mother, widowed sister, and her children.

Hugo opened his mouth to yell something—to taunt the other man and make him come back and fight—but he shut his mouth without uttering a sound. Because he agreed with Clark's accusation.

Hugo and the Maiden

If he truly loved Martha, he would want her to have what was best for her. And Hugo wasn't best for anyone—especially not a woman.

Instead of leaving her here with a man who loved her, he was going to take her as his wife without ever telling her the truth: that he was a lying whore incapable of love.

If he were a better man, he'd steal a boat and row himself across to the mainland and disappear from her life.

But he wasn't a better man, and there was no way on God's green earth that he was ever going to let Martha go.

Chapter 24

"So, Mrs. Buckingham."

Martha smiled at her husband of barely four hours. "So, Mr. Buckingham."

Hugo grinned back at her, the expression uncharacteristically joyful and boyish. "I'm sorry our wedding was such a rushed affair," he said as they walked from the Norseman Inn and Public House up Wick's High Street.

"There is always too much work to be done during the harvest to take more than a few hours away," she reassured him. "That's why most weddings take place in the winter or spring."

"I have to admit that I'm happy that we got into Wick before the shops closed. I'm not sure how much we'll be able to get today."

For the wedding Mr. Stogden had loaned him a coat and neckerchief, but he'd changed back into his own clothes right before they left.

Martha's clothing—everything except what she'd been wearing the night she'd been trapped in the Gloup with Hugo—had burnt in the fire, along with all her possessions, so the island women had contributed to her wedding ensemble. While the gesture was a kind one, the outfit was hideous. Still, even dressed in ill-fitting near rags she was happier than she'd been in her entire life.

Guilt had tried to worm its way into her day over and over since she'd woken feeling joy at the thought of becoming Hugo's wife.

How dare she feel such happiness when her father had been dead not even two weeks?

The sharp pain that accompanied that thought was enough to make breathing difficult. But each and every time she began to spiral into despair, she'd hear her father's voice: *I love you too much to ever want you to grieve for me, Martha.*

Jonathan Pringle had despised society's insistence on imposing mourning periods.

Why mourn our loved one's death when we should be celebrating the joy they brought to our lives?

Hugo and the Maiden

Martha had reminded herself of her father's words repeatedly throughout the day.

The wedding had taken place early and the wedding breakfast that Joe and Mary hosted was more like a wedding tea. In Martha's opinion, it had been lovely and perfect and just the right amount of time to avoid any maudlin emotions to build up.

And then the three of them had piled into the *Louise* and Jem Packard had taken them across the firth and into Wick Bay.

And now Hugo wanted to take her shopping.

"Are you sure you can afford buying all of us clothing, Hugo? The women were very generous, and I have—"

"Buying a few outfits of clothing won't beggar me." He squeezed her hand and they both winced as Cailean—too busy staring in shop windows—almost walked into a lamp post. "He's going to injure himself if he's not careful," Hugo muttered.

Martha was behaving like a gawking yokel, herself. When was the last time she'd even stepped foot in an actual town? As for buying a brand new dress? Well, that had never happened.

"If you are sure, Hugo," she said.

"I'm sure, darling. You would look lovely in a burlap sack, but the three of us bear more than a passing resemblance to a trio of scarecrows." He cocked his head at her. "What does one call a collection of scarecrows?"

"Hmm. A fright?" she suggested.

His low chuckle warmed her body through, even though the wind was a bit chill. "What about a scare, no wait, that has the same word. A startle?"

Martha smirked. "A tatterdemalion?"

Hugo laughed. "I surrender. I thought—"

"Hugo?"

They turned at the rare sound of Cailean's voice. He was pressed up against the tiny bow window of a sweet shop.

"Go on in and tell the clerk what you want," Hugo told him as Martha wandered to look through the bookstore window right next door. She gorged on the sight of shelves and shelves of books.

"Martha?"

"Would it be all right if I just looked inside?" When he didn't answer, she turned. He was smiling down at her with the oddest—almost tender—look in his eyes.

"I'll go get Cailean his sweets and we'll sit on that bench right there"—he pointed to a bench across from a toy shop—"and wait for you."

"Are you sure? I don't want to—"

"I'm sure."

I promise I won't be more than—"

"Here." He shook several coins from a fat leather pouch into his hand and held them out to her. "Will that be enough for a book or two?"

"Hugo! That's far too much, I could never—"

He closed her fingers around the coins and lifted her hand to his mouth. "Take all the time you want, darling." His low voice did disturbing, exciting things to her body. He kissed her fingers, his lips hot even through the thick cotton of her gloves. "I'll be out here feasting on Turkish delight if you need me."

***

Martha looked from the boxes piled in the corner of her room to the stack of three books on the nightstand and felt almost giddy.

And then she immediately felt ashamed that she was taking such pleasure in material possessions. But it had been *so* long since she'd had a book that wasn't dog-eared, or stained, or something that she'd not already read a dozen times.

As for her new dresses? This was the first time in her life that she had not one but *five* new gowns, none of which she'd sewn herself. New ankle boots, two pairs of slippers, two hats, a new cloak, four pairs of gloves, and on and on.

She'd been too shocked to do more than gape as Hugo had ordered around the elated saleswoman, the pile of garments growing and growing.

Hugo had purchased only a few articles of clothing for himself. "I have lots of clothing in London." Irritation had flickered across his features. "Hopefully."

Cailean had been far less interested in new garments than in the book Martha had bought for him. It was a reading primer with the most beautiful pictures she had ever seen. She was determined to teach him to read now that they both would have time.

They had topped off the magical day with a delicious meal in the small inn's only private parlor. Afterward Hugo and Cailean had gone down to the taproom.

Hugo and the Maiden

And now Martha was waiting for her husband to come to her. Her husband.

Martha hugged herself, her fingers stroking her new feather-soft muslin nightgown. It was one of the few garments that she'd chosen for herself, too shy to allow Hugo to select such an intimate thing for her.

She had brushed her hair until it shone, and it hung in a pale blonde froth down to her hips. Martha knew it was her only beauty. She was neither pretty, nor ugly, but average, except for her corn-silk hair. But the way Hugo had looked at her that night in his lean-to had made her feel beautiful.

There was a light knock and then the door opened. Hugo stepped inside and then saw her and froze, his expressive, dark eyes flickering up and down her person before settling on her face. He locked the door without looking away from her.

She wasn't accustomed to seeing him with such short hair or wearing clothing that fit and flattered his magnificent body.

He looked handsome and virile in snug buckskins, a black coat that molded to his broad shoulders, and a white cravat that was an attractive contrast to his tanned face.

"You look lovely," he said, closing the distance between them in two strides.

He stopped so close that Martha had to crane her neck to look up at him. She could smell smoke and spirits. Beneath that was the faint masculine earthiness that seemed to be distinctly Hugo's own scent.

He lifted a hand and cupped her cheek. "I have been looking forward to tonight."

"M-me too."

"I hope you don't mind that I only took the one bedchamber for us."

"Er, should I mind?"

"Lots of married couples don't share the same room—at least not beyond a few hours on selected nights." His shapely mouth curved into a smile that made her breathing quicken. "But I will want you in my bed all night. Every night." He leaned close and whispered, "I will want to make love to you often."

Martha's lips parted, but nothing came out.

"You will have your own chambers wherever we live, of course, but we shall always sleep together."

She moistened her lower lip, which felt unaccountably dry.

Hugo's gaze dropped to her mouth, his eyes darkening. "Undress me, Martha."

Martha jolted at the quiet command. "Oh."

He nodded encouragingly at her, waiting patiently as her shaking hands reached for the buttons on his coat. As she unfastened them, he carded his fingers through her hair. "You have the most beautiful hair I have ever seen."

She'd heard similar things in the past, but never had mere words caused her entire body to heat.

"Breathe, sweetheart."

She cut him a quick glance, both annoyed and aroused by the lazy confidence in his hooded gaze.

Once the last button was undone, he cupped her face in his hands and lowered his mouth over hers.

His kisses were light and teasing and he smelled and tasted so good that Martha felt intoxicated. She didn't realize he'd coaxed her mouth open until she felt the smooth flick of his tongue against hers. She shuddered and grabbed his biceps, wanting—no, *needing*—more.

Instead of pulling her closer, he stepped back, his eyes glinting with gentle amusement and something else. Desire?

"Help me take off my coat."

The garment was tightly fitted, but not ridiculously so and she was able to peel it from his shoulders when he shrugged. Martha laid it over the clotheshorse at the foot of the bed and turned to find him waiting.

She fumbled her way through the buttons on his waistcoat, intensely aware of his silent gaze. When she reached for his cravat, she risked a look up at him.

He was no longer amused; he smoldered.

"My wife," he murmured, sounding dazed. He yanked off his cravat and tossed it aside, his movements no longer languid, but abrupt and impatient. "I wanted to take my time and seduce you slowly, properly." He pulled his shirt over his head and it joined his neckcloth. "But I want you too damn much, Martha." He gave a soft snort that sounded like disbelief and held out his hand; it was shaking. "You see that?"

Before she could answer—not that she knew what to say—his hand dropped to the ridge tenting his leather breeches and he pressed the heel of his hand against it, grimacing as if he were in pain. "Get on the bed."

Her sex—already sensitive and swollen—pulsed at his low, rough command as she hastened to obey.

He sat on the bench in front of the small dressing table and removed his new boots with a few rough jerks, throwing them to the floor with loud *thunks* before pushing down his stockings and standing.

Their eyes locked as he undid the closures on his fall and then quickly flicked open the four buttons beneath. His movements were practiced yet sensual—as if he'd disrobed in front of women countless times and was comfortable displaying his body.

Martha didn't want to think about how many lovers he must have had to gain such confidence and competence in the bedchamber.

He shoved down his breeches and drawers in one graceful motion and when he stood, his erection jutted long and thick from his narrow hips.

She knew her mouth was open but couldn't make herself close it.

Hugo strode toward her, his shaft bobbing, and reached for the hem of her nightgown. Martha lifted her hips without being told and he raised the garment up over her head, throwing it to join the other clothing.

His eyes glittered as they traveled down her body, lingering on her stiff nipples. "So bloody beautiful," he murmured as he climbed up on the bed. "Lie on your back, Martha."

When she complied, he nudged her thighs apart and knelt between her legs. "You do this to me," he said, sliding his palm around his erection, his tone almost contemplative. They both looked down as he pumped himself, a bead of moisture appearing at the very tip.

Martha was frightened of his size, but her body craved him—desperately—and she ached with need.

His lips curved into tiniest, smuggest of smiles—as if he could see the contents of her wicked mind. He ran his other hand, hot and calloused, up the inside of her thigh, delving into her curls when he reached the top. He traced her lips, his stroking too maddeningly light.

As she'd done the other night, Martha opened her legs wider and lifted her hips in silent entreaty.

He groaned, released himself, and gracefully lowered his torso, shoving her legs even wider to accommodate his wide shoulders. "You're driving me mad," he muttered, and then opened her with his thumbs, the tip of his tongue peeking between his lips. He made a noise that sounded like he was in pain and then lowered his mouth over her.

She squeezed her eyes shut at the unbearable bliss of his hot, wet mouth and caressing tongue. His forearms kept her thighs pinned and spread while he ruthlessly worked her toward her climax.

Martha bucked and thrust and writhed, shameless in her passion. And then he pushed his tongue inside her.

"Hugo," she cried out, shocked and aroused in equal measures at the erotic invasion.

He didn't pause, the primitive rhythm of his thrusting a promise of what was to come.

The second orgasm was upon her before she knew what was happening. Unlike the headlong rush of the first, this was a brutal punch of intense pleasure that shattered her.

He slid a finger inside her and she gasped as her inner muscles contracted around him.

"Mmm." He kissed and nibbled the tender skin where her thigh joined her sex and then moved up beside her, until they were hip to hip, and claimed her mouth.

Martha gasped; that was herself she tasted on his tongue.

"Sweet, aren't you?" He sucked her lower lip into his mouth as he rubbed his erection against her hip. "Touch me, Martha."

Martha had been dreaming of touching him for weeks—never had she expected the astounding silky softness of his skin. Or the heat of him.

He closed his hand around hers and gave a low growl of approval. "Just like that, darling—tight." He released her hand and palmed her mound, gently squeezing her sex. "Mine." He pushed two fingers inside her, working her with languid pumps. "All mine."

With each stroke of her hand, she spread more and more moisture down his shaft, until he was slick with it. He grunted and thrusted his hips, pushing into her tight, wet fist.

It was challenging to ignore her own pleasure and concentrate on bringing him to his release, but she wanted to see him come apart.

"So good," he muttered. And then he did something to her with his thumb, and a blissful sensation ambushed her yet again.

Martha bucked and cried out. "Hugo."

He groaned. "Oh, Martha. I wish you could see how beautiful you look right now," he said in a husky voice, his hand stilling while she shuddered, boneless with ecstasy.

He waited until she came back to herself before removing her limp hand from his erection, making her realize that she had stopped stroking him.

Martha reached for him again. "I want—"

"No." His jaws were tight enough that she could see the muscles and sinews beneath the skin "I can't wait any longer to get inside you." He positioned his body over hers and cut her a quick, concerned look. "It will only hurt for a moment, darling, and then I promise I'll make you feel wonderful." His slick, hot crown pressed against her entrance, hard and insistent. "Do you want me, Martha?"

"Yes … please, Hugo," she begged, as if some wanton had gained control of her mouth.

He breached her with a quick, firm thrust and she cried out, more in surprise than pain, although there was considerable discomfort.

He was panting, like he'd been running, his pupils huge. "Mmmm, Martha. So wet and tight for me," he growled against her temple, his biceps bulging as he held himself still.

Martha squirmed beneath his far larger body as she stretched to accommodate him. He was big and it hurt more than she'd expected. But she wanted him—wanted *this*—no matter how uncomfortable it was.

"Can you take the rest of me?" he asked in a strained voice.

She bit her lip and tilted her hips.

"Good girl, open yourself for me," he praised as her knees spread wider.

He gave her his length slowly, entering her inch by inch, not stopping until the ridged muscles of his abdomen pressed against her stomach and it felt like he was poking her spine.

"Relax your muscles and let your body adjust. You'll be fine in a moment," he soothed, kissing her temple. "And breathe, darling, breathe."

Martha took a deep breath, and then another. He was right: the initial pain was gone; what remained was only a vague ache and the sensation of fullness. Regardless of the discomfort, she reveled in their joining; this is what both their bodies had been designed to do. She felt more like a wife right then than she had earlier that day, when she'd spoken her vows.

He kissed her brow again. "Better?"

"It's lovely." And it was.

He smiled and his shaft flexed inside her.

Martha's lips parted. "Did you do that?"

"Who else would be doing it, darling?" He flexed again and again, jerking against her swollen sheath.

Martha tightened her inner muscles, the action sending ripples of pleasure through her body.

Hugo groaned. "You're a fast learner, sweetheart. Are you trying to break me in two?"

"Did I hurt you?"

"Only in the most delicious way. I'm going to move in you, now."

Martha could breathe more easily when he withdrew, but she immediately missed him.

He slid back in, faster this time, burying himself to the hilt.

"So good," he muttered. And then he began to move, his strokes slow and measured, each one leaving more pleasure in its wake than the one before. The long, lean muscles of his flank bunched beneath her hands as he filled her again and again, his body angled in such a way that he grazed her core with each thrust.

"Come once more, for your husband," he said, and then reached between their bodies and drove her toward yet another climax.

He moaned when she contracted around him, his thrusts becoming less controlled, until his hips pounded into her with the unrestrained force of a winter storm.

Martha forced her heavy eyelids up, desperate to watch as he gave in to his climax.

His jaws clenched and his dark eyes locked with hers. "Going to come," he growled, and then rammed himself deep, holding her in a punishing embrace while he kept her full and impaled, his shaft pulsing and thickening as he flooded her with a hot rush of seed.

Martha drifted for a moment, reveling in the feel of his hard, hot body on top of her and inside her. A body which gradually became heavier and heavier, until he was no longer supporting his weight on his arms. Instead, he crushed her into the mattress, his breathing deep and even.

He'd fallen asleep.

Hugo and the Maiden

She smiled and slid her arms around him, reveling in a moment of complete happiness.

"I love you, Hugo," she whispered.

***

Hugo shifted to get more comfortable and something beneath him groaned.

He opened his eyes and stared directly into the sky-blue eyes of his wife.

"Did I fall asleep on top of you?" he mumbled thickly as he rolled aside.

"Just for a minute. It was ... nice."

Her voice was breathy and high—nothing like the Martha he knew.

That's because this wasn't just a fuck for her, you dunce. It was her first time; you need to act like a lover.

Hugo scowled; how the hell did a person act like a lover?

Talk to her, comfort her ... make sure you didn't hurt her.

It was that last thought that woke him from his stupor.

Hugo turned on his side and pushed up onto his elbow. Her face was turned away from him, so he took her chin and turned her back. "Martha?"

She was blushing fierily, but she smiled, too. "Hugo?" she said in a mocking tone.

If she was smiling and teasing him, it couldn't have been too bad. Could it?

"Did I hurt you? I meant to go slower, to be more—"

"No, you didn't hurt me—except for a moment or two at the beginning."

He supposed it was too much to hope that she might have enjoyed it. Did virgins enjoy their first time? Virgins were not a subject he had much experience with.

"Regrets?" he asked.

She shook her head.

"Good. Because you can't undo it."

"I don't want to."

"Good," he said again, because he could think of nothing else.

She yawned. "I'm so sorry," she said, flushing. "That's rather rude."

"I'll forgive you. This time."

"I don't know why I'm so tired."

"Because I wore you out, darling. I'm going to take it as a compliment." He pulled the blankets up around her.

"Mmm. Thank you, Hugo." She turned onto her side and snuggled down into the covers, pushing her bottom against his groin.

"Get some sleep, sweetheart."

He waited until her breathing became regular and then rolled onto his back and stared at the yellowed plaster ceiling.

His jaw tightened as he recalled what he'd done: he'd spent inside her. He never done that before, at least not inside a woman. It had been careless, no matter that they were married.

Why? You're married. That's what married people do: have children.

Married. Children. Hugo swallowed a hysterical laugh. Bloody hell. He couldn't wrap his mind around having a wife yet, and he sure as hell couldn't wrap his mind around having a brat.

You'd better start wrapping because she'll want them. A lot of them.

Those had been her words.

His half-hard cock twitched at the thought of putting a baby inside her. Hugo snorted; well, at least one part of his body was thrilled.

Shame flooded him at the snide, unworthy thought.

Children were necessary for Martha's happiness and he'd already vowed to do everything in his power to ensure she never regretted her decision to marry him. That meant children.

Besides, while it was true that he'd not wanted children in the past, he could imagine having them with Martha. He might lack the ability to love, but he could support and care for children and bloody well make sure that no child of his ever felt unwanted. And Martha would be such a wonderful mother that she'd make up for his emotional deficiencies.

He turned to look at her sleeping form, thrilling at the knowledge that she was his wife. He could have her every night, as often as they both liked—and he would use all his skills to make sure that she wanted him often.

He smiled at the thought. Being married wasn't going to be bad, at all.

You think that now; imagine how wise you'll feel when she figures out how you make your money.

She won't; I'll make sure of it.

Hugo would have cause to remember those words before too long.

Chapter 25

Hugo had to admit that the journey south with his two companions was both amusing and eye-opening. Although he'd not done a great deal of traveling himself, he had seen more of the country than Martha and Cailean combined.

Events and sights that he normally wouldn't have noticed—an overturned mail coach on the side of the road; a cow pasture filled with hundreds of long-legged white birds; and a village fair, complete with a traveling theatrical troop—all captivated his companions.

Although he'd hired a post chaise—an expenditure that had bothered his frugal wife—the trip had still been long and grueling.

Even his enthusiastic traveling companions were road-weary and exhausted when their carriage finally rolled into London five days later.

Hugo had enjoyed the journey, especially Martha and Cailean's innocent enjoyment, but his worries about London and what he'd find at Solange's had never been far from his mind.

But now that he was in London, and closer to discovering what happened with each mile, he couldn't help wishing that he was still back on Stroma.

Maybe they should just keep going. They could go to Dover, hop a packet, and explore the Continent for a few years. Now that the war was over, plenty of English people were traveling.

Hugo perked up at the thought. Why not? If they went someplace fresh and new, then Martha would never need to know about his past or what he did for a living. He wasn't wealthy, but he'd squirreled away enough in the bank to last a few years.

If Laura hadn't managed to somehow steal it.

Hugo gritted his teeth and thrust away the thought. Instead, he returned to the dream-tour of the Continent he'd just been building in his mind's eye.

One day the money will run out and then you will need to earn more.

His fairy tale image began to flicker and get ragged around the edges.

And you only know one way to make money.

The fantasy shimmered, and then dissipated like a puff of smoke.

There was no escape for a man like him—no running away from who he was. The unavoidable truth was that he could either own a whorehouse or he could work in one.

He needed to stay and fight for what was his. If he could regain control of Solange's then he wouldn't have to earn money on his back.

You can just earn it off other people's backs.

That was true, and Hugo refused to feel bad about it.

Instead of dwelling on Solange's, he forced himself to enjoy the last bit of their trip, watching Martha's expressive face as they traversed the city, the streets becoming cleaner, the houses bigger, and the people more affluent with every street they passed.

As they turned off David Street onto Berkeley Square, Martha's eyes threatened to roll out of her head. "My goodness," she breathed, cutting Hugo a quick glance. "Surely we aren't going to be staying—"

The carriage rolled to a gentle stop, cutting off her words.

She gawked out the window. "Who *are* these friends of yours, Hugo?"

Hugo just smiled.

The front door to Lady Selwood's monstrous house opened and Joss himself came trotting down the front steps.

Hugo hopped out of the carriage without bothering to lower the steps. "Jocelyn my dear boy!" He grabbed Joss's arm, which was the diameter of a full-grown tree, and pulled him away from the post chaise. "Not a word about my business or Solange's," he said through gritted teeth.

Joss, a man who was phlegmatic to the point of resembling a wooden carving rather than a human being, merely cocked one eyebrow and moved toward the carriage. He flipped down the steps while nodding to the postilion who'd dismounted to help unload the baggage. "My servants will take those," he said, sounding for all the world like a lord of the manor rather than a prizefighter-turned-whore-turned-groom.

Two liveried footmen scurried toward the carriage and began removing their few pieces of luggage.

A charming smile transformed Joss's harsh, almost brutal, features and he offered Martha a hand. "Hello, you must be Mrs. Buckingham."

Martha's cheeks were a fetching shade of pink as Joss handed her from the carriage. She was so blooming and pretty in her sky-blue traveling costume that Hugo could scarcely look at her without wanting to tear off her clothes and mark her as *his*.

The possessive impulse—one he'd experienced frequently over the past week—rocked him to his core, but he no longer tried to fight it.

"And you must be Mr. Gormley," Martha said, smiling in a way that exposed that sweet little dimple in her cheek. "Hugo has told me all about you."

Joss glanced at Hugo and chuckled. "Has he?"

"Only the good things, Joss. It took less than two minutes," Hugo couldn't resist adding.

"Hugo," Martha chided.

"This is Cailean Fergusson," Hugo said as the enormous young man climbed from the carriage, stretching and yawning.

Joss's eyes widened and Hugo smirked. He doubted that the huge man had to look up at another person very often.

"Welcome, Mr. Fergusson," Joss said, the title making Cailean blush just as wildly as Martha. Joss held out his arm to Martha. "May I have the honor?"

"Of course."

Hugo and Cailean followed them up the marble steps. A servant dressed in the dark, sedate garb of a butler stood on the landing, his expression reserved but welcoming.

"This is Butterbank," Joss said as they entered a foyer that could have held Martha's little cottage twice over. "I thought you might like to freshen first. We've brought dinner forward a bit as I'm sure you'll all be starving."

"Dinner before eight o'clock? How savage." Hugo smirked. "But thank you, we appreciated your thoughtfulness. You go with Butterbank," he told Martha, "I need to have a word with Joss, but I'll be right up."

She nodded, her eyes wide, as if she didn't want to miss even a bit of the splendor surrounding them.

Once they'd gone up the stairs, Hugo turned to Joss. "Melissa said you'd be gone by the time we arrived," he said rudely.

Joss gave him one of his opaque looks—the sort that had always gotten under Hugo's skin. "I apologize for still being in my own house, Hugo. Would you like to have this conversation in the foyer or perhaps we could go to my study?"

"Ooooh," Hugo mocked childishly. "Your *study*."

Joss turned on his heel and strode away without speaking.

Hugo had to trot to keep up with the towering man's stride. "Where are we going? You have your study on the ground floor?"

"No, but this way is faster, so we'll take the servant stairs."

"You're probably more comfortable using these, anyhow—aren't you?" Hugo taunted as they passed through a nondescript door into a narrow, functional stairwell.

"I can't tell you how much I've not missed you," Joss said as he climbed the steps with a grace that was unusual in a man so large.

"When are you leaving?" Hugo asked.

"Don't worry, I've booked passage on a packet on Wednesday."

Well, that was good, at least; he'd only have to put up with the insufferable man for a few days.

Once they reached the second floor, Joss led him down an elegant corridor. A maid came out of a room, spotted them, dropped a curtsey, and then scurried off toward the servant stairs.

It irked Hugo how quickly and easily Joss had adjusted to a life of wealth and luxury. Not only had he married one of the richest women in London—an American heiress who was also the widow of the Earl of Selwood—but his new wife was one of the most beautiful women Hugo had ever seen. He'd met Lady Selwood when she'd come to the female side of Solange's several years back.

Hugo had been within moments of getting the lovely countess naked when Joss had barged in and spoiled all his fun. Hugo suspected Joss still held a bit of a grudge over that near miss.

Joss opened a magnificent, intricately carved door and motioned Hugo into a room that took his breath away: vibrant jewel tone carpets, walls lined with books, heavy, comfortable leather furniture, and a fireplace large enough to roast an entire ox.

"Just what is it that you study in here, Joss old man?"

Joss ignored the question. "Something to drink?"

"I'll have whatever you're having."

"That almost tempts me to ingest poison," Joss murmured.

"Har har, you are as droll as ever."

Hugo inspected the magnificent landscape that hung over the fireplace while Joss dispensed their drinks. "What are you doing in London, anyhow?"

"Visiting my new niece and checking on several business matters for my wife."

Hugo accepted the crystal glass that Joss dwarfed with his huge hand and took a sip. "Very nice. So," he said, once they were both seated. "Have you gone to Solange's?"

"I did," Joss said.

Hugo heaved a sigh. "Are you going to make me pull the words out of you?"

"I saw Laura. I didn't tell her I'd heard from you—or about you, rather—I just asked her how things were."

"And?"

"I could see how things were," Joss admitted. He pinned Hugo with his disconcertingly sharp gaze. "I take it Melissa told you about Bev Davies."

Hugo gritted his teeth. "Yes, they're partners."

"Not any longer."

"What?"

"From what I could tell, she no longer owns any of it. She's just working there. Although I doubt she has many clients; she looks ill."

"I don't care if she's on death's bloody doorstep," Hugo snapped. "Are you telling me she lost the whole damned place to Bev—my half *and* hers?"

"It looks that way. Partnering up with the man who runs the worst gaming hells in the city isn't a wise decision for anyone, but especially not a woman of Laura's proclivities."

"She's on the gin again?" Hugo guessed.

"Yes."

"And Solange's? The employees?"

Joss's expression was grim. "Nobody looked happy. I've not been around the place in several years, so maybe that accounts for the lack of familiar faces, but I didn't know any of the servants. In fact, the only person I recognized was Laura."

There was only one reason to fire excellent servants, and that was to hire cheaper ones. Some of the servants had worked at Solange's for more than twenty years—employees that had been with the place through four different owners."

"Bastard," Hugo muttered. "That would be Davies's doing."

"The place already looks … well, it's only a few months but it looks down at heel."

Hugo wanted to yell. Instead, he asked a question he'd been dreading, "I know about Bev's other houses. Please tell me he hasn't begun to run virgins out of Solange's?"

"According to Laura they aren't."

"Do you believe her?"

"I don't know," Joss admitted. "What are you going to do, Hugo? You know how Davies is: he doesn't have partners. At least not for long. Laura is lucky that she's still among the living. I don't know what she told him about your half of the business, but I'd wager you won't be getting any money out of him."

Hugo swallowed down the bile that threatened to choke him. He knew Joss was right; now that Bev controlled the place, he would never let it go. He'd kill Hugo before giving up even a penny.

He turned his glass in his hand, gazing abstractedly at the liquid. Like every other Welshman in the city, Hugo had known Bev Davies all his life. Bev had started off as a pimp in St. Giles, quickly expanding his operations into the rest of the city over the next forty years. He now owned over a dozen brothels, gambling hells, and gin houses. If it was illegal, then Bev had a hand in it.

"What are you going to do?" Joss asked again.

"I'm not going to rush into anything. Right now I have an advantage in that Laura doesn't know I'm back—neither of them do."

Joss nodded. "Well, tell me if you need any help."

That offer surprised him. "Thank you." The words almost choked him. "I figure it will take some time to unravel this mess before I decide."

"You don't want to simply confront Laura?"

"The woman is a liar."

"She's in a bad way, now. Bev has put her to work—a full schedule."

Hugo wanted to feel malicious pleasure at the news that Laura was once again on her back, but all he felt was anger; the woman was too old to be doing such work. Not only would it be hard on her physically, but she wouldn't make much money: it was a sad but undeniable truth that most men didn't want old whores.

Hugo knew, without a doubt, that Bev would kick her out and she'd be working back alleys within a year or two.

He forbade himself from pitying her because all this mess was all her bloody fault.

Hugo and the Maiden

"Do you need money?" Joss said the words quickly, as if he thought Hugo would be offended.

Instead, Hugo was oddly touched by the other man's generosity. "I have some tucked away unless Laura managed to get into my bank account." He'd left more hidden in his suite of rooms at Solange's, but he doubted Laura had left that.

"Well, you can stay here as long as you want. Alicia wanted you to know you would be doing us a favor since an empty house always seems to fall apart faster."

"Please thank her for me," he said, for once managing to keep any snideness from his tone. The woman didn't even know him but seemed determined to show him kindness.

"She keeps a skeleton staff here no matter whether the place is empty or occupied, but please feel free to engage more servants if you need any."

"Even though she doesn't visit?"

"I suspect that she keeps it staffed just for my infrequent visits to see my sister and brothers. She hates England and will probably never come back." His lips quirked into a wry smile. "She claims she doesn't want to sell it because the current market is a poor one." He shrugged. "I don't argue since she's far smarter and more knowledgeable on such topics."

Hugo could hear the pride in Joss's voice as he boasted about his clever wife.

"I take it your wife knows nothing of what your plans are?" Joss asked.

"Neither of them do," he said sharply. "And I plan to keep it that way."

Joss gave a disbelieving laugh. "Good God, Hugo. How can you keep such a thing from her? Don't you think she will—"

"If I recall correctly, Joss, you weren't exactly in a big hurry to tell *your* wife about your past as a whore, either?"

"The situations couldn't be more different. First, I didn't marry Alicia without telling her the truth. Second, we weren't married while I worked at Solange's so I wasn't still doing that sort of work."

"I don't plan to *do that sort of work*, either," Hugo shot back.

Joss cocked his head, his expression quizzical.

"What?" Hugo demanded, even though he hadn't said anything. "You don't think I can just manage the place?" He snorted. "That's assuming I can even get back in the door without Bev killing me."

"I'm just wondering if your clients will allow you to *just manage*."

"They can hardly force me to fuck them, can they, Joss?"

"What will you do if a particular"—Joss coughed the words *royal duke*—"returns and demands your services?"

Hugo gritted his teeth. "I shall explain I have retired."

"And you think he will take *no* for an answer?"

"He will have to."

"That will be an interesting conversation."

The royal duke in question was a long-time client of Hugo's. The man didn't visit Hugo more than a few times a year, but when he did, he expected Hugo to drop everything—including his breeches—and obey his summons.

It had been a good six months since he'd last heard from his royal highness; the newspapers claimed he was somewhere on the Continent. Hopefully he would stay there. Maybe Hugo would be fortunate and could sort out this problem with throwing royalty into the mix.

He snorted, and then realized Joss was staring at him. "What now?"

"Even if you don't take clients, you'll still be—"

Hugo scowled. "It's none of your affair, Joss."

"I don't like you very much, Hugo—and I know you don't like me much either—"

"Something less than *much* and rapidly diminishing the more you pontificate."

"I'm not pontificating. I'm just pointing out that such a deception won't come without a cost. She seems an intelligent and lovely young woman and—"

"And you know nothing about her." Hugo set his glass down with a thump. "She's not a sophisticate like your wife—this sort of thing would ... well, it would crush her. Her father was a bloody vicar for Christ's sake!"

"And Mel's husband was a curate."

"I. Don't. Care." Hugo stood. "I appreciate you allowing us the use of your house, but if it comes with your advice attached, I'll summon a hackney and we can move to a hotel right bloody now."

Hugo and the Maiden

Joss raised his hands in a placating gesture. "Don't fly into a pucker, Hugo. Of course I won't say a word. But what if they ask me where it was that we worked together?"

"Cailean won't ask you a thing—the lad doesn't speak much. As for Martha, you can tell her that we met through Exchange business."

Joss laughed. "I don't know a thing about buying and selling stocks."

"Either does she, so she won't ask specifics."

"Do you plan on lying to her for the rest of your life?"

"If need be."

Joss sighed. "Fine, Hugo. Whatever you want. I just hope you know what you're doing."

So did Hugo.

Chapter 26

"Hello, Laura."

Laura's shriek was the most satisfying sound Hugo had heard in months.

She squirmed in Hugo's arms, but he held her easily while he shoved a rag into her mouth. He was shocked by how much weight she'd lost; holding her was like clutching an armload of hangers.

Once her cheeks were bulging with cloth Hugo grabbed both her wrists, lifted her arms, and then nodded to Kenny, who was standing nearby with a thick cloak.

They rolled her up like a rug and Hugo carried her into the decrepit old coach he'd hired. He lowered her onto the seat and sat beside her, holding her propped upright.

Kenny shut the door, climbed on back, and the wheels started rolling.

Hugo peeled back the cloak just enough so that he could see Laura's wide, red-rimmed gaze.

He clucked his tongue and carefully tucked some of her brittle blonde hair behind her ears. "Didn't expect to see me back here, did you?" Hugo smirked when she tried to speak around the mouthful of rag. "No, no, you don't need to talk just yet. There will be plenty of time for that shortly." He chuckled. "Someday—not tonight, of course—I will have to tell you about the lovely journey that I took thanks to you. But for now, just rest assured that I am back and going *nowhere*. You, however—but I've gotten ahead of myself. I've been watching you these past days and nights, darling, because I wanted to see the state of things at Solange's before we had our little chat."

Laura's eyes widened and she began making noises.

"What I learned surprised me—and not a pleasant surprise, either. It appears you've gambled away not only your half of the business, but also managed to transfer my half to Bev Davies—a man whose hobbies include torturing and killing people. It seems like the only way I'll ever work at Solange's again will be on my bloody back."

Two fat tears slid down her cheeks, which only infuriated Hugo more.

Hugo and the Maiden

"Fifteen years of hard work gone without a trace. Well done, you sodding bitch." Hugo shoved her away. He'd never struck a woman before and he'd be damned if he allowed Laura to drag him down any further.

They rode for a while in silence while Hugo glared out the window into the London night and struggled to get himself under control.

When the carriage slid to a halt a quarter of an hour later, he was almost calm. He turned back to Laura, who was quietly sobbing behind her gag.

Hugo experienced a pang of remorse.

And then instantly wanted to punch himself in the face.

How dare you feel sorry for this gin-soaked, card-obsessed, duplicitous slattern? he demanded of himself, giving vent to a muffled growl of fury before he flung open the carriage door.

The air stank of rotting fish and the eye-watering stench of the Thames at low tide.

"Carry her inside," Hugo told Kenny as he navigated the buckled cobblestone, passing below a tattered wooden sign proclaiming: *Drunken Duck Tavern, Est. 1687.*

The front door swung open before Hugo reached it, exposing an almost painfully handsome young man named Daniel Charters. Like Kenny, he'd also worked at Solange's before Laura had sacked him and a dozen other servants in her quest to save money.

"Everything is ready, Mr. Hugo."

"Thank you, Daniel."

The inn had been one of the busier hostelries on the water for decades but had closed when the silt made this part of the river inaccessible to big ships. The owner had been pitifully grateful to rent the derelict building to Hugo for a few nights, no questions asked.

Only one of the inn rooms on the second floor was lighted and Hugo went inside, pleased to see that Daniel had covered the window as he'd asked.

Hugo had been tempted to throw Laura into Newgate—naked, as she'd done to him—and let her kick her heels in some true squalor and misery, but the deciding factor had been his aversion to visiting the rancid jail in order to speak to her.

"Put her on the pallet," he told Kenny.

The moment the giant man put Laura down she began to thrash. Hugo leaned against the wall, crossed his arms, and waited for her to free herself from the cloak.

Once she'd done so she pulled the rag out of her mouth and pressed her back against the wall, her blood-shot eyes darting from Hugo to Kenny to Daniel like a cornered animal.

"If not for me you'd be dead," she said, her voice hoarse from screaming into the gag. "He wanted—"

"Shut up," he said, more than a little surprised when she obeyed. He jerked his head at Daniel. "Daniel had some very interesting things to tell me."

She scowled at the gorgeous young footman. Hugo knew for a fact that Daniel didn't swing toward the ladies so that must have doomed him as far as Laura was concerned.

"You can't believe him, Hugo. He's just angry I fired him."

"Because *you* sold the bloody place to a bastard too cheap to pay a decent wage, you gin-soaked, worn-out slattern," Daniel shot back.

Laura opened her mouth to argue.

"Shut up, Laura," Hugo said again. "You should be grateful that you're here in this filthy little room and not floating in the Thames, locked in Newgate, or currently headed toward warmer climes" He narrowed his eyes. "Now, tell me *how much*? How much did it cost for Bev to get his hands on my bloody business?"

Laura caught her lower lip in her teeth. "I don't know exactly—"

"An estimate."

Laura named an amount.

"Holy fuck!" Hugo yelled. He felt as if every nightmare he'd experienced in his entire life had returned all at once. "Are you bloody mad? How in the name of hell did you manage to lose so much?"

Tears slid down her ravaged cheeks. "He let me punt on tick, didn't he? And before I knew it ..." Her shoulders sagged. "At first he just said he'd take payments. But there was interest, too. I gave him almost *everything* and it still wasn't enough. And ... and—"

"And you continued to visit his gaming hells?" Hugo guessed.

She shrugged.

"He wanted you to keep playing, didn't he."

She didn't need to answer.

"So once you were over your head he gave you the option of getting rid of me and then signing over the business?"

Hugo and the Maiden

She chewed her chapped, peeling lip and cut him a quick, sly glance.

Hugo pointed at her. "Don't lie to me, Laura. Because if I learn you've lied—"

"It was Cowan's idea to get your half."

Hugo gave an ugly laugh. "You mean he was faking the grand passion he claimed he felt for you?"

"Yes, he used me!" Her face twisted into a scowl. "Does that make you happy?"

"As a matter of fact, it does a bit. So, the dumb bastard thought you'd be able to sell the place if I wasn't around, eh? It must have come as quite a shock to him when he learned you were in debt up to your neck."

"It's worse than that."

"What do you mean?"

"He's one of Bev's bastards."

"So what? That's not exactly rare. I understand Bev's got more brats running around the rookeries than that bloke from the Bible."

"It turns out that Bev is makin' noises about getting' old," Laura said. "He's talking about choosing an heir and he'll pick the one who impresses him the most."

"Ah," Hugo said, comprehension dawning. "Solange's would be quite a prize for Cowan to bring home to dear old Da." He studied her miserable face. "But you didn't know about any of that, did you?"

"No. At least not until—well, not until after it was done."

"You bloody fool."

Laura didn't bother to deny it.

Go on," he ordered.

"Cowan said that if I could get rid of you, he knew a forger who could help with the deed. He said once it was all mine then I could sell the place, pay off the money to Bev—with some left over—and we could get married. He said that he earned enough from his work with Bev that I never needed to work again."

"I'm guessing it wasn't Cowan's plan to have me arrested?"

"No, he wanted you dead." She locked eyes with him. "I went behind his back and arranged this with a bloke I knew. I couldn't do it, Hugo. I couldn't have you killed."

"I'm touched. Finish the story."

"Things didn't go the way Cowan said."

Hugo gave a bitter laugh.

"The forger didn't fix all the documents in my name, he used Bev's." Her face twitched, her eyes haunted. "When I found out, I tracked Cowan down. He laughed at me—the things he said—" She choked on a sob. "I threatened to tell and—and—" She swallowed convulsively. "He beat me so hard I pissed blood for a week."

Hugo shook his head in disgust.

"So you were gone, Bev owned your half with nobody to dispute it, and I still owed him all that money. I signed over my half two days later."

"How could you be so bloody stupid, Laura? Didn't you think—"

"I thought Cowan loved me!" Her words echoed in the dank room. "I thought maybe I'd finally gotten lucky. Why not—it wasn't as if Cowan were anything special. Melissa married a bloody lord and got out of the business—both her and Joss married into the aristocracy. Was I asking too much to marry the bastard son of a criminal?" She pinioned Hugo with her ravaged gaze. "Was I?"

Hugo gritted his teeth against the pity that stabbed at him. She deserved *nothing* from him but scorched earth retribution.

Based on what he'd observed the past few nights as he'd skulked around Solange's their clients had already begun to scatter. It was physically painful to see the business he had poured his life into—for years—falling apart.

And all because of *her*.

He sneered. "So now you work for him?"

"I only work two nights a week and he lets me live there, although I had to move into a smaller room. He said he'll let me stay as long as I pull my weight."

Which, judging by her sickly pallor, significant tremors, and the bones pressing against her grayish skin, wouldn't be long.

He shoved his hand into his hair and pulled until his eyes watered. Christ. His head was bloody spinning. What, in the name of God, could he do to salvage any of this?

"Hugo?"

"What?" He had to force himself to look at her.

"If Bev learns you're back, um, well—"

"Why do you think I haven't just strolled into Solange's?" Hugo snorted. "Of course, I didn't have any idea of the extent to which I was fucked until talking to you, sweetheart."

Laura's pale cheeks flushed slightly, making her look like a feverish corpse.

"Do you know the name of the man who forged my name?" he asked.

She swallowed and then nodded again. "But if you put me in front of a judge, I'll say it was you that signed it, Hugo." She gave a slightly hysterical laugh. "I'd not survive the day if I ever tried to drag Bev or one of his men into a courtroom. Even if he didn't kill me, I'd never survive a journey in the belly of a convict ship."

She was right on both counts.

Hugo had to clench his hands behind his back to keep from grabbing and shaking her. "In my room there was a—"

"Strongbox under the floorboards," she finished. "I took it. I'm sorry," she said, dully.

Hugo closed his eyes and clenched his teeth against the impotent rage threatening to boil over. He'd kept five hundred pounds in banknotes tucked away in that box, not to mention a great deal of jewelry and other valuables—all of which he'd hidden close at hand in case of an emergency. Gone. All of it gone. He laughed weakly and opened his eyes to find Laura staring.

"What are you going to do, Hugo?"

"I have no bloody idea."

Chapter 27

Martha was dreaming that she lived in a house with over one hundred cats.

"Darling?" one of the cats said.

A warm hand slid over her belly, the touch jolting her awake. She opened her eyes to find Hugo smiling down at her.

"Let's take this off, Martha. Sit up a bit, love."

Her body responded even though her brain was still half-asleep. "I was having the strangest dream," she said, lifting first her hips and then her arms as he raised the nightgown over her head.

He shrugged off his robe and it slithered to the floor with a soft *hiss*. Martha had left a candle burning on a table by the door and it was the only light illuminating the huge bedchamber. She wished that he'd lighted more; as immodest as it was, she adored looking at him when they made love.

"What was your dream about?" he asked as he climbed the padded stepladder they needed for the high bed.

"I dreamed that I lived in a house with over one hundred cats."

Hugo chuckled, the sound low and sensual. "Maybe that was a premonition; I'd say Cailean is moving in that direction. Spread your thighs for me, sweetheart."

Martha instantly complied, her sex already pulsing at the thought of what he was about to do.

He stroked up her thighs, his fingers grazing her mound. "I missed you today," he said, his voice oddly tight.

Martha pushed up onto her elbows, trying to see his face. "Is everything all right, Hugo?" The candle was behind him, casting his face into shadow. He didn't sound ... right.

"Everything is fine, darling." Hugo pushed her legs wider and pinioned her thighs with his forearms before opening her. He made a low growling sound. "More than fine," he murmured.

And then he proceeded to tease orgasm after orgasm from her body.

Somewhere around the fourth or fifth, Martha grabbed his hair, needing to yank hard to stop him. "Hugo."

He allowed her to pull his head back, but he still stroked her swollen lips with his fingers. "What?" he all but snarled.

Martha couldn't see his face, but she could feel his glare.

"What is wrong?"

"*Nothing* is wrong." He thrust two fingers into her and scissored them.

Martha cried out at the stretch exquisite, her hips bucking for more.

"Am I not giving you pleasure, Martha?"

"Of course you are giving me pleasure, but …"

"But what?" He began to pump her with deep, deliberate thrusts.

"But—" Martha gasped as his finger touched something exquisitely sensitive inside her.

"You're so beautiful and responsive, Martha. It makes me happy to give you pleasure—to give you orgasms. Please, let me make us both happy."

Martha wanted to tell him to stop—she wanted to know what was bothering him—but his mastery over her body was greater than her selfish desire for more.

He added a third finger, driving into her harder. Her hips lifted to meet each thrust and take him deeper. The sensation within her was subtly different than any other she'd experienced—more visceral and slower to build.

Martha bit her lower lip, but she couldn't restrain the keening, primitive noises pouring from her mouth as he relentlessly drove her toward bliss.

"Let me hear you," he ground out, his breathing hard from the sheer physicality of what he was doing to her. "Don't hold back. Scream and yell; come apart for me."

His words were the last straw and she shattered.

"Yessss," he hissed as she spiraled out of control. "Come for your husband, darling."

Martha lost track of time and was lazily drifting in a haze of pleasure when Hugo gently turned her onto her stomach and then lifted her onto all fours. "Up on your hands and knees for me, sweetheart."

Once she'd complied he shoved her legs wider with his knee. "So beautiful." His voice was almost feverish, but his hands were as steady and commanding as ever. "Rest your head and shoulders on the bed for me," he said, gently pressing her down. "Yes, just like that."

He had never taken her this way before—the way animals mated—and it felt wicked and primal to be so open and exposed to him.

"I wish you could see yourself, Martha," he said, as if reading her mind. "You are entrancing." He stroked the slick folds of her sex, his caresses almost hypnotic. "I ache for you, lover."

Martha shivered at both his words and the sheer carnality of her pose. He probed her with the tip of one finger and her back arched as she shamelessly thrust her bottom against him, her knees spreading wider, her hips tilting.

He chuckled darkly. "Such a needy little thing, aren't you?"

Martha wanted what he was offering too badly to care about her pride or modesty. "Yes, Hugo, I'm needy—for you."

He pushed his thumb inside her and stroked something that made her whimper.

"Mmm. So tight and wet and ready to be filled."

Her body clenched at his filthy words and he growled his approval before replacing his thumb with something far thicker and hotter. "I love this so much, Martha." He sounded almost … anguished. "I want you to know," he said, entering her with only his crown and gently pulsing his hips so that he breached her over and over, "that I have never felt this way with any other lover."

Pleasure and jealousy swirled in her belly at his words. She loved that she was special to him, but she hated the thought of him doing this with others.

He caressed her hips as he stroked deeper, but still not deep enough. The rush of desire she felt for him—to be taken and dominated by his far larger and stronger body—shocked her. Later, when she wasn't in the grip of passion, the violence of her emotions would worry her. But right now, she needed him with a hunger that threatened to consume her.

"Please, Hugo."

He hilted himself with one long, hard thrust.

Martha sucked in a harsh breath at the depth of his penetration.

"It feels different this way, doesn't it?" He stroked from her waist to her shoulders, the caress emphasizing her bowed, submissive

Hugo and the Maiden

position as he kept her stretched and full. "Deeper and more ... primitive."

He was right on both counts. And even though the pleasure bordered on pain, Martha loved it and needed more.

"I'm going to be selfish and take you now," he warned. "Hard and fast."

Martha thought about the multiple climaxes he'd just wrung from her body and wondered at his definition of *selfish*.

"Tell me you want it," he asked as he withdrew slowly, inch by inch. "Beg for it."

"Please, Hugo, I want—"

Her words were the proverbial match to a fuse. "Take it," he grated, slamming into her hard enough to move her up the bed.

Martha groaned. "More, please."

"Take it all," he growled, giving her his full length with each savage stroke.

His hips drummed faster, harder, his grunts and snarls becoming maddened as he claimed her over and over and over again. By now they'd made love so often—often three or four times a night—that she knew the signs of his impending crisis.

His thrusting became wilder and less controlled. "Martha—I need—" His fingers gripped her hard enough that she would have bruises tomorrow. "I need—" And then he shouted her name and buried himself, his body jerking with each jet of hot seed.

She closed her eyes and reveled in his primal claiming.

The spasms gradually diminished and came farther and farther apart, until he was still. And then he sighed deeply and relaxed.

Martha slid forward, until she was lying on her stomach, with Hugo sprawled on top of her. He was heavy, but not unpleasantly so. The hard, sweaty muscles of his stomach and chest molded against her back and his shaft was still buried inside her, half-erect.

It was ... heaven.

He shifted slightly, exhaled—the sound one of profound contentment—and then became boneless with sleep.

"Hugo?" she whispered.

He didn't so much as twitch.

Martha couldn't help smiling, even though she was more than a bit unnerved by his almost frenzied behavior. He was always an energetic lover—also vulgar and without shame—but he'd never been so frantic before.

Something had happened to him today. Not that Martha could have any idea *what* as she had barely seen him during the daylight hours since their arrival in London a week ago.

He disappeared every morning before she woke and only returned home after she'd gone to bed, slipping in beside her while she slept and waking her with his skilled, passionate lovemaking.

"I'm sorry, darling," he'd said the third night, after she'd asked if he would ever eat dinner with her again. "Things should slow down … soon."

"Have you met with your business partner?" She wanted to ask the woman's name, but decided it was not her affair. If he wanted her to know, he would tell her.

"Not yet, but soon. I promise you it won't always be this way. Why don't you and Cailean explore together, for now, and then next week I'll engage a leasing agent to show us some properties?"

For the first few days Martha and Cailean had occupied themselves discovering London, walking for miles and visiting historical sites that she had never imagined she would get to see in real life.

But two days ago, when she'd gone down to breakfast, she'd learned from Richard the footman that Cailean had left even before Hugo that morning.

Martha had been beside herself with worry until Cailean returned before dinner, clutching a filthy, battered, and bleeding cat. Martha loved animals—all animals—but the mangy feline had a face that only its mother—or Cailean—could love.

It was missing half of one ear from an old injury and the bend in one of its back legs wasn't quite right. Most daunting was its entirely white right eye, which seemed to look right into Martha's soul as she helped Cailean bathe the beast.

She had never bathed a cat before and would never do so again. Her arms looked as though she'd climbed through a dozen rose bushes. Cailean, who'd borne the brunt of the cat's ire, looked even worse.

Once the animal was free of grime, its coat was actually an attractive black and gray tortoiseshell. But that was the only attractive thing about it.

Hugo and the Maiden

Butterbank had located a small medicine chest and Martha had tended to the poor creature's injuries.

Clean, dry, and full of milk and a bit of liver, the cat had slept soundly in front of the kitchen hearth. Not until the following day had she learned that Cailean had slept right beside her.

Any ambivalence Cook or Butterbank might have had about the new addition to the kitchen—whom Cailean dubbed Maggie—dissipated when Maggie presented Cook with an obviously well-fed rat.

After the cat incident Martha had asked Hugo to have a talk with the younger man and make sure he wasn't venturing into dangerous parts of the city. No matter how huge he was, he was still a gentle, kind lad who wouldn't hurt a fly. Martha could not be comfortable thinking about him exploring some of the parts of London that she'd seen from the window of a hackney.

Remarkably, Cailean was transfixed, rather than daunted, by the size and complexity of the city. Indeed, he seemed almost at home.

So, the only one of the three of them who had nothing to occupy them was Martha.

In addition to the housekeeper, there were at least a half-dozen maids—for the kitchen, the bedchambers, the common areas—a footman, the butler, and even a cook.

They'd been married almost two weeks and she'd never even cooked Hugo a meal! It just didn't feel right.

Never had Martha believed that she could become bored with too much leisure time and too many books. It seemed profoundly ungrateful to admit that—even in the privacy of her own head—but it was true.

Martha sighed and closed her eyes, even though she wasn't in a hurry to go to sleep and wake up alone again tomorrow morning.

Not surprisingly, rest eluded her.

It wasn't until the early hours of the morning that she finally identified the emotion that had emanated from Hugo in almost suffocating waves: it had been despair.

Chapter 28

Bevan Davies sat behind the desk that used to be Hugo's, his big feet propped up on one corner.

He was of middling height, his build whipcord lean, like Hugo's.

He was not a handsome man, but his craggy face was strangely compelling. He almost always smiled, although it never reached his dark brown eyes. Hugo estimated his age to be somewhere around sixty, although he had lived a hard life and probably looked older.

Bev had spun such a web of lies around his origins that nobody knew when he'd first arrived in London. His accent was still Welsh, but with a big helping of St. Giles thrown in for good measure.

Being Welsh and growing up in St. Giles meant that Hugo had known of Bev Davies from an early age. He even recalled the man coming to the pitiful shack his parents had called home. His father had bowed and scraped whenever Bev visited, but his eyes had glittered with hatred after Bev's visits.

"Bev Davies is a worse friend than enemy," Hugo recalled him saying to one of Hugo's elder brothers.

After Hugo's father sold him to Mr. Caton—who'd taken him away from St. Giles—Hugo hadn't seen Bev for several years.

He'd been eighteen when he next ran into him. At the time Hugo had been working in a birching house which Bev had systematically destroyed before purchasing for a greatly reduced sum. He'd asked Hugo to continue working for him after he'd taken over the business.

Finding the right words to decline Bev's offer—and not end up face down in the muck—had been one of the most nerve-racking experiences of Hugo's young life.

And here he was, tangled up with Bev all over again, but for far larger stakes.

"Well, well, well. If it ain't Mr. Hugo Buckingham. I was wondering when you'd come to see me."

Bev's lack of surprise greatly displeased him. While Hugo hadn't hidden his presence in London, he'd not advertised it, either. And he'd

Hugo and the Maiden

not yet released Laura, so Bev's source of information had been somebody else.

No, he didn't like that one bit.

"Hello, Bev," Hugo said. He had to look up since somebody had sawed a good six inches off the chair legs.

"Drink?" Bev gestured to a bottle and two none-too-clean glasses beside it.

It was only eight in the morning.

"Thank you," Hugo said. No reason to antagonize the man by rejecting his offer of hospitality, no matter how spurious.

Bev poured the liquor and then shoved the glass across the desktop, spilling some and forcing Hugo to stand and fetch the glass.

"Thank you," he said, feigning a drink, his nostrils burning at the harsh smell of cheap brandy.

"What can I do for you?" Bev grinned, the expression knowing. "If you're here to talk to your old partner I'm afraid I haven't seen her in a few days. It seems she took an urgent trip ... somewhere."

So, he'd guessed that Hugo had taken Laura. Well, no surprise, there.

"No, I'm here to talk to you. I wanted to tell you that I never signed the papers for the sale of my half of the business." He had decided on the bold, suicidal approach on his way over this morning.

Bev's black bushy eyebrows shot up. "I'm confused. Are you saying that Laura forged your signature?"

"That's exactly what I'm saying."

"How was I supposed to know that?"

"I don't think you did," Hugo prudently lied. "But, if I were to take the matter before a magistrate, I can prove that I was abducted and tried in a false court so that Laura could gain control of my half of the business, not to mention significant personal assets that were seized from my rooms here."

"Hmm." Bev rocked back on two legs of his chair, his expression one of exaggerated concern. "That's quite a tale. And you say you can prove this?"

"Yes."

Bev let his chair fall with a loud *thump,* his smile ... unfriendly. "Why do I feel like you're threatening me, Hugo?"

"I'm only telling you that we were both victims of Laura." *And your scheming son, all with your knowledge and encouragement, no doubt.*

Hugo wisely left out that part.

"I *will* pursue this matter through legal means. Or ..." Hugo hesitated.

"Or?"

"Or we can make some sort of arrangement."

Bev stared hard enough to burn holes through his head.

And then he threw his head back and laughed.

And laughed.

Hugo couldn't help the slight shiver he experienced at the other man's reaction.

Bev owned a half-dozen brothels—and now Hugo had an idea how he'd accumulated so many—but they were the sort of places where a man would go in with a hard cock and come away with a case of crab lice. At best.

Solange's was ... well, it was so different from the bawd houses that Davies ran as to constitute a different species, entirely.

Was Hugo insane to be here today, confronting Bev head-on, using his suspicions as a bargaining chip?

Probably. But what else did he have left? If he couldn't regain his stake in this business his options were grim. He could pursue the matter in the courts, but that would take time and Bev would bleed him of money—if he didn't actually bleed him of blood—and there would be nothing left of Solange's if he ever did get his hands on it.

Or he could sup with the Devil.

Bev leaned back in his chair after he'd caught his breath and said, "Did I ever tell you I offered to buy you from your pa?"

Hugo could only stare.

Davies smirked. "Aye, yer ma worked for me in my very first house." He chuckled at Hugo's shocked look. "Flora was a prime article in her day. Yer pa met her when he came to work for me. And then he stole her away."

Hugo wasn't sure he believed the man. His parents had worked in a brothel? His mother had died when he was thirteen and his father had sold him soon after—not that he'd ever exchanged more than a dozen words with his father in all his years. In truth, he knew nothing about his parents. Besides, why would Bev lie?

"Er, what kind of work did my father do for you?"

Hugo and the Maiden

"He wasn't a whore, if that's what you're thinkin'. No, Evan Dinwiddy were a tough lad but he weren't a pretty one." Bev's eyes crawled over Hugo like insects. "Not like you."

Hugo thought Bev must be the only man or woman in the entire city who would call him *pretty*. He somehow doubted the other man's regard for him would do him any good.

"No, he didn't look like you, but then Evan weren't yer da."

Hugo had always suspected that. "Do you know who was?" he asked, not that he cared.

"Coulda been almost anyone since she was workin' at McBride's when she fell pregnant."

McBride's was an Irish brothel that was neither the best nor worst of its kind.

"In fact," Bev said with a sly grin. "You might even be mine. Flora was past it by then, but I plowed her a time or two for old time's sake."

Hugo squeezed the arms of his chair rather than fly across the desk and squeeze Bev's neck.

Bev smirked, as if he knew what Hugo was thinking. "Evan liked to ride his high horse, but he never could put bread on the table. He weren't above whorin' out his wife—although she had to go all the way to McBride's to ply her trade so's nobody in the old neighborhood would know." His dark eyes glinted. "He wasn't above whorin' a boy he'd raised as his own son, neither. Though he waited until after yer mam died to do that, dint 'ee?"

Hugo hadn't believed that an old wound could still cause him such pain.

He'd been wrong.

"Why did you want to buy me?"

Bev grinned.

Hugo recoiled. "Christ. Even though I might be your son?"

Bev's grin just broadened. "You were a right temptin' morsel back then, Hugo. I was willin' to risk my immortal soul for a taste."

Hugo felt like throwing up.

Bev shrugged. "But Evan refused. He claimed it was 'cause he didn't want that life for any of youse. But I know the real reason was that he hated my guts because I had yer mam first and she always did fancy me more." He gave a bawdy laugh. "I woulda paid more than that old whip maker for you, but Evan Dinwiddy had a head like a fuckin' brick." He cocked his head at Hugo. "What about you, eh? You got a brick for a brain, too, Hugo?"

"I must have to have taken Laura Maitland as a partner."

Davies found that amusing. "Aye. Never do business with women, that's one o' my rules." He gave Hugo a mocking look. "Another is never do business with anyone who's got the fever. And that's Laura."

"I thought it was only for gin, I didn't realize the extent of the gambling."

"That sounds like an oversight on your part, mab."

Hugo knew he was right; he was no crime lord like Bev. All he knew about was fucking and running whores.

"You used the word *were* when you mentioned my father. Is he dead?"

"Aye, he went in that spate o' typhus six or seven years back." He scratched his head, his expression reflective. "Seems two or three of your brothers went off to war, one got transported," he chuckled, "for real, that was. Your sister Nell died not long after Evan sold you. Moira and Susan came to work for me." He shrugged. "But they've been gone some years now. I couldn't say where any of them are."

That was just as well. The last thing he wanted was a family reunion.

"But you didn't come here to reminisce, now did ye?"

"No."

Davies waved a hand around the room. "I've wanted this place for decades. Since before you were breeched." He chewed the inside of his cheek, his expression ... bemused. "And now I got it."

"I can't help noticing that you don't look very happy about that."

Bev pushed out his lower lip. "Naw, I ain't. You see, I ain't never lost money before."

"Solange's is losing money?" It hadn't in all the years Hugo had worked there.

"Aye." Bev's jaw shifted from side to side as if he were chewing on something tough and gristly. He gave Hugo a look that made all the hairs on his body stand up. "I don't like losin' money, mab."

And Hugo didn't like Bev calling him *mab*, the Welsh word for son, but he kept that to himself. "No, I can imagine."

"I don't like ... failure."

Hugo waited quietly.

Hugo and the Maiden

He scowled. "I can't seem to keep these high steppin' punters."

Hugo wanted to suggest that the way to keep wealthy clients was not to extort them, but he doubted that would go over well.

"I can see what you're thinkin'," Bev said, smirking. "And you're right. I was plannin' on squeezin' a few of 'em. But only those with stacks o' vowels in my bloody safe."

Yet another reason Hugo wanted to strangle Laura, who'd insisted they extend ridiculous credit to several of their customers, amounts the men would never be able to repay. He'd considered extorting those bastards himself.

Bev swung his feet back onto his desk. "I've always had a soft spot for ye, Hugo. Why, you might be my own blood, after all."

Hugo hoped he hid just how disturbing he found that.

Bev grinned, exposing more than one black stump. "And that's why I'm gonna make you an offer."

Bloody hell. Here we go.

Hugo forced a smile. "I'm all ears, Bev."

Chapter 29

Martha was in the bookroom when Hugo returned from his meeting with Bev.

He had not come directly from Solange's but had made a few stops along the way.

He paused a moment just inside the door to admire her. She was curled up on the window seat, so enrapt by whatever she was reading that she didn't even hear him enter. She wore a dark blue wool dress with a fluffy cream-colored shawl draped over her shoulders, the color remarkably close to that of her hair.

The gown wasn't especially fashionable—it was one of the few he'd bought for her in Wick—but the severe color and prim cut were the perfect foil for her fair coloring. He swallowed as he drank in the sight of her. Today he had secured their future. It would be a long, difficult year ahead, but at the end of it he would regain his half and would immediately turn around and sell it and get out from under a business that he no longer really wished to operate. It wouldn't be enough money to last the rest of their lives but should last for a good, long time.

But all that was still far away. A year of managing Bev—not just Solange's—stood between him and freedom.

Did it infuriate him that he'd struck a bargain with the very same man who'd defrauded him in the first place?

Yes.

But other than a long, expensive court case that he likely wouldn't survive, he could think of no other way to recoup his investment.

If there was one thing he'd learned in life, it was not to rail against the impossible.

Solange's, under Bev's management, was hemorrhaging money at an alarming rate. Hugo was confident that he could not only halt the flow but reverse it.

He had made his deal, and now he wanted to celebrate his future with the only person he was interested in spending it with.

"Good evening, darling."

Hugo and the Maiden

Martha's head jerked up and she immediately smiled, her blue eyes lighting up for him in a way that nobody else's ever had. It was more intoxicating than a glass of the finest brandy.

"You're home early." She glanced out the window. "It's still daylight."

As he strode toward her, her eyes dropped to the huge box in his hands.

"From now on I'll be able to adhere to a much more reasonable schedule, sweetheart." He set the big pink box on her lap.

"What's this?"

"It's for you."

"Oh, Hugo, you've already bought me too—"

"Shhh, I bought this for me. Open it," he ordered.

Her fingers shook as she lifted the lid and pushed back the layers of tissue paper.

She gasped and looked up at him as she lifted the gown from the box. "It's the most beautiful thing I've ever seen. But—but wherever will I wear it?"

"You'll wear it tonight when we go to the theater. But first, we shall go out to dinner, and I know just the place."

Her gaze flickered from the yards and yards of pale-yellow silk in her hands to Hugo. "Really?"

He grinned at her enthusiasm. "Really."

She frowned.

"What is it?"

"It's just that I'd like Cailean to come—he's never seen a play."

"Of course he can come, darling."

"But I've not seen him all day; he's taken to drifting in right before dinner.

Hugo didn't like the sound of that. "I'll talk to him and mention he should be home at a more reasonable hour." Just listen to him—he sounded like a pillock.

No, you sound like a father.

Hugo ignored the startling thought and said, "If he shows up in time, splendid. If not, then tonight will be just for the two of us." He gave her a long, lingering kiss. "And this is only the first of many evenings, Martha. I shall be able to spend more time with you and Cailean." He kissed her again. "Things are going to change from now on—for the better."

***

The days sped by with alarming speed and before Martha knew it, more than a month had slipped away and they were still living in Lady Selwood's house.

Guilt ate at her. Other than the few hours she spent working on reading and writing with Cailean—he was turning out to be a veritable wizard at both—her only real duty was to find a house to lease, and she'd not done so.

Hugo worked all day, and even some evenings, so he'd entrusted her with finding their new accommodations.

But it was an enormous responsibility, and she didn't want to choose unwisely and burden Hugo with a house he disliked, even though he claimed he would like whatever she chose.

But it was time—past time—to make a decision.

Martha looked up from her list of possible houses and glanced across at Hugo, who was reading the newspaper. It was just her and her husband in the breakfast room since Cailean had gone out at first light—as usual—although he'd been much better at coming home at a reasonable hour.

Husband. Even though they'd been married for almost six weeks the word still sounded exotic.

Her husband *looked* exotic, too.

Unlike all the businessmen she'd seen on her trips around the city, Hugo garbed himself almost entirely in black—black skin-tight pantaloons, black linen, and glossy black hessians that even had black tassels.

Martha had been startled the first time he'd come down to breakfast so uniquely accoutered. Surprisingly, she adored his somber wardrobe, which made his rather stark features look stern, dangerous, and mysterious.

Love, pride, and desire welled up in her as she stared across the table at him. Her love for him was so overpowering that she felt a sharp prickling behind her eyes.

Hugo looked up and smiled. "You are giving me a quizzical look … wife." His eyelids lowered slightly at that last word, reminding her of how he'd looked last night in bed: wild and sensual as he'd managed to shock and please her.

Her cheeks heated. "I'm just thinking about what I have planned for the day," she fibbed.

Hugo and the Maiden

"And what is on your schedule?"

"Mr. Duncan will be here around one and he has two more houses for me to look at."

"Ah, how is the search going?"

"I think I have it narrowed down to three houses, unless one of these today is better." She wanted to pick a house that wasn't just comfortable and convenient to the Exchange, but also close to a church where she felt at home. The closest church to Lady Selwood's house felt more like Rotten Row than a religious sanctuary. Most of the congregants paid more attention to what their neighbor was wearing than what the vicar was saying. And the vicar and his wife had dressed as luxuriously as their wealthy parishioners.

She'd found the entire experience disheartening. Especially when she'd seen the effect of the scene on Hugo, who had come to church with her for the very first time just this past week.

Although he'd been visibly amused watching the crowd, she'd seen the cynicism in his dark gaze. Martha could only hope that he would trust her enough to attend another service at the tiny church she'd recently discovered.

"When shall we go look at them?" Hugo asked.

"Hmm?"

"The houses," he gently reminded her.

"Oh, you will come look at them with me?"

"Of course, I will, sweetheart."

"I can ask Mr. Duncan if he can arrange for us to go tomorrow, if that is suitable?"

He reached across the table and took her hand. "Imminently, darling."

Martha loved it when he called her that. Or sweetheart. Or love, or any of a dozen pet names he used on her.

"I hope your family isn't holding off on visiting until I find a suitable house, Hugo. Lady Selwood wrote me the most delightful letter assuring me that I should treat this as our home. I will feel much more comfortable inviting them to have nice long visits with us when we are in our own home, but surely they may come and stay at least a little while? How you must miss them."

"I don't miss them nearly as much now that I have you, Mrs. Buckingham."

She hesitated.

"What is it, sweetheart?"

"I hate to be a pest, but now that you have finished sorting out matters with your ex-partner—" Martha couldn't help scowling at the thought of the woman who'd tried to have Hugo sent away for seven years and attempted to steal the property they jointly owned. Rather than seek prosecution, Hugo had generously allowed the woman to go free after she'd signed over the requisite papers. Martha knew she should be proud of him for such Christian kindness, but she believed the woman deserved suitable punishment for her criminally dangerous actions.

"Yes, my dear?" Hugo prodded.

"Oh, I was wondering if you happened to write to any of your siblings? I know you said only Susan and Johnny ever come to London. Is there any chance either of them might be visiting? Would you like me to write them and extend invitations?"

"Er, as a matter of fact, I got letters from both Susan and Johnny just a few days ago."

She frowned. "I didn't see them come in with the mail."

"They came to my office. I thought it best to use that address as we won't be staying here permanently."

"Ah, that makes sense. Now you need to remind me: Johnny—he's only a little older than you?"

"Yes, just a year." He paused and then said, "I'm afraid Susan is in a delicate condition, so she won't be traveling. She passed along her love and said she is eager to meet you."

"Might I write a letter to her?"

"Of course. How kind of you, darling. Once you've written it, I'll put it with mine."

"And Johnny?" she asked. "You invited him, as well?"

"Yes. He … er, he'll be here next week."

Martha clapped her hands. "Oh, Hugo! You wretch—you were keeping this to surprise me."

"Yes, it was a surprise," he said.

"Will he be staying long? Which rooms shall I put him in? Should I—"

"He's only here for a day, I'm afraid—not even overnight."

"Just one day? You can't convince—"

"We can try once he is here," he assured her, "But his employer is a demanding taskmaster so it's likely that we must be satisfied." His eyes flickered over her gown. "That is a very pretty dress, my dear. Did you get it from the shop I suggested?"

Martha glanced down at her dress, needing to remind herself what she was wearing. "Yes, I did. I'm pleased you like it. I hope you don't think I've spent too—"

"What did I tell you about worrying about money?"

He'd threatened her with a shopping trip—promising to go with her and buy ten times as many garments if she didn't purchase at least a dozen new gowns for various occasions. Martha knew he was not speaking in jest. His own dressing room was stuffed with a staggering amount of clothing.

"I know, Hugo, it's just that I feel guilty to have so many nice things."

"Blame it on me."

She chuckled.

"Ah drat," he said, grimacing as he folded up the last section of newspaper and set it aside.

"What is it?"

"I just recalled that I have a business dinner tonight. It only came up yesterday and I forgot to tell you when I got home last night." He gave her his wicked smile. "I'm afraid I had other matters on my mind."

This was the third time this week that he'd had to be away at one meeting or another. She understood why, of course. Many of the men he dealt with only visited London to do business. And since they came without their wives it made more sense to engage in meals that revolved exclusively around business.

Martha hoped she hid her disappointment. "Of course, I understand, Hugo."

"You're such an understanding wife." He lifted her hand and kissed the tips of her fingers. "Tomorrow—after we look at the houses you've selected—I won't return to work and we can spend the rest of the day together."

"That would be lovely!"

"One of the men who will be at dinner tonight is part owner in a theater. Shall I see if I can get tickets for the three of us? Or maybe we could invite Albert, too?"

"I shall send a message to Albert and ask if he is free. I can't wait to tell Cailean."

"Speaking of the lad, I understand we now have *three* kitchen cats and a new cur, in addition to Fergus, skulking around the mews."

"Are you very angry about that, Hugo?"

Hugo laughed. "Of course not. As far as pastimes go, it's a lot more innocuous than some I could name." He kissed her hand again and released it with visible reluctance. "Well, I'd better be off, darling. Remind Albert when you send him that message that we have that meeting after breakfast tomorrow."

"I will." Martha stood and walked with him to the door. "Do you think this new lawyer will be able to help Albert sort out his problems?"

"I hope so." He gave her a very chaste—for Hugo—kiss. "I'll miss you tonight, darling. I will wake you when I return, no matter the hour." His eyelids lowered. "I shall make it worth disrupting your sleep."

Martha pursed her lips, her face invariably heating.

"Ah," he said, giving her jaw a fleeting caress. "There's the blush I adore."

Once he'd left the breakfast room Martha couldn't help noticing how empty it felt without him.

***

Hugo shrugged on his overcoat and took his hat and walking stick from the hovering footman.

"Thank you, Richard," Hugo said. "I'll be out late tonight, so don't wait up. I've got my housekey."

"Very good, sir."

Richard opened the door for him, but a sharp yipping sound made him pause. Hugo frowned as the racket grew louder. "What the devil is that?"

Richard's lips twitched. "Er, I believe that would be Mister Cailean, sir. He just returned about half an hour ago."

Hugo closed his eyes briefly. "Please. Tell me he didn't bring home another dog."

Richard laughed. "No sir. He brought back a cat this time."

He groaned.

The commotion—now identifiable as the yowling of more than one cat—grew louder.

"No, Felix!"

Hugo and the Maiden

Hugo jolted at the sound of Cailean's voice. The boy spoke so rarely that Hugo forgot what he sounded like.

"Come back!" The sound of thudding of feet came from the hallway that led to the kitchen. A few seconds later Cailean shot from the corridor as if he'd been fired from a gun. In front of him, gaining ground, was a soaking wet, gray streak.

Man and cat disappeared down another hallway.

Hugo turned to Richard, who was clearly having a difficult time controlling his laughter.

"What was that?"

"Mr. Cailean was giving the new cat, er, Mouser, I believe he named him, a bath."

"I didn't think cats liked baths?"

"They don't, sir. One of the other cats—Maggie or Mr. Whiskers—took a dislike to Mouser, so that was complicating the process."

It was Hugo's turn to laugh. "I'm going to leave before I get drawn into this."

Once he was outside, he pulled on his gloves and commenced walking.

Hugo never took a hackney directly from the house; the last thing he wanted was a direct connection from where he lived to Solange's. He always walked a few blocks before hailing a cab.

As he crossed the square, he berated himself. Why, in the name of all that was holy, had Hugo told Martha that his brother would visit? He must be going mad.

He groaned loud enough to startle a passing housemaid, who made a wide arc around him.

Now he would need to find somebody he trusted to act as his bloody brother. Who the hell would *that* be? Hugo walked in silence for several blocks, racking his brain.

He was no closer to coming up with a suitable candidate a quarter of an hour later, when he raised his cane to hail a hackney.

"Where to, gov?" the driver asked.

"Solange's."

The driver smirked. "Startin' early, eh?"

Hugo ignored him and climbed into the passably clean carriage.

He tossed his hat and cane onto the opposite seat and closed his eyes; he was so exhausted. It wasn't the work that was tiring him—

operating Solange's was so much easier without Laura interfering—but the strain of keeping his two lives separate.

He had hoped to spend more time with Martha but undoing all the damage that Laura had done was taking more time than he'd anticipated.

Fortunately, Bev had been as good as his word and handed him complete control, not showing his face once in the month since Hugo had taken charge.

"My mug ain't the sort to make toffs come clamberin' in, is it?"

No, it wasn't, although Hugo didn't say that.

"I'll sign over your half of the business if you can make this place pay, every month, for a year."

Since Bev Davies hadn't needed to give Hugo so much as a penny, he'd leapt at the offer.

Another part of his deal with Bev involved Laura. Hugo had been tempted to give her a taste of her own medicine, but, at the end of the day, she was too bloody pathetic to be worth the effort. But he refused to put up with her at Solange's. Although Hugo despised himself for even bothering, he'd extracted a promise from Bev to give her work at one of his other brothel's.

His request had greatly amused the old criminal. "Yer soft in the head, Hugo. I was going to kick her onto the street, where she belongs."

Not that the witch had shown any gratitude.

In fact, the last Hugo saw Laura—when he'd gone down to the Drunken Duck to release her—she'd hurled invectives as the hackney carried her away.

"Oi!"

Hugo opened his eyes to find the driver glaring in at him. "We're 'ere."

He paid the man and climbed the familiar steps to the regal off-white mansion that took up a large chunk of the short street. From the outside it looked no different than any other grand house, but there were few men in London who didn't know what the walls contained.

Solange's also owned the building next door, which had been converted into more luxurious rooms and a huge ballroom that was used for larger frolics, like the debauches commonly known as Roman Nights, one of which was scheduled for this coming Saturday.

Hugo and the Maiden

Hugo gritted his teeth; he'd have to lie to Martha about a business dinner, yet again.

Roman Nights were exactly what they sounded like: orgies. They were also some of the busiest nights of the year, which meant all hands on deck. It wouldn't only be Hugo working Saturday night, but also Andrew, Moira, and Enid, his most trustworthy employees, who usually functioned as managers in his absence.

Hugo had stopped finding orgies amusing at least ten years ago and was dreading Saturday. Mostly because it would be an exercise in tedium. But there was always a possibility for volatile situations whenever you tossed a hundred or so wealthy patrons in with four dozen whores—half of whom he'd bring in from two other exclusive brothels—and then poured endless amounts of liquor on the situation.

The front door opened before Hugo reached the landing and Daniel stood inside the foyer, looking magnificent in his dark green and black livery. "Good afternoon, Mr. Hugo."

"Anything I need to know about?" Hugo asked as he handed him his hat, cane, and coat.

"Mild altercation in the Gold Room, Sir Lawrence Blackheathe and Mr. Alan Percival kicked up a bit of a dust. But Mr. Andrew was here and had the matter smoothed over in a tick."

"What were they fighting about?"

Frank's lips twitched. "Er, it was over Maisie, I believe."

Hugo rolled his eyes and Daniel laughed.

"The mail has already been taken to your study, sir."

Hugo gave him his gloves and opened the panel door that was off to one side of the grand entryway. "Where's The Book?" *The Book* was the daily ledger.

"Mr. Andrew brought it by half an hour ago."

Hugo looked at his watch. "Go tell Maisie to be down here in an hour. An hour," he repeated.

"She won't like that, sir."

"I don't care."

Maisie was one of the house's most expensive and popular whores, and she was also its biggest pain in the arse. Hugo had nobody to blame for her except himself since he'd been the one to hire her.

"Very good, sir. Shall I send up coffee?"

Hugo paused and stared at Daniel, an idea blooming in his head.

Daniel eyelids lowered fractionally over his coffee-colored eyes as Hugo studied him.

He was a beautiful lad and if Hugo hadn't been a happily married man, he might have taken him up on that come-hither look. As it was, he wanted something entirely different from him.

"How old are you?"

"Er, twenty-nine on my next birthday."

A little young, but the dark hair and brown eyes were a good match—even though the real Johnny was fair-haired like both Hugo's parents. "I have a business proposition for you, Daniel. Join me for dinner in my study later and we can talk."

Daniel nodded, his handsome face puzzled. "Of course, sir."

Hugo loved his study. It wasn't the biggest or nicest room in the two buildings that made up Solange's, but, in his opinion, it was the most elegant. It reminded Hugo of the drawings he'd seen of the toff men's clubs he'd never be allowed to—places like White's, Brooks's, or Boodle's.

Luxurious but slightly worn carpets covered the dark wood floor; comfortable leather chairs and sofas were scattered about the room; and the walls were lined with hundreds and hundreds of books. Since claiming the room for himself Hugo had discovered there was nothing more delightful than working while surrounded by books.

Thankfully, the room had escaped Laura's recent predations. She had maintained both her suite of rooms and office in the newer building, so most of the damage—gaudy furnishings, tasteless art, and whorish color schemes—had occurred in that part.

Hugo had made changing those rooms back to their original state one of his first priorities, along with re-hiring valuable staff like Daniel. And he'd also made an effort to personally meet with each of their clients to assure them that business had returned to normal at Solange's.

Many of those who'd left had come back quickly when they'd learned Laura was no longer in charge. And even more had returned after Hugo had put out the word that Bev was not an active partner.

And then there had been those who'd come back for his services, in particular.

Hugo had put off most of those meetings while he'd actively engaged in recruitment. As arrogant as he was about his sexual abilities, he knew that all his clients, with a very few exceptions, would be

Hugo and the Maiden

pleased if he could hand them over to an equally skilled employee. Especially if that person was younger and more attractive.

To that end, he'd hired two new men and four women. Well, to be honest, he'd poached them away from two competitors, which hadn't been difficult. Working for Solange's had once been the aim of any smart, ambitious whore.

He'd gradually eased his best customers into accepting his new employees, although it hadn't been as easily done since people seemed to think they deserved a reason for why he wouldn't fuck them.

He could have told them that he had married. But—after they had stopped laughing—most of his clients would tell him they didn't care, since most of them were married, too.

But Hugo had no intention of advertising his recent marriage. In fact, he planned to make sure that *this* part of his life and the part with Martha never got within miles of each other.

Hugo turned his mind to the prior night's bookings and was just finishing up with the account book when there was a knock on his door.

A quick glance at the clock showed that an hour and a half had passed. He scowled. "Come in."

Even Hugo, as jaded as he was by working with beautiful woman, caught his breath whenever he saw Maisie Hudder.

But he easily squashed his admiration. "You're late."

"I'm sorry, Hugo." She smiled blandly and teetered across the room on her high-heeled slippers. She was dressed in a snow-white silk dressing gown that made her raven-black hair and startling blue eyes all the more attractive.

And then there was her body...

Well, the woman wasn't their most sought-after employee for no reason. She lowered herself into the chair across from his desk with the sinuous grace of a cat, her gaze heavy lidded, her smile lazy.

"The next time I summon you and you don't arrive on time you can pack your things and get the hell out. Understood?"

Her eyes widened in surprise.

"Do. You. Understand?"

The fragile architecture of her white throat flexed. "Yes, Hugo."

"Good. Now, what's the problem with Percy and Blackheathe?"

A smug smile tugged at her sinful lips. "They both want to offer me a contract."

Hugo bit back a groan, hoping he hid his irritation. "So, which one do you want?"

"Neither."

He frowned. "Then—oh, let me guess, they're behaving like two skunks pissing over who gets you. But, instead of piss, they're throwing jewels at you?"

Her smile grew.

Hugo leaned across his desk. "Do not *fuck* with my business, Maisie."

Her smug smile slowly drained away.

"You know the way things work: if you want to accept an outside offer, then do it. I won't have you turning the place into riot just so you can collect more baubles. Understood?"

Her plush lower lip quivered. "Understood."

"I want you to stay away from both of them for a while." Hugo turned to the appointment book that he usually kept locked in the safe but had been looking at earlier. He turned to the page of appointments for tonight and ran his finger down the list. "It looks like Amhurst will be here tonight and he inquired after you the last time." He closed the book with a snap and looked up. "I want you to attach yourself to him like a barnacle. He is one of our best clients; make him happy. Extremely happy."

"I will. I'm sorry, Hugo." Her enormous blue eyes glassed over with tears.

Hugo wanted to clap. Instead, he stood and came out from behind his desk, offering her his hand and helping her to her feet. "Don't be sorry, darling—just be a good girl from now on, hmm?"

She pressed her lush body against him before he knew what she was doing, her hand running from his chest to his flaccid cock. Maisie frowned when she felt physical proof of his lack of interest. She caressed him with her palm. "Can I make it up to you, Hugo? I'll do anything you like."

Hugo gently but firmly removed her hand from his groin. "Save your enthusiasm for Amherst, darling."

"Don't worry, Hugo—I wouldn't tell your missus."

Hugo took her by the shoulders and held her at arm's length. "Who told you I was married, Maisie?"

She shrugged. "Everyone knows."

Hugo and the Maiden

How in the world did people hear about his marriage? He'd not told a soul. Maybe they were just guessing, based on the fact he no longer took clients. Whatever the reason, he didn't like talking about his wife while at work. It felt too much like he was soiling her, even if nobody ever saw Martha's face or knew her name.

He looked down into Maisie's sly eyes. "As appealing as your offer is," he lied, "I've got a pile of work waiting for me." He escorted her to the door.

She stood on her tiptoes to kiss his cheek. "Thank you for being so understanding, Hugo."

As he watched her teeter off on her ridiculous heels, he was tempted to plant a boot in her fleshy arse for believing she could play her tricks on him. Instead, he shut the door and went back to work.

Hugo was half-way through the mound of bills and other correspondence when another knock disturbed him.

"Yes?"

The door opened and Daniel entered, a large tray in his hands.

Hugo shoved his hair off his forehead and glanced at the clock. "Lord, dinner already? Well, come in and make yourself comfortable," he said. "And you'd better lock the door behind you. What I want to ask is for your ears alone."

Chapter 30

Mr. Duncan glanced at his watch. Yet again.

"I'm sorry," Martha said. "Something must have happened to keep him." Hugo was already an hour late and the estate agent had become increasingly fidgety. "If you have another appointment, you can always leave me with the key. I know he will come."

"Well..." He chewed his lower lip.

"It will be fine, Mr. Duncan. Perhaps you could leave all three keys and we can drop them off later?"

"I normally wouldn't do that, but I'm afraid I only budgeted two hours, as you requested. However, if you are sure that you will be all right here by—"

The front door opened, and Hugo entered, his black overcoat and top hat dotted with diamonds of water. His dark eyes flickered dismissively over the agent before they landed on Martha and softened. "I'm so sorry, darling. I'm afraid I got tangled up in something of a riot."

"Oh, goodness," she said.

"Is that over on Haymarket?" Mr. Duncan asked.

Hugo nodded absently, taking Martha's hands in his. "Forgive me?"

"I thought you were coming from the Exchange," Mr. Duncan said.

Hugo turned slowly to the agent. Whatever the other man saw on Hugo's face made him recoil.

"Er, not that it's any of my affair," he mumbled.

Hugo made a low humming sound of agreement.

"Mr. Duncan needs to be somewhere shortly, Hugo. He said he could leave us the keys and we could drop them by later."

"Now that your husband is here, I'd be happy to stay and—"

"That's a capital idea." Hugo held out his hand.

Mr. Duncan hesitated.

"Is there a problem?"

"Er, no, no, of course not. Um, if you'll just—"

"I'll have a servant run them over later this evening."

"Very good, sir." Mr. Duncan gave them both a nervous smile. "Well, then, I suppose—"

"Thank you for your time," Hugo said.

"Thank you so much," Martha said warmly, her face hot at Hugo's rudeness.

Once the door shut behind him, Hugo heaved an exaggerated sigh. "Thank God for that. I don't know how you tolerate that old stick, Martha."

"He's quite nice, Hugo. You needn't have been so sharp with him. He was—"

He slid his arms around her and lowered his lips over Martha's. The kiss was both gentle and firm, and he took possession of her mouth in a masterful way that left her breathless when he finally pulled away.

"Let's not talk about Duncan," he whispered, his eyes sparkling.

Martha blinked up at him, a bit dazed. "Oh ... well, all right."

He took her hand. "Come, show me which room is going to be our bedroom."

"Hugo!"

"What?" he asked as he all but dragged her toward the stairs. "It's the only room I'm really interested in."

"You say that now," she said, breathless as she tried to keep up, "But you will change your mind when you find the study too small or the fireplace in the dining room too drafty."

"Which door?" he asked when they reached the landing.

"The one at the end."

Martha laughed when he darted forward, almost yanking her off her feet. He flung open the door to a large bedroom.

"The dressing room connects to—

Hugo drew her toward the bed. "Lie down, darling."

"Hugo," she shrieked as he pressed her down on the bed, which had a Holland cover over the mattress, just like all the other furniture in the house.

"I want to test out the room," he said, untying her cloak and pushing it back before taking her reticule and tossing it onto a nearby chair.

"But—"

"Hmm?" He pulled up the skirts and petticoats of her navy-blue walking dress.

"What if somebody comes?"

"Oh, somebody will be coming."

"Hugo!"

"I do love it when you yell my name, darling." He thrust up her skirts and then grinned. "You are wearing my present."

Her blood pounded in her ears as he stared at her. "One of the many gifts you insist on showering me with."

"Oh, my love, this gift isn't for you—it's for me."

Martha scraped up her courage. "Do you like it?"

He nodded, his expression entranced as he reached out to run his hands over the whisper-thin muslin. "The woman at the shop said these will soon be all the rage."

These were a pair of drawers that were similar to men's inexpressibles, but with little frills on the leg openings.

He traced her cleft with one finger, up and down, up and down. The thin fabric barrier somehow made her feel even more exposed. "So pretty," he murmured.

Martha's sex tightened as he pressed harder, parting her lips and lightly flicking her core while his other hand stroked up her bare thigh and beneath the fabric.

Martha gave a startled yelp.

"Sorry, sweetness," he murmured, his gaze moving between her face and what his hands were doing. "Is my hand cold?"

"A little," she said in a shaky voice.

"Do you want me to stop?" His eyes glinted with wickedness.

"No."

***

Hugo gazed down on his gorgeous wife as she lay before him, a veritable banquet of femininity.

He drank in her parted lips and flushed face, teasing her sweet little pussy through the material until she made a damp spot on her pretty new drawers.

"Spread a bit wider for me, darling."

As always, she turned the most delightful shade of pink.

But she obeyed him.

Hugo and the Maiden

"Good girl," he praised when she opened for him. He loved the pink drawers on her, but they were a nuisance when it came to easily accessing her body.

Still, he was creative; he could adapt.

He grazed her clitoris, making her moan. She was wet for him, her body already trembling with need. His wife; his vicar's daughter with the soul of a courtesan.

Thank the Lord.

He flicked open his fall with one hand, not pausing his caressing. She spread wider without being told and Hugo slid his hand inside his drawers and drew out his prick.

Martha's slitted gaze fixed on his plump crown which had thrust back his foreskin and was slick with evidence of his desire.

Hugo pumped himself as he pushed a finger into her tight heat. "Fuck! Martha."

She clenched at the vulgar word, but he knew she was titillated, rather than offended, like those times he slipped and took the Lord's name in vain.

"So wet and ready for your husband," he praised, giving her a lascivious smirk while he stroked them both.

Hugo knew he wouldn't last long—he never did the first time he took her. And he'd take her again—once in every house she showed him. Martha was not the sort of woman you could have just once.

She was fortunate that old Duncan had buggered off, because Hugo had planned to mount her whether the man was there, or not. He smirked as he imagined Martha's terror at being caught. But he knew she wouldn't have denied him.

Every night in their bed she came to him with a hunger as voracious as his own. After the first few weeks—when she'd gotten over her shyness—she had actually approached him. The first time he'd woken to her hand stroking his shaft he'd almost wept at the sheer perfection of her—of his life with her. All the lying and sneaking were worth it if he could have her. And keep her.

Hugo pushed aside one leg of her drawers to expose her to his greedy gaze, mesmerized by the sight of his glistening fingers stroking her tender folds. *Christ.* He'd never seen anything so beautiful in his entire life.

"Please Hugo," she begged, squirming.

"As you command," he said, bringing their bodies closer.

He watched himself enter her; his gaze riveted to where they were joined as he made her feel every inch. "I wish you could see what I'm seeing, Martha." He filled her completely and held her full, giving her a moment to adjust before withdrawing slowly. "You look so beautiful taking me." The sight of slick skin on slick skin was almost as exquisite as the feel of her.

"Hugo." The sound of her moaning his name was more erotic than a gamahuching from any other woman.

"Yes, darling?" he asked, his voice hoarse as he began to work her with deep, deliberate strokes.

"Please, more."

He smirked and reached down to caress her bud. She groaned, her hips lifting off the bed as she muttered something he couldn't make out. He quickened his pace, giving her what she wanted.

"Oh—oh—" She gasped, her tight sheath clenching so damned hard it almost hurt.

Her rhythmic contractions shoved him over the edge, and he gave in to his need, driving into her with savage thrusts before hilting himself and then emptying his aching ballocks deep inside her sweet body.

Hugo's arms turned to water and he collapsed on top of her, his chest heaving. As chilly as the day was, she felt like a furnace beneath him. As his fogged brain cleared, the last few minutes came back to him in a rush. "Was I too rough, love?"

"You were perfect. As always."

The warmth that flooded him at her words astonished him. Why was it that just a little bit of praise from Martha was more powerful than the effusive flattery of every lover he'd had, combined?

"So were you, darling," he murmured against the damp skin of her throat. "I hate to be impulsive, Martha, but I don't think we need look any further; I adore this bedroom. I think this is the house for us."

She chuckled weakly, her body shaking. "Oh, Hugo." She slid her slender arms around him and gave him a rib-bruising squeeze. "I love you so very much."

Hugo opened his mouth to tell her he felt the same—that he'd die for her, that she was the best thing to ever happen to him, that marrying her had been the smartest thing he'd done in his entire life.

But, as always when it came to saying the simple four-letter word, it was as if he'd suddenly eaten lye. His throat thickened and his mouth went as dry as a desert.

Instead of baring his soul, Hugo held her, hoping to God that what he gave her would continue to be enough for her.

Chapter 31

Hugo *hated* Roman Night.

This—he decided as he watched an overweight, pasty, septuagenarian marquess chase three giggling whores who were (barely) dressed as the Three Fates around the Roman ruins in the ballroom—was the last time he would attend one.

"That's the fifth time you've looked at your watch in the last ten minutes, sir."

He turned at the sound of Daniel's voice and snorted. "If you don't want to end up servicing one of our drunken, randy clients I advise you to stay in the foyer, my good lad."

"I'd take your suggestion, but I drew the short straw tonight."

"Ah, Micky and Jonathan tricked you into working the ballroom, did they?"

Daniel laughed. "So, am I still to come to your house next week, sir?"

Hugo's face heated at the memory of what he was paying the younger man to do. What the hell was happening to him? He'd picked up a conscience somewhere—probably from prolonged association with Martha—and it was spreading like a bloody disease.

"Yes. And you'd better practice calling me Hugo before then."

"Of course, si—er, Hugo."

"You've memorized the information I gave you?" Hugo asked.

"I have ... brother." Daniel grinned.

Hugo snorted. "*Hugo* will be more than sufficient, Daniel." He was about to reach for his watch when he recalled that he'd just done so.

"Quite a bacchanal," Daniel observed, standing beside Hugo in a parade rest position that gave away his past in the army.

"You've never wanted to join in?" Hugo asked. "You'd make a hell of a lot more money than running errands and delivering messages."

Daniel's gaze flickered across the room and settled on a naked woman lying spread eagle on a settee. An exceedingly drunken man was

Hugo and the Maiden

rogering her while at least seven other men looked on and shouted suggestions and encouragement.

Daniel turned back to Hugo. "I don't think so, sir. I was raised Catholic."

Hugo threw back his head and laughed. "Well, I don't think—"

A hand landed on his shoulder. "Hugo?"

Hugo turned to find Andrew, his second in command, dressed in a toga that had seen better days. His eyes looked a bit … wild.

"What's wrong?" Hugo asked, immediately serious.

"Er, there's a gentleman with Maisie in the Aegean Room."

"Lord Amherst?"

Andrew shook his head slowly. "No."

Hugo ground his teeth. That *bloody* Maisie. "Well, *who*, then—it had better not be Blackheathe or Percival?"

"I don't want to say, sir. But, er, he wants to see you."

Hugo felt the hairs on the back of his neck lift.

Fuck. He could only think of one person who would have such an effect on the normally calm Andrew.

"Stay here and keep an eye on these fools," he ordered, and then cut his way through the revelers toward the exit.

The Aegean Room was one of the more expensive suites on the male side of the brothel. Four men dressed in clothing that was neither flash nor expensive stood outside the room and Hugo recognized one of them.

"Bloody. Damn. Hell," he muttered.

And then he pasted on a smile and approached the man. "Gibson, isn't it?" he asked, even though he knew good and well that was his name.

Gibson—one of the most expressionless people Hugo had ever met—nodded. "Buckingham, right?"

Hugo laughed at the bland dig. "Yes. He, er, wants to see me?"

"You wait here until the woman comes out."

"Just one in there?"

Gibson nodded and then continued to appear bored as drunken aristocrats and naked whores romped past them. Anyone looking his face would never believe Gibson was observing a full-blown orgy with some of England's most powerful and wealthy citizens.

But then, given the man he served, everyone here was as significant as a speck of fly shit.

Hugo's mind raced; how did one go about denying a man who was second or third in line for the throne of England—Hugo could never remember which—anything he asked for?

He was still pondering that question a quarter of an hour later when the door to the Aegean Room opened and Maisie stepped out. She was wiping her puffy, reddened lower lip with one delicate finger, her expression as vapid as ever. She gave Hugo a half-smile. "He said he wants to talk to you."

Hugo stared at her so hard he should've been able to see into her brain; did she know who it was that she'd just gamahuched?

Gibson took Maisie's arm and led her away from the door.

His royal highness was buttoning up his trousers when Hugo entered the room. He greeted Hugo with a smile that was remarkably genuine considering their disparate social stations. "Hugo, old man!"

Hugo gave a full court bow, something he did with exquisite grace.

"No need to stand on ceremony with me," the duke said, his bulbous blue eyes glinting with pleasure at either Hugo's person or his gesture of obeisance, Hugo wasn't sure which.

The other man had taken a beating in the newspapers lately, so a little respect probably went a long way to soothing his battered nerves and pride.

"Come, sit."

Hugo viewed the fact that the duke gestured to the chair next to his, rather than the floor between his spread thighs, as a positive sign.

"Thank you, your royal highness."

"How have you been, Hugo?"

"I have been well."

The duke nodded briskly, "Capital, capital. Quite a nice gel that—what was her name?"

"Maisie, sir."

"Hmm, yes." His magnificent mustache moved from side to side, his fingers drumming on the arm of the chair. Even though Hugo had been inside this man's body countless times he still had no idea what went on in his head.

Hugo and the Maiden

"I'm leaving for the Continent soon," the duke suddenly barked. "Probably saw that in the demmed papers." He muttered that last part more to himself, and then his vague blue gaze sharpened and pinned Hugo to his chair. "I shan't be coming home for ... well, not for some time." His slack features suddenly became firm and stern. Kingly, almost. "I'll come back next week—one last time."

"Er, shall I reserve Maisie for you, sir?"

The duke laughed, but then his eyes narrowed as his jaw flexed, his eyes hungry as they moved over Hugo's body. "One last time, Hugo," he repeated.

Hugo swallowed. "Er, that's—"

The duke nodded vigorously. "Jolly good, jolly good."

The door to the room opened, as if somebody beyond it was attuned to the royal attention span. It was Gibson and he held the door open and gestured for Hugo.

Hugo turned to the duke, but the older man was looking at his watch. Only the clenched fist that rested on his thigh gave away the duke's tension.

Again, he opened his mouth to tell the duke that he would not be here next week—that he wouldn't be in the city. Better yet, that he wouldn't even be in the country.

Or perhaps he should just tell him that he was married. The duke had a wife and he even seemed to care for her, in his own strange way. Surely he would—

"Time to go," Gibson said, his cold gaze on Hugo.

No, Hugo thought as he bowed low to the duke and then walked toward the door, his feet like lumps of lead, *the time to go was before I ever stepped foot into this damned room.*

Chapter 32

Martha, Albert, and Cailean were in the breakfast room when Hugo went down the following morning.

"Hugo, what are you doing up so early? You didn't come home until after four o'clock. You couldn't have had more than three hours sleep."

Hugo didn't tell her that he'd not even slept that much. Instead, he kissed her cheek and then nodded at Albert and Cailean. "Good morning, Albert, young Cailean." He grinned at the huge lad. "Nice to see you for a change."

The boy flushed and gave him a shy smile.

"Coffee, please," he said to Richard.

"Aren't you hungry?" Martha asked when Hugo sat down without filling a plate from the buffet.

"I need to have a few cups of coffee first." He turned to Albert before Martha could try to feed him; she was adamant in her belief that a healthy breakfast was critical to a healthy body. Normally Hugo agreed with her, but this morning he thought he might vomit if he tried to eat.

"How were things with Mr. Williams?"

Albert smiled. "He is confident that I can get control of the patent with the proof I've given him. In fact, he knows of my ex-employer and said there have been accusations in the past. He is a brilliant man" His chin wobbled and a distinctly emotional expression slid over his face. "How can I ever thank—"

"Excellent news," Hugo boomed, not wanting the younger man to thank him—yet again—for loaning him a bit of money and introducing him to a competent lawyer.

"I told Albert that we selected a house with ample room and that he should consider coming to stay with us until his legal troubles are over. Cailean and I would adore having a Londoner show us the best places."

Hugo was both proud and amused that she was trying to do a favor for the cash-poor young man and make it seem as if Albert were the one doing a favor for her.

Albert's freckled face flushed at the offer. "Oh, I'm sure the two of you must be tired of—"

"What an excellent idea, Martha." He turned to Albert. "I'm afraid my business is eating up a great deal more of my time than I'd like at the moment. You really would be doing all of us a favor."

"I would want to pay for—"

"We can discuss that later." Hugo cut in. "You must stay with us until the patent issue has been settled. These things can sometimes drag on for months—even years."

Albert frowned.

"Not that it will in your case," Hugo hastened to assure him.

"Well, it you are sure—"

"We're positive." Hugo turned from the younger man to the fourth occupant of the table. "I've not spoken to you in almost two days, little brother. Have you brought home any new houseguests—perhaps a carthorse? Some pigeons?"

Cailean gave one of the hushed, huffing laughs that Hugo found so endearing, his huge shoulders shaking with silent amusement.

"Cailean has been finding homes for some of the animals," Martha said.

"Is that so?"

"Lord Bellamy's stablemaster said he needed a good mouser and also that his daughter had taken a liking to Emma—the little black dog."

"Ah." Hugo turned to Cailean. "You don't mind if they go to somebody else?"

Cailean shook his head, his expression calm but firm, as if he'd considered the character of the people and was satisfied. That was probably a good thing since the animal head count seemed to grow weekly.

"Well, you are an excellent judge of character," Hugo teased. "You liked me on sight, didn't you?"

Cailean snickered.

"I've told Cailean that he needn't worry there won't be enough room as our new home has a large back garden," Martha said.

Hugo had to smile at that. The house they'd chosen had a big enough garden, but it wouldn't hold all the animals Cailean collected. "I'm sure we'll manage," he said, topping up his coffee and taking another sip, beginning to feel more awake.

"Will you be able to come to services with me today, Hugo? You needn't if you're too tired. Cailean and Albert are joining me, so I shan't be alone." She hesitated, and then added, "It is a new church."

"Oh?"

"Yes, St. Olav's. Do you know it?"

"I can't imagine there is a Londoner who doesn't, my dear. I shall be delighted to attend services with you today."

The door opened and Richard approached Hugo with a salver. "I'm sorry to interrupt, sir, but this message just came for you and the messenger is waiting for a reply."

Hugo ignored the tightening in his gut at the familiar cheap parchment and broke the sickly gray wafer.

I want to see you immediately. Don't keep me waiting. B.

He swallowed down the bile that surged in his throat at Bev's terse message. What in the name of God had happened now? He'd left Solange's after the party was, for all intents and purposes, finished, although there were always the inevitable stragglers.

A quick perusal of the ledger last night had shown they had made more money than ever before from the ridiculous orgy.

Something must have happened after he left. Something bad.

Hugo looked up to find three sets of eyes regarding him curiously. "Er, tell the messenger that I shall be over within the hour."

"Of course, sir."

Once Richard had gone, Hugo said to Martha, "I'm sorry, darling. It looks like I shan't be able to go with you, after all."

Martha smiled, but he could see she was disappointed. "Do you think you will be home for dinner?"

"I'm sure I will," Hugo said, hoping to God he was right.

***

Just like the last time there were two sneering ruffians flanking the door to Hugo's study at Solange's.

But this time, Cowan Morgan—Bev's bastard son, Laura's manipulative ex-lover, and the man who'd helped to defraud Hugo of his life's work—was one of the men.

Cowan said something to Jac Evans when he saw Hugo and the men laughed in a way calculated to be offensive.

Hugo ignored them and reached for the door handle.

"Not so fast, *Mr. Buckingham*," Cowan said, grabbing Hugo's upper arm with his meaty paw.

Hugo and the Maiden

Hugo grinned up at Cowen, who had a good six inches and three stone on him, and then turned his head and licked the back of the other man's hand.

Cowan yelped as if Hugo had struck him and yanked away his hand.

"Did you *want* something from me, Cowan?" Hugo asked with a leer.

Jac—a deceptively jovial-looking bloke whom Hugo knew had killed at least two men—shook his head, grinning from ear to ear. "You're a one, you."

Cowan scrubbed the back of his hand against his breeches, scowling. "He's a sick sod bastard who likes takin' it up the arse, is what he is."

"How flattering that you are so interested in my arse and what I put in it, Cowan."

Jac chortled and opened the door. "Go on in, 'Ugo, 'ee's expecting ye."

Hugo winked at Cowan and struggled to leash his fury as he was admitted into his own goddamned office as if he were a lowly bill collector.

Bev was sitting behind his desk, poring over a ledger. The safe behind the desk, where Hugo kept all the important documents and account books, was open.

Hugo had been aware that Bev had the combination—it was his business, after all—but he felt physically violated to see evidence of the other man's ownership.

And there wasn't a damned thing he could say or do to stop him.

"Sit." Bev hadn't bothered to look up when Hugo entered.

Hugo sat.

The clock on the mantel ticked softly as Bev finished the page he was reading. When he was done, he closed the book without a sound and finally looked up.

"You had a visitor last night."

As an experienced whore, Hugo was good at hiding his thoughts. But this question surprised him so much that it took him a fraction of a second too long to respond. "Er, visitor?"

Bev's eyes narrowed.

"Oh, yes—a *visitor*. Er, how did you know?"

"It's my business, Hugo."

Red-hot fury churned in his belly at the man's words. Hugo forced a smile. "That it is."

"So, what did he want?"

"The same thing that everyone else wanted. He spent an hour with Maisie and then left."

"Yes. But what did he *really* want?"

"As far as I know, that was all."

Bev leaned back in his chair and chuckled. "Oh, mab. You'd have to live in the world a whole lot longer than you have to lie to me."

"I'm not lying."

Bev slammed a ham-sized fist on the desk, making everything on top of it jump. "Don't lie to me!"

Hugo knew exactly what a rabbit felt like when cornered by a fox. He was momentarily frozen with fear. But if he bowed to this man once, he would never get off his knees.

"I'm not lying," he repeated calmly.

"Cowen!" Bev bellowed.

The door opened and Bev's ugly son stuck his shaggy head in. "Aye?"

"Bring her in."

There was a scuffling sound in the foyer, a feminine whimper, and then Laura came stumbling into the room.

He'd only seen her a month ago, but already she looked ten years older.

"What's this?" Hugo asked Bev, turning away from the cringing woman.

"While nobody wants to take her for a ride anymore," Bev said, sneering at Laura, "it turns out the slut is still good for somethin'."

Hugo experienced an almost overwhelming desire to kick Bev's ugly head right off his shoulders.

Bev turned his cold gaze on Laura. "Which one of my employees did his royal highness want to go ridin' with, pet?"

Her eyes darted around the room, never settling on anything for long. "Hugo."

"Good lass," Bev praised. "Now get out."

Laura moved with remarkable speed for a woman in her condition. She wrenched open the door but then turned. "I'm sorry, Hugo." Cowan yanked her out of the room and shut the door.

Bev chuckled. "I have to thank you for convincin' me to keep her around."

Sometimes Hugo hated himself.

"What do you want from me?" he asked.

"I think you know the answer to that."

"It was one of my few conditions that I would no longer take clients," he reminded the man, as if he might have forgotten.

"Aye, that's true. But now I'm changin' our agreement."

Hugo clamped his jaws shut, afraid of what might come out if he opened them.

Think of Martha. You're no longer alone, you have her to take care of—not to mention Cailean.

"Hugo, Hugo, Hugo." Bev chuckled and shook his head. "After so many years what does it matter if you take one last punter? And Laura already told me that it's his royal highness who takes it up the arse, not you. How difficult can it be to put a duke on his knees and bugger him?" He laughed even harder. "Hell, I know men who aren't even sods who'd pay good money for the chance."

"Why do you care, Bev? He doesn't pay more than anyone else."

"Don't worry about my motives, Hugo—that's not your concern."

"True," he conceded. "But it is my concern where I shove my prick. And I won't do it."

Bev's eyes narrowed and he cupped a hand up to his ear. "I think I misheard you."

"Our agreement was that I'd manage Solange's for you, not whore for you. If it comes down to that, I'll leave."

"Well, see—that's a problem."

Hugo refused to be baited and play Bev's fool.

When he didn't reply, Bev smiled unpleasantly. "You've made a deal with me. That means you don't get to decide when our arrangement is over, Hugo—*I'm* the one who makes that decision."

"Are you going to force me to fuck him?"

"Nah, I'll just have a chat with your pretty young wife and tell her what her husband does for his crust."

Hugo was only startled for a second. And then he gave a dismissive bark of laughter. "You think she doesn't already know what I do?"

"As a matter of fact, I know she don't." Bev chuckled. "Such a friendly, trustin' little bird—came all the way down from some godforsaken island in Scotland with her clever husband, who spends his days playin' the 'Change."

"You stay the hell away from her!" Hugo was halfway across the desk when Bev produced a small pistol from thin air.

The older man clucked his tongue. "Now, now, don't get emotional, Hugo. Ain't no place for that in business. Why, if I were to get emotional, I might be offended that you'd attack me after all I done for you. If *I* got emotional, I might find my finger twitchin' on this trigger. All sorts o' bad things might happen if I were to let my emotions control me." His thin lips tightened. "You might disappear. So might that wife of yours and the big lad who's touched in the upper works."

Hugo stared.

"Aye, I know about your little household. I know about the ginger-hackled boy and his patent." He grinned. "I might be interested in putting a bit o' blunt into such a clever device." His smile disappeared in a heartbeat. "Now, you listen to me, you uppity sod: you get your arse in here when the old duke returns and you give him the bloody ride of his life."

Hugo stared at the other man and considered his motives. Trying to extort money from a royal duke for patronizing a whorehouse would be like trying to extort money from the average person for breathing. The entire nation knew the royal dukes patronized whores—not to mention kept mistresses and fathered bastard children on them.

But it would be an entirely different story if one of them were discovered with a man. His mind boggled at the power Bev would have over the duke if he could get proof of sodomy.

"You're going to try to extort money from him—or is it something else? A royal favor?"

Bev just smiled at Hugo's accusation. "That's none of your affair, mab. The only thing you need to worry about is gettin' your prick hard and into his arse. I'll take care of the rest."

"And if I refuse then you'll tell my wife what I do for a living."

"Nah, I won't tell her." Bev leaned across the desk, his eyes like twin pits that led straight down to Hell. "I'll kill her."

Chapter 33

Martha was tossing and turning when she heard the door to Hugo's bedroom close. She sat up and peered at the clock on her nightstand; it was after two in the morning. Poor Hugo must be exhausted.

But as tired as he was, he always came to her. He had spoken in earnest on their wedding night when he'd told her they would share the same bed every night.

Martha listened to the sounds of him moving around his dressing room and imagined his reaction to her news. She laid a hand over her midriff; it was far too early to feel anything, of course, but it just made her feel close to her baby to touch her stomach. Which was silly since she was already as close to her unborn child as a person could get.

She smiled at that thought and yawned yet again. Her eyelids were so heavy she couldn't keep them up. She'd just sleep for a minute, until Hugo came in...

Martha jerked, awakened from a deep sleep by ... something. She opened her eyes to darkness and silence and felt the bed beside her; it was empty. She pushed herself up and leaned close to the clock: it was after three. And she was alone in their bed. Not once since they'd married had they not slept together.

Martha chewed her lip. She'd just take a peek in his room; she wouldn't wake him if he were sleeping. He'd barely had any sleep last night and was probably exhausted.

She pushed back the covers, swung her legs off the bed, and shoved her feet into her slippers before shrugging into her dressing gown and tiptoeing toward the connecting door. She laid her ear against it for a moment; all was quiet.

Martha twisted the knob and pushed. Nothing happened. She twisted harder and leaned her shoulder against the door. It didn't budge.

That was ... odd. Perhaps one of the servants had accidentally locked it and that's why Hugo hadn't come in. He knew that she always locked the door to the corridor because he found it amusing that she was so worried about servants walking in on them when they were in flagrante, as he liked to say.

That's what must have happened.

She unlocked the door to the corridor and padded down the hall to Hugo's bedchamber. His door wasn't locked so Martha slowly pushed it open. Hugo hadn't drawn the drapes and the faint light from the square illuminated the room.

"Hugo?" she whispered, shuffling toward the bed, which was in the shadows. Only when she reached the foot end could she see it was empty.

Martha frowned. Had he not come home? Then who would have been in his room at two o'clock in the morning? Her skin prickled. What if somebody had broken into the house? What if they were still in the house—still in this room somewhere? Martha backed toward the door.

"What are you doing in here?"

She yelped and spun around.

Hugo was standing in the doorway, backlit by the dim light in the corridor.

"You scared the life out of me." When he didn't answer, she stepped closer until she could see his face. He looked haggard, far older than he'd looked only this morning. "Hugo? Is something wrong?"

"No."

"Why didn't you come to bed?"

"I went downstairs to the bookroom." He tossed several folded and sealed sheets of parchment onto a nearby table.

"You look so very tired. Perhaps—" Martha reached out to touch his face, but he jerked back.

"I'm glad you're awake."

He didn't sound glad; he sounded ... grim.

"What's going on?"

He brushed passed her, his eyes turned away as he headed to his dressing room. "I just came home to get some things," he said, lighting several candles in the big holder as well as a candlestick.

"Things? Are you going somewhere?"

"Yes, I am." His broad shoulders were tense beneath his shirtsleeves as he carried the candlestick into his dressing room.

Martha stood like a statue, waiting for ... something.

When he came out of the dressing room, he had a valise in one hand and a coat in the other.

"What is going on?"

"I told you, I'm leaving. And tomorrow you'll be leaving, too."

Martha gaped; who was this stranger? His eyes were hard and cold, his mouth thin and mean. She reached for him, as if touching him would help her understand.

Hugo knocked her hand away. "Don't," he snapped, his jaws flexing. "This isn't working, Martha."

"Wh-what isn't working?"

"*This*. Us. This marriage." He looked away. "I can't do this—I'm not made for it."

"But—I don't understand."

He turned on her in a way that reminded her of Lily's male otter—vicious and feral. "Do you know where I really work every day?"

She opened her mouth.

"I'm a *whore*, Martha."

Martha felt as though she'd opened a door to a raging furnace. She took a step back. "I don't—"

"I don't go to work at the Exchange; I go to work at a brothel. I've been working there for over a decade—that's the business I co-owned with Laura Maitland, my *business partner*." He snorted, as if the words amused him. "I've been whoring since I was fourteen. That is how I've earned all my money, Martha: having sex with anyone who will pay enough—man or woman." His dark eyes glittered as he glared at her, clearly waiting for a reaction.

Martha heard what he was saying—heard the actual words—but they made no sense.

"Cat got your tongue?" His face twisted into a sneer. "Don't worry, I don't want you here any more than you want to stay. The good news is that I spent the day arranging your travel." He pointed to one of the letters he'd just thrown onto the table. "All the details are in there. I already spoke to Albert several hours ago and he will come tomorrow and help you and Cailean prepare to leave."

"Leave? And go where?"

"To France. Joss and his wife will help you find a suitable house. I've already set up an account for you. Joss will explain everything when you arrive. You will just have to—"

"I'm not going anywhere."

It was his turn to blink. And then his expression turned cold—so cold that she shivered under his gaze. "You are my wife and will do as you are told." He raked body her body with a hard, dismissive look before settling on her face. "You can go willingly or unwillingly. But you will go." His mouth flexed into a nasty smile. "And don't think that crying will change my mind."

Martha hadn't even known she was crying, but when she felt her cheeks, they were wet.

"All those nights you've been gone you were d-doing—" she swallowed "*that?*"

He laughed, and it was not a pleasant sound. "Are you trying to say *fucking*, sweetheart, because—"

"Don't! Don't you ever call me *sweetheart* using that tone—making the word sound so, so *ugly.*"

"I *am* ugly. So is what I do for a living; you'd better face the truth, *sweetheart.*"

"Why did you marry me?" she asked hoarsely.

"Haven't you figured that out yet? Your father bribed me to take you off Stroma. In return, he saved me from McCoy. That was our agreement. At first, I'd hoped that I could fob you off on Clark, but you ruined that escape for me so I was forced to marry you. I might be a whore, Martha, but I don't go back on my word." He gave her a look of pure distaste. "But I'm sick of it—sick of you—sick of this life, and I'm finished pretending, about all of it."

"Why are you saying—"

His eyes glinted dangerously, and he grabbed her upper arms, squeezing her so hard that she whimpered. "Don't you understand, you little fool? I love my job, Martha—all aspects of it. I love spending my days and nights fucking beautiful women"—he grinned evilly—"and also beautiful men, sometimes both at the same time." He snorted when she flinched. "You wouldn't believe the things I do—the perversions I enjoy. That's who I am. How could you ever believe I would enjoy such bland, milk and water sex with you after I've had some of the most gorgeous, sensual women in Britain?"

His words pummeled her like fists, and it was hard to breathe. "You've done this while we were married?"

"Oh, yes, darling. Tonight, I was with two women—exquisite, skilled women who were a pleasure to service. Every single night I've come from some other lover's bed before doing my duty with you." He shoved her away. "But I'm done pretending to be happy in this farce of a marriage and I'm done with you. Your father coerced me to marry you, but he said nothing about having to live with you."

"Ev—" She choked, swallowed, and tried again, "Everything you told me on Stroma—and since then—was all a lie?"

"Every single word of it, from what I like and who I am to where I came from. I don't have a loving family." He gave a bark of bitter, almost wild, laughter. "Although I didn't lie about how many of them there were. I *did* have eight brothers and sisters and not one of them ever gave a damn about me.

"Either did my mother or father. I haven't seen any of them since my father sold me to my first *lover*—an old man with a penchant for whippings, by the way—when I was fourteen. Not even my name is real; I changed it when I was eighteen." He smirked. "You're actually Mrs. Brian Dinwiddy."

Martha could only stare.

He spun away from her, as if too repulsed to even look at her, and strode back into his dressing room. "Only pack one small valise for both you and Cailean. I'll send the rest of your belongings separately. Joss will meet your packet and—"

"I'm not going to France. We've just signed the papers for the new house and—"

He stepped out of the dressing room and stared at her. "I'll tell Duncan we don't want it."

Her head spun. "*Why* are you doing all this?"

He flung an armful of clothing onto the floor and stalked toward her. "Haven't you been listening to me? I cannot live this dual life any longer. This was never meant to be, Martha. But I will take care of you—you never need to worry that you will be in want—"

"Something must have happened today. You were fine earlier—*we* were fine—"

His eyes blazed. "Don't bloody argue with me!" he thundered.

Fear and confusion threatened to choke her, but she refused to step back—to flee. She held her ground. "No. I won't leave. I took vows before God, Hugo. Those vows mean something to—"

He grabbed her by the arms again, but this time he shook her so hard her teeth rattled. "Goddammit, Martha! I don't want you. Is that so hard for you to understand? You sicken me! The best thing you can do is get the hell away from me." He dragged her by one arm toward the connecting door, unlocked it, and then flung it open. "Don't you dare defy me, Martha," he said, glaring down at her. "Be ready to leave tomorrow or there will be the devil to pay." He thrust her into her room—their room—and then slammed the door hard enough to rattle her teeth. She heard the tumbler turn as he locked the door.

Martha stood where she was, rooted to the floor; this couldn't be happening to her.

Except ... it just had.

She clutched her belly—where their baby was even now growing—and stared at the connecting door. His words from only moments before rained down on her like a hail of sharp stones, over and over and over.

Martha slapped a hand over her mouth to stifle the piteous cry that broke out of her, but it was no use, her tears would not be contained or controlled. She sank to her knees as sobs racked her body.

As she wept, she willed the connecting door to open, silently begging Hugo to come back. If not to apologize, then at least to explain. If she could only have a few more minutes to talk to him...

Surely he wouldn't just leave—

Somewhere a door slammed hard enough that she could feel it through her knees. Bootsteps passed by her bedchamber and receded down the corridor, until, once again, the house was shrouded in silence.

He wasn't coming back.

**

Hugo barely made it to the chamber pot behind the attractive screen before dropping to his knees and casting up the contents of his stomach.

He continued to heave until there was nothing left, and then he pushed himself to his feet and slumped against the wall.

He could hear Martha's sobbing through the connecting door and took three steps toward it, his hand reaching for the handle before he knew what he was doing.

No. You think you are being cruel, but you are saving her life, Hugo. This is the only way.

The sour taste of bile coated his tongue and burned his throat. His stomach clenched and he retched again. But nothing came up. His hands shook and the pounding in his head was so severe that his vision tinged with red, as if the blood vessels in his eyes had exploded.

Hugo and the Maiden

Hugo snatched up his valise and all but ran from the room; he had to leave now, before he broke down and begged her to forgive him for all his cruel, brutal lies. But that would be as good as a death sentence for the only person he had ever loved. He'd been selfish when he took her off Stroma; he needed to be strong now.

A hysterical, half-mad laugh broke from him at the exquisite irony of it all. He finally loved somebody—somebody who loved him in return—and he'd just destroyed everything in order to save her life.

You could have gone with her.

Hugo scoffed. Sure he could go with her, and when the paltry amount of money he'd saved was gone a year or two years from now then he could drop to his knees to earn more.

Solange's was *his*. He'd sweated and bled for it. There was no way in hell he was giving up everything he'd worked for. Not without a fight.

And what will you have if you win this fight?

He'd have a way to support his wife in comfort for the rest of her life.

But you won't have Martha.

"Goddammit!" he yelled, slamming his valise to the ground, his voice echoing up and down the empty street. He grabbed his aching temples and squeezed, slumping against the nearby lamp post.

He had no idea how long he stood there before his head no longer felt like it would explode. Once he could see without red blurring his vision, he picked up his bag and walked. And walked.

But the time he stopped—an hour and a half later by his watch—he was several miles away from his destination. Only then did he realize that he'd forgotten his overcoat, his hat, his walking stick, and his gloves.

The early morning was cold, but it was nothing compared to the chill inside him. He'd spent yesterday making sure that he decimated any possible future with Martha. Everything that he'd loved about his life—*everything*—was now gone. Hugo swallowed down his horror; he'd done what he had to do, and this was the last time he'd allow himself to wallow in his pain and self-loathing.

It would be dawn in another hour, so Hugo turned and trudged toward Solange's and the life he'd always known he'd end up with.

Chapter 34

"Martha?"

She startled at the sound of her name and looked up into Albert's concerned green eyes.

"I'm sorry," she said, forcing a smile—not a very good one if Albert's expression was anything to go by. "I missed what you said."

"I said that Fergus just bit Butterbank."

"Oh, dear. Where is Fergus now?"

"Cailean took him out to the carriage house."

"Is the bite bad? Should I go fetch the medicine chest and—"

"No, no," he soothed. "It's just a nip, but he said Fergus wasn't allowed back into the house."

"Well, I can't blame him," Martha said, abstractedly. "I'll tell Cailean to keep him outside until we leave."

Albert dropped to his haunches in front of her chair and took her hands in his. "What happened, Martha? Hugo seemed so very grim when he came to me yesterday. I've never seen him like that before—not even when we were in the hold of that horrible ship."

Martha was grateful that Hugo hadn't told Albert the truth. She didn't care if Albert knew what Hugo did for a living, but she didn't want to face his pitying looks at being abandoned.

She swallowed and thrust the unbearable thoughts away. "You don't have to accompany me, Albert. I know this must be hard on you. You've only just found a new job and—"

"You took care of me when I needed help—remember? And I owe Hugo everything, Martha, so if he wants any favor in the world then he has it. Besides, the lawyer says I'll not be needed here for weeks—perhaps months—and Mr. Haskins says I'm the best clerk he's ever had and that he'll take me back whenever I return."

Martha nodded. Not because she agreed, but because she simply didn't have the energy to argue.

"But won't you tell me what went wrong?" Albert persisted. "You both seemed so hap—"

The door opened. "Excuse me," Butterbank said, "but there is a Jonathan Buckingham here to see you, ma'am."

Hugo and the Maiden

Martha stared blankly, her mind stumbling like a drunken sailor. Just what in the world was *this*?

"That must be Hugo's brother," Albert said when she failed to respond to the waiting butler. "I know now isn't the best of times, but don't you want to meet him, Martha?"

Martha shook herself from her daze. "Yes, Albert. I'd like to meet Hugo's favorite brother. Show him in, Butterbank."

The man who walked in the door a moment later had the same dark coloring as Hugo, but other than that, the men couldn't have been more different. Jonathan Buckingham—or whatever his name was—was one of the most gorgeous men she had ever seen. As much as she loved Hugo—and she did, despite the horrid things he'd said to her—her husband was not classically handsome. This man was a veritable god.

"What a pleasure to meet you, ma'am," he said, bowing over her hand in a courtly fashion. "Hugo has told me so much about you in his letters."

Martha turned to Butterbank, who was hovering in the open doorway. "Would you have tea sent up, please?"

"Of course, ma'am."

Once the butler was gone, the smile dropped from her mouth and Martha locked eyes with the handsome stranger. "Now, perhaps you might tell me who you really are, *Jonathan*."

A short time later ...

"—and so he asked me to be here on Monday at noon," Daniel finished, sliding a finger between his immaculately tied neckcloth and muscular neck and gently tugging, as if he'd tied it too tight.

Albert turned to look at Martha, his face a mask of utter perplexity. "I don't understand, Martha. Why would Hugo do this?"

Martha felt a glimmer of hope for the first time since Hugo had ejected her from his bedchamber the night before. "To make me happy," she said. "When did you last talk to Hugo about coming over here today?" she asked Daniel.

"Er, that would be Saturday night." For some reason, he blushed.

Martha worried her lower lip as she considered that information. Hugo had still been trying to conceal his double life—his lies—barely two days before he experienced his dramatic about-face.

She stared pointedly at Daniel and he shifted uncomfortably in his chair. "Ma'am?"

"Tell me what happened?"

Daniel's eyes flickered from Martha to Albert and back. "I don't understand what you mean?"

"You say you are a friend of my husband?"

"Yes."

"Where did you meet?"

Daniel opened his mouth, and then shut it.

Martha smiled tightly. "It's all right, Daniel. I know where Hugo works—and it's not the Exchange."

"It's not?" Albert asked when Daniel said nothing. "Martha, what is going on?"

Martha ignored his question. "Hugo is your employer, isn't he?"

Daniel sighed. "Yes, ma'am."

"What happened yesterday?"

"I, er—" He gave her an anguished look. "Lord, ma'am. I don't know what to say."

"Hugo told me the truth about his family last night. Why didn't he tell you not to come here today?" Martha asked.

"I'm guessing he probably had one of the servants leave a message for me in my room." The skin over his high cheekbones darkened. "Er, I slipped out last night and spent the evening at a, er, friend's house and I didn't go back home before coming here."

Ah, that made sense. "Tell me what happened yesterday, Daniel."

"Ma'am, I can't—"

"I shan't tell Hugo and jeopardize your job, but I want the truth from you. If you tell me everything you know, I won't tell Hugo that you came here today."

Daniel pondered his choices for a moment before saying, "Bev Davies called Hugo in yesterday. I don't know what it was about—I don't," he insisted at the skepticism he likely saw on Martha's face. "But I *do* know that Bev brought Laura into the office while he was with Mr. Hugo."

"Laura Maitland?"

"Yes."

"And who is Bev Davies?"

Hugo and the Maiden

Daniel groaned and dropped his head into his hands. "Mr. Hugo will kill me."

"Martha, would you *please* tell me what this is all about?" Albert asked.

"Hugo is the owner of an exclusive brothel."

"*Brothel?*" Albert yelped.

"Yes. The brothel is the reason his scheming business partner arranged for Hugo to be falsely arrested. He managed to regain control of the business since returning to London and—what?" she asked Daniel when he opened his mouth, but then shut it again. "Why do you look like that?"

"It's just—well, Bev owns the business now and Hugo manages it."

"All of it?"

Daniel nodded.

Martha struggled to digest that information. Why would Hugo have lied about that?

"Brothel?" Albert repeated, and then turned to Daniel. "And you, er…" Albert's pale, freckled skin darkened as his eyes flickered over the much larger man's body. He cleared his throat. "You work for him?"

"Not like that," Daniel hastily assured him. "I'm a footman there."

The two men held each other's gaze, something unspoken passing between them.

"What is the name of the brothel, Daniel?" Martha asked when it seemed they'd both fallen into a trance. "I'm afraid my husband did not mention it."

Daniel pulled his gaze away from Albert with visible reluctance. "Er, it's called Solange's."

"Hugo owns Solange's?" Albert squawked. "That's the most exclusive—" He pulled a face and turned to Martha. "I'm sorry. We shouldn't be talking about such a thing in front of you."

Martha snorted. "It's a bit late for that."

Albert shook his head. "This is—you must be—" He made a sound that was half disbelief and half frustration. "Surely when you say that Hugo owns the business that means he doesn't actually, er *work* there?"

"Yes," she said softly. "He does."

"Actually—" Daniel started, and then stopped when the two of them turned to him.

"Actually what?" Martha asked.

"Um, Hugo doesn't take clients."

All the blood in her body rushed to her head. "What?" she asked, her voice over-loud judging by the way both men jolted.

"Hugo doesn't take clients," Daniel repeated. "At least not since he came back."

Martha struggled to breathe.

"Martha?" Albert slipped from his chair and crouched down in front of her, looking up at her with knitted brows. "What is it?"

"Say it again, Daniel—what you just said," she ordered.

"You mean about Hugo not taking clients?"

Martha squeezed her eyes shut. "No one?"

"Not a one, ma'am."

Hysterical laughter bubbled up inside her.

"He doesn't," Daniel insisted, when she opened her eyes and stared at him. "Not even when people pester him, which happens often. Everyone has commented on it. I'm the only one he told about you, but everyone speculates that he must, er, well, that he must have somebody. And then there is the fact that he no longer lives there, when—"

The door opened and it was Butterbank again, holding a silver salver. "I beg your pardon, ma'am, but a *person* is insisting on speaking to you."

"A person?" Martha stared at the battered, grubby calling card on the tray: Laura Maitland.

She glanced up at the butler and swallowed. "Um, are you sure she's not looking for Mr. Buckingham?"

"She specifically asked for you."

"Oh. Well, please show Mrs. Maitland in."

The door hadn't even closed before Daniel said, "Laura! What's she doing here? I don't think this is a good—"

"Why not?"

"Because ... well, just because."

"Won't you tell me what is going on?" Albert asked yet again, looking from Martha to Daniel and back. "Why would Hugo's ex-business partner want to talk to you?"

"I think we're about to find out," Martha murmured as the woman herself entered the room.

Martha didn't know what she'd been expected from the co-owner of an exclusive brothel, but the gaunt, gray-skinned wraith who entered the room wasn't it.

Laura Maitland studied Martha with the same intensity, her bloodshot eyes flickering over her person. Martha knew the woman must be wondering what it was about her that had caught the attention of a man like Hugo.

The two men stood, and Laura recoiled when she recognized Daniel. She scowled up at him. "What are *you* doing here?"

"Please, have a seat, Mrs. Maitland," Martha hastily said, as it looked like Daniel was about to say something unkind.

Laura didn't look away from Daniel, and Martha could see the woman was reconsidering her visit.

"Please," Martha repeated. "I'd like to know why you are here."

Laura jerked her gaze from Daniel and lowered herself into the proffered chair, her body vibrating with tension. "I take it you know who I am?"

"You are the person who had my husband wrongfully abducted and transported."

Laura's pale cheeks tinted, but she didn't look away. "Yes."

"Why are you here?" Martha repeated.

"Because I was there yesterday—at Solange's—when Bev brought Hugo in to threaten him."

Martha sat bolt upright. "Threaten him? Who is this person—this Bev?"

Laura glanced at Daniel. "Shall I tell her?"

He pursed his mouth, clearly unhappy.

"Yes, you should," Martha said when Daniel refused to answer.

"Bevan Davies is one of the most powerful criminals in London. I made a plan with Bev's son Cowan—one of his many bast—er, baseborn children—to, um, steal Hugo's part of the business." The muscles in her peaked face tightened. "I thought Cowan loved me, but he was just using me to get his hands on Solange's, which he then delivered to his father." Laura Maitland shrugged at the betrayal, but Martha saw pain in her eyes. "I know that Bev made a deal with Hugo. If he could operate the business at a profit for a year, he told him that he'd sign over the half that was once his and—"

"*How* do you know all this?" Daniel's handsome features were twisted into a sneer. He turned to Martha. "You can't believe her, ma'am. She's a lying, thieving, conniving—"

"Thank you, Daniel. But I'd like to let her finish."

Daniel's mouth snapped shut and he cut Laura a venomous look.

"He's right, Mrs. Buckingham—I'm all that and more. A cheap whore, a degenerate gambler, and I'm too fond of blue ruin by half. But I am telling you the truth about your husband. I know all about his deal with Bev because Cowan still comes to the Hen Roost." She swallowed and glanced away. "That's where I work now."

"I thought he threw you over?" Daniel asked. "I've heard him say—"

Fire blazed in the colorless woman's eyes. "You needn't rub it in! I know what Cowan Morgan says about me, Daniel." She deliberately turned her back on him. "You're a decent woman," she said to Martha, "and I know Hugo wouldn't want me to tell you too much about our trade—"

"He wouldn't want you in the same room with her," Daniel muttered.

Laura's mouth tightened, but she continued, "Daniel is right that Cowan despises me. But he still comes to me. Suffice it to say that I do things for him that most of the other women refuse to do." Her throat worked as she swallowed. "Demeaning things."

"I'm not going to judge you for what you do to earn a living," Martha said softly. "You needn't go into any detail. It sounds like what you're saying is that you've heard things from this Bevan Davies's son about my husband?"

"Yes. About Hugo, and about a lot of other things, too."

"Like what happened yesterday?"

She nodded. "Cowan was laughing about it last night—crowing about how Bev had brought the mighty Hugo Buckingham low. He, er—"

"Go on," Martha encouraged.

"He's blackmailing Hugo to, er, service a very powerful client—somebody Bev will be able to squeeze for a great deal of money and other favors."

Martha's face scalded at the word *service*. "Who is this person?"

Laura turned to Daniel. "Do you know who I mean?"

"I can guess," Daniel said.

Hugo and the Maiden

"Who?" Martha demanded.

When Laura said the name Martha's jaw dropped.

"Good God!" Albert gasped. "You have *got* to be bloody joking!"

Martha had never heard the gentle man swear before.

Daniel shook his head.

"I don't believe this," Albert said to Martha. "Any of it. Tell me you don't, either? Hugo would never—"

"He already admitted as much to me, Albert."

Albert blinked, poleaxed.

"What did this Bevan Davies blackmail Hugo with?" Martha asked Laura, although she was beginning to suspect.

"At first he said that he'd tell you that truth about what Hugo did."

"How did he know I wasn't already aware?"

"Bev has had somebody watching Hugo since he learned he was back. Hugo isn't known for being, er, well *tractable*, so I'm sure Bev decided that he'd probably need to have some leverage over him at some point. That's how he found out that Hugo was married." Her brow furrowed. "Cowan mentioned something about a man who was showing you houses?"

"Yes, we have an agent," Martha said numbly.

"He's the one who talked to Bev's man about you."

Mr. Duncan knew all about them—Martha had spent hours with him and had doubtless told him everything.

"But I don't understand," Martha said. "Hugo came home and told me the truth about everything last night. So how—"

"Bev said he would kill you if Hugo didn't do what he ordered."

The two men shot up from their chairs, both loudly chastising the other woman for telling Martha such a thing.

Martha's mind went back to last night—as it had been doing ever since Hugo had shoved her from his bedchamber—to all the cruel things Hugo had said to her. Now it was blindingly clear what he'd been doing: he wanted her to leave London and stay gone.

He'd said all those things to protect her—true, it was a misguided and foolish and predictably arrogant male response to danger—not to hurt her. He would have known that she would never leave him without extreme provocation.

He hadn't meant any of it. He'd said what he had because he *cared* for her.

"Martha?"

She looked up to find Albert squinting down at her.

"Hmmm?"

"Are you *smiling*?"

Her smile grew into a grin. "Yes."

His ginger eyebrows drew down. "But—"

"I'll tell you later," she promised. She turned to Laura, who was arguing heatedly with Daniel.

Martha cleared her throat and the two turned to her. "You still haven't said why you've come to me, Mrs. Maitland?"

"I came because I wanted to help—but I knew Hugo would never trust me."

"And you shouldn't either, Mrs. Buckingham," Daniel said, giving Laura a look of blistering contempt. "She's a liar."

Laura sighed. "Daniel's right."

"Perhaps. But I'd like to know what kind of help you have in mind," Martha said.

"Cowan always talks when he's, er, well, when he lets down his guard. Two weeks ago, I heard about something big. Something that wouldn't just put Bev and all the rest in jail—it would put their necks in nooses." Her gray eyes glowed with an emotion Martha couldn't identify. "It gave me an idea. An idea that could get Bev out of Hugo's hair for good."

"And why would you want to help Hugo?" Daniel demanded, asking the question that Martha was about to ask.

Laura ignored him and leaned closer to Martha. "I lost *everything* because of Bev Davies."

Daniel snorted. "And whose fault is that, Laura?"

"It's mine," she snapped. "I know that. *I'm* the one who went to his vile gaming hells and stayed night after night at his tables—I won't try to place the blame on Bev for my own weakness. But I know now that he had his eye on Solange's ages ago; he was determined to get it. He came after me because he couldn't ensnare Melissa or Hugo because neither of them is as weak and stupid as I am." Her lips thinned. "It's true that I'm the one who hanged myself. But Bev is the one who handed me the rope, inch by inch. You want to know why I would help you?"

Martha nodded.

Hugo and the Maiden

Laura smiled, and the hatred in her bloodshot eyes was a frightening sight. "Because the man who is trying to destroy your husband—and your marriage—has already destroyed my life. And I would dearly love to repay the favor."

Chapter 35

Hugo stood in front of his looking glass, putting the finishing touches on his neckcloth, and deeply regretted that he was not a drinking man.

The last five days had been the most unpleasant in his life. More unpleasant than his first weeks with Mr. Caton or his time on the convict ship.

Martha's eyes as they'd looked that night—shattered and betrayed—were never far from his mind.

He told himself that the chaos in his head would settle after this business with the duke was over tonight.

Either that, or he'd be dead—depending on what he did, which he'd not yet decided.

He placed a plain silver pin in the soft folds of his cravat, turned away from the mirror, and took one last moment to collect himself before going to work. It was likely to be a long evening. But then they'd all been long since that last, nightmarish night with Martha.

Hugo exhaled, rolled his shoulders and let himself out of his room, locking the door to the same suite he'd lived in before Laura sent him on his journey. Although she'd found his money and cache of valuables, she'd left the contents of his large dressing room untouched. He suspected that she would have gotten rid of that, too, given enough time.

Four days ago, Hugo had sold everything of value except three outfits of clothing.

Because he had always purchased the very best, even a quick sale had yielded him almost five hundred pounds.

He had deposited the five hundred, along with the rest of his money, into Joss's bank and then sent him a detailed letter explaining what he'd done. No matter what happened tonight, Martha would have enough money to take care of both her and Cailean for at least five years.

Hugo knew that if he died tonight Joss and Mel would both help Martha and Cailean. Perhaps they'd give her a job at one of the orphanages they were so fond of opening. He smiled; Martha would love that.

Yes, he had taken care of every last detail.

He grimaced. Well, except one.

Not until three o'clock Monday afternoon—after he'd thoroughly wrecked his marriage and moved back into Solange's—had he recalled that he was supposed to have met Daniel at Lady Selwood's.

When he'd finally found Daniel, the younger man's shocked expression told Hugo just how rough he looked. "I forgot to tell you that—"

"I went to the house, but nobody was there," Daniel interrupted. "I assumed something had happened to change your plans."

Well, you could say that.

"I'll still pay you for your time," Hugo had promised.

"You don't—"

But Hugo hadn't been in any mood to debate the matter. "I'll be in my study and don't want to be disturbed." He'd locked the door and hidden away from the world until half past five, when he'd gone to Lady Selwood's house.

He'd told himself that he wanted to make sure Martha was gone. But what he'd really hoped was that she'd defied him and he'd find her curled up in her favorite window seat reading. Cailean would be making a racket in the kitchen with some new cat, and his little dog Fergus—a wiry-haired terrier cur who would give his life for the lad—would be patrolling the back garden and keeping it safe from squirrels.

But he'd known even before Butterbank opened his mouth that Martha and Cailean were gone.

"You just missed them, sir. They left a short while ago."

"Good," he'd said, the last of his hope dying inside him. "I'll have somebody come by next week to pack up the rest of our things."

So, that had been that. Hugo had given an order and Martha had obeyed him. He told himself that he was relieved—and he was—but he also felt as if somebody had reached into his chest, crushed his heart, and ripped out his lungs.

It had been a struggle to breathe as he'd walked down the steps of Lady Selwood's house.

And breathing hadn't gotten any easier in the days since.

As he pondered the night ahead and prepared to sacrifice himself for a business that he no longer wanted, Hugo wondered if breathing was really worth the effort anymore.

***

Just to complicate matters, Solange's was busier than ever that night. Hugo could hardly walk five steps before some punter accosted him.

It was not quite midnight and Hugo was bloody exhausted. The duke rarely made it to Solange's until after one, which meant Hugo still had an hour to wait.

He surveyed the crowded card tables without really seeing them until raised voices pulled his attention to the back of the room—to the table that always seemed to attract every young, spoiled, and drunk aristocrat in London.

Tonight was no different.

Hugo ground his teeth as he watched the five men harassing the dealer, an older woman named Irene.

Irene had been dealing cards longer than most of the young bucks had been breeched and she didn't look flustered so much as irritated. As Hugo watched, one of the younger men reached over and swatted her on the arse.

Hugo spat out an especially vulgar word and stalked toward the table. He stopped between Irene and her harasser. "Good evening gentlemen," he said, needing to raise his voice to be heard above the raucous shouting and laughing. "It's time for Irene to take her supper break. I shall step in for her."

The arse-slapper was Lord Elwood Yates, the youngest son of the Duke of Montrose. God save him from younger sons.

Lord Elwood blinked owlishly up at him, weaving in his chair. "Oh, I say ... Buckingham. I was—*hic*—I was on a run."

Hugo gave the empty baize in front of the younger man a pointed look and the rest of the players erupted with jeers and laughs.

Hugo bared his teeth at the feckless aristocrat. "Well, let's see if we can't get you running in another direction, shall we?"

It took him less than half an hour to disperse the men in various directions—most toward expensive rooms and even costlier whores. Lord Elwood—who'd lost consciousness about ten minutes into the play—Hugo poured into a hackney and sent home.

Hugo and the Maiden

He'd just finished sorting out that mess when Daniel came toward him, his expression tense. "Excuse me, sir, but you're wanted in the Diamond Suite."

So, the time of reckoning had arrived. Hugo felt a mad urge to laugh, but he was afraid he wouldn't be able to stop.

"Oh," Daniel added, "and I just thought you'd want to know that Mr. Davies just arrived."

Hugo did laugh at that, but the sound had no amusement in it. "Was he by himself?"

"Er, no, he had Jac and Gary with him."

As Daniel stared at him, Hugo couldn't help noticing that the younger man looked almost as sick as he felt. "Are you unwell?" he asked as he strode from the card room and headed toward the grand staircase that led to the suites.

"Er, no," Daniel said, trotting along beside him. "I'm fine, sir."

Hugo started up the stairs and then stopped when he realized that Daniel was still with him. "Was there anything else you needed?"

"Uh, no, sir."

"Well, then you'd best get back to the door. It is going to be one of those nights." And then some.

Daniel hesitated, but then nodded. "Yes, of course sir."

Hugo watched the younger man leave and then turned and resumed his journey. It was only one flight of stairs, but it felt like a thousand.

On the second-floor landing Hugo turned right and headed toward the Diamond Suite. It was the most opulent set of rooms in the men's side of the house.

Like its name, the Diamond Suite glittered with crystal chandeliers, cut mirrors, and gilt furniture, aping the grandeur of Versailles.

Unbeknownst to many patrons, every room at Solange's had a small, secret room attached—usually referred to as a panel crib in the brothel trade. In the rougher, less savory whorehouses a male employee often hid in a panel crib, waiting for an opportune moment to pop out and rob a punter. At Solange's, the panel cribs had comfortable benches or chairs and were used by clients who paid to watch others.

Tonight, Hugo knew it would be Bev who was watching and that he'd wait to pop out until Hugo was balls-deep in his royal highness. Oh what a night of drama old Bev had planned!

Outside the Diamond Suite were the usual four guards. Hugo wondered if it was his imagination, or if Gibson gave him a harder-than-usual look.

He smiled. "Mr. Gibson."

Gibson ignored his greeting. "You can go in now," he said, nodding to one of the others to open the door.

Just like the time before, the duke was buttoning his breeches and Maisie was getting up off her knees when Hugo entered. Hugo dropped a low bow and forced a confident smirk he wasn't feeling. He jerked a dismissive nod at Maisie.

"I hope Maisie was to your liking, your royal highness," he said, the words for the whore's ears.

"Yes indeed, lovely, quite lovely." The duke's bulbous blue eyes looked uncharacteristically sharp tonight, even though his voice was as lazy and languid as ever. He gestured for Hugo to come closer, and Hugo didn't stop until he stood between the duke and the panel crib peephole.

Bev could probably still hear what he said, but Hugo was blocking both his and the duke's faces. Hopefully it would take a few seconds for Bev to figure out that things weren't going as planned.

Not that Hugo had known what he was going to do or say until the words began to pour out of him. "This is a trap, your royal highness," he said in a voice barely above a whisper.

"Eh?" The duke cupped his hand to his ear. "What's that?"

Hugo wanted to scream. Instead, he said in a marginally louder voice. "I said it's a trap. There's a man hiding behind a second of wall—right behind me—and he is going to—"

"*Stop where you are!*" The muffled yell came from the direction of the panel crib.

Both Hugo and the duke jerked at the sound of smashing glass, which was followed by a *thud* that seemed to shake the very building.

"*You are under arrest by the order of His Majesty, King George III, for—*" A deafening *bang* cut off the rest of the sentence.

Part of the wall exploded, showering the room with splinters of wood, just as the door to the suite flew open and Gibson and his three henchmen rushed in, using their bodies to form a wall between the panel crib and the duke. "Your royal highness—are you—"

"I'm fine," the duke said. "Go help the others." He didn't take his eyes from Hugo's face.

Hugo and the Maiden

A strangled cry, some vulgar shouting, and another loud crash came from the other side of the wall.

"It sounds like they might need it," the duke added drily.

Gibson jerked out a nod and his three men ran out into the hall. Gibson stationed himself just outside the door, leaving it open.

"My visits to Solange's have always pleased me," the duke said, loudly enough to be heard by anyone still listening. "As has your loyalty and respect for my privacy." He paused, and then added in a far softer voice. "I knew you would not disappoint me, Hugo."

That was a hell of a lot more than Hugo had known.

"I shall miss your services greatly."

Hugo had always thought the duke was rather vapid. But right then, intelligence and resolution shone in his gaze.

Before Hugo could come up with a response another man in non-descript clothing arrived at the door and Gibson let him through.

"Well?" the duke demanded.

"All went as planned, sir."

"The weapons?" the duke asked.

"Our agents seized the guns and captured seven men—two employed by Davies and five with the radicals. One man died while trying to escape and another got away, but we have reason to believe that he was badly injured and hope to apprehend him before the night is over."

Hugo blinked. *Guns? Radicals? What?*

"What were their names?" the duke asked, straightening the cuffs on his coat.

"They refused to tell us." The messenger's smile was grim. "But we'll find—"

"*Hugo, you bloody bastard!*" Bev and his four captors stopped in the open doorway. The crime lord's lip was bleeding and one of his eyes was swelling.

Hugo forced an insouciant grin he was far from feeling and sauntered toward him. "Going somewhere, Bev?"

Bev thrashed like a wild beast, all but foaming at the mouth. "You bastard! You think you'll get away with this?"

"Now, now, Bev." Hugo thoughtfully stroked his chin. "What was it you said about not allowing one's emotions to get the better of one?"

Bev snarled and launched himself at Hugo. His burst of energy startled his captors, and he broke free and grabbed Hugo's coat lapels, slamming him up against the wall as if he could put him through it. "You'll be bloody sorry!" Spittle flew from his mouth. "You'll not get away with double crossing me. I've got a long reach and I'll—"

Hugo smashed his head into the bridge of Bev's nose and heard a sickening crunch as Bev crumpled, blood spurting from his nose.

Two huge men grabbed him beneath the arms and yanked him to his feet and then hauled him like a sack of potatoes, the iron heels of his hobnail boots scratching grooves in the glossy wood floor.

"Enjoy your trip, Bev," Hugo called after him, adjusting his crushed cravat and coat with hands that shook.

He turned to the duke. "Can somebody tell me what the hell is going on?" he demanded, not giving a damn that the man across from him might one day be his sovereign.

"Come here, Hugo."

Hugo stopped in the same place he'd stood only a few moments earlier.

"You and your wife have not only rendered immeasurable aid to your country, but I am personally in your debt."

"My wife?"

The duke didn't appear to hear him. "If you ever need anything, you may take this to my house in Kew." He extracted a folded and sealed piece of parchment from his breast pocket.

Hugo took the document and stared blankly at it, his brain beginning to understand—if not comprehend—that Martha was somehow behind this.

"Thank you, your royal highness." He swallowed, hesitated, and then looked the duke squarely in the face. "Er, I'm afraid that I, personally, can't provide your royal highness with the usual, er, services tonight. However, we do have a new—"

"I would rather go without."

Hugo felt oddly flattered by the other man's words.

The duke's lips flexed into a faint smile. "By the by, congratulations on your marriage." He cocked his head. "I must admit I was surprised."

"No more than I was, sir."

Hugo and the Maiden

"Your wife is an admirable young woman who appears to love you a great deal." His expression turned almost wistful. "You are a fortunate man."

"Yes," Hugo said. "I am the most fortunate of men." Or at least he had been, before he destroyed it all.

The duke laid a hand on Hugo's shoulder. "My advice to you is to treat her like a queen."

Hugo bowed again and then watched as the duke limped toward the door. He waited until the other man was gone before collapsing into the chair he'd just vacated.

"Bloody hell," he muttered, his entire body shaking as the tension he'd been suppressing all day—hell, all week—surged through him.

He glanced at the huge bed just across the room and briefly considered crawling beneath the covers and sleeping for a week.

But no, he needed to find his wife and get to the bottom of this.

And he needed to tell her something; something that was long overdue.

Chapter 36

Hugo saw the faint glow in the sidelight next to the front door and leapt out of the hackney cab before it even rolled to a stop. He flung the fare at the driver, ignoring the man's outraged squawk when coins struck the side of the old coach instead of his outstretched hand.

Hugo had come from the house on Berkeley Square with his heart in his throat. If Martha wasn't here, he had no idea where he'd find her.

He ran up the steps, slipping on the smooth stone and almost pitching himself through the glass beside the door. He pounded on the heavy wood, grabbed the handle, and shoved.

Miraculously, the door swung open and he stumbled into the small but elegant foyer, which held two people and one very excited dog leaping straight up into the air like a bouncing ball, over and over and over.

But Hugo only had eyes for one thing. He reached for Martha, but she beat him to it.

"Hugo!" she yelled as she slammed into his chest hard enough to knock the air from his lungs.

Hugo squeezed her tighter than the metal rings around a barrel, burying his nose in her hair and inhaling the sweet scent of his wife. "Oh God, darling—I'm so sorry for those terrible things I said. I didn't mean—"

"I know—I know, Hugo," she murmured, kissing and squeezing and petting him.

He held her at arm's length so he could look at her precious face. "You know? But how?"

Tears streamed from her magnificent blue eyes but she was smiling. "You were only trying to protect me. You wanted me to go so that Bev didn't—"

Fergus gave an earsplitting howl and bolted toward the corridor that led to the kitchen.

"Fergus!" Cailean shouted, sprinting after the little dog.

"What the devil is that all about?" Hugo asked Martha.

"I don't know."

"Did you just get here?" he asked Martha.

"Only a minute before you."

"Where did you come from?"

"We were staying in a house that Mr. Gibson arranged for the three of us. He said it wasn't safe to come back here until they'd arrested Bev Davies."

Hugo frowned. "Where is Albert?"

"He got here before us. We needed to go and get Fergus from Lady Selwood's—the stablemaster was keeping him for us. Maybe that is what Fergus heard in the kitchen, Albert?"

Bev's words from Solange's slammed into him: *I've got a long reach, you'll be sorry.*

"Christ!" Hugo yanked open the front door. The hackney was still at the curb, the driver crouched in the street looking for the coins he'd thrown. Hugo shoved Martha toward the carriage. "Go wait in the cab, Martha. Tell the driver to leave if I'm not back in five minutes."

"But Hugo—"

"I'm going to see what Fergus ran after."

"It is probably just Albert."

Hugo thought about Fergus's spinetingling howl. "I want to make sure," he said, giving her a gentle push. "Just go."

He slammed the door before she could argue, grabbed the candlestick off the console table, and followed the sound of Fergus's barking. Some of the wall sconces were lit in the long hallway, which explained why Cailean hadn't fallen on his arse.

He turned a corner and could see the kitchen dead ahead. The door was open and Fergus jumping up and down, his frenzied yapping interspersed with snarls. Hugo skidded to a halt just inside the door. He stared at what Cailean was staring at: Albert trussed up like a gamebird in the corner of the kitchen.

But Albert wasn't looking at Cailean or Hugo.

Albert's bulging eyes were staring at something right behind—

Hugo whirled just as cudgel came down. Pain exploded in his shoulder as the heavy club clipped his shoulder instead of cracking his skull. Hugo stumbled back, ran into a chair, and went sprawling onto his arse.

Cowan—or at least he thought it was Cowan Morgan, although his hair was matted with blood and his face so swollen on one side that he didn't even look human—limped toward him and raised the huge club again.

"Nooooo!" Cailean leapt between Cowan and Hugo faster than a lad his size should have been able to move. But Cowan, for all his injuries, was quick enough to pivot and he swung the raised club at Cailean instead of Hugo.

The club struck Cailean in the upper arm and the lad screamed as the blow knocked him back several feet and he careened into the pot rack before sliding to the floor.

Dozens of pots clattered on the hard floor of the kitchen, the din deafening.

Cowan turned and started back toward Hugo, just as a black and white streak shot across the room and struck him in the crotch. The big man's scream was even louder than the pots.

"Get it off! Get it off!" he shrieked as he staggered backward, striking at Fergus with the club, but hitting his own knee rather than the small, squirming dog. He howled in pain and flung the club away, slapping at Fergus with his huge hands.

But Fergus's jaws had locked tight. His wiry body hung a foot off the floor and thrashed back and forth as he savaged Cowan's jewels.

Cowan rammed his pelvis into the counter, squashing Fergus against a cupboard door while he fumbled with the knife block.

Hugo leapt over the tangle of kitchen chairs that had brought him down, lunging for Cowan's club just as something gray fluttered at the edge of his vision.

It was Martha, and she held a large vase over her head as she ran toward Cowan.

"Martha, be caref—"

She smashed the vase against the back of Cowan's skull with all the strength of a woman who'd spent the first twenty years of her life doing hard manual labor.

Cowan grunted and crumpled, the knife slipping from his limp fingers with a clatter as he slid to the floor, trapping Fergus beneath his huge body.

Hugo snatched up the club and strode toward the fallen man. "Get back, Martha," he said when she reached for Cowan's shoulder to turn him over and free poor Fergus.

She jerked back her hand and took a step back.

Hugo and the Maiden

Hugo kicked the knife away from Cowan's outstretched hand, raised the club, and nodded at Cailean, who'd crawled to the fallen man on his hands and knees. "Go ahead and turn him over."

Cailean grunted with the effort of rolling the huge man onto his back.

Fergus squirmed free of his prison and gave a joyous yip as he leapt into Cailean's waiting arms.

Drool and blood leaked from the corner of Cowan's mouth and more blood oozed from a nasty cut over his eye.

Hugo lowered the club. "Go untie Albert," Hugo told Cailean, and then turned to his disobedient wife. "And *you*. I thought I told you to wait in the carriage."

Before she could speak—and likely argue—Hugo grabbed her with the hand not holding the cudgel and yanked her close, squeezing a startled squeak out of her as he stared down into her wide blue eyes.

"Never mind," he said, kissing her hard on the mouth. "What I meant to say was *I love you, Martha Buckingham.*"

She stared up at him, poleaxed.

"Oh, and also thank you for saving the day with that hideous vase." He gave her another kiss, this one a bit more thorough, and then pulled away. "But the next time you thrust yourself in the middle of danger I'm going to put you over my knee. Understood?"

Martha's smile grew slowly, until it illuminated the kitchen. "Yes, Hugo."

Hugo snorted; he wasn't fooled for a second by her demure tone and meek expression. "We shall talk more about this later," he promised. "In great detail. Is the hackney still outside?"

"I paid him to wait."

"I'm going to stay here and watch over Cowan. Take Cailean with you and go tell the driver he needs to fetch the nearest Watch. And then come right back here."

"Yes, Hugo."

He kissed her, and then waited until the two of them left before turning to Albert, who was rubbing the circulation into his wrists. "Need a doctor?" he asked.

Albert shook his head and then winced. "Just a bit of a goose egg. I'll be fine."

"What happened?"

"I came in through the kitchen—my key didn't work on the front door—and he must have been waiting."

Cowan moaned, the eye that wasn't swollen shut opened a crack and his hands went to his bloody trouser front. He whimpered, clutched his jewels, and then whimpered again.

"Fancy seeing you here, Cowan."

Amazingly, Cowan's battered face twisted into a sneer when he saw Hugo looking down at him, holding his club. "You filthy sod bastard."

Hugo grinned. "I'm glad to see that almost having your prick ripped off hasn't dimmed your sunny nature. Why are you here?"

"Where the hell else could I go?" Cowan shouted, and then winced at the pain it must have caused his head."

"Is that a trick question?" Hugo asked, genuinely confused. "How about the Continent? The Liverpool docks? Calcutta? Just about anywhere else but here?"

"The bloody soldiers have seized everyone I know and everything I own. I got away from them at the harbor, but there were more waiting at Bev's place. I ain't got any money. I'm bloody trapped and will probably swing for this. So I figured I'd come here and kill your whore wife and—"

Hugo kicked him in the side and Cowan screamed.

"Now, now. Mind your manners, Cowan," Hugo said, his foot twitching to kick him again. And keep on kicking until he was no longer a threat to anyone.

Cowan clutched his side and glared up at him, fury and hatred burning in his eye.

Hugo heard movement behind him and turned to find Martha, Cailean, and Fergus. "The Watch is on their way," she said.

Hugo slipped his arm around her and smiled.

"You go ahead and smile, Buckingham," Cowan shouted through his swollen mouth. "You'll get *nothing* out of all this, you dumb bastard."

Hugo kissed Martha's cheek and then looked down at the raving man. He was tempted to tell him that he was wrong—that he got *everything* out of what happened tonight: Martha. But he decided that Cowan didn't deserve to even hear Martha's name.

Instead, he said, "Is that so?"

Hugo and the Maiden

"Yeah, that's so. There won't be no Solange's in a few months. Bev already sold the buildings—the money has changed hands and the new owner takes possession at the end of the year." He laughed, and then gasped and grabbed his side.

As Hugo stared down at the bloody, hateful man at his feet he considered the news he'd just heard and what he felt about it.

It took him a moment to identify the emotion: it was relief.

Hugo handed Albert the club. "Keep an eye on him until the authorities come." He then looked away from Cowan, turning his gaze to something infinitely more beautiful and worthy: his wife.

"Shall we go wait in that charming little sitting room, darling?"

"I'd like that, Hugo."

He tightened his arm around her, and she melted against him.

"Don't you understand? Solange's is gone!" Cowan shouted after him. "Everything you ever worked for. If you want it back, you'll have to spend every penny you have on lawyers and waste years of your life chasing it through the courts."

Hugo smiled down at Martha. "I don't care about Solange's anymore," he said, just loud enough for her ears. "And I can think of a much better way to spend the rest of my life."

Chapter 37

Several hours later ...

"Laura?"

Martha gave him an exasperated look. "Hugo, that's the fourth time you've said that."

"I know, I know," he said. "But ... *Laura?*"

Martha laughed. "Yes, it was Laura who came up with the plan."

He kissed her nose and then his dark gaze lowered to her chest.

Martha looked down and saw the blanket had slipped and that one breast was exposed. She hastily covered herself.

"Oh, Martha."

"Oh, Hugo." She smiled at his petulant tone and pouty look. "Do you want to hear the rest of my story or look at my breasts?"

"Can't I do both?"

"You didn't seem to be able to do both half an hour ago when we came to bed."

He smirked. "You're probably right. So, it was Laura's plan to approach our sovereign's brother and tell him that he was about to be a victim of extortion. For sodomy."

"Well, when you state it so *baldly* I suppose it does sound a bit, er, audacious."

"Yes, just a bit. Especially when one considers who Laura is, what Laura is, and where Laura now works."

Martha didn't want to feel pity for the woman who'd been responsible for Hugo's captivity, but Laura Maitland was a broken creature. While Martha couldn't quite bring herself to forgive Laura, she respected her for doing her best to right the wrongs she'd done Hugo, even though she would never be able to restore everything she'd stolen.

"Laura was the first one to admit she would never be allowed anywhere near his royal highness," Martha said.

"And so *you* decided to be the messenger."

"We *all* decided I should go."

He snorted. "I still can't believe Daniel was part of this mad plan and kept it from me. I'm his *employer*."

Hugo and the Maiden

"It wasn't so mad, since it worked," she pointed out.

Hugo slid an arm around her bare shoulders and pulled her close. "I know it worked—and I'm grateful. But you could have *died*, sweetheart. Cowan was demented enough to kill you."

"But I didn't die. And the duke didn't get extorted, and Mr. Davies wasn't able to sell the guns to the radicals, and you no longer need to work for that dreadful criminal."

"You're right—yet again, darling." He kissed her. "Now tell me about your meeting with the duke; *that* I need to hear"

"First I had to speak to a gentleman named Gibson."

"Ah, yes, Gibson."

Martha didn't tell him that Mr. Gibson kept her locked in a windowless room for six hours while he questioned her. Over and over and over. Nor did she tell him that she'd never been so terrified in her entire life.

There was no reason for him to know any of that.

"Once Mr. Gibson ascertained that I wasn't lying, the duke came to see me." She'd waited almost twenty-four hours before the duke finally came. Martha suspected they'd kept her in that windowless room so that nobody would ever see the two of them together.

"He was very polite and asked only a few questions about everything that I'd already told Mr. Gibson, so I assumed he'd informed the duke thoroughly." She hesitated, and then said, "He seemed far more interested in my relationship with you."

Hugo gave a noncommittal *hmmm*.

Well, what else could he say? What *was* there to say? Her husband had been a royal duke's *lover*. He had worked as a prostitute all his life; he'd had hundreds, if not thousands, of lovers—male and female.

And there wasn't a thing Martha could do to change that.

She strove not to be judgmental or jealous or hateful, but unpleasant emotions roiled in her belly while she'd sat there looking at a man who'd been intimate with her husband. Those same feelings were stirring right now as she looked at her beloved Hugo and thought about all the people who'd known his magnificent body and enjoyed his magical skills.

"Martha?"

Fear, shame, and defiance lurked in his beautiful dark eyes. "I want you to know that I went to the duke last night and told him *no*. It is who I was, not who I am."

His words rendered her boneless with relief. She sagged against his body and pressed her face into the hardness of his chest, kissing his silky, hot skin and nuzzling him until her lips brushed against a small, hard nipple and he jerked.

"Mmmm." She fastened her mouth over the little bud and sucked.

Hugo shivered. "Martha," he warned.

She reluctantly detached herself from his delicious body and looked up at him. "I had hoped that was what you would do, Hugo. Thank you."

"I didn't do it for you, Martha. I did it for us. You are the only good thing that has ever happened to me. And just like you, the vow I took means something to me." His arm tightened. "I will be faithful to you until I die, Martha—even if it means I have to go hat in hand to Melissa's bloody husband and beg him for a job wrangling orphaned French brats." He kissed her and then held her gaze. "But there is nothing I can do about all the years behind me."

"I know that, Hugo." Martha swallowed, struggling to find the right words. "I'm not going to lie and claim that learning the truth about your past won't take time to understand and adjust to, but I love you and nothing will change my mind about that." She opened her mouth, but hesitated.

"What is it, darling?"

"You really mean it? I mean about the orphanage?"

He traced her lower lip with his thumb, his eyelids heavy. "Yes. I'm very serious about finding another way to make money. I'll dig ditches before I sell myself again." His mouth quirked into a smile. "My body now belongs only to you."

Her eyes burned and she blinked rapidly.

"Please don't cry," he begged.

She gave a gurgle of a laugh. "I'm just so happy." She shoved her face into his chest again and sniffled.

Hugo stroked her shoulder and held her close. "Tell me the rest of your story, Martha."

"There's not much else," she said, her voice watery. "Laura had heard Cowan complaining that his half-brother—Elis, I think his name is—had impressed their father by bringing guns from France to sell to some group here. We all agreed that was something the government should know. Gibson and I both argued to arrest them all beforehand, but it was the duke who wanted to catch Davies in the act, so to speak."

Hugo snorted. "Ah, the dramatic approach."

"Hugo?"

"Hmmm?"

"Will you try to get Solange's back?"

"No. That's over. Cowan was right about it taking years and lots of money. It would make for a miserable life." He sighed. "I'm not happy about it, Martha—it took years to earn enough to purchase my half and I poured even more money into the place during the three years I was co-owner. It ... pains me to let it go. But it pains me even more to have you associated with such a place."

Martha hesitated, and then said, "Thank you, Hugo. I shouldn't care to think of you continuing to work in such a place, either. I don't believe it comes without cost." She smiled. "And I don't think it would be good for our child, either."

***

Hugo blinked. "I'm sorry, darling—did you say *our child?*"

She nodded, her soft hair tickling his chin.

Hugo straddled her blanket-covered body and grabbed her shoulders. "Our child?"

"I know you said you didn't want children, but—"

"Our child?"

She laughed. "You're doing it again—sounding like a demented parrot."

Hugo crushed her against him for the third time that night. "How could you think I wouldn't want our child? Whatever I said back on Stroma—before we were married—was spoken in ignorance." He kissed her head, squeezing his eyes shut and inhaling her scent, which intoxicated him. "When did you learn this, sweetheart?"

"The day you told me to leave."

Her words were like a punch to his heart. "Oh, darling. I'm so sorry. How terrified you must have been."

"It was not a good night."

Hugo released her so he could see her face.

"No," she said, before he could speak. "Don't apologize again. What you said that night hurt me—greatly—but you did it for the best of reasons." Her lips twisted. "However misguided. I forgive you for the pain you caused me." She gave him a chiding look. "Just never do it again."

He gave a breathless laugh. "I will be a model husband for the rest of our lives."

"I hope not, I like you the way you are."

Hugo shifted so that he could strip the blankets off her.

"Hugo! What are you doing?"

"I want to see your belly."

"But—"

He pushed open her thighs, knelt between them, and laid his head on the gentle swell of her stomach.

"*Hugo.*"

"Now you sound like a demented parrot," he teased. "I can't hear anything," he said a moment later, and then pushed up onto his elbows to meet her gaze.

She laughed. "What did you expect to hear?"

He shrugged. "I don't know a thing about babies or childbirth." He left unsaid his only knowledge of subject, which was avoiding making clients pregnant. "When will you show some sign of your condition?"

"It's early—only six weeks. It will be a few months."

Hugo stroked the soft skin of her belly as his brain struggled to absorb the fact that there was—at this moment—a child beneath his hand. His child. *Their* child.

He experienced a sudden rush of primal pride and his cock— already half hard from being so close to her—throbbed as he imagined her swollen with his baby.

"Do you want a boy or a girl?" she asked, interrupting his primitive preening.

"Either is fine. What about you?"

She smiled down the length of her delicious body at him. "I just want a fat, healthy baby."

He stared at her stomach as he caressed her, utterly stupefied that a tiny human would be living in there for nine months—he knew that much about babies, at least.

"Hugo?"

He looked up. "Yes, darling?"

"Won't you tell me about your family—about what happened to you?"

Hugo and the Maiden

He groaned and rolled onto his back, the raging erection he'd been sporting already shriveling. "It's so sordid, Martha." Not to mention humiliating.

"Is it too painful for you to speak of it?"

For years his father's abandonment had bled like an open wound. But now?

"No, it's just an old ache now."

She scooted down the bed, until they were shoulder to shoulder, and then took his hand in her much smaller one. "Please?"

Hugo sighed. "When I was fourteen my father took me on a hackney ride across London. My mother had died just the week before and—" He snorted and turned back to the ceiling; it was too difficult to tell this story while looking into her beautiful eyes. "The one thing that Bev Davies gave me was the truth about my parents—and about me. I didn't learn until a month ago that my mother was a prostitute before marrying my father. She gave up whoring for years, until desperation forced her back. I was conceived during that time."

"Oh, Hugo."

"You'd have thought that I would have guessed years ago. After all, I looked nothing like my father and shared few characteristics with my siblings, or even my mother." He shrugged. "I had always believed that my father disliked me because I was such an inconvenient afterthought. He wasn't cruel to me. In fact, he just ignored me until that hackney ride."

Hugo could still recall his anticipation that day. Perhaps his father might start to like him? After all, Hugo was the only one who still lived at home and Evan Dinwiddy had seemed broken by his wife's death—maybe they would help each other through their grief?

He almost laughed as he recalled how naïve he'd been.

"He took me to a whip-maker, a man named John Caton." Hugo chewed his cheek, wondering how to phrase what came next.

"That is who taught you to braid," she said softly. "You mentioned once that he … whipped you."

"Yes." Hugo still remembered that first time, although he'd forgotten the dozens, if not hundreds, of others over the years that followed.

He turned to her again. "There are people—a great many—who find sexual pleasure in either whipping or being whipped."

Martha swallowed, her chest rising and falling too quickly for a person at rest.

Hugo took in her signs of distress and shook his head. "I don't think you want to hear this, darling."

"I want to know about you, Hugo."

He traced the graceful line of her throat down to her breast and caressed her nipple as he considered what he was about to say.

"Caton bought me because he liked men—very young men."

"Boys," she corrected, her eyes suddenly fierce.

"Very well, boys. But don't fret over me, Martha—I wasn't a virgin when I went to him and I knew what he wanted from me. My life at home had always been difficult. There was never enough food, my mother was ill for a long time before she died, and my father expected me to work. I was a slender lad until I turned eighteen or so—not good for manual labor—and it didn't take me long to discover that I appealed to certain men." He met her gaze, which was direct, but wary. "What I'm about to say will doubtless sound wrong—sinful—"

"It's not my place to judge you, Hugo."

"But you are, aren't you?"

"I did at first. Those first few days after you told me the truth, I was angry, hurt, and—yes—disgusted," she admitted. "I was so very shocked and caught by surprise, some of the things you mentioned had never even entered my mind. But once I stopped being so furious at you for leaving, I thought about what my father would say. You know how he was—he *never* judged others."

Hugo nodded; the vicar had been a truly kind, good soul. But Hugo suspected that even he would have blanched at Hugo's past.

"My father never believed in using the Bible as a weapon or hectoring people for their sins. He believed in loving others and doing no harm. I think the only person harmed by the things that you did—and that were done to you—was *you*."

"Perhaps," Hugo said, not in any hurry to play the victim in her eyes. "Until you, I had always viewed fu—er, sex—as a way to make money. That's all that mattered to me: who paid the most."

As Hugo let her absorb that, he considered the fact that he enjoyed using the word *fuck* when they were in the heat of passion—he adored shocking her—but that it felt wrong and crude to use it in conversation.

Hugo and the Maiden

"Why am I different?" she asked. Her voice was steady, but he heard the pain and confusion beneath it. She was genuinely trying to understand him, but it was a lot for anyone to comprehend, especially a woman who was hardly more than an innocent.

"At first I didn't know why," he said. "On Stroma, when I couldn't stop thinking about you, it bothered me. No," he amended, "it terrified me, although I refused to admit it at the time."

"You were scared?"

"I'd never had such strong feelings—such a relentless desire—for anyone. I wanted you, badly, but I didn't want to hurt you or ruin your life. That was also a new consideration for me." He gave her a wry smile. "I'm sure you remember what I was like when I arrived that night."

She chuckled softly. "You were horrid. But also very …"

"Yes?" he prodded.

She dropped her gaze, her cheeks fiery. "I couldn't look away from you. Your b-body was so beautiful and unlike anything I'd ever seen. And when your blanket slipped—"

It was Hugo's turn to laugh. Amazingly, he also felt his own face heat at her compliment. "Ah, you remember that, do you?"

"You were so naughty."

Hugo smiled down at his love. "And you were so cruel."

She snorted, but the smile faded from her face. "Finish your story, Hugo."

Hugo sighed. "Caton made it clear my first night the way things would be between us."

By that time Hugo had already been with many men, but those had been furtive back-alley encounters. Caton owned his body outright and had the leisure and opportunity to use him fully.

"He liked to, er, well, whip me and then use me."

She bit her lip, and her eyes became glassy.

He groaned. "Don't cry for me, Martha. It's a sign of what a bad man I am that I really didn't suffer all that much during the years I worked off my debt. He knew how to handle a whip and never damaged me in any permanent sense. He was quite old when he'd bought me and took me less and less as time wore on. My last year with him was—well, it was quite possibly the easiest year of my life up to that point." Only after he'd spoken did he realize how pitiful that sounded.

"Oh, Hugo."

He kissed her. "He taught me a trade and I was good at it. I made enough money to buy my freedom. He wanted me to stay." Indeed, he'd offered to give Hugo his business if he remained and took care of him. "But I was young and arrogant and, by then, I knew I could make a great deal more money elsewhere."

"With your body?"

"With my body," he confirmed. "I worked at several places before I managed to get a position at Solange's. It was one of the most exclusive brothels in the city. Melissa Griffin cared about her employees and it was the safest place I had worked, by far." He shrugged. "And the rest you know—I worked there until I could buy into it."

"And you never saw any of your family again?"

"No. Bev told me that two of my sisters had worked for him, that my father—or the man I thought of as my father—had died some years back, and the rest of my siblings he knew nothing about."

"Was your mother at least kind to you?"

He considered his mam, whom he'd not really thought about for years. After a moment, he shook his head. "I know it is terrible, but I can't even recall her face. She was ill—I suppose it was consumption—for years. She was always tired, worn down, and joyless. She was never cruel to me—neither of them was—but I was just a burden to her. I don't think she had enough of herself left to love any of us. It was a hard life, Martha. That's why—" He bit his lip, not wanting to talk about losing Solange's.

"That's why you were so determined to hold on to your business—you didn't want to be poor again."

Hugo nodded. "Until I met you, possessions were the only things that made me feel safe or happy. I thought if I could surround myself with enough *things* then I would finally feel secure. But I now know that would have never happened. I would have always needed more, more, more." He stroked his fingers through the soft hairs at her temple. "Now ... well, I don't give a damn about expensive clothing or a grand house stuffed full of fine things."

"Do you really think you can be happy operating an orphanage in a foreign country, Hugo?"

He smiled down at the love of his life. "I don't think you quite understand what I'm saying, Martha. When I thought I'd lost you—that

Hugo and the Maiden

I'd thrown away what we had—I realized that the only thing I needed for happiness was *you*. I'll be happy living anywhere, doing anything, as long as we are together, my darling."

Epilogue

A Small Village in France
Several Years Later

"*Non, non, ne tenez pas le chien par la queue, Yvette. Il n'aimera pas ça.*" Hugo said to the angelic-looking three-year-old girl who was risking life and limb by holding Fergus's tail.

Martha smiled at both Hugo's coaxing tone and his French. While all three of them had become far more fluent in the language over the last seven years, Hugo still had the most dreadful pronunciation. Sometimes she suspected that he wore his sheer Englishness as a badge of honor.

Once he'd detached the unwitting cherub from imminent canine danger, he carried the little girl back over to the group of children who were currently listening to a story before they took their afternoon nap.

"I'm sorry, Monsieur Yougo. Yvette is a sneaky one!" Sandrine said in charmingly accented English. She was one of the five women who lived and worked at their small orphanage. Hugo, Martha, and Cailean had all learned French, but they asked that their employees learn English so their young charges would learn both languages. All the children would one day have to work for a living and being bilingual was a valuable, and lucrative, skill, as the three of them had quickly learned.

Once he'd deposited the little girl, Hugo strode across the lawn of what had once been the country home of the de Courtney family. While the grounds were still lovely, much of it had been allowed to return to nature. What lawn remained was dotted with dandelions—which the children adored—and only raggedly trimmed.

Martha knew that the lovely estate was a mere shadow of what it had been when it belonged to the de Courtneys, but she liked to think that it was far more beloved by the children who had come here to heal and begin new lives.

Although Melissa and Magnus had originally purchased the house and land and employed Hugo and Martha to operate the orphanage, they had been able to buy the property after Albert's first factory began production three years ago.

Rather than pursue his interest in Solange's, Hugo had used the ducal favor he'd been granted to ensure that Albert gained speedy control of his patent. Not only that, but the man who'd tried to steal his idea and condemned Albert to transportation was now, himself, a resident of the southern colonies.

Over the years Albert had applied for more patents than Martha could count and was currently constructing a second larger, factory several miles outside London. While he made his permanent home in England, he still visited them three or four times a year and always brought his employee and dear friend—Daniel Charters—with him on his trips.

Last year Albert had invested money in yet another of Magnus's ventures, a school that would teach older children both practical skills as well as mathematics and sciences.

Hugo dropped into the chair beside her with a sigh, and then patted his knee. "Come here, Fergus old boy," he cajoled. "She didn't hurt you—well, maybe your pride," he amended with a chuckle as the old dog walked stiffly toward him.

Hugo scooped him up and Fergus immediately settled in for a nap, the first of several he'd take today.

Hugo turned to her. "How are you feeling, darling?"

"Big."

He chuckled and set a hand on her belly. "And Annette is sure it's not twins?" he asked, not for the first time.

Annette was the woman who served as midwife and nurse for the little village that was only a mile from the chateau.

Martha set her hand over her husband's and squeezed. "She is certain it is just one very large boy."

Like her other pregnancies, this one had been free from sickness or discomfort—until this past month. Not only was it full summer, but she was already one week past her due date. She was ready to have this baby.

"When is Cailean supposed to return?" she asked him.

"I made him promise to be back two full hours before dinner." Hugo picked up the newspaper he'd been reading before he'd gone to rescue Fergus from Yvette.

Cailean had taken the older children—those five to eleven—out to the large barn at the edge of the property. In the years since London, he'd expanded his menagerie exponentially.

The barn was his animal hospital, where he kept anywhere from twenty to fifty or more animals at any given time. Most of the animals were those he rescued—dogs, cats, and wild creatures like rabbits and birds—but the people of the village had begun bringing him farm beasts several years ago when they heard about his facility for healing.

Twice a week he took a group of children—including their daughter, Elizabeth—with him to help. Martha suspected that having seven little humans underfoot was more of a burden than any great help, but Cailean loved the children and they adored him.

He still rarely spoke, and when he did, it was usually to one of his patients, rather than a person, but Elizabeth could always get a word or two out of him. At almost six years of age, she was her father's daughter when it came to her gregarious, fearless spirit.

"Oh," Hugo said, removing the glasses that he'd finally admitted he needed on his thirty-ninth birthday. "I forgot to tell you that Mel wrote to say Laura finally agreed to marry that blacksmith—I can't recall his name—"

"Jacques."

"Yes, that was it. Mel said the man's daughters adore her and she is enjoying being a grandmother." He turned back to his paper and Martha smiled. She was both relieved and amused by his attitude toward the woman who'd stolen his business and sent him on a journey to New South Wales that had ended on an island in northern Scotland.

The third year they'd been in France, Hugo had sought her out one day when she'd been working in the nursery, her favorite part of the job.

"There you are!" He'd been breathless, as if he'd run to find her.

"Is anything wrong? Is it Elizab—"

"No, no, nothing like that. She's fine—Cailean's watching her."

Elizabeth had been almost two at the time and the French women had dubbed her Mlle Comète because of her comet-like speed when it came to shooting through a room.

"I just thought of something." Hugo had lifted her to her feet and slid his arms around her.

"Oh, Hugo—I can't right now, I'm the only one here watching the—"

"Not that, my wicked wife."

Hugo and the Maiden

As ever, she'd blushed when he teased her about anything intimate.

"No, I was just thinking about seeing Laura when we go and visit Melissa and Magnus next month."

"Oh, Hugo—I was hoping you were getting less angry with her. You know that we—"

He'd laid a finger over her lips. "What I wanted to say, is that I should probably be thanking her for what she did."

"*What?*"

"If she hadn't sent me on that dreadful journey, I never would have met you."

Martha had immediately teared up. "I think that's the most romantic thing you've ever said to me."

She still remembered his lovemaking that evening. He'd been intense—even more passionate than usual—and she was convinced they'd conceived their younger daughter, Amelia, that night.

Ever since then, he'd seemed to take almost a proprietary interest in Laura's life.

Martha was grateful that he'd let go of his anger, no matter how justified. Anger, jealousy, envy—and a raft of other negative emotions—were always more corrosive to the bearer than the target.

Hugo wasn't the only one who had wrestled with such problems over the years.

Martha had suffered through terrible months during their first year of marriage, unable to forget all the beautiful and skilled lovers Hugo had enjoyed before her. She'd been stunned by her capacity for jealousy—an emotion she'd not had much experience with until then.

It had been Melissa who'd helped her accept her husband's past.

"Hugo and I are very much alike," the beautiful redhead had said after Martha finally broke down and asked the other woman if Magnus, her husband, had ever been jealous of the men in her past. "It was always a job to us," she explained. "I knew other women—and a few men—who fell in love with their clients, or came to care for them, but that never happened to either of us. I know it is difficult for most people to understand, but the act of physical love is meaningless if there is nothing else to go with it." She'd laughed. "I once compared it to other activities—eating a meal together or playing cards—and poor Magnus almost fainted."

Martha could certainly understand the man's reaction. The things she did with Hugo were unlike any card game she'd ever played.

Melissa's smile had faded, and she'd given Martha a direct, unflinching look. "What you should remember is that when it comes to love, you were Hugo's first and only. Nobody ever touched his heart until you."

Her words had been a revelation. Hugo had said something similar, but she'd been unable to push aside her jealousy and *listen.*

Martha would probably always feel a twinge when she thought about all the people he'd shared his body with, but the thought no longer rode her like a demon. She was the only one to have his heart.

As she looked at him now—bespectacled, with a few strands of silver threading through his striking black hair—she experienced the same overwhelming love for him that she'd felt all those years ago on Stroma.

It made her shiver when she thought about all the things that could have happened to keep them from being together. If the sailors hadn't mutinied and the journey had gone as planned. If the ship had struck the rocks at a different angle and trapped the men inside. If Cailean hadn't found Hugo in the darkness and rescued him. If her father hadn't coerced Hugo into taking a chance on a vicar's daughter. If Martha had chosen the safe fork in the road and stayed with Robert Clark.

And a thousand other things that might have happened to keep her from spending her life with this most wonderful man.

As if feeling her eyes on him, Hugo looked up and smiled, his expression quizzical. "What is it, my love?"

Martha quickly swallowed back the tears that always made him anxious for her, even when she tried to convince him they were borne of joy.

Instead, she gave him the cheekiest smile she could muster. "I was just thinking how grateful I am to be married to you."

He perked up at that and folded the paper without taking his eyes from her. "Is that so?" His wicked black eyebrows arched. "Er, how grateful, exactly?"

Martha laughed and smoothed a hand over her huge belly. "Not *that* grateful." She cocked her head. "I've come to realize that you are almost the perfect man for me."

He coughed. "Excuse me, darling? But ... *almost?*"

"Well, I had always set my heart on a different last name."

Hugo and the Maiden

"You don't like Buckingham? It's a princely name," he chided. "And a great deal nicer than Dinwiddy."

She gave a dreamy sigh. "True, but I'd so fancied being able to call myself Martha Higgenbotham."

Hugo's delighted laughter woke up Fergus, who gave them both a disgusted look, jumped down from his lap, and stalked off in high dudgeon.

Hugo stood and held out his hands. Martha took them and he lifted her to her feet as if she weighed no more than a feather.

"You'll just have to settle for me, instead, darling." He slid his arms around her and brought her close, until her round stomach pressed against his flat one. "Because I love you, Martha Jane Buckingham, and I am never, ever going to let you go."

And then he kissed her.

Dear Reader:

I hope you enjoyed Hugo and Martha's adventure and had a fun time in northern Scotland and London.

As I write this, it is 2021 and the entire globe has gone through a year that will likely get its own chapter in future history books. I must admit that it was a relief to escape modern troubles and live in the early nineteenth century this past year.

I had a lot of fun researching this book and became especially fascinated with the island of Stroma.

The island maintained a tiny population for centuries—there are stone structures in evidence that are thousands of years old—but the last residents finally abandoned Stroma in 1997. (see Wikipedia's article on Stroma for lots of interesting tidbits) The island's only inhabitants now are sheep, puffins, and other birds (and probably a few otters!).

Through the miracle of Google Maps you can look at the satellite view of the island and see that Stroma's lighthouse, church, and houses—many still filled with possessions—are all that remain of the tiny, once-vibrant community. It is a ghost town floating in the North Sea.

As writers often do, I went down a research rabbit hole (several, actually) and had some interesting correspondence with a hard rock miner about the geology of Stroma. I learned a lot about cutting flagstone in the early nineteenth century and had a large section in the book about Hugo's life as a flagstone cutter. Alas, it hit the cutting room floor.

I also had fun researching otters, which can indeed be very vicious, albeit cute, little animals. Otters have made their way onto lists of animals (including humans) which can behave violently for no apparent reason.

The Gloup (taken from the Old Norse word 'gluppa' meaning chasm) is an actual geological feature on Stroma. Although I've altered the caves to fit my purpose they really were used for distilling and storage of contraband and nicknamed "the malt barn".

I like to keep my books steamy and sexy and a character like Hugo would have made free use of the sexual slang at the time. Phrases like "getting your corn ground," and "horny," "dick," and "pussy" were all in use in the nineteenth century, although they have a contemporary flavor. One of my most precious research sources on the internet is Jonathan Green's Oxford Dictionary of Slang. Not only can you find the earliest use of slang words, complete with timelines, but there are also links to sources.

Although I have a royal duke in the story, I deliberately left the character unnamed because he is a product of my imagination. Bevan Davies's blackmail scheme would have been a serious threat at the time since homosexual behavior was still punishable by death under the Buggery Act of 1533. The last execution for sodomy wasn't until 1835.

If you've read other books by me, you might have noticed that I like to write stories about commoners. While dukes (and their modern equivalent, billionaires) are exciting and exotic, I believe love flourishes in all social strata and the "little people"—even sex workers like Hugo—deserve their place in romance, too.

Estimates for the number of prostitutes in nineteenth century London vary greatly, but even if you believe the conservate numbers, there were still a shocking number of people, men and women, who earned their money as sex workers.

While I strive for historical accuracy, this is first and foremost a romance novel. If you are interested in any of the places, people, or events mentioned in my books I always recommend you consult a primary or reliable secondary source if you wish to learn more.

What am I working on next?

Well, I have a full schedule ahead for the next year.

In addition to writing another ACADEMY OF LOVE novel, the last book in THE MASQUERADERS, a third book in my LIGHTNER AND LAW series, I am also starting a new series for Kensington Publishing. It is called THE WILD WOMEN OF WHITECHAPEL and will feature three Regency ladies who work at Farnham's Fantastical Female Fayre, an all-female circus.

The first book in the series is THE BOXING BARONESS, a book with—you guessed it—a heroine who is a professional boxer. You can look out for that in 2022.

I love hearing from readers. Is there a character you'd like to know more about? Questions about this story? Upcoming stories? Stories you think *need* to be written? If so, you can drop an email to: minervaspencerauthor@gmail.com or leave a comment on my website, www.minervaspencer.com Or just pop in to say 'hello'.

As always, I ask that you take a moment to write a quick review—even just a few words—if you liked my work. I don't pay for reviews, so I rely on my lovely readers to share their genuine opinions and help browsing readers decide to give my books a try.

Until my next book, I wish you all the best and lots of great reading!

S.M. LaViolette

Keep reading for a sneak peek at THE FOOTMAN …

Chapter One

London
1802

Iain Vale was examining a marble statue of some poor armless bloke when the door beside it flew open and a whirlwind in skirts burst into the hall.

"I *will not!*" the whirlwind yelled before slamming the door, spinning around, and careening into Iain. "Ooof." She bounced off him and stumbled backward, catching her foot in the hem of her dress in the process.

Iain sprang forward, reached out one long arm, and caught her slim waist, halting her fall. He looked down at his armful of warm female and found surprised gray eyes glaring back at him. Her mouth, which had been open in shock, snapped shut. Iain hastily righted his bundle and took a step back.

"Who the devil are *you?*" the girl demanded, brushing at her dress as though his gloved hands might have soiled it.

"I'm the new footman, Miss."

The gray eyes turned steely. "Are you stupid?" She didn't wait for an answer. "I'm not a *Miss*. I am Lady Elinor, your employer's *daughter*."

Iain's face heated under her contemptuous eyes. He'd been spoken down to many times, but never quite so . . . effectively.

"You are welcome, *Lady Elinor*."

"What?" she demanded. "*What* did you say?" Her eyes were so wide they looked to be in danger of popping out of their sockets.

"*I said*, 'you are welcome, my lady.'"

She planted her fists on her slim hips. "I'm welcome for what?"

"For saving you from a very nasty fall," he retorted, unable to keep his tongue behind his teeth even though he was breaking every rule in the footman's handbook. If such a thing existed.

The unladylike noise that slipped from her mouth told Iain she was thinking the same thing. "You are an intolerably insolent *boy*. Not to mention the most ignorant footman I've ever known."

Iain couldn't argue with her on that second point.

"Besides," she added, looking him up and down, "I wouldn't have needed your clumsy rescuing if you'd not been listening at keyholes."

Listening at keyholes? *Why the obnoxious little*—

Iain had just opened his mouth to say something foolish and most likely job-ending when the door Lady Elinor had exited so violently opened and Lady Yarmouth stood on the threshold. Her gray eyes, much like her daughter's, moved from Lady Elinor to her newest footman and back again.

"What is going out here, Elinor?"

The girl scowled. "I have just asked our new footman to run away with me, Mama."

Iain's jaw dropped.

Lady Yarmouth's lips thinned until they were pale pink lines. She raked the younger woman with a look designed to leave her quaking in her slippers. Her daughter glared back, un-quaked.

"Come back inside this instant, Elinor." The older woman turned and retreated into the room without waiting to see if her daughter obeyed.

Lady Elinor gave an exaggerated sigh and rolled her eyes at her mother's back before limping toward the open doorway. She stopped and turned back to Iain before entering the room.

"You'll catch flies if you don't close your mouth." She slammed the door in his face.

Bloody hell.

***

Iain yawned. It was almost three in the morning and the festivities showed no sign of abating. Other than his encounter with Lady Elinor earlier, the evening had been quiet. Disappointingly quiet not only for his first ball, but also his first day as footman.

The only other entertainment had been watching an overdressed dandy cast up his accounts on his dancing slippers while trying, and failing, to make it to the men's necessary.

Iain adjusted the lacy cuffs of his fancy new shirt and examined the stranger who looked back at him in the ornate mirror. The black livery made him appear taller than his six feet and the well-tailored coat spanned his shoulders in a way that made him look lean and dangerous rather than scrawny and puppyish. His wiry red hair had been cropped to barely a stubble and was now concealed by a white powdered wig that gave him dignity. Of course his freckles were still there, but there was nothing he could do to hide them—unlike his age.

"You don't look five-and-ten, Iain," his Uncle Lonnie had said upon seeing Iain in his new clothes earlier today. He'd then grinned and squeezed Iain's shoulder. "Go ahead and give us yer story one last time, lad."

The story was one his uncle had concocted when Iain first came to work in Viscount Yarmouth's household three months ago: Iain was nineteen and had spent six years in Mr. Ewan Kennedy's household, two as a scrub boy, two as a boot boy, and two as a footman, even though he was unusually young for that last position. Uncle Lonnie also told Lord Yarmouth that Iain had come to London seeking employment after Mr. Kennedy died and there weren't any other suitable positions in the tiny town of Dannen, Scotland.

That last part was the only *true* part of the whole story. Dannen was more a collection of shacks than a real village and there'd never been any Mr. Kennedy, nor any work as scrub boy or footman. Iain had written the letter from "Mr. Kennedy" himself, under his uncle's direction.

"Admiring your pretty face?"

Iain yelped and jumped a good six inches. Female laughter echoed down the mahogany-paneled corridor. He turned to find Lady Elinor behind him, her small, almost boyish, frame propped against the wall in a very unladylike manner. Her white gown looked limp and tired, as if it were ready to go to bed. Her hair, a nondescript brown, had come loose from its moorings and fine tendrils wafted about her thin, pale face. Only her large gray eyes held any animation.

Iain drew himself up to his full height and glared over her shoulder at nothing. "How may I be of service, my lady?"

"Oh, stuff! You're angry with me, aren't you?" She didn't wait for an answer. "I'm sorry for being beastly earlier. I was wrong. Pax?" She held out her hand and limped forward. Iain stared, not because of her limp—he already knew she was lame—but because of the gesture. Surely a footman wasn't permitted to shake a lady's hand?

Besides, he hadn't forgiven her. His mother and uncle both accused him of being too grudging and slow to forgive. He looked down at her little hand and chewed his lip. Maybe they were right; perhaps it might be advisable to *appear* to forgive her. He'd just decided to say 'pax' when Lady Elinor grabbed his hand.

"Don't be angry with me. I apologized."

"I'm not angry," he lied, tugging not so subtly on his hand to free it from her grasp. He suspected it would not do to get caught holding the hand of the daughter of the house at three in the morning, or at any other time of the day or night, for that matter.

"Why aren't you in there," he gestured with his chin toward the ballroom, "dancing? Er, my lady," he added a trifle belatedly.

She snorted and hiked up her dress, exhibiting a shocking amount of leg. "With this?"

Iain gawked. He'd seen girl's legs, of course, but never a *lady's* leg. Her stockings were embroidered with flowers—daisies, perhaps. His groin gave an appreciative thump as he studied the gentle swell of her calf. She had shapely legs for such a tiny thing.

She dropped her skirts. "Are you ogling my limb?"

"What do you expect if you go around hiking up your skirt like that?" The words were out of his mouth before he could stop them. Iain squeezed his eyes shut and waited for her to start screeching. But the sound of giggling made him open them again.

She eyed him skeptically. "You're not like the other footmen."

What was Iain supposed to say to that?

"You look *very* young. How long have you been a footman?"

"Today is my first day."

"You shan't keep your job very long if you argue with any other members of my family. Or ogle their limbs."

His face heated and he pursed his lips.

She looked delighted by whatever she saw on his face. "How old are you?"

"Nineteen, my lady."

"What a bouncer!"

"How old are *you*?" Iain bit out, and then wanted to howl. At this rate, he would be jobless before breakfast.

"Sixteen." She stopped smiling and her eyes went dull, like a vivid sunset losing its color. "But I might as well be forty. I shan't even have a Season."

"I thought all young ladies had at least one Season." What drivel. What the devil did *he* know about aristocrats, Seasons, or any of it? It was as if some evil imp had taken over his body: some pixie or spirit determined to get him sacked. Or jailed. He clamped his mouth shut, vowing not to open it again until it was time to put food in it.

Luckily his employer's daughter was too distracted to find his behavior odd.

"Tonight was my betrothal ball." Her shapely, shell-pink lips turned down at the corners. "Why should my father go to the expense of a Season when he can dispose of me so cheaply without one?"

It seemed like an odd way to talk about a betrothal but Iain kept that observation behind his teeth.

"The Earl of Trentham is my betrothed," she added, not in need of any responses from him to hold a conversation. "He is madly in love."

The silence became uncomfortable. Iain cleared his throat. "You must be very happy, then," he said when he could bear it no longer.

Her eyes, which had been vague and distant, sharpened and narrowed. "He's not in love with *me*, you dunce. He is in love with a property that is part of my dowry. Some piece of land that is critical to a business venture he and my father have planned."

Iain's flare of anger at being called *dunce* quickly died when he saw the misery and self-loathing on her face.

"Lord Trentham will have his land, my father will get to take part in the earl's investment, and I? Well, I will have—" She stopped, as if suddenly aware of what she was saying and to whom she was saying it. She glared up at him, her gray eyes suddenly molten silver. "Why am I telling *you* any of this? How could you ever know what it is like to be an ugly *cripple*? You will never be forced to marry someone who is twice your age. A man who views you with less pleasure than he does a piece of dirt." Her mouth twisted. "I am no more than a broodmare to him."

Her expression shifted from agonized into a sneering mask. Iain hadn't thought her ugly before—plain, perhaps—but, at that moment, she became ugly. Fury boiled off her person like steam from a kettle and Iain recoiled, not wanting to get burned.

She noticed his reaction and laughed, the sound as nasty as the gleam in her eyes. "What? Do I scare you, *boy?*"

Iain felt as if she'd prodded him with a red-hot iron and he took two strides and closed the distance between them, seething at the undeserved insults and bile. He stared down at her, no idea as to what he planned to do. Not that it mattered. The second he came within reach, her hands slid up the lapels of his jacket like two pale snakes. He froze at her touch but she pushed closer. Small, firm mounds pressed hard against his chest.

Breasts! Breasts! a distant, but euphoric, part of his mind shrieked.

His breeding organ had already figured that out.

Iain looked down into eyes that had become soft and imploring.

"What is your name?" she asked, her voice husky.

"I—" He coughed and cleared his throat. "Iain, my lady."

"Would you like to kiss me, Iain?" It was barely a whisper and Iain wondered if he'd heard her correctly. He cocked his head and was about to ask her to repeat herself, when she stood on tiptoes and pressed her lips against his.

Iain had kissed girls before. Just last week he'd done a whole lot more than kiss with one of the housemaids in the stables. But this kiss was different. It was a gentle, tentative offering, rather than a taking. To refuse it was somehow unthinkable. He leaned lower and slid his hands around her waist, pulling her closer. She was so slim his hands almost spanned her body. She made a small noise in her throat and touched the side of his face with caressing fingers, her pliant body melting against his.

"You bloody *bastard!*"

The girl jumped back and screamed just as Iain's head exploded. He staggered, his vision clouding with multi-colored spangles and roaring agony. When he reached out to steady himself on the wall, he encountered air. A foot kicked his legs out from under him and he slammed onto his back, his skull cracking against the wood floor.

"Lord Trentham, *no!*" Lady Elinor's voice was barely audible above the agonizing pounding filling Iain's head.

A body—Lord Trentham's?—dropped onto Iain's chest with crushing force. Soft but powerful hands circled his neck and squeezed.

"You rutting pig, how dare you touch *my* betrothed?" The choking eased on his throat just before a fist buffeted the right side of his head. "How *dare* you put your filthy hands on your betters?" Another blow slammed into his left temple.

"*Stop it! Stop this instant, he did nothing wrong. It was me!*"

"I'll deal with you next, you little whore," the earl said, his tone even harsher than his words as his fists cracked against Iain's head over and over again. Iain's mouth filled with blood and he struggled to spit it out before he choked on it. And then a knee jammed between his thighs and he screamed, the world going black.

"*You're going to kill him!*"

Iain retched and Trentham scrambled off him, clearly wishing to avoid becoming drenched in blood and vomit. Iain rolled to his side and cupped his hands protectively over his aching groin, his stomach convulsing until there was nothing left to expel.

He wanted to die.

"What the devil is going on here?"

Iain distantly recognized Lord Yarmouth's voice.

"Make him stop, Papa, he will kill him!"

"I will certainly make him *wish* he were dead," Trentham snarled just before a foot made contact with Iain's side.

"*Ooof!*" Iain groaned and rolled away, unwilling to take his hands from his groin and risk more gut-churning abuse.

"Trentham, what is going on?" Yarmouth asked again.

"This lout was in the process of mounting your bloody daughter when I caught them."

"That's not—" Lady Elinor began.

"Silence!" her father roared.

"Is this the kind of household you run, Yarmouth? Has this happened before? Is she even *intact*?"

"I assure you, Trentham, this is the first time such a thing has happened. Look at her. Do you think she poses much of a temptation to any man?" The viscount continued without waiting for an answer. "Besides, this is a mere boy. I told Lady Yarmouth he was too young to be fit for the position. We shall discharge him immediately and forget this ever happened."

"I won't forget it, Yarmouth. And I won't marry this lout's castoffs—not unless my doctor examines her and swears she is intact. And I want *him*—" a kick glanced off Iain's shoulder—"put where he belongs."

"We did nothing wrong, Papa. It was just—"

"Another word from you, Elinor, and you will regret it most severely." The viscount's normally soft voice was thick with disgust and rage. A pregnant pause followed his words before he spoke again. "Very well, Trentham."

"*Papa, no.* It was only a kiss. He didn't even want to, I begged him—"

"*Enough!*" The word was followed by a loud crack and a muffled cry.

"I want him taken in for attempted rape," Trentham said, his voice suddenly cool and collected.

"Very well," the viscount said. "Thomas, Gerald, take him. You can put him down in the cellar while one of you fetches the constable."

Four hands closed around Iain's arms and began to lift. He struggled weakly against their efforts, squirming and thrashing his way across the plush carpet.

"You incompetent fools." The Earl of Trentham's voice came from behind. "Let me ensure this piece of rubbish gives you no trouble." Something hard slammed into Iain's head and the world faded to black

Who are Minerva Spencer & S.M. LaViolette?

Minerva is S.M.'s pen name (that's short for Shantal Marie) S.M. has been a criminal prosecutor, college history teacher, B&B operator, dock worker, ice cream manufacturer, reader for the blind, motel maid, and bounty hunter. Okay, so the part about being a bounty hunter is a lie. S.M. does, however, know how to hypnotize a Dungeness crab, sew her own Regency Era clothing, knit a frog hat, juggle, rebuild a 1959 American Rambler, and gain control of Asia (and hold on to it) in the game of RISK.

Read more about S.M. at: www.MinervaSpencer.com

Minerva's OUTCASTS SERIES

<u>DANGEROUS</u>
<u>BARBAROUS</u>
<u>SCANDALOUS</u>

THE REBELS OF THE *TON:*

<u>NOTORIOUS</u>
<u>OUTRAGEOUS</u>
<u>INFAMOUS</u>

THE SEDUCERS:

<u>MELISSA AND THE VICAR</u>
<u>JOSS AND THE COUNTESS</u>
<u>HUGO AND THE MAIDEN</u>

VICTORIAN DECADENCE: (HISTORICAL EROTIC ROMANCE—SUPER STEAMY!)

<u>HIS HARLOT</u>
<u>HIS VALET</u>
<u>HIS COUNTESS</u>

THE ACADEMY OF LOVE:

<u>THE MUSIC OF LOVE</u>
<u>A FIGURE OF LOVE</u>
<u>A PORTRAIT OF LOVE</u>
<u>THE LANGUAGE OF LOVE</u>

THE MASQUERADERS:

<u>THE FOOTMAN</u>

THE POSTILION
THE BASTARD

THE BACHELORS OF BOND STREET:

A SECOND CHANCE FOR LOVE (A NOVELLA)

ANTHOLOGIES:

THE ARRANGEMENT

Made in the USA
Middletown, DE
05 August 2024